MW00654970

The Kate Fox Mystery Series

Stripped Bare

Dark Signal

Bitter Rain

Easy Mark

Michaela Sanchez Southwest Crime Thrillers

Echoes in the Sand

The Desert's Share

The Nora Abbott Mystery Series

Height of Deception

Skies of Fire

Canyon of Lies

Standalone Thrillers

The Desert Behind Me

Never miss a new release! Sign up to receive exclusive updates from author Shannon Baker.

Shannon-Baker.com/Newsletter

As a thank you for signing up, you'll receive a free copy of

Close Enough: A Kate Fox Novella

To Dave: The only person I want to isolate with.

1

Rebuilding your life is like remodeling an old house. You don't know whether to knock down walls or put up more. I preferred old, trusted houses to new builds, but maybe I was due for a change. That's what gnawed at me as I wrestled the sheets in the middle of the night.

The sliver of moon cast shadows on my bedroom ceiling. An occasional 'yote howled and an answer bounced back across the hills, but mostly the cottony sound of isolated prairie floated through the open window, along with the pleasant, slightly damp smell of spring. The shadow of the old cottonwood two-stepped alone in the May breeze, the sway of its branches a reminder of my singlehood.

Maybe the worst part of being single was my seven brothers' and sisters' determination to pair me up. Being alone wasn't so bad and certainly not what kept me awake. My heart hurt for the loss of the family I once had. My husband, Ted, now anticipating the birth of his first baby with another woman, and my niece, Carly, gone.

I rolled to my side battling the familiar frustration of not being able to help Carly. With both her parents dead, Carly had run away on my watch just over a year ago, on the cusp of her eighteenth birthday.

After an eternity, sleep finally pulled a soft blanket over my head.

A jangle wrenched it from my face. I gasped, disoriented. I didn't know how long it had taken for the sound to burrow into my consciousness, but I grabbed for the phone, swiping the screen and smacking my lips to wet my mouth.

I think I croaked, but it sounded nothing like "Grand County sheriff." Probably more like, "Gphsh."

A young woman's frantic voice slapped me awake. "Help me!"

Lightning flashed behind my eyes. "Carly?" I saw her, tall and thin, long legs bare between her cutoffs and cowboy boots, blond hair flying in the summer breeze.

The woman yelled, too panicked to speak coherently or even hear me. "Shit! Here he comes!"

The image of Carly faded. It wasn't Carly on the phone. Some other girl in trouble. "Wha—?" I kicked the down comforter off my legs.

She screeched over my question. "I don't know what he wants."

I swung my legs to the floor. My heart still believed this caller was Carly, and I so wanted to run to her. "Who—"

The rumble in the background—maybe wind rushing through a car window—made it difficult to hear clearly. "Please help me. We need you!"

I blinked Carly's image away. "Where—"

The caller couldn't have heard me because she never stopped shrieking. "I'm on my way from the rez."

The voice sounded young. Before I asked another question, she gasped.

She shouted and her voice cracked. "No!"

A shard of panic splintered my heart. "What's happening?"

No voice. Only rushing wind.

"Hello! Hello!" *Come back. Let me help.*

Another intake of breath, a grunt. The roaring stopped. A fluttering on the other end. The line went dead.

By this time, I stood beside my bed, reaching for the light switch, my bare feet absorbing the cold from the wood floor. "Who—?"

Panting in the chilly air, my heart battering my ribs, I blinked in the bright room and tried to process the call.

I'm on my way from the rez, she'd said. *We need you.*

2

It took less than five minutes to throw on my brown sheriff's
uniform, lace up my boots, grab my jacket and gun, and fly
down the porch steps to my cruiser. The Lakota reservation of
Antelope Ridge lay just over one hundred miles north of
Hodgekiss. I had a head start because my cottage was nestled
on a shallow lake seven miles north of town. It would take me
over an hour, with my light bar dancing, to reach the reservation. But the caller said she'd *left* Antelope Ridge Reservation
and was heading my way. Or at least, that's what I decided
she'd meant. In the darkness of predawn, I strained to see
oncoming lights.

My headlights and the swirl of the blue-and-red flashers
cast garish light on the prairie as I sped down the empty highway. The sliver of moon had set and dawn wouldn't put in an
appearance for another couple of hours, so I had to strain to
peer into the barrow ditches on either side of the highway for
signs of a wreck. The caller wasn't Carly, but I kept seeing her
freckled face. My breath caught at the irrational image of
Carly trapped in the mangled steel of a wrecked car.

Antelope Ridge Reservation was well outside Grand County's jurisdiction. As a sovereign nation of the Lakota Sioux, it had its own government and law enforcement. Grand County didn't even share a border. We bumped up against the southern edge of Spinner County, and Spinner's sixty-nine-mile length ended at the reservation's doorstep, the line between Nebraska and South Dakota. It was a desolate stretch from Hodgekiss to the rez. If someone had an accident, they could lay out here for unseen hours, maybe even a day.

After nearly twenty minutes of squinting into the darkness along the road's edge and spotting nothing but weeds, a prick of light caught my eye up ahead. I goosed my already speeding cruiser, and when I drove close enough to make out a vehicle on the side of the road, I braked, jerked to the left shoulder, and stopped.

An old silver-and-red ranch pickup—looked like a twenty-year-old flatbed Ford F-150—idled on the roadside. Its headlights shone on the underside of a car one hundred feet away in the pasture. The car, upended like a turtle on its back, had taken out the three-strand barbed wire fence. Nothing moved near the wreck. In my short tenure as sheriff, I'd handled several wrecks, always fearful I'd see someone I knew, or find a grisly scene. So far, I'd been lucky that all injuries had been minor. I prayed tonight would be the same. I jumped out, leaving my car door open, and raced toward the rolled car.

Diving to my knees, I squinted through the shattered driver's window, my eyes adjusting and making out a few details in the shadowed interior. My sigh of relief sounded harsh in the dark silence. No body, no terrible carnage, just an empty, overturned car. I pushed myself up, surveying the nighttime prairie for a body that might have been thrown.

The pickup driver's hard voice came to me from the road above. "No sign of anyone." A heavyset man in a black cowboy hat, wearing jeans, cowboy boots, and a brown jacket, stood next to the passenger side of the pickup, arms folded.

Of all the people who might arrive on the scene, he was near the bottom of my choices. I tossed him a chin by way of acknowledgment.

Rubbing my hands to warm them from the dewy ground, I hiked back to my cruiser and leaned inside. With a punch, the glove box flipped open, and I pulled out Big Dick, the flashlight long enough to pole-vault with and heavy enough to club a yeti. I grabbed my own brown coat and stepped from the car, ready to deal with the Spinner County sheriff. He made no effort to meet me, so I marched the few yards to his pickup.

"Howdy, Lee." I tried to sound, if not excited to see him, at least not disappointed. "What do you know about this wreck?"

The hangdog face drooped lower in the jowls. "What're you doing out here?"

They say it's coldest right before dawn, but Lee Barnett's greeting made it even frostier.

I zipped my coat, the one that matched his. "Heard there might be an accident. Came to check it out."

He seemed almost angry. "Dispatch? I never heard anything."

He wasn't driving his sheriff's Bronco, so how would he have heard a call over the radio?

Since he wasn't a well of information, I jogged down the barrow ditch and up the other side. With the bright beam of the flashlight, I again searched for someone thrown from the car and was thankful I didn't see anyone. Back down on my knees, I studied the broken window and driver's seat. No blood.

Help me! The terror in her voice had sent ice through my veins. *Here he comes!*

Who? Had he got here before Lee? Or had the girl run

away? Did someone arrive to save her? I spun around, casting the light over the hills to the west, then back across the highway to the east, catching Barnett's progress toward me.

Big Dick's light ran over the metal as I circled the car. Even if you didn't count the crushed roof, this puppy wasn't a showroom special. Mostly rust with a few patches of paint that might be a faded red in bright sunshine, enough dents that textured it like oatmeal, but the logo on the back told me this heap was a proud Mercury Marquis, plenty old enough to vote. No license plate. Not surprising.

"What are you doing out here?" I asked when Barnett joined me.

It took Barnett so long to answer I quit expecting his reply. "Out patrolling."

I raised an eyebrow at the beater pickup and his jeans. "Not officially?"

He probably wanted to tell me it was none of my business; instead, he gave an impatient snort. "Saturday night off the rez, they run away if they see the cop car. This way, I can get a handle on who's causing trouble."

Right. And in a rural county with a population in four digits, no one knows who drives that particular pickup. Not to mention the wrinkles on his cheek that looked suspiciously like pillow creases. Still, not my business what the Spinner County sheriff does on a Saturday night, or technically, Sunday morning.

"How long have you been here?" I shimmied into a gap between the hood and the ground and pointed my beam to where the VIN tag ought to be, not shocked that it was AWOL.

"Just got here." He stood with his legs wide, arms crossed.

"Wreck is pretty far off the road. Wondering how you happened to spot it in the dark." Okay, yeah, I didn't mind needling him.

He sneered. "Lucky, I guess."

I wanted to ask him exactly what I'd done to make him act like I'd stolen all his crayons. But I knew the answer.

It had started with running against my ex in the general election last fall. The four adjoining counties that made up the sheriff's association were more a good ol' boys club than a professional co-op. I fit in about as well as sauerkraut on a cupcake. The other two sheriffs were friendly, at least.

Winning the election had been a long shot for me, since Ted was coming off two successful terms. But my family pulled out the stops campaigning, and with eight brothers and sisters, cousins, aunts, uncles, nephews, and nieces, that's a fair number of stops pulled. Ted's affair with Roxy might have soured some folks, at least enough to outweigh my lack of experience and worse, being a woman.

The driver's side door had popped open several inches during the crash, and I lowered myself to my belly and snaked toward the Mercury for a close-up of the other place VINs are posted. Big Dick's light showed where the number had been scratched out on the door edge. I played the light across the ripped seat and the cracked dash with yellow foam rubber squeezing out like pus from an infected scratch. No blood. The light revealed nothing under the seats. No purse, jacket, suitcase, or anything else strewn about.

Barnett watched but didn't offer conversation. I straightened and stepped back. My palm rested on the underside of the Grand Marquis, detecting warmth in the chilly air.

We need you. Help me, please.

What did she mean? Was the call intended for me? Or maybe she meant Ted, the previous sheriff?

I retreated to the trunk, which had sprung open, but no trunk-trash littered the pasture. Dried mud clung to the chipped red paint outlining an absent plate, like maybe it had been removed not long ago.

Barnett followed me and acted like I was a skunk in the grain bin. "No one is coming back for this piece of shit. There's no identification on it anywhere."

Dawn crept on the eastern ridge with enough gray light that I made out Barnett's sagging features. "You checked?"

He didn't look at me, but turned to the empty western pasture. "Of course I checked. No VIN, no registration." Didn't he say he just got here?

Still surveying the scene, I trudged past Barnett, back across the ditch to the highway, and waited for him to climb to the road. "Did you pass anyone on your way here?"

"Nope."

What a guy.

I cast the flashlight in front of Barnett's pickup on a dusty set of tire tracks. They swung out from the west side of the road, across the highway and faded quickly, but not before they traced a U-turn heading north. "'Cause there's a track."

Barnett's voice hardened like cement on a hot day. "Someone picked up the driver and took him back to the rez." He brushed his hands together as if he'd solved a mystery.

I don't know what he wants. Jagged blades of fear in her voice.

If Barnett was right, who picked up the driver? The man chasing her, or a savior? Kidnap or rescue?

My cheeks tingled with cold as I followed the dusty tire tracks, flashlight like a hound's nose, to where Barnett stood. He watched me with distaste. "Ask Ted. He'll tell you this is what Indians do."

I scanned the dark hills to the west. "If you didn't pass anyone, whoever drove this car is still here."

Barnett ground his jaw. "Maybe I did pass someone heading north, now that I think of it."

Warm hood. Tracks leading north. Barnett completely unhelpful. There wasn't much to go on here.

Barnett spoke with the authority of a man who'd been sheriff since before I had my driver's license. "I'll get Schneiderman to tow this piece of shit. But no need to wake him. I'll call after sunrise."

With Big Dick pointed to the ground, I surveyed the roadside. "Thanks. But I'll get it."

He focused on me like a border collie on a sheep, waiting for me to step across the invisible line. "It's closer to Potsville than Hodgekiss."

I edged next to Barnett, leaning over to study the ground with my flashlight. "But Potsville is the county seat of Spinner, and Hodgekiss is my county seat."

The hound dog face remained passive, but his eyes schooled me. "Ted and I always did the most logical thing."

There. A footprint. "Bingo!"

Barnett planted his cowboy boot on the print and scraped his sole sideways, spraying gravel.

I stopped short of shoving him. "What the hell are you doing? That was a footprint!"

He glanced down between his feet. "I don't think so." He pulled his phone from his shirt pocket inside his jacket. "I'll call Schneiderman now."

If I winged Big Dick, would it hit Barnett's head before he ducked? Probably not, and I didn't want to damage my buddy Dick. I swung the light up and lit the back of a billboard. Not exactly a billboard, but a seven-by-seven-foot piece of plywood nailed to plank scaffolding. The front side of that sign showed a hand-painted picture of a cow and the background of grassy hills. In white letters, it said, "Welcome to

Grand County, Best Cow Country in the World." To the bottom right of the cow, in bold black, it read, "This Is No Bull."

"Looks like we're in Grand County," I said. "I'll take care of it."

Barnett didn't hide the irritation in his gravelly voice. "There's nothing to handle here."

Please help me.

Her words ricocheted in my head, sending a jolt through me.

Not sure why I didn't tell Barnett about the phone call. Well, yeah, I was sure. He wanted to make me look bad so Ted could get elected next time. He'd find a way to sabotage the investigation to make me look like a fool, and this girl might need help. The less Barnett knew about my business, the better.

He had a point, though. This looked to be nothing more than an abandoned car with no sign of foul play. Except I heard Carly's voice in the other girl's words, pleading with me to help her this time.

I didn't talk to Barnett. No sense in pretending we were friends.

He followed me while I leaned close to the ground. "What is it you're looking for?"

I mumbled to make it clear I didn't need or want his help. "A clue about the driver."

"The only clue you're gonna find is a Budweiser can or some coyote-eaten puke. No telling how long this car's been here. Maybe a couple of days. I haven't been out this way since last Saturday night's patrol."

That didn't account for the still-warm hood. "Maybe so, but it won't hurt to check things out while I wait for the sun to come up."

Barnett's voice ground like sand on a shovel. "Like I said, rez car. They abandoned it for us to clean up—like they do everything. We tow it, sell it for scrap. I'll make sure Grand County gets its share of the proceeds."

Too bad I hadn't brought some gloves or a cap. It might smell all fresh and growy, like spring, but before the sun got around to its job, it felt more like winter out here.

Please help me.

Was she safe or in danger? The dusty tracks held no answers.

The first birdsongs floated on the air. Barnett leaned against his pickup, arms folded, the annoyed set of his face clearer as the sun bloomed in the east.

Enough of his silent disapproval. "Feel free to head back to Potsville."

He faked a breezy tone we both knew was full of crap. "Nope. It's bad practice to leave one officer alone."

Since all the Sandhills sheriffs were the lone law officers in counties the size of small states, that was a bogus remark.

"Suit yourself." By now the sun shed just enough light so I could expand my search. I walked across the highway to the east, shutting off Big Dick and stowing him in my utility belt. Damn. I hadn't slipped my gun into my holster. I often forgot to carry it. Honestly, I hated it.

I didn't want to go back to the car and get it now because it would look amateurish in front of Barnett. Why didn't he just go home and leave me to it?

Because he wanted to be a jerk. He was pretty good at it.

I searched the ditch along the road, really hoping *not* to find a body. When my phone chirped I jumped and pulled it out of my coat pocket all in one move.

"Hi, Sarah." My sister-in-law and best friend.

She sounded like a bowl of cold manure. "I've been

throwing up for two hours. I know I'm probably waking you up, but I'm miserable. Tell me about the date you went on last week."

Coming on to five months pregnant, Sarah had morning sickness daily, along with noon and night sickness. I turned my back on Barnett and hunched over to talk to Sarah. "I'd love to distract you with my latest failure, but you laughed so hard when I told you the first time, you peed your pants and made me promise not to tell you again."

Sarah sounded more pathetic than I'd ever heard her. "I changed my mind."

At least I had a good excuse to save me from a humiliating memory. "I can't. I'm on a call."

"Oh. Th-th-th-that's okay." She suddenly burst into tears.

Whoa. Sarah hated tears, sympathy, all that squishy girl stuff. It's something we had in common. "Sarah. Jeez, stop. I'm sorry. I'm really, really sorry."

"Damn it." She sniffed and cried again. "I hate this fricking hormonal rollercoaster. I cry all the time."

A stabbing ray of sunshine burst over the hill. The pasture came alive in green, and the birds increased their volume. The air stilled, hovering in a lull before the day started in earnest.

But right now, I was letting down my best friend, ticking off a coworker, not helping someone who'd asked for my help, and generally not living up to any great potential. So I compounded my loser streak by offering stupid comfort. "You're about to enter your last trimester. It won't be long before you have your baby."

That elicited another bout of tears. "What the hell was I thinking? I can't be a mother."

I couldn't help it. I laughed. "Get some perspective. You and Robert will be the best parents ever. I've really got to go.

She sniffed a final time. "Okay. I'll eat a saltine and think about your miserable love life to cheer me up."

When I put my phone in my pocket, I was surprised to see Barnett had crossed the road and was standing by me.

He eyed the pocket where I'd deposited my phone. "First thing Sally does every morning is call her girlfriends. They can chatter on for hours, like hens, you know."

Since I couldn't hit him, I stared at him with as much disdain as I could muster. "Maybe you don't understand loyalty to friends."

He raised his lip in a snarl. "I know about friends. But you women have to talk it all out. Men, we do what needs doing."

Growing up in the middle of nine kids, I'd learned how to keep my mouth shut when I'd rather punch someone in the face. I turned from Barnett.

The dawn vanished when I thought of the anguish in the girl's voice. *No!*

I put my head down and walked north on the highway.

Barnett snarled at me, "Now what are you doing?"

Ignoring him might feel good but wouldn't be right. "Going to walk out this way for a bit and see if she left some clue."

He followed me. "What makes you think it's a she?"

I walked with my head down. "Just a guess."

He caught up with me. "I'm telling you—"

I flipped my head up and glared at him with Dad's Look. The one he gave us right before he put us on prison rations.

Barnett stopped talking.

We staged a standoff. I kept walking because I knew he wanted me to quit, and he stayed with me because he knew I wanted him to leave. What a pair.

After a quarter mile Barnett stopped, panting at the exercise. "This is bull." He spun around and stomped past the

Grand County sign, never acknowledging the irony of "This Is No Bull" painted in the corner, and launched himself into his beater pickup.

Smiling with grim satisfaction, I kept walking north until he'd sped over two or three hills.

Then I jogged back to my cruiser, fired her up, and did a U-turn too. I headed back toward Hodgekiss.

I didn't want to give up searching for the girl, but Barnett was right. I wasn't a TV Indian scout who could put an ear to the ground and hear hoofbeats. It wasn't as if—

I slammed on my brakes.

3

Hurray for dewy May mornings, fresh grass, and damp sand. I pulled to the roadside, jumped out of the cruiser, and trotted a few feet ahead. The sandy tread of two-inch-wide tires laid a track across the highway.

To the west, the track curved across the wet pasture. To the east, it ribboned over the highway to a gravel road. From there, it slipped off the gravel road and wound on top of a crest of hills across an empty pasture. Seemed awfully early for someone to be zipping cross-country on a dirt bike.

If the bike had been coming from the abandoned car, its destination lay over those eastern hills. I hadn't heard an engine while at the accident site, but whoever drove this bike might have used Barnett's exit to mask his getaway. I hurried after the trail cut through the dew.

The pasture opened up before me with a tall ridge about two hundred yards away. No cattle dotted the meadow, only grass, purple spiderwort, and yellow coneflowers.

Green, wet, and high enough to cover my ankles, the grass had a good start on summer's forage. Dew soaked my boots before I made it halfway to the hills, while the birds provided an ever-more boisterous soundtrack. There was nothing as beautiful as sunrise in the spring and summer on a grass-covered hill, the air coming alive with growth, the sky blue enough to taste.

I trudged up the hill as the early morning sun brushed back the night's chill. If memory served, the old Olson Ranch headquarters hunkered on the other side of this hill. No one had lived there for ten or fifteen years, and I'd only been there once as a high school freshman, when Danny Duncan had hijacked me, driven me to the crumbling buildings, and threatened to leave me there if I didn't kiss him. I didn't tell him he hadn't needed to waste the gas. I'd have kissed him without the drive.

I picked up my pace and, before long, reached the top of the hill and paused before starting down the other side. The ancient barn stood alongside decrepit wooden corrals. The old one-story farmhouse still had chipped and peeling paint. I hadn't remembered the other giant pole barn and what looked like a cookhouse. Actually, there were quite a few things I hadn't remembered, including an open structure that resembled a huge carport, the roof covered in military-type camo covering, with two pickups and a shiny green tractor parked underneath.

I inhaled in surprise. "Would you look at that."

The more my eyes adjusted, the more I understood. What appeared to be old and abandoned was repaired, renewed, and disguised. Below me, a whole ranch headquarters stretched out. A ranch I knew nothing about. Way up here, snugged against the county line, over a half hour's drive from even the smallest town, someone had set up a ranch head-quarters.

The Nebraska Sandhills are like a grass-covered Sahara Desert. The region takes up one-fourth of the state but boasts fewer than five thousand people. That's .95 people per square mile. A surprisingly abundant bird population, despite a dearth of trees. Groundwater bubbles to the surface, creating multitudes of shallow lakes that wax and wane through wet and dry years. If you aren't comfortable with your own self for company, you probably ought to keep driving on through.

My county, Grand, accounted for about fifteen hundred of those good folks, and I was related to more of those than is seemly. With the cow-to-people ratio of about sixty to one, we knew a whole lot about everyone else. Or, at least we believed we did.

If someone was determined to keep this construction project under wraps, it would take a lot of stealth, but it could be done. For instance, Barnett and I had been hanging around the car and walking the road for quite a spell and hadn't seen hide nor hair of a vehicle.

You'd need to arrange for materials and equipment to be delivered at night, when no one would notice. But even then, it seemed strange that word hadn't spread about who bought this ranch. Usually, if an outsider poked his head around here, someone would end up talking to him and find out his story.

The Olsons, the last owners, were old before I'd even been a thought, so I didn't actually know them. My knowledge about this ranch could fit in a shot glass: The once mighty Olson ranch had been reduced to a bunch of smaller ranches. The last Olson, Oscar, passed away with no children of his own. I'd heard a distant nephew inherited the place.

Apparently, that nephew had been busy.

From my vantage on the hill, the sun highlighted rolling hills far into the distance. Nothing but sky so blue it hurt my eyes and empty pasture, except for the ranch below me. I started down the hill, picking my way through the clump grass and sand on the eastern slope. My breaths, boots swishing through the grass, and the birds broke the heavy silence of the morning.

Two newish, if dirty, white Ford F-250 pickups were parked under the carport, and a spectacular old muscle car nestled between them, along with the shiny John Deere. Not many Sandhillers sprang for a tractor this extravagant. I could retire on what that baby cost. I rested my hand on the car, suspecting it was an expensive classic. Not being a classic car expert, I couldn't tell the year, but it sported a Roadrunner decal and Plymouth logo. It had less dust on it than the dresser in my bedroom.

There was no movement on the ranch. No cattle or horses in the corrals. No rooster crowing or chickens clucking. Not even a dog barked. Could be no one lived here. Maybe the nephew built this place from a fortune he had stashed. Might be he wanted a romantic Western homestead to visit on long weekends. Except it looked more like a movie set for the Dust Bowl than a weekend getaway. A curious contrast between expensive vehicles and purposeful dowdiness.

The buildings huddled between two ridges of rolling hills. A windmill with solar panels attached stretched above the barn, waiting for the first morning breeze. On the eastern ridge, immediately above one of the houses, a brown camouflage-painted tank, probably a water cistern, perched like a gargoyle overlooking the compound. It probably held about three thousand gallons, and the only reason I knew that was because I'd had to replace the cistern at Frog Creek a few years back. Course, I'd positioned that one well away from the house and corrals in case it sprung a leak. It's easier to lay some pipe than it is to repair flood damage.

The tracks led across the compound to a dirt bike resting against the big house.

It felt eerie walking into the ranch yard with no signs of

life, like a ghost town. My boots ground on the dirt of the central compound. Greening weeds with a smattering of grass, what was probably the previous Mrs. Olson's lawn, surrounded the house. All of the buildings, including the cookhouse and a few others with new construction made to look aged, were arranged in a merry-go-round formation along with the barn, like a modern version of circling the wagons. One of the smaller buildings might have been a chicken house with a small fence encircling it. But if any fowl lived there, they were oddly silent for daybreak.

I walked to the dirt bike resting against the house. Heat radiated from the engine. The single-story ranch house was nothing fancy, but it had a new coat of beige paint with white splotches smeared on top to look like peeling paint from a distance. A concrete slab porch led to what looked like a solid metal door with a small window for a peephole. Maybe, since the nephew didn't live here full time, he wanted the house secure. Most homes in the Sandhills didn't even have locks, but a city dweller wouldn't be comfortable with that. I knocked on the door.

I didn't wait for an answer but instead wandered to the side of the concrete porch to peer into a window. I leaned close, put my hands around my eyes, and squinted inside the dark house.

Yikes! A pair of eyes stared back at me.

I jumped away from the window and to the side of the house. Instinctively, I reached for my gun before remembering I wasn't carrying it. But I'd reached for it. Maybe I would get used to it, after all.

Since I had no weapon, I lowered my voice to the tough-girl range. "Grand County sheriff. Just want to talk to you."

Hot air close to my ear leaked a whisper. "Then talk."

How I didn't scream was a mystery, but I did jump and

spin around. A thin man, maybe fifty, in a fluffy camo bathrobe stood with his hand in his pocket. The bulge could easily be a gun. He wore leather moccasins, looking new from Lands' End, and his dark hair plastered to one side of his head and shot up straight on the other. A thick dust of black whiskers covered a pointy chin. He must have seen me coming and hid for the ambush. "What do you want?"

I lifted my eyebrows and indicated his hand, trying to act way cooler than I felt. My heart banged against my ribs. "Got something in your pocket?"

He studied me with skepticism. "No."

This was going well. "I'm Kate Fox, Grand County sheriff," I repeated.

"Yeah, so?" This guy wasn't easily intimidated. Not that I had much intimidation potential right then.

He could shoot me, bury me behind the cistern, and no one would know. I held up my hand in an "easy" gesture, and he tensed the arm that led to the hand in his pocket. I made steady eye contact. It might be cliché to say he had the beady eyes of a rat, but that's what struck me. I kept my voice slow. "There's an abandoned car on the highway, and I followed dirt bike tracks here. I wondered if someone picked up the driver."

"No." He glared as if I were an idiot. "Now leave."

I cocked my head and smiled with deliberate falseness. "The tracks are fresh."

He mimicked my fake expression. "I went for a ride."

"You look like you just woke up."

He glanced at his robe. "Do I?"

A bolt slid on the front door and it opened inward, followed by a woman's voice sounding low and sleepy. "Marty? What's going on?"

I wasn't buying her clueless, confused tone, betting she'd been the eyes behind the window.

Marty's voice didn't soften. "Nothing, baby. Go back to bed." Marty made his way to the doorway as if to defend the homestead. The door opened to a room hidden in shadows. I couldn't see anything beyond a scratched round table near the door, the kind used for keys and mail.

A blond woman, maybe forty-five, with a good inch of dark roots at her scalp and hair as attractively arranged as her husband's—assuming she and Marty were married—appeared behind him. She wore a cotton nightgown that hit below her knees and didn't leave me guessing about her pudgy form underneath it.

She blinked at me. "A cop?" One elbow knocked into Marty's rib while the other hand was hidden behind her back. "What did you do?"

They both spoke with a nasal twang, their words a hard accent we only heard on TV shows like *The Real Housewives of New Jersey*. Not that I ever watched it, but when I lived with Mom and Dad last winter, my nieces and nephews tuned in when they visited.

He swung his arm to shove her elbow away, and the gun he'd been hiding slipped out of his pocket, the barrel pitched my way. I ducked against the wall.

He spoke pointedly to her. "I've been riding my dirt bike."

She sneered at him. "You've been..." She stopped and nodded. "R-i-ight. Like you do every morning." The toothy grin leveled at me looked less than sincere.

She grabbed the barrel of his gun and yanked it toward the ground. "Put that away."

Marty jerked away from her but kept the gun down. "Back off, Rhonda."

She shot him a look that could stop a buffalo stampede. She pulled her arm from behind her nightgown and sat a pistol on the table inside the door. Rhonda looked to be far more hospitable than Marty.

When Marty backed up to set his gun inside, she turned to me. "What do you want?"

Another gun? How many did they own? I'd sauntered into an armed camp.

I started a new tack. "I think a woman might need help. I wondered if she came here."

She nailed me with dead brown eyes. "We finally got so the goddamned chickens don't wake us up at the crack of dawn, and now you bang on our door with this bullshit?" She held out her hand and waved it around the yard behind me. "No fool is here except you. So you can turn around and leave."

This was about as far from a Sandhills welcome as a body could get. For one thing, any Sandhiller worth his salt would have been up an hour or two ago. Not to mention the inhospitality of getting shot in your boots on the front porch. "Sorry to wake you."

She waved her hands in a shooing motion. "Move along."

I would've loved to turn tail, but that wasn't my job. It's not normal to hold up visitors, especially law, even if I didn't carry my badge or gun today.

Obviously, Marty had been the charmer of the two.

I couldn't have been less prepared for this encounter. Every experience was a chance to learn and improve, if I didn't end up getting killed along the way. I pulled up a big ol' bluff, like they didn't scare me. Walking unannounced onto someone's ranch might be rude, but I was the sheriff. Seemed like I ought to know what was happening in my county. "How many people live here?"

Rhonda scanned the yard behind me. "Where's your car?"

"On the highway." I pointed to show where I'd followed the tracks.

Behind her, a door slammed. Marty whipped his head over his shoulder and disappeared into the dark house.

Rhonda tilted her head, let her eyes travel down to my boots and up to my wild curls corralled by my ponytail. "You're trespassing."

She was starting to get my dander up. "I'm investigating an accident. Now, can I get your names?"

She leaned closer to me, invading my space in an aggressive way. I could probably slap some cuffs on her and take her in for threatening me. It would be an iffy charge at best, and considering I had no car to put her in, no gun to back me up, and really no reason to escalate the situation, I didn't think too hard along those lines.

Voices rose inside the house. Sounded like Marty and a younger guy. I jerked to the right, glancing behind Rhonda in time to see a tall, skinny kid with bushy dark hair shoot down the hall and through another door. It slammed, and then heavy footsteps stormed down stairs.

Rhonda pushed me and stepped over the threshold, pulling the door behind her. I nearly shoved her back before remembering who had the firepower. She kept her face close to mine, and I nearly gagged on a wave of garlic-laced morning breath. "You come back here with a search warrant and probable cause, and I'll tell you whatever I'm legally obligated to explain. Until then, get the hell off my property." Sounded like she had experience with the United States legal system.

But the bike and hidden kid? And what about the caller? I leaned around Rhonda again, trying to peer through the slit between the door and jamb. "Is someone else here?"

She snicked the door closed behind her. "You're too nosy."

She was right, but this was what the county paid me for, despite the perspiration and terror. I met her deadpan face with The Look. "I'm concerned about a citizen in distress, and I want to make sure everything is all right."

She took a step forward and bumped me back with her chest. "We haven't seen anyone."

At least the gun was on the other side of the door.

A car engine sounded in the quiet morning. Rhonda's eyes sharpened and she trained her attention on the road leading to the compound. Within seconds Barnett's beat-up pickup rumbled to stop in front of the house.

Rhonda's eyebrows, too dark for the blond she tried to pull off, dipped to hood her eyes. "Now what?"

Barnett slid out, all six foot two and 250 pounds of mean, and sauntered to my side. He held out his hand to Rhonda. "Don't believe we've met."

"It's a growing club," I said, relieved he'd shown up and had a gun.

Rhonda mimicked Barnett's Western drawl. "Don't believe I care. How the hell did you get past the lock?"

"Bolt cutters." He pulled a padlock from his brown coat pocket and held it out to her.

She snatched the lock from him and sniffed as if smelling spoiled fish. "Of course, you farmers carry bolt cutters at all times."

I didn't enlighten her about Sandhillers. We were ranchers, and calling us farmers, as Dad would say, is fightin' words.

She scowled and pointed at me, acting as if she wished her finger were a gun. "Arrest him for destruction of property."

Barnett beamed one of his I'm-an-asshole grins, except this time I didn't mind. "Thought we had an officer in trouble here. It's in the line of duty."

I tipped my head his way. "Lee Barnett, Spinner County sheriff."

"Fuck me." Rhonda threw her head back at the cloudless spring sky. "Haven't had my damned coffee this morning and I've got two cops on my doorstep."

Coffee sounded mighty fine. If she'd been a decent Sand-hiller, we'd all be enjoying a cup right now.

Barnett stood with his legs apart, hands on his hips. Probably confident with his weapon in his holster on the back of his right hip. "How about you give us the names of everyone living here, show us some ID, and we'll be on our way."

Rhonda folded her arms across her chest, hiking up her nightgown above her knees. With a sneer, she said, "How about you go to hell."

Barnett's arms popped to his sides and he lunged at her. "I ought to take you in for obstruction."

Rhonda didn't flinch but instead laughed. "Okay, Deputy Fife. You try that and see what a shit storm of legal trouble you land in."

I held up my hand. Much as I wanted them corralled behind bars and to know why they barricaded themselves in the hills, I figured we'd gone far enough for now. We could return and go all Waco on them later if we needed to. "All right. If you think of something, give me a call. That's Kate Fox, Grand County sheriff." Of course, I had no business cards to hand out, in the unlikely event they'd consider calling.

Rhonda gave me that dead stare.

Barnett didn't seem inclined to leave.

I turned around, hoping I wouldn't get shot in the back by either of them, and breezed to Barnett's pickup. I climbed inside and watched Barnett and Rhonda stare at each other for a few more seconds. Movement behind the window caught my attention. The sun spoked a ray into the house and someone pulled a shutter closed inside. Not blinds or curtains, a solid shutter. With a slit about the right size for a gun barrel and another for a peephole. These folks were ready for Armageddon.

Barnett stomped back to the pickup, threw himself inside, and gunned the engine, spraying gravel in Rhonda's direction. I glanced in the side mirror to see her flipping us matching birds with both hands.

Around the first curve from the house, we came across a steel-paneled gate with a loose chain dangling from one side where Barnett had cut the lock.

A thought occurred to me. "Why are you here?"

Did he hesitate? "Sally sent me to Ogallala to pick up a prescription. I saw your car on the road and figured you'd come this way. Why are you here?"

"I followed dirt bike tracks."

"And?"

"Interesting folks." Would they have shot me if he hadn't arrived?

"Damned preppers."

There were a few ranchers around who believed the end of the world loomed, or distrusted the government enough they hid and stayed off the grid. If I wanted to live independently, grow my own food, create my own energy, keep my own company, I couldn't pick a better place than the empty spaces in the Sandhills. Even then, I think I'd want community around me. The settlers staked claims in this lonesome region less than two hundred years ago, but they stayed semi-sane by having barn dances every now and again.

Rhonda and Marty seemed more like thugs than end-timers. "Do you know anything about them?"

Barnett sped down the gravel road, rattling my bones as we bumped over the washboards. A platoon of semi-trucks, the kind that would haul building equipment and tractors, would cause wear on a gravel road like this. His voice warbled with the rough road. "Didn't know anyone took over after old man Olson passed. This is all new to me."

It didn't seem an accident that these folks retrofitted a sizeable compound without anyone in Spinner or Grand County passing along gossip that wafted its way to either Barnett or me.

"You're new to the job, so listen to wisdom here. The car belongs to some drunk Indian. End of story."

I hated that he sounded so pleased I hadn't found anything. "Something was going on inside the house that Rhonda didn't want me to see."

Barnett huffed and shifted his gaze back to the road. "They're spooks. They wouldn't want you to see if they had tomatoes sitting on the kitchen counter. It's all a big secret to them."

I didn't tell him about the hot dirt bike or the kid fighting with Marty. And I certainly didn't mention the single car key on the table where Rhonda had set her gun. The key attached to a fob with the three lines of the Mercury logo.

4

The sun declared full-on morning by the time I returned to my cottage. I was more than ready for strong coffee. Too bad I hadn't remembered to buy any. Yeah, I'd taken to calling it a cottage on the lake instead of a dumpy little house stuck out in the country. It made me feel as if I'd purposely sought this solitary life and career as county sheriff. I didn't like thinking of my choices as consolation prizes for a failed marriage and losing the ranch I loved.

I shouldn't scoff at my progress, though. In the year since Ted and Roxy had jerked the rug out from under what I considered a near-perfect life, I'd gone from unemployed, living with my parents, and unsure how to move on, to being Grand County sheriff, owning a home on a lake, and most days, feeling some optimism about life.

After growing up one of nine kids in a cramped and chaotic house, I treasured the peace of Ted's and my home at Frog Creek, even after Carly moved in the last year. I loved my family, but trying to eke out any privacy at Mom and Dad's resulted in nine months of frustration. The solitude at my new house might weigh a little heavy at times, but generally, it suited me fine.

Glowering clouds gathered in the west like giant dark beasts, so I'd best enjoy the sunshine while it lasted. Buck naked, I wandered across my spring grass, goose bumps running over my skin despite the sun. Pride swelled when I greeted the seedlings breaking the crust in my garden.

After admiring my green thumb, I retreated to the house. Because I had no neighbors, I'd taken to dressing on my screened porch, and I pulled on my brown uniform while watching the ducks bobbing on the lake. The birds raised a ruckus in the three old elms that stood sentry at the edge of my yard. Leaves that were buds a week ago now spread with summer's promise.

The threatening storm clouds accented the blue sky stretching over Stryker Lake. "Lake" being a generous term for the puddle barely long enough to get a good head of steam to ski and only deep enough to keep an outboard engine from spewing up sand. A coyote trotted, his yellow coat waving in and out of reeds at the water's edge. Aside from the raucous gossip of the yellow-headed blackbirds, no sounds carried on the soft breeze.

Heaven. Or lonely. Depending on the day and my mood. Today my thoughts tumbled.

Were Rhonda and Marty hiding the driver? Had the driver returned to the rez unharmed?

Barnett's conclusion that the abandoned car didn't necessarily mean trouble made sense. No blood or anything to identify the owner. No emergency 9-1-1 calls, or dispatch would have notified us both.

However, Barnett hadn't heard the caller. *Please help me.*

What about the key on the table? It could belong to any ranch vehicle. Not the pickups or the muscle car, but an old

Mercury could be stored in the barn. Or the key on the fob might not necessarily belong to a Mercury. The key to Mom's VW Vanagon hung on a BMW ring.

I jumped back to Marty and Rhonda. From what I knew, all the Olsons were towheads. Blue-eyed, big-boned Swedes. Neither Marty nor Rhonda—proven by her dark roots—fit that description. Why all the secrecy and the fortified compound?

Was the girl in trouble? All of this stirred up my constant worry about Carly. Why had she run away in the first place? Where was she? Was she safe? The same questions that looped constantly in the back of my brain now thrummed insistently. Before I stuffed my feet back into my damp boots, I padded into the house to retrieve my phone and punched Baxter's number.

He answered before the second ring. "Is everything all right?" Glenn Baxter was a classmate of Carly's father from military school and took a keen interest in Carly's safety. Since he owned one of the largest cable news networks in the country, I'd gratefully allowed him to pay for a top-notch investigator to track down Carly. After a little over a year, he'd only uncovered meager leads.

Hearing his confident voice calmed me a little. "Fine. Just checking in."

"Whew." He sounded relieved. "It's getting late, and I was afraid something happened."

"What?"

His voice floated over the miles. "You usually call earlier on Sunday mornings."

I wasn't aware I had a schedule or that Baxter kept track. Since most weeks I didn't go to the courthouse on Sundays, maybe that's when I worried the most. I didn't know how I felt about Baxter knowing my schedule better than I did.

It sounded as if he sipped something, and I stepped one foot into a boot, suddenly in a hurry to get to the Long Branch and some of Aunt Twyla's chest-hair-growing java.

"I'm always happy to talk to you, of course, but I've got no news," he said.

Even though I knew he'd have called me if he had anything to report, hearing it disappointed me. The ducks paddled into the middle of the lake, keeping a good distance from the coyote prowling the shore. "Is the investigator still in California?"

Carly's mother, my oldest sister, Glenda, had died of cancer when Carly was only twelve. Two years after that, not long after her father, Brian, had remarried that thorn in my side, Roxy, he'd crashed his Cessna 182 into a hill. If that tragedy wasn't enough, just over a year ago, Carly's beloved granddad had been murdered. I hadn't seen her since. She'd called me once last January, and though she sounded sad and lonely, she was safe.

She'd convinced herself that her father's death wasn't an accident and, for some reason, she'd run away to find his killer. I didn't believe in a phantom murderer and figured Carly's quest had more to do with her grief than with reality. What I knew for sure was that I missed her, worried about her, and wanted her safe.

Baxter scolded while I looked out on the lake. "Obsessing about Carly isn't good for you. I'll let you know if we find anything."

The coyote pounced on something, probably a mouse. "It's just..." Just what?

"I know." He sounded as if he actually *did* know. All the frustration, the anger at her running away, the fear she'd get hurt, my aching desperation not to lose her forever.

Both feet in my boots, I clumped down the porch stairs

without lacing them. "You don't think someone really killed Brian, do you?"

Baxter and Brian had been as close as brothers, having attended military school together. Baxter didn't rip open his chest and let his heart spill all over me, but I knew Brian's death had been a blow. He sighed, probably because we'd been over this question so many times. "No. I don't think someone tampered with her father's plane and caused it to crash."

I climbed into the cruiser. "See? When you say it out loud, it sounds ridiculous."

His voice on the other end, like strong coffee with thick cream and a splash of Irish whiskey, loosened my tight chest. "She's confused and in mourning for her parents and grandfather. She's smart enough to evade the investigator, but we'll find her, or she'll come home soon."

The engine fired up with a roar. "If the investigator is as good as you say, why can't he find her?"

"He is good. Maybe Carly is hanging out with other young people. They would cover for her. From everything you've told me, Carly is smart and resourceful. She's fine."

He asked about my family, I asked about the latest celebrity gala, and we chatted for several minutes while I maneuvered the cruiser down my bumpy country road and the clouds dropped lower. As he always did, Baxter lopped the jagged edges off my worry. When I started to feel guilty about taking up too much of his time, I said, "Let me know if you hear anything about Carly."

"Kate." We both paused for no reason. Finally, he said, "It'll be okay."

He had a way of putting my fears for Carly in a bag and tying a string around the top. Containing them somehow. It wouldn't hold forever, but for now, I could go on. I repeated

Dad's favorite saying and Baxter joined in, having heard it from me. "It'll be okay in the end. If it's not okay, it's not the end."

The quiet comfort Baxter offered lasted long enough for me to turn from the lake road to the highway. That's when a doe decided to play chicken with my Charger. She sprang from the barrow ditch on the left and bounded in front of me. I slammed on the brakes, the seat belt slicing into my shoulder. I flinched, ready to feel the impact of flesh and steel.

I must have squeezed my eyes shut for a split second because I opened them to see her dashing off to the west, like Bambi after a butterfly.

My blood racing, heart pumping, breath sucking, all I could think of was the Mercury Marquis on its roof. I remembered the caller's plea. *Help me!*

"I'll try," I answered, then felt foolish for talking to the windshield. I started back down the road.

Since I didn't know the caller's identity or if she needed rescuing, my first priority was to find out about the preppers. If I could come up with some probable cause—and heaven only knew what that might be—I could check out their ranch headquarters. Find out if the girl was there.

On my way into town, I called Dad's cousin Stormy at R&S Auto. Stormy worked on cars, tractors, and haying equipment, sharpened ice skates and mower blades, and on slow afternoons, played pitch in his oily back room with some of the old ranchers who'd retired and moved to town. Someone answered and then hung up.

A minute later, my phone rang. "Sorry, Katie. I'm not used to this phone. It hangs up every time I answer the damned thing."

I'm pretty sure the whack I heard was his wife, Donna, slapping his arm. I'd seen her do it a hundred times. "Stormy!"

He sounded contrite to me. "Pardon my French." Donna had even less tolerance for cursing than Dad.

I warmed at the thought of them going through their same routines after forty years of marriage. "I've got an abandoned vehicle off the highway north at the county line. Can you tow it to town for me?"

"No can do. Brenda shelled out that pumpkin last night, and me and Donna are on our way to Broken Butte to see it."

More commotion on their end, and Stormy followed up. "Donna says it's a granddaughter, not a pumpkin or an *it*. But I can get 'er towed first thing tomorrow mornin'."

That would have to do. It only took ten minutes from my front porch before I slowed my speed on the edge of town. A closed sign hung in the Long Branch window, and the few other businesses in Hodgekiss were dark. Tuff Hendricks's pickup was parked at a wacky angle on Main Street, but that was probably from last night.

Backing the cruiser into its spot close to the courthouse back door, I gazed up at the still-sunny sky. It'd be nice to enjoy the morning before the rain hit. Too bad I couldn't still saddle my old roan, Cactus, and ride the hills. Ted still owned Cactus. Carly's mare, Burner, was a full sister to Cactus, five years younger. Ted insisted I let Burner stay at Frog Creek, safe and sound until Carly returned for her.

I couldn't find Carly. But maybe I could find the other missing girl. Giving one last glance of regret to the blue sky and sunshine, I unlocked the courthouse door and clambered up the back stairs in the mausoleum silence of the century-old building. I hadn't ever seen a ghost here, but it seemed possible they'd lurk in these halls. I didn't exactly run to my office, but I didn't waste any time slapping on the lights in the windowless cubby at the end of the corridor. I booted up ol'

Bessy, my computer, and connected to a 70s rock music station, setting the volume low.

Ethel Bender, the county assessor, kept the records on who owned property in Grand County. Betty Paxton, the county treasurer, collected taxes on the properties. Either of them could probably rattle off owners without taking time to consider. Unfortunately, on a Sunday, my best option seemed to be public records online. It didn't take me long to find the free website and punch in *Grand County*.

My phone rang and I was concentrating so hard I didn't check the caller ID. I recognized my mistake as soon as I said, "Sheriff."

Louise, my older sister, sounded like tiny vise grips squeezed her vocal cords. "Why aren't you out here?"

Might be better to pop back out to the Olson place and face Marty and Rhonda and their firearms than Louise when she was stressed out. Luckily, she couldn't strangle me through fiber-optic line. "Something came up. I'm not going to make it today."

"Something...?" Sputter, sputter. "No. I've got this listed in the program. 'Four County Sheriffs Compete in Wild Cow Milking.' It's the grand finale. The others are here."

Big doings were underway today at the fairgrounds in Grand County. Rog and Kendal Dugan's little girl, Scarlett, had been born with a rare disease I couldn't pronounce, and since Rog worked as a hired man on a local ranch, they didn't have much to see them through the long trial ahead. Louise had arranged a committee to put together the mother of all fundraisers. It would start with a barbeque beef lunch, all food donated and free-will offerings accepted. It moved on to a team roping competition and ended with a wild cow milking contest.

I winced as if warding off the blows. "I didn't plan an accident. Even you know that official sheriff business needs to come first. Milo, Pete, and Lee will still give a good show." And they would, but I'd get the real blue ribbon for avoiding that particular activity in which no one would emerge with dignity intact.

Louise had some more to say, including accusing me of lying to dodge my civic duty and how I had never been a team player and how disappointed Dad would be in my behavior. By way of penance, I listened until she wore down, then apologized again and tried not to feel too relieved when I hung up.

With three older sisters and one older brother, and three younger brothers and one younger sister, I was the ultimate middle child. I missed the wise, calm authority of Glenda. As second oldest, Louise took it upon herself to mother the rest of us, who had no intention of letting her get away with it. Diane, the next oldest, held the Overachiever card. She managed a big bank in Denver, drove the BMW whose key fob Mom used, and lived in a McMansion. Like Louise, Diane felt a certain proprietary right to direct my life.

It's no mystery why I relished privacy and solitude.

Bessy, the computer, had taken a nap while Louise burned my ear, so I woke her up with a jiggle to the mouse and continued my search. The site allowed me to zero in on the renovated ranch and get an eagle's view of the buildings. On my screen the large carport didn't sit in the middle of the ranch yard, and the barn had a much smaller footprint. The date on the images showed the photos had been taken three years ago. I experimented with the site, trying to get it to cough up the new owners. I could search for names or addresses. I had no address for the ranch, and inserting section, township, and range didn't get me anything. I tried variations of the Olson name to search for owners, but that netted me zero information.

I sat back while Led Zeppelin climbed one tall stairway. Dad knew everyone and kept their family trees planted in his memory. He might know the nephew's name who inherited the Olson place. Or maybe the name of the ranch, or even if and to whom it was sold. He was at the fairgrounds. Along with a good chunk of the population from the four-county region.

With a big enough crowd and my well-honed Louise radar, I might be able to slip in and out with no one getting hurt. And by no one, I meant me.

5

There were maybe twenty thousand things I'd rather do than glad-hand at the fundraiser and perform in the grand finale by trying to squeeze a few drops of milk from a rangy cow and run it across a finish line.

At best, I'd end up with cow manure slathered down my clothes and mud in my hair. At worst, my skull would be smashed by a well-placed kick. In the middle loomed humiliation, broken bones, and missing teeth, not to mention being forced to hang out with Lee Barnett and pretend we were amiable colleagues.

I couldn't see where being in the cow milking would help the Dugans much, since everyone there already paid an entrance fee. And my embarrassment wasn't an extra charge. This kind of event was mostly good public relations so I could get reelected.

I cruised three miles east of town to the fairgrounds.

The thirty acres of mostly sand and some scraggly grass featured a rodeo arena at its center. The wooden stands, painted every five years or so by the 4-H clubs, rose on the south side. The crow's nest towered on the north. Chutes and holding pens clustered on the east and west ends.

Pickups and stock trailers ringed the arena, where those who couldn't climb the stands or wanted the privacy and comfort of their vehicles could watch the action. Farther out from the arena people parked their stock trailers. Others rode horses or wandered around the grounds, visiting and teasing friends.

Cars and SUVs filled the dirt parking lot in front of the metal 4-H building several yards from the arena. Grimy kids chased each other through a half-dozen packed picnic tables where people enjoyed beef sandwiches. The entire fairgrounds rang with good cheer, like the Fourth of July.

If Marty and Rhonda were the kind to mingle with their neighbors, they'd be here, too. They were definitely not like us. Who were they, and why had they moved to Grand County? If Dad didn't know anything, or more likely wouldn't tell me, maybe someone else would. Eldon Edwards's ranch shared a few fence lines with the Olson place. He'd have been a good one to talk to, if he hadn't been murdered a year ago last April. Since Eldon had been Carly's granddad, thinking of that sent me full circle back to her and one step more to the girl on the phone.

Rain clouds edged closer but still looked a ways off. Cursing rain was something you never did in the Sandhills. Our main industry was grass. Tall, green pastures of lush grass fed cattle. And cattle ruled the Sandhills economy.

The beautiful spring morning might have helped draw out this big crowd. Even if plenty of folks out here didn't have two nickels to rub together, that didn't stop their generosity. Between the roping fees, the free-will contribution for the food that was prepared and provided by volunteers, and the donated silent auction items, this day would probably net the

Dugans ten thousand dollars. Knowing their neighbors cared about them enough to pull off this kind of shindig might offer some comfort. It was all we could do.

I wandered into the 4-H exhibit hall and the smell of beef barbeque, warm and savory. I wanted to ask everyone here about the Olson place and Marty and Rhonda. But the last thing I needed was the likes of Aileen Carson banging on Rhonda's barricades with a basket of muffins to welcome them to Grand County. I scanned the crowded building for Dad.

Guilt balled in my gut. Why was I working so hard to avoid helping Louise? Would it really kill me? I made a deal with myself. If I ran into Louise before I finished up official business, I'd go ahead with the wild cow milking spectacle.

Holding a plate of beef barbeque, Dad stood alone by the silent auction table containing one of Mom's hand-sculpted butter dishes. Someone would probably bid ten dollars for that dish, not knowing that in a gallery in Santa Fe, it would go for seven times that amount.

Before I took more than three steps in Dad's direction, a friendly voice caught me. Josh Stevens, a dark-haired man a little older than me, maybe thirty-six, seemed surprised he'd gained my attention. He stood six foot four, thin but muscular, with a generally serious face. Josh Stevens reminded me of Abraham Lincoln, only nicer looking. His grin surprised me, since I'd always thought of Josh as dour. But that might've been because I first met him last January, when he wasn't at his best.

He stared for a moment, as if hunting for conversation. "Looks like it's gonna rain."

Even though I knew exactly what the clouds looked like, I acted as if the impending storm was news to me. "We can always use the rain."

He nodded. "Makes the grass grow." And we came to the

end of that conversation. After a moment, he started another riveting topic. "So. Ready for the cow milking?"

I dodged. "How's Enoch getting on?"

Josh latched onto the conversation. "He's having a sandwich outside. He'd love you to come say hi."

Enoch, Josh's elderly father, spent some of his days mired in memories and confusion. Seeing him alert would be nice. "Of course. I need to talk to Dad first and I'll be right out."

Josh stood a moment longer, then smiled again. "Okay, then. I'll go on out and tell him."

I stepped back on the trail to Dad, only to find him missing. Dang. A quick scan of the 4-H building didn't cough him up. The line for food dwindled and nearly dried up, and a hunger pang punched my gut, so I altered my plan. I'd turned into an opportunistic diner since living alone.

Louise had recruited a slew of family to help out. I stepped up to Aunt Twyla, Dad's sister who owned the Long Branch. Her long dark hair was pulled back from her hard-living face and dangled between her shoulder blades. On the back side of noon, her usual hangover had probably started to lift.

With her scratchy voice, she barked at me. "Grab you a plate."

I didn't feel like I had time to sit and eat a whole meal. "Just a sandwich, thanks."

She huffed her disapproval but thrust the tongs into the loose beef and plopped it on the bun and shoved it at me. I lifted the bun lid, held the sandwich out to Uncle Bud, who towered over her.

He ladled sauce on top. "Ready for the cow milking?" He let out a belly laugh, no doubt picturing me covered in slimy manure.

My return chuckle was meant to be good natured and

noncommittal. I retreated outside. Clouds were falling into formation for their march on our afternoon.

I had taken one bite of the tender shredded beef slathered in Aunt Twyla's tangy sauce, when my nephew, David, fifteen and with all the geeky charm of a toad, slapped me on the back.

"Hey, I need you to come to my Lifestyles class on Wednesday for career day."

I mumbled around my sandwich.

His braces gave him a big-lipped lisp. "Sorry, forgot to tell you. No big deal, just a fifteen-minute talk about what you do."

I managed to swallow. "I—"

"Oh, and you're supposed to do PowerPoint." He loped off with a posse of equally awkward teens.

Another bite of pure Sandhills beefy deliciousness. I caught the flash of a familiar brunette ponytail disappear around the side of the 4-H building. Stuffing a few more bites of the sandwich in my mouth, I followed her.

I rounded the building, not liking what I found. Sarah bent over, her arm propping her on the wall of the building, her head down, and her whole body heaving. Glad I'd managed most of my sandwich, I tossed the last of it in a trash can and hurried to her.

I put my hand on her back. "Don't tell Twyla her sauce made you sick."

She sounded shaky. "Not even. All I did was smell the potato salad and Tigger rebelled." Tigger was the name Sarah and Robert gave to their unborn baby.

"Potato salad doesn't smell." When I thought about it, though, I supposed onions and mustard might turn a sensitive nose.

She gagged. "Tigger is going to kill me. If you loved me,

you'd pull this parasite from inside me and protect me, like in first grade."

Sarah and I had been practicing roping a fence post when Grady Brown ran by and pushed her. I roped that little brat and tied him to the merry-go-round, and Sarah and I were about to run him like a horse in a round pen when Mrs. Macomber stopped us.

Sarah and I were always on the same team. "That one got me prison rations and a week of extra chores."

"Wish you could help me now."

Me, too. "I love you, but the friend contract clearly includes Tigger under my protection."

Her shoulders relaxed, the puking over for now. "You're the best aunt."

Yeah, that's why Carly had run away. "I'll grab you some water."

She pushed herself from the wall and pulled a tissue from her jeans pocket. "Thanks."

Barb Houser stopped me on my way back and wanted to know if I thought drug dealers from Omaha were targeting our kids. With a little sympathizing and uh-huhing, I was able to get away from her fairly quickly.

I stepped around the side of the building. No Sarah. Probably felt better and got tired of waiting for me. I'd say a quick hello to Enoch and try to track Dad.

Several picnic tables were scattered around, and Josh waved at me from the one farthest away. Sharp-faced Enoch, with his dandelion wisp of hair fluffing in the breeze, scowled my way. I took it as an invitation, since Enoch wasn't prone to happy faces.

Between me and Josh was a table filled to overflowing with kids sitting on laps and everyone else squeezed together. The adults leaned into the center of the table, obviously cussing and discussing something engaging. The very definition of trouble in Grand County.

My immediate Fox clan—most of us, anyway. With brothers and sisters, various spouses, and offspring, we'd grown into an intimidating army. Even Diane managed to visit from Denver, and the youngest, Susan, a student at the University of Nebraska (Go Big Red) sandwiched into the mix.

My heart squeezed a drop of acid into my gut when I noticed my not-so-loyal clan had admitted a new member. Roxy. For the younger Foxes, that might make sense. They'd consider Ted family, and since he had a new wife, she'd belong, too. I thought my family ought to be more discriminating.

Roxy was sitting right next to Sarah, who looked more alive than she had a few minutes ago.

As I approached, Jeremy, second youngest, poked his head up and spotted me. He spoke loud enough to drown out the others. "Anyway, I've always said Nebraska should stick to the running game."

Good try. Except this wasn't what they were arguing about because everyone in Nebraska knows the Huskers needed to keep the ball on the ground. Whatever they'd been arguing about, obviously, they didn't want me to know. I stood at the head of the table, giving them each a one-second eye interrogation, using my Super Sheriff investigation skills. "Okay, what's going on?"

Sarah's wan smile looked guilty. "Roxy saw me puking and offered me saltines she keeps in her purse."

"Great. But that's not what I mean."

Michael, twin to Douglas and the wheeler-dealer of the group, found a smarmy grin. "What? We're having some good family time. Join us."

Even if I could squeeze onto a bench, which I couldn't, I

didn't feel welcome. So I stood like a thistle in a rose garden, staring down at them.

Diane gave an exasperated huff, something she seemed practiced at, probably from a million corporate meetings she manipulated to her will. "For fuck's sake."

My sister-in-law Lauren squeaked at the curse. Susan rolled her eyes. Most ignored it.

Diane shook her head in annoyance. "Here's the deal. It's time you start dating. You're highly marketable. We're trying to figure out your best option."

Boom.

That was not what I expected. My jaw dropped, and I stood like a lump of biscuit dough. I snapped my mouth closed, blinked to make sure this wasn't a nightmare, and spun around.

A hand clasped my bicep. I'd have welcomed a hungry wolf if it'd rescue me from this batch of backstabbers, but I settled for Louise. Shaped like an overripe pear, she wore her hair in a strange perm like she'd stepped out of Grandma Ardith's high school yearbook. "The other sheriffs are waiting for you."

I didn't pause to consider the timing. Louise offered me escape from a deep, boiling stew of humiliation, and I gladly jumped for it.

I dragged Louise away at a clip faster than she was used to, causing parts of her to undulate like an abominable belly dancer. I finally asked, "Why are they waiting for me? The wild cow milking is the last thing."

Louise caught her breath and slowed to zero mph. "There's this other thing."

Remembering why I came to the fairgrounds in the first place, I scanned the crowd for Dad. "Whatever it is, I can't. I'm working."

Louise hammered her fists on her hips. "Liar."

Fine. Maybe she could help. "Have you heard anything about the Olson place?"

Louise disseminated information like a one-woman social media site. Her eyes lit up. "Is there trouble?"

I leaned closer, like I wanted to share something juicy. "Has Norman delivered fuel there?"

She practically salivated. "What's going on?"

I played Louise like a piano, except I couldn't read music. "What do *you* think is going on?"

She paled. "It's drugs, isn't it? The kids are having parties out there. Barb was right. You can't tolerate abandoned buildings hidden out in the hills. Have you been out there?"

I needed to shut this down. "I'm just yanking your chain. There's no drug house out there."

Louise wasn't ready to quit the trail. "It's a meth house, isn't it? Some dealers from Omaha think our kids are naive."

I laughed, pretending I'd set her up and she'd fallen for it. "You're too easy. Honestly. There's nothing going on out there."

She glowered at me. "When will you ever grow up? Now you owe me."

She paused and a warm breeze ruffled her sweat-damp hair. A heavy scent of hay, horse, and manure wafted over us. She considered a group of teenagers including her son, David, and his older sister, Ruthie. Louise's eyes narrowed as if she had MegaMom X-ray powers to hear them.

I looked closer. The bushy dark hair. The kid from Marty and Rhonda's place. He stood taller than most and hung on the outside of the circle with his head dipped, looking at his shoes. A couple of the others leaned toward him as if trying to hear his words. I jerked against Louise, attempting to steer her toward the knot of kids.

Apparently satisfied her kids stayed on the straight and

narrow, Louise picked up her pace and spouted words at me like a deranged garden sprinkler. "We thought we could raise a bunch for the Dugans with this. And the other sheriffs agreed, except Lee Barnett balked a little, but Milo convinced him. And it's going to be fun and you'll see, it's all okay."

I pulled up short. "What did you do?"

She wouldn't look me in the eye and instead waved to Newt and Earl Johnson, two bachelor brothers around Dad's age.

I grabbed one of her chins and forced her to look at me. "What?"

6

Louise huffed. "Pie throwing. We wanted the dunk tank instead, but Shorty Cally said it has a leak from when we used it for Principal Barkley at the after-prom party."

I swiveled on my boot and started in the opposite direction. I couldn't hang out in a pie booth now. I needed to talk to that kid. He knew Rhonda and Marty, probably his parents. He might know something about the abandoned car and the caller.

Louise grabbed hold of my arm and, since she had the weight advantage, used my momentum to propel me toward the group of three men standing next to a folding table weighted with whipped cream–topped pies.

May Keller, a tough rancher old enough to have played craps with the first Pharaoh and looking like she'd been mummified alongside him, sat behind the table taking money. The line snaked back several yards. Louise was right; slathering the local law enforcement with pastry would be lucrative for the Dugans and their daughter. How could I say no?

The bushy-headed dude would hang out with my nieces

and nephew and I'd catch up to them later. Ruthie and David would give me the skinny on the kid.

Louise deposited me in front of Milo Ferguson, Choker County sheriff, Pete Grainger, Chester County sheriff, and Lee Barnett, whose Basset hound expression hadn't improved since this morning. They'd been sharing a joke, but their easy laughter faded, replaced with their public faces.

I peered over Louise's head, pinpointing the group of kids, making sure I knew who else hung out with them. When I gave my attention to the sheriffs, I caught Barnett following my gaze.

Milo rested his arms on his potbelly, worrying a toothpick in the corner of his mouth. Pete stood next to him, strung tight like a spring, with a dark complexion and brown hair. His friendly smile, eager as always. I tipped my head in greeting. "Gentlemen."

Pete, sugar to Barnett's vinegar, held out his hand. I shook it, not having to tilt my head much for eye contact. His military buzz cut and crisp uniform made him look like a Marine, but his cheeriness eased the severity. "I propose we go in order of age. That's you first," he said.

I jerked my hand from his. "Way to throw me under the stampeding hooves. I thought you were my friend."

Milo buried the toothpick in the side of his mouth. "Pete's everybody's friend. But he ain't stupid."

"I've got a better idea." I lunged toward Milo, and before he could defend himself, I pulled a small plastic tube from his breast pocket. I thumbed the lid off, shook out two toothpicks, and handed them to Louise. "We draw straws."

"Great idea," Louise said. She was trying to get in my good graces again.

The three middle-aged sheriffs didn't like that as much as sending me to slaughter first, but they agreed. Louise snapped the toothpicks. She turned her back to us and hunched over to line them up in her fist.

Barnett cast a mean smile. "Surprised you interrupted your investigation to join us."

Milo lifted his eyebrows at me. "Got a case?"

Barnett laughed, but his jowls hung low and his belly didn't jiggle. "I'll say. A rez car left on the highway by a drunk Indian. Fox thinks some woman was abducted by aliens or something. She's like a bloodhound sniffing around the country."

Pete and Milo both looked at me for an explanation. "The car rolled off the highway and landed on its roof."

Pete, always a burn of energy, seemed to intensify. "Anyone hurt?"

I shook my head. "No blood. There's no ID on the car and nobody around."

Milo sucked on a toothpick. "No blood and if it's from the rez. Well."

The other three obviously agreed with this assessment, and even Pete seemed to relax a bit. I didn't want to go any further. "Do either of you know anything about the new buildings at the Olson place?"

Pete's deeply tanned face looked blank. Milo shrugged. Barnett laughed again. "She's all spooked about some preppers moving in. Got the solar panels and windmill and whole nine yards."

Milo grunted as if building up momentum in his big belly to form words. "Yeah. I've got some preppers in Choker County. They mostly keep to themselves."

Pete's conversation shot out of him, making me wonder if he could share some of his overabundance of firepower with Milo. "Never give me trouble. They don't want anything from me, and I leave 'em alone."

Barnett harrumphed. "We all wanted to be Dirty Harry when we started. But be careful or you'll end up more Barney Fife."

That's what Rhonda had called Barnett. It had obviously stung, and he wanted to pass it on.

Pete's wife, Tammy, hurried over and wound an arm around him. I always thought Pete had lucked out with Tammy. Though Pete had a plain, almost homely face, and might be considered on the short side, Tammy was a beautiful blonde from Omaha who he'd met in college probably thirty years ago. I liked that in this case, the good guy got the beauty queen.

She gave Pete a peck on his cheek. "I have a clean shirt for you in the pickup."

Milo guffawed. "Ain't that sweet. Gloria told me not to kill my fool self and went off to spend the day with her sister in Broken Butte."

Barnett grunted. "I didn't tell Sally about this."

Tammy hugged Pete tighter. "The kids wouldn't miss seeing their dad tangle with a wild cow. Watching him get pied is a bonus."

Pete laughed in delight. "Always after their old man." Pete's oldest son was an All-State quarterback for Chester County Consolidated High School, and Pete's daughter had enough 4-H trophies to shingle a house. They seemed like a nice family, and Pete never missed an opportunity to brag on his kids.

Louise whirled around like she'd performed a magic act.

The line to throw pies grew. My youngest brother, Jeremy, gave me a thumbs-up with a devilish grin. If I'd had doubts before, now I knew I'd be a sticky whipped cream mess in a matter of minutes.

Louise thrust her hand out, and Barnett snatched the first

straw, keeping it hidden. I picked next, then Milo. Pete Grainger, always polite, took the remaining straw.

Relieved at the long piece he'd drawn, Milo held his up first. "How 'bout that."

Pete looked worried but slowly opened his palm and held out his hand. Tammy slapped him on the back, and they shared a chaste kiss. She dabbed lipstick from his lips.

I moaned. Milo and Pete both hooted when I showed my sliver to be slightly shorter than Pete's.

A whispered "Shit" slithered from Barnett's lips. He tossed his draw onto the ground.

A soft bump to my leg drew my attention to Kyle Red Owl, our shared deputy, as he bent over to pick up Barnett's straw. Not more than a few inches taller than my five-three frame, Kyle was made of muscle and gave the impression he could spring into action at any moment. Guess Marine training did that for a person.

Kyle held up Barnett's straw and laughed, his teeth white against his dark skin. "As the old Lakota say, 'Age before beauty.'"

Milo cringed and pulled in his neck, as if expecting an explosion.

It came in the form of Barnett's booming voice. "Don't need Indian-speak to tell me this draw was rigged."

Good ol' Pete. He held up his hand. "Whoa there, Lee. We all did it fair and square."

Tammy's smile slipped, and she backed away as if Kyle smelled bad. She caught me watching her and brightened again.

Barnett lowered his eyebrows and shifted a ray of anger from Kyle to me. "Isn't this your weekend off? Why did you take the call this morning instead of Red Owl?"

I'd hoped this wouldn't come up. I opened my mouth to

answer, but Kyle got there first. "I was at a sweat for the youth of Antelope Ridge."

Milo eyed Barnett as if to see whether he ought to dive for cover. But Pete spoke with concern. "Is everything okay?"

Kyle nodded, worry lodged in the wrinkles on his forehead. "I hope so."

Barnett exhaled. "You're kidding me." He swung his head from Milo to Pete and back to Milo. "We need a deputy we can trust, not one who runs off to the rez at the drop of a hat."

A few people stopped to stare at us and more started milling our way, sort of like school kids expecting a fist fight.

Although he spoke in a soft voice, steel knifed through Kyle's tone. "I'm on the clock now, Sheriff Barnett."

Barnett sneered. "Admirable." To Milo and Pete, he said, "Told you we need to have Ted back." He glared at me in challenge.

Since Kyle had taken Saturday off, he'd arranged to come to the office on Monday. I didn't really need him, but I figured he could use the wages. My budget didn't have a lot of wiggle room, but making a deputy as happy as possible paid off in terms of availability when I needed him. Along with Kyle being qualified, reliable, and experienced, another big incentive for providing job satisfaction and keeping him on the force, was that as long as we had Kyle, we wouldn't need to hire another deputy. Namely, Ted.

I wanted to brain Barnett, and I suspected Kyle might be close to throwing the first punch. I stepped forward, hanging on to calm by the tiniest thread.

Louise clapped her hands in her annoying way. "Lee, you step on up there and we'll get going."

I tugged Kyle's arm and pulled him a few steps away, turning my back on the other sheriffs. "Why don't you patrol the highway?"

Sun soaked into his black hair, and his dark eyes questioned me. "Now?"

I tipped my head toward the other sheriffs. "I think we've got enough lawmen here already."

He considered the other sheriffs. "I don't really match the set, huh?"

I could commiserate about being odd man out, but what good would that do? "They like you well enough when you give them a weekend off."

Kyle's shrug acknowledged the truth. "My uncle Lloyd Walks His Horse served two tours in Vietnam. One guy in his unit, he served with him both times. This guy, a white guy, always called Lloyd Chief. But Lloyd, he doesn't let it bother him. The guy makes fun of him all the time, never treats him like a true brother. And one night, they get in this terrible firefight. Lots of casualties, lots of soldiers hurt. This white guy gets injured pretty bad. Uncle Lloyd, he takes a hit to the shoulder, but he's like a Dog Soldier. Man, he's fighting and hauling his comrades out of danger, like some kind of Lakota legend."

The other sheriffs looked at me with impatience. I tried to hurry him along. "So your uncle saved the white guy, gained his respect, and now they're friends."

Kyle's eyes traveled to Barnett. "No. Lloyd saved a lot of brothers that day. But the guy that disrespected him, he never made it out."

At only twenty-eight, Kyle had been in the Marines and spent a couple of years in the deserts of the Middle East. He probably had a few stories of his own.

I wanted to show I supported him despite Barnett's jabs. "Did the sweat go well?"

His dark eyes clouded. "Sometimes feels like a losing

battle. But some of those kids, they've got light in them. Gives me hope for the tribe, you know?"

Except he looked more sad than hopeful, kind of how I felt when I thought about Carly. "Wish they knew how big the world is and how full of possibilities."

Kyle nodded and walked away, and I turned back to the pie throwing, anticipating Barnett getting creamed.

Louise bustled over to Barnett with a plastic tablecloth. "Quit being such a baby. It's for a good cause." She wound it around his neck like a barber's cloth and snatched his cowboy hat from his head, showing thinning grayish hair, damp with sweat. He plodded to the chair set up thirty feet from the pie table and flopped down. He threw his own version of The Look to the people in line, but no one backed away.

The first pie throwers were giggling grade school girls. I tried to hide my disappointment when they missed.

Then a pie flew through the air and smacked into Barnett's face, cream coating his hair and splashing onto his brown pants. It was followed by two more in rapid fire, like an automatic baseball pitching machine gone haywire. The sixteen-year-old boy tossing them wore a maniacal grin in direct contrast to Barnett's murderous grimace.

Louise grabbed the fourth pie before he launched it. "You can't throw after you already hit him. I'm going to charge you double for those other two, and you're banned from any more today."

Barnett didn't bother to lick the cream from his lips, and it looked like rabies frothing his mouth. If I were that kid, I'd be heading for the hills.

The kid laughed, all teeth, long legs and arms. "So worth it." Barnett had probably picked him up for speeding or underage drinking.

Barnett jumped up and stomped forward, untying the

tablecloth. "Your turn, Fox." He thrust the cream-soaked cloth at me, and I barely grabbed hold before he shot toward the line.

He pushed my brother, Jeremy, out of the way at the front and fished in his pocket, coming out with crumpled bills. He thrust them at May and palmed a pie.

He didn't smile as he waited for Louise to tie on my bib. Forget about the sticky cream clotting in my hair and drawing flies. When Barnett shot that pie at me, the plate might break my nose.

Barnett's chin twitched like Clint Eastwood right before he pulled the trigger.

7

With no escape possible, I allowed Louise to tie the tablecloth around my neck. Like a prisoner facing a firing squad, I sat, gritted my teeth, and stared Barnett in the eye.

His eyes gleamed like a killer jack-o'-lantern, and I knew I was toast. He drew his arm back, the pie resting on his open palm.

"Ka-tie, Ka-tie, Ka-tie." A chorus erupted to the right of the pie table. My family. From what I could tell, the whole herd, including all brothers and sisters, a handful of nieces and nephews, Bud and Twyla, and even Dad, joined in the chanting. "Ka-tie, Ka-tie, Ka-tie."

It must have worked like some kind of Fox voodoo, because when Barnett launched the pie, it sailed wide. I felt the wind as it whizzed past my head and landed in the dusty weeds behind me.

My peanut gallery erupted in cheers.

Barnett reached for another pie, but Louise shot an arm out and stopped him. "You'll need to get to the back of the line if you want to try again."

At that signal, the Foxes crowded in behind Jeremy, and

the line tripled in length. Barnett's Clint Eastwood sneer scorched me, but not for long, as a fluffy plop of canned whipped cream collided with my noggin. Jeremy lifted his arms in triumph. Sticky, but not having my eyes blackened or my nose broken, I laughed, wiped and licked the fluff from my face, and stood for Louise to untie the bib.

Louise handed me a damp towel and turned her attention to Pete. Onlookers and his family teased, and the whole thing began again.

I scanned the crowd for the teens and located Ruthie and David and a few of their friends threading their way through the stock trailers. I scrubbed at a spot of cream on my chest and started after them.

My sister Diane called to me, and even though that made me want to run the other way, I waited for her to catch up to me. "Did you decide who I should marry?" My question came out snarkier than I expected.

Diane wore khakis and a golf shirt embroidered with her bank logo. Her expensive blond haircut looked perfect, despite the breeze tugging it, each strand landing exactly right. She had the tight, toned look of someone who worked out regularly with a personal trainer. If I was the black sheep of the family, Diane was definitely the Golden Fleece. She flashed remarkably white teeth. "Learn to take a joke."

She was right. I could hang on to the insult, but why? In a few days, there would be something else to be offended about. If I didn't let it roll off, I'd spend my life angry or alone. I rubbed a dried bit of cream from a strand of hair. "Thought you were heading back to Denver this morning."

The loudspeaker crackled and Bill Hardy test, test, tested. He'd been announcing rodeos and ropings since before I could say yee-haw.

"Welcome, welcome!" He launched into a corny joke,

thanked everyone for helping out the Dugans, and empha-
sized that the Calcutta on the roping would be split fifty-fifty
with the family, so be sure to bid it up.

Diane rolled her eyes at Bill's drivel. "Kimmy and Karl
wanted to stay for the barbeque. What the hell? We'll get
home at bedtime and I need to stay up late to prep for a meeting, but, when you're a single parent, you make sacrifices."

Yeah. I wouldn't know, not having any kids of my own.
"How are the anniversary plans coming?"

Mom and Dad's anniversary was coming up, and Louise
wanted a family get-together in town. Diane insisted we all
contribute and give them a getaway weekend instead. She'd
promised to plan it and make reservations, and we'd all
agreed. Except for Louise, of course.

Diane waved her hand. "It's coming together."

One problem I didn't have to worry about. "Great."

"So." She hesitated, and I knew this wouldn't be good. "You
know Poupon?"

Uh oh. Poupon was Diane's three-year-old Standard
Poodle. When someone asks a question they know you can
answer, you should back away. I tried, but she kept up
with me.

"He's been getting out of the yard, and I hired a fence
company to install an underground electric fence. The kind
that works on a collar. But they can't do it for two weeks. I was
going to leave Poupon with Mom and Dad, but Mom's
working on a new sculpture, and now that you're not living
there, well, he needs more attention."

I looked over my shoulder, backing away faster.

She slipped around me to look into my face. "So I left him
out at your house."

I stopped. "What? I can't keep a dog. I'm hardly ever
home."

She wouldn't hear it. "He's really easy. Doesn't need much. It's only for two weeks."

"No, I..."

Bill Hardy's voice rang over the fairgrounds. "What do you get when you give an alligator a vest?"

Diane raised her chin and focused behind me. "Kimmy! Karl! Time to go."

"An in-VEST-igator!" Groans accompanied the stupid punch line, and Bill introduced the first ropers.

Diane started to leave, blowing me a kiss and saying, "Thank you. I owe you."

"Wait!"

She turned, eyebrows raised.

I held firm. "I refuse."

She had the nerve to laugh at me. "You don't refuse."

I rubbed my sticky fingers, feeling less than powerful with bits of cream sticking on me. "I do now. Bad things happen when I'm put in the care of living things."

The annoyed exhale and drop of her arms dismissed my argument. "Get over it. Carly ran away because she's willful. You aren't to blame."

Why did she assume I was thinking of Carly? I hardly talked about her, so my family shouldn't know she was always on my mind. "She was my responsibility."

Diane walked away, pausing only long enough for her end of the conversation. "She's probably living it up in California."

I lunged at her and caught her arm. "California? How did you know she's there?"

Diane lasered my arm with her supersonic eyes, and when I didn't let go, she wrenched it free and made a face at the sticky spot on her arm. "I didn't know. It just seems that if I ran away, I'd go someplace warm."

I meant to question her further but she walked away, shouting at Kimmy and Karl.

Someone chuckled behind me.

I turned around to see Kyle with his eyes twinkling.

"Aren't you supposed to be patrolling the highway?"

He held up his hands, still grinning. "On my way, boss."

Before he left, Roxy waved from a few yards away on a straight path toward me. On instinct, I swung to look behind me to see who she wanted. Oh, please lord. No one was there. She came at me like a tornado. I altered my course to follow the teens and swerve away from Roxy. It didn't work.

"Kate. Wait. I want to talk to you." Roxy jiggled and wiggled on her way to us.

I lowered my eyebrows at Kyle to indicate he should be going, but he folded his arms across his chest and waited to see what bee Roxy had up her bonnet.

Knowing prying eyes watched every time I met Roxy in public, I plastered on a polite smile. The mature and forgiving cheated-on ex-wife, that's me.

Roxy caught up to me, all out of breath. She nodded a greeting to Kyle, then patted her pregnancy-swelled boobs. "Whew! I can't believe how much expecting a baby takes out of me. Normally, I wouldn't be winded at all."

I waited, trying not to wish expecting a baby would take more out of her than her wind.

"I'm glad I found you. I heard that Trey Ridnoir is on his way to the roping. He'll be here pretty soon. Ted brought in a mare he wants to sell, and Trey agreed to ride her in the roping to show her off. But he needs a partner. Ted and I knew you'd be perfect."

"Me?" I couldn't help the outburst. I hadn't roped since Ted had kicked me off Frog Creek when I served him divorce papers.

"You should ask me," Kyle said, his eyes still holding a mischievous gleam.

Roxy and I both stared at him.

He took us in with his gaze. "Yep. I learned to rope from my uncle, Lloyd Walks His Horse. He won the Indian Rodeo All Around eight years in a row."

Roxy tilted her head. "I think I've heard of him."

Oh, brother.

Spurred on, Kyle continued. "One time, when I was a kid, I followed Lloyd around at the finals. I noticed that every time he was up for an event, like saddle bronc or steer roping, he'd go to the stock pen first and sing. Only it was so soft I couldn't hear what he sang. So when I asked him about it, he told me he sang to each animal according to who they were, and the stock appreciated it so much, they helped him out."

On the loudspeaker, Bill Hardy commiserated with a missed throw. "Let's show the hard-luck cowboys how much we appreciate their effort." He couldn't seem to help his stupid jokes. "What kind of music do bunnies like best?"

Roxy's eyes stayed riveted on Kyle as if she were listening to the Dalai Lama.

Bill answered himself. "Hip-hop." More groans.

Roxy nudged Kyle. "Finish your story."

"Uncle Lloyd, he taught me the song especially for the steers. Only I don't do it much because it doesn't seem fair."

Roxy blinked and gave me a tentative smile. "Is he serious?"

All I could do was look at her and silently thank Kyle for pointing out what an airhead she could be.

She laughed. "Oh. I get it."

Kyle chuckled. "Indian stories." He saluted me and took off.

I tipped my head to her. "Thanks for thinking of me. But

I'm working today." I did my best Diane imitation and glided away, looking over my shoulder to shoot her a wave.

On the trail of Ruthie and Company, Louise collided with me. "Thanks so much for helping out at the pie throwing. We made a couple of hundred."

Pleased and feeling like a hero, I said, "Since I'm out here already, I could participate in the wild cow milking."

She looked startled. "Oh, that's okay. I understand you've got important county business."

She...understood? That didn't sound like Louise. But I'm not one to look a gift horse, or a wild milk cow, in the mouth. I trotted off before she changed her mind.

By now the wind had picked up and the dark clouds lumbered closer. The seventies temperatures held, though, so the day progressed in cheery fashion. The steers in the holding pen occasionally bawled, and horses whinnied over the sounds of the crowd. If not for a missing girl and an abandoned car, mysterious headquarters hidden in the hills, and my family meddling in my life, it would be a grand day.

I wound through the parked stock trailers and horses, twisting around pickups, and country music competed with Bill Hardy's corny jokes as I looked for Ruthie and her gang. My guess was the kids found someone's pickup and were having a private party.

Part of me hoped so, just to loosen Ruthie's halter a little. She was that bossy kind of older sister who took house rules so seriously she sucked the warm out of a sunny day. A little healthy trouble would do her good. But only a little.

It took a few minutes to find the bunch. I was disappointed the bushy-haired kid wasn't among them. David and his herd either got bored or were chased away by the older and cooler kids. I didn't have to try hard to sneak up on them. They were huddled in the bed of Ostrander's new half-ton, passing around a cigarette.

When I popped around the fender, Ruthie nearly passed out. "Oh, jeez. Oh, jeez. I didn't. I wasn't."

I kept my face neutral.

She teared up. "Don't tell Mom."

This girl could use some lessons in harmless teenaged rebellion or she'd never break out of her mother's mold. Carly had been inching Ruthie toward loosening up, but when Carly hit the road, Ruthie buttoned back tight.

I studied the other four kids. My detective's nose didn't pick up any pot or beer. Rodeos and kids on their own could lead to any manner of mischief, and it wouldn't hurt to check them out. I had them each hand over their pop cans for a good sniff, and if they had vodka or anything else in there, I couldn't tell. After clearing them, I assured Ruthie I wouldn't tell Louise that some of her friends snuck a cigarette in Ostrander's pickup.

"Earlier, I saw you talking to a dark-haired guy. Tall, kind of cute. Who was that?"

Melanie Ostrander giggled. "You thought he was cute?"

Dusty Hardy made a face like he'd stuck his nose in road-kill. "Dude, please."

Ruthie shrugged. "I thought he was okay."

The others poked her and laughed and generally acted more like junior high kids than upperclassmen. I gave them a "settle down" kind of glare. "Who is he?"

"Max?" Melanie ventured.

"Max who?"

Ruthie spoke for the group. "Don't know. He kind of walked up and started talking. That's all."

"What did he say?"

Dusty's eyes widened. "Is he a fugitive? Drug dealer or gang killer or something?"

Sheesh. "Far as I know, he's just a kid. I hadn't seen him around before and wondered if you guys had."

Ruthie answered in her Sunday school voice. "He wanted to know if Kyle Red Owl was around. We told him we didn't know, and he wandered around a little while, then left."

Interesting. I'd ask Kyle about him tomorrow.

Bill Hardy broadcast over the arena. "Give 'em some love. You'll get 'em next time, fellas." The crowd dutifully applauded, and I started toward the 4-H building and my cruiser. "Stick around, folks, for the wild cow milking. We've got one more team to go and then the Sandhills' finest will show you what they're made of."

The chutes squealed, shouts flew from the stands, clapping. "And that's how it's done, folks. Shorty and Willy Cally in seven seconds!"

Wow, that time ought to win the whole thing. I'd have to remember to congratulate them on their performance. As Ted used to tell me, an elected official is always campaigning.

Admittedly, when I ran for sheriff, I wasn't sure I really wanted the job. Sure, I needed employment after leaving Frog Creek, and this gig paid better than most in the county when you factored in benefits, which most ranch jobs didn't have. One main motivator for me, and I didn't tell anyone this, was taking the job away from Ted. There. I wasn't proud of that.

Since then, though, I'd settled into it. I might even say I liked being sheriff. At least temporarily. Maybe I'd run again in three years.

Bill Hardy's voice traveled over the fairgrounds. "Coming up, the event you've all been waiting for. Be thrilled, be amazed, be very entertained as the sheriffs from the four-county region compete in the wild cow milking."

I should have insisted I participate in the cow milking. That kind of thing generated a wealth of goodwill.

Since I'd thrown away that opportunity, I needed to round up Dad and see if he had any insights on the Olson place. I paced toward my Charger, grumbling inwardly about Diane manipulating me again and about my family planning my life.

"How many teenagers does it take to screw in a lightbulb?" Bill Hardy fired up the mic again, then answered himself. "Whatever."

After the obligatory groan, he said, "And here they are, for your ultimate Sandhills' entertainment. Milo Ferguson from Choker County, Lee Barnett from Spinner County, Pete Grainger from Chester County, and our very own from Grand County, Ted Conner."

8

Didn't that just frost your tomatoes? No wonder Louise let me off the hook so easily. She'd already recruited Ted. What a family. I'd have thought that when I divorced Ted, they'd have chosen my side. But no. Seemed the whole caboodle of them picked Ted and slipped Roxy into my place. Even Sarah, my best friend since kindergarten, huddled with Roxy like pregnancy twinsies.

I growled at the wind and mentally flipped the bird at the gray clouds, yanked my door open, and threw myself inside the cruiser. I drummed the steering wheel and stared out the windshield while my adult self got the upper hand.

At a population of fifteen hundred people, give or take a prepper or two, there weren't a lot of social circles to choose from. Of course, Ted and Roxy were a part of the group. Honestly, as a married couple with a baby on the way, they had a lot more in common with most of my clan than I did. Even if that hadn't been the case, why would I expect or even want anyone to carry a grudge for me? I lugged around enough for the whole family, and I hoped I'd shed it soon.

Which was the best reason for me to quit the pity party and get back to my job.

I backed out of the space, watching the dust as it danced and whirled around my cruiser, and drove slowly from the fairgrounds. I radioed Kyle and told him to go on home, transfer the calls back to me.

I drove into town. Dad's old Dodge pickup was parked next to Mom's Vanagon in the wide dirt patch between them and their neighbor, Beverly. When we all lived at home, this area looked like a parking lot with our various beater cars and, at any given time, a few friends. My family's coming and going had felt constant and almost always annoying when I'd lived here last winter, but it made me a little sad to see only my parents' vehicles there now.

My cruiser didn't do much to make the place seem homey. Kimmy and Karl had left the old go-cart on the weedy front yard, but even that seemed lonely. I let myself into the kitchen.

The red polka dot motif and *I Love Lucy* charm always made me appreciate Mom's sense of humor. She rarely cooked and had never been domestic, preferring vegan protein shakes and herbal tea. When she took time to eat or drink. For her, the kitchen was a weigh station between her basement sculpture studio and her bedroom behind the living room.

This afternoon, she sat in her silk kimono, her long waves tamed into a gray braid down her back. One hand curled around a steaming ceramic cup of tea, her face looked rested and her smile radiant.

With the clouds outside, the kitchen felt cozy, despite being the biggest room in the house. Counters lined the west wall, and a butcher-block island added needed workspace. When the family gathered, which happened often, almost everyone gravitated to the kitchen.

Dad stood at the counter, patting out hamburger, his ever-present travel mug of coffee close by. Not tall, Dad had a lanky build, his jeans hung loose and his gray hair brushed the back of his T-shirt. He looked tired, probably worked all night, but he had a ready smile for me. "Katie! Let me make you a burger."

I waved him off. "No, thanks. I've got to get home soon. Diane said she dropped Poupon out there, and I want to make sure he hasn't eaten the furniture."

Mom patted the top of the picnic table that not only served as open dining for Foxes and associates of all kinds but also as psychiatrist couch. "You can sit for a minute."

I pulled one of Mom's hand-thrown coffee mugs from the cabinet and poured coffee, then joined her at the table. "You must have finished your piece."

A soft glow shone in her eyes. "I am pleased with it."

This was my favorite Mom. The normal woman, who'd worked hard, rested, and felt satisfied with her life. She'd probably stick around for several weeks or months before she started a new sculpture. When you were seven years old and the manic phases hit, followed by the lows, it could throw your life into chaos. At thirty-two, you accepted the good times with gratitude. "I'd love to see it."

She sipped her tea. "In a few days."

Dad washed his hands and joined us at the table. "You say Diane dropped her dog off?"

I bristled. "Never asked, didn't bother to see if I had plans. Just, boom, the dog's at my house."

Mom tugged on her braid. "You can't be too hard on her. It's always been this way, and it'll be hard to change the rules now."

Dad brewed coffee strong enough I should wear boxing gloves to manage it. "What rules?"

Dad chuckled and looked at Mom for the explanation.

She sat back and crossed her leg, bouncing it lazily, letting the silk of the kimono flap. "You've always been the one they go to. All of them. You help them out without asking much in return."

Dad agreed. "It's one of the great things about you. You understand the importance of family."

What? They couldn't be talking about me. Most of the time, I tried to avoid family. That's one big reason I loved Frog Creek so much. I stayed out at the ranch in my own little world and could usually use work as an excuse to get out of too much family time.

Mom smoothed the silk on her thighs, as if luxuriating in the texture of the fabric. "If you want them to quit relying on you to help them out every time, it's going to cause some disruption. It's okay, if that's what you choose. You aren't obligated to pick up the slack for your brothers and sisters, but be prepared for some fallout."

Dad placed a hand on Mom's. "There is nothing wrong with being there for your family."

That was what served as an argument between Mom and Dad. I switched gears. "I stopped by to ask if you know anything about the Olson place."

He looked puzzled. "I haven't heard anything for several years, why?"

I had to give up on the sludge in my cup. "A couple with a teenaged kid moved in there. Fixed up the house, put up a pole barn, but camouflaged it to look aged."

His eyebrows shot up. "How did you find out?"

I told him about the wreck. "I thought maybe they knew about the driver."

Mom's concerned eyes drilled into me. "Did they?"

I shook my head. "No. I'm not sure what to do about that." I explained about no sign of foul play and no ID and really, no reason to investigate. "What really chaps me, though, is the attitude of the other sheriffs."

Mom didn't generally care for authority, and she lowered her voice, like a dog giving warning. "How do you mean?"

I regretted bringing it up, and normally, I wouldn't have. But I was feeling a little raw from this afternoon at the fairgrounds. "It's like they've decided the car is from the rez and they don't care."

Mom's lips tightened. I assumed her inner yogi was advising some version of "if you can't say something nice, don't say anything."

Dad sighed. "It is a shame that racism and bigotry take so long to wash away. It's better than it used to be, for sure. But it can still be bad. Usually, the two cultures stay separate."

I knew that was true. The reservation lay about a hundred miles away from Hodgekiss, and yet we had no Lakota families living here and hardly ever saw a Lakota person. "I can't believe it was even worse than this."

Dad winced. "I remember when I was a little kid, there was a tipi village in Broken Butte. In that area just north of the depot. Seemed like a lot of tipis, but I was little. They had no running water or sewers, no electricity. They lived there year-round."

"Why didn't they live in houses?"

He looked at me like I missed the point. "It wasn't allowed. Don't know if there were laws against it. But I remember the signs downtown, at the drug store and the American Legion. 'No Indians Allowed.'"

I was speechless. Tears stood in Mom's eyes.

Dad stared at his coffee. "There are a lot of good people, Indians and white. But there is a lot wrong."

I took my cup to the sink and washed it. "I need to see about Poupon."

Dad met me at the door. "You know, that Kyle. He's a good guy. I think you hiring him might help everyone."

I kissed him on the cheek. "I didn't hire him because he's Lakota."

Dad nodded. I waved at Mom and headed back to my car.

The whole morning played back. The call. The wreck. Weirdos Rhonda and Marty. Even weirder Max. Maybe they had nothing to do with each other. But I'd bet they did.

With Sunday sliding away and no real reason to investigate anything, I thought about what I ought to do. More than likely, Barnett had made the right assessment. Just because Marty and Rhonda lived off-grid and didn't conform to Sandhills' norms didn't mean they were criminals. Almost everyone in the Sandhills kept guns handy. Rhonda and Marty hadn't actually pulled them on me.

I wrangled the cruiser up the bumpy dirt road that ran along Stryker Lake. Everyone I knew was out at the fairgrounds whooping it up and helping out a neighbor. Like a miserable troll, I pull up in front of my hovel and turned off the engine.

The cooling late afternoon air filled my lungs when I stepped out, and I leaned on the warm car, craning my head to watch the sun flirt with the western clouds. The blackbirds chirped a jaunty tune, and fresh scents of green life tickled my nose. Not bad. Not bad at all.

Just a little lonely. My phone appeared in my hand and Baxter's number started to ring before I gave it much thought. Over the last few months, I'd called Baxter more frequently, not always about Carly. It wasn't unusual for him to call me out of the blue, telling me something he thought I might find interesting. He gave me a different perspective than the Sandhills point of view, and I'd grown to enjoy his take on things.

He answered on the second ring. "Did you know saguaro cactus only grow in the Sonoran Desert?"

"Um. No. Guess I didn't."

"I'm watching a documentary on climate change that we probably won't air. I may not sleep for a week."

See? Not normal Sandhills conversation. "Why won't you air it?"

"Not our style. They'll sell it to National Geographic, so don't worry. You'll still get to be terrified by it."

"Not unless I hook up to satellite TV." I had the crickets and frogs in the summer and movies and books all the time, didn't see much use for a lot of television.

"Sacrilege." He paused. "What do you do to relax?"

He already put a smile on my face. "I love to saddle up and trot off across the hills."

"I'd rather hang from my thumbnails."

"It beats watching depressing documentaries."

"Television is the perfect anesthesia." He changed the subject. "What's on your mind this evening?"

Sunlight reflected on the ripples frolicking on the lake. "Releasing irritation and insult and breathing in peace."

He laughed. "That sounds very Zen."

"That's Mom's influence. Truth is, I'm out of sorts with my brothers and sisters and trying to get some perspective."

"So you called me? The man who has no family and steers clear of emotional entanglements."

"Exactly. You can encourage me to revel in my independence and singlehood."

I imagined him in his office, the sun already set, the lights of Chicago's skyline bright. "Independence is in your DNA. But, I won't tell you singlehood is good for you."

That dropped a stone inside me. "I thought I could count on you for solidarity."

Sounded like he eased himself into a comfortable position. "For me, it is. I work twenty hours a day, and when I'm not working, I'm thinking about work. I don't spend any time at home. I'm around people enough I don't get lonely. It's a life I'm comfortable with. You, on the other hand…"

Clouds blocked the sun, and a chill rose goose bumps while I waited for him to continue.

"You aren't married to your job, even if it is a big part of your life. You love your family, and I know you won't accuse me of being presumptuous when I say that your divorce and Carly's disappearance crushed you, even if you won't show it."

I popped back. "A crushed woman wouldn't get up every day and go to work, buy a house, plant a garden."

"Here, I'm guessing, but I'm convinced I'm right. You value loyalty and commitment above self-interest. Since you married Ted and vowed to love him no matter what, you're hanging on to him because you think that deep devotion is admirable."

"I don't—"

He didn't let me interrupt. "But suffering isn't noble, not if there's nothing to be gained. And believe me, I've met Ted Conner. He's not worth it."

"Because I'm not interested in dating doesn't mean I'm burning a candle for Ted." I hated the tightness in my voice.

"Then what?"

A chilly breeze ruffled my hair. "I'm enjoying freedom from having to take care of someone. I don't miss cooking a meal every night or doing dishes while someone else watches TV."

He fired back. "Not all men think a woman is domestic help."

"Yeah, well, you live in Chicago, not the Sandhills."

"What about kids?"

Sucker punch. I gritted my teeth and fought the image of Roxy and Sarah and their growing baby bumps. "There's time for that." Wasn't there?

He brightened his tone. "Okay, big brother lecture over."

I was ready for a new topic. "Thanks. I don't need any more brothers."

"No. You need a date."

Back to that already? "That's it. You don't get to mention this to me until you have a date."

That stalled him. "Okay. I have a wager for you."

This wouldn't be good. But he knew I couldn't resist a challenge. "What?"

"If I go on a date first, you'll have to watch the five documentaries on climate change and population growth I've rejected this month."

That ought to be motivation. "And if I go on a date first, you have to take a half-day trail ride."

"Those are high stakes."

"Deal?"

He sighed. "Deal."

"Okay, now I want to know how Diane knew Carly is in California."

Silence. Then, "Diane? Your sister?"

"She said Carly was probably living it up in California. How would she know that?"

Baxter didn't often sound unsure, but he hesitated. "I think maybe she manages funds for the nonprofit our class from Kilner set up." Kilner Military School was where Baxter and Carly's father, Brian, met and became like brothers. "If I remember, Brian had us set it up at Diane's bank because she was his sister-in-law."

I hadn't known that. "Still, how would she find out about Carly?"

Again, a little hiccup in his response. "Well, Carly's been tracking our classmates for some reason. Maybe one of the board members said something to her."

Leads. Everywhere. I was ready to book a flight to California tonight. "Who? Where? I can go out there now and find her."

He sighed. "You can't. The investigator already checked out those leads, and Carly is ahead of him."

I felt like yanking my hair out. "Why didn't you tell me?"

"Look, the investigator is doing his job. I told you she was in California. Try not to worry."

"Who else is on the board?"

No wishy-washy stumbling this time. "Leave it, Kate. The investigator is good. If anyone can find that girl, he can."

He was right. California is a big state, and I didn't know if Carly was north, south, east, or west. Baxter wasn't about to give me names of board members.

Baxter and I said our goodbyes, and I hung up and stared at my phone. Acceptance of the situation ground like shells in an egg salad sandwich.

Time to deal with the next episode of *Leave It To Kate*.

My boots clumped up the cement porch steps, and I pushed open the screen, crossed the porch, and burst into the house, worried I'd find shoes, furniture, and books chewed and scattered by a stressed poodle.

I scanned the neat room, finally settling on the giant pile of fluff on my leather couch. Poupon opened his eyes but didn't lift his head from the throw pillow.

"Oh, no." I took two steps across the room and fastened my fingers on his collar. "First rule of Kate's house: no dogs on the furniture."

With a gentle tug, he rolled to his feet, stretched his front legs long, and then lunged forward to give the back legs equal time. Diane kept Poupon's creamy-colored fur immaculately groomed in the classic way, with poofs on his head, ears, around his chest, and from his knees down.

"Poor guy. How are you gonna be tough if she's got you all dandied up?" I scrubbed the top of his head, and he allowed it.

I wandered into the kitchen, not really hungry, but thinking if I cooked a meal, it would be ready by dinnertime and I might want to eat by then. I'd finally scored a refrigerator manufactured in this decade, something I'd coveted for years, and it remained empty, save for a small jar of mayonnaise, lettuce nearing the end of the line, and two eggs. I'd already eaten the pickled green beans my sister-in-law Lauren gave me. My freezer contained hamburger and steaks, another sibling contribution. This one from Robert and Sarah from their last butchered beef. I pulled out a package of burger and plopped it in the microwave to defrost.

The light illuminated the kitchen, and I stood in front of the window as the meat carouseled. Poupon sat by my side, his head level with my hip. Without realizing it, I'd buried my hand in the fur at his head and massaged, my mind turning over Rhonda and Marty and the kid and the Olson place.

I poked the button to shut the microwave off. "You need a walk."

Poupon seemed amenable and followed me outside with his usual arrogant aplomb. With barely a sniff of indignation, he stepped, not leaped, as any self-respecting lab would, into Elvis, my 1973 Ranchero.

We maneuvered down the road toward the highway. "A drive, a walk, you don't really care, do you?"

Poupon sat with his regal posture and watched the oncoming road without comment.

In fifteen minutes I turned right on the gravel road leading to the Olson place. Maybe the kid came home after the roping.

I could justify showing up out there by saying I'd heard he was looking for my deputy. Thin, sure, but Poupon thought the idea had merit.

By the time we pulled up to the locked gate, the clouds looked like pregnant whales waltzing in a brisk wind. I sat in front of the gate, impressed with Rhonda's quick replacement of the padlock.

Poupon sat next to me in the bucket seat, no less interested in the immobile steel than he'd been with the open road. A personality must be locked somewhere inside him, but he did a good job resisting it

"How 'bout that walk I promised you?" No response, not even a turn of his head when I opened my door and climbed out, holding it open for him. I closed my door, walked around Elvis, opened the passenger door, and gave him a personal invitation. This time, he daintily stepped out.

I trudged, Poupon strutted, and in several minutes, we'd made it to the top of the hill overlooking the compound. Nothing stirred below. I checked for sandburs and thistles before settling myself amid the faded gold grasses from winter and the lengthening green of spring.

The Olson headquarters stretched below me, the barn doors closed against the buffeting wind. Both white pickups were parked under the covered cement pad. The sweep down the hill to the valley floor looked like an ocean with the grasses swaying like waves. The valley wound beyond the buildings to the north, following the natural trough between two ridges, until I couldn't see it. Green tinges in the winter grass promised spring, and the vastness of the landscape required deep breathing to take it all in. Another ridge rose behind the headquarters, and another beyond that, with no trees to break it up, only one barbed wire fence in view. It was a cow's paradise. For me, too.

I pulled my jacket closer. Poupon sat next to me, head high, tongue hanging out in a most impolite way. What birds hadn't settled for the night kept to themselves, so the night seemed to press out the day with heavy silence.

After a time, I quit wondering about Marty and Rhonda and their kid and practiced my cowboy Zen by letting the Sandhills weasel under my skin and hug my heart into acceptance and contentment—a step closer, anyway.

In dusky light, the bang of a door whipped me back to attention. Voices rang out, though I couldn't make out words. The sounds ricocheted against the hills. The kid shot from the house with Marty close on his heels. Marty shouted while the kid stomped across the yard holding a plate.

Rhonda popped out the door and stood with Marty, tossing off sharp words.

The kid didn't stop or turn but kept an angry pace toward the chicken house. He opened the wire gate and walked across the empty chicken yard, setting the plate down by the door. With jerky movements, as if angry, he fiddled with what looked like a padlock, eventually pulling it loose, dropping it on the ground, picking up the plate, and slipping inside.

On the front porch, Rhonda slid an arm around Marty. He pulled her close and they leaned together, their heads turned toward the chicken house. It shocked me when she rested her head on his shoulder in a tender, domestic moment.

I draped my arm around Poupon's back, grateful for even his minimum companionship. He tolerated for half a second, pushed himself to his feet, and started back toward Elvis.

Guess we were done with our stakeout.

9

———

Morning brought the smell of rain and damp air sneaking through my window along with gray light and the bright notes of blackbirds and robins, maybe a few sparrows and chickadees to round out the choir. I'd had my normal battle with the bedsheets and, as usual, come out the loser. Worrying about Carly and the preppers had looped with thoughts of Ted running against me in the next election, still three years away. There was the ever-present worry of financial ruin and finally, indignation and embarrassment that my brothers and sisters discussed my dating life. Or lack of it.

Still, mornings always boosted my spirits. Worries didn't loom as large in the light of day. What's not to love about a spring morning in the 'hills, even with the threat of rain? On my way to the front porch to get a good dose of morning, the lump on the couch startled me.

Poupon. I'd forgotten him. "Off the furniture."

He opened his eyes, raised his head, and oh-so-slowly, as if he hated mornings as much as Diane, the sister who slept through stampeding mustangs, he slid his front legs on the floor, stretched, then stepped his back legs off. Without eye contact, he followed me to the front porch and dutifully descended the steps when I held the screen door open.

Giving Poupon his privacy, I hurried to the kitchen to rustle up coffee and maybe breakfast. I wanted to get to the courthouse to be there when Stormy towed the car in. But I remembered not only did I not have coffee, I'd left the hamburger in the microwave. I'd zapped it too long, and the edges had turned a rubbery gray. The sniff test came out negative for spoilage, but I didn't want to risk death over a half pound of ground beef.

Definitely time for Twyla's witch's brew and a cinnamon roll. No, not a roll. I needed to start eating better—said the woman who lived alone and caught random meals, a most unbalanced diet.

I let Poupon inside, fed him, and had a serious discussion about staying off the furniture, but when I popped out of the shower, he'd climbed back on the couch. Dressed in my brown trousers and crisp official shirt, I hesitated at the front door. If I left him in the house, he'd probably sleep most of the day on the couch. I could run home at noon and let him out. But what if I got busy? There's always the potential for disaster with being a sheriff, though mostly I had ample time to cruise around, stop for coffee, even spend whole days working cattle or in the hayfield.

"Come on." Poupon gave me a bored expression. I added more insistence. "Let's go." Still nothing. I clapped. "City life has spoiled you. Around here, we get up and get after the day."

He ignored me until a gentle tug on his collar convinced him I wasn't going away. He hopped off the couch and followed me out. He might have been insulted I only offered him the back seat of the cruiser, not shotgun, but he didn't argue.

The ten-minute drive to town allowed me to convince

myself that today, I'd start off right. Oatmeal. Maybe yogurt and fruit. I couldn't guarantee Twyla stocked anything that healthy, so I'd settle for eggs. No toast. Definitely not a cinnamon roll.

Damp sand and rain-heavy air greeted me as I stepped from the cruiser. The morning smelled musty, like humidity intended to stick around long enough to soak everything. I crossed the highway and hip-checked the glass door of the Long Branch. Two doors opened off the vestibule. One headed into the bar, the bigger and more interesting of the Long Branch division. The other, letting out the smells of bacon and sausage, with a coffee-infused benediction, was today's choice. I shoved into the restaurant side, my mouth watering and my eyes rolling back into my head at the promise of liquid life.

A shriek ambushed me. "Oh my God! Look, Ted, it's Kate!"

No. No. Oh my God, no.

Roxy stood in front of the cash register. She grabbed my hand as if we were reunited twins separated since birth and yanked me toward her. I pulled back but couldn't slip out of Roxy's death grip. Aside from her affair with my husband that ended my marriage and left me homeless, almost everything else about Roxy torqued me.

Her loud laughter probably made everyone in out-state Nebraska turn to see me floundering to escape.

I jerked my hand from her grasp but, because of a lifetime of Dad's training, couldn't help from forcing a polite smile.

Ted, my tall, broad-shouldered, Ben Affleck look-alike of an ex-husband, stood behind Roxy and offered a sheepish smile, as if apologizing for Roxy's extravagance. I bet he did that a lot.

Because I allowed myself to be distracted by Ted, Roxy had an opportunity to throw her arms around me. "We never get to see you!"

"Not like yesterday at the fairgrounds." I tried not to stare at her boobs swelling from the top of her maternity T-shirt. Her belly didn't make a dent in the shirt yet, and it seemed unfair her already impressive breasts should get a jump on the baby bump. It also rankled me that unlike Sarah, who had a wrung-out, pasty look from her constant morning sickness, Roxy glowed.

Roxy released me and grabbed my hand again. She pulled me down the narrow aisle between red molded plastic booths lining one side with windows and the other side a dark fake-paneled wall. Most of the booths held several diners, and I nodded and smiled good morning on my way. Roxy fairly bubbled. "Looky who happens to be here."

She stopped at a table littered with egg and syrup-smeared plates, paper napkins crumpled up, and empty heavy ceramic coffee mugs. Trey Ridnoir, all spiffy, hard-chested, well-groomed, and ready for business in his state trooper blue and gray, smiled up at me. A flush crept up his neck to his cheeks.

Roxy looked from one of us to the other, her amply lip-sticked mouth in XXL grin. "What a coincidence. I mean," she put a hand on her hip, "do you come in here for breakfast a lot?"

Only like every other day. Oh dear God. She was setting me up. My cheeks burned with a combination of humiliation and rage that left me tongue-tied.

Thankfully, Trey kept his senses, despite his cherry complexion. He stood—all six foot one of muscle—and fished in his pocket for a tip. "It's great to see you again." Had Roxy let him in on the matchmaking, or was he blindsided, too?

I managed one sentence. "What brings you up this way?" Trey lived eighty miles south in Ogallala. We'd worked together on a murder last winter, but I'd only seen him a few times since.

He nodded at Ted, who'd joined us in the middle of the restaurant, amid the rapt attention of the breakfasters. "Ted invited me, and since I couldn't make it up to the roping yesterday, I thought it would be fun to catch up." He shifted his gaze to Roxy, shooting her an accusatory glare.

Roxy was too old to play coy, but that didn't stop her. "Well, I thought you hit it off last winter with that awful railroad incident. But you haven't had a chance to see each other since."

What the hell was she talking about? If Trey had wanted to call me, he knew where I was.

Our smiles contained an extra thick layer of awkward sauce.

Roxy waited for our conversation to spark, and when it didn't, she goosed it. "Did you know that Kate has eight brothers and sisters and they're all named for the Academy Award winners of the year they were born?"

Trey looked way more amazed than it warranted. I didn't know Trey well, but enough to know he was toying with Roxy. "No way."

What could I possibly add to that fascinating fact?

Roxy pushed again. "Now that Sarah is going to have a baby, Kate is going to need some new friends." She patted her stomach. "Life changes so much when a little one arrives. And you two have so much in common."

"Really? What?" Trey overdid his surprised reaction to the point of melodrama and still, Roxy didn't understand he was teasing her.

Roxy's eyes tilted to the sky. "Oh, well, you both like art, because Kate's mother is an artist and you studied art in college." She paused. "And you both went to college." She shrugged, her boobs doing a happy dance I hated. "Oh, who's kidding? You're both single."

I regretted not having my gun in my holster so I could shoot myself, or Roxy, or both of us.

My savior appeared in the form of my five-foot-two, rusty-voiced, hangover-toughened Aunt Twyla. "Do your sparking someplace else. We got a breakfast crowd here wanting their eggs."

That was the break I needed. "I've got to get to the courthouse anyway. Stormy is towing a car in. Good seeing you." I wasn't sure you could technically call what I did running, but it was no stroll.

Fat raindrops helped cool me as I threw myself into the cruiser and turned it up the hill. So much for coffee and breakfast, but getting to work might help soothe the burn of Roxy and Ted trying to set me up.

Poupon shared my outrage when I spouted off. "As if I can't find my own man. Not even that. As if I need to pair up. This is too much. Too damned much."

We pulled into my parking spot behind the courthouse, the Mercury Marquis nowhere in sight. Poupon seemed content to make a den in the back of the cruiser, and I had to resort to a sharp clap to command him out. He did his front legs down, stretch, step out like the King of Sheba bit to show me what he thought of my orders.

The smell of scorched coffee greeted me when we climbed the stairs from the back door of the courthouse toward the main floor, where Ethel Bender's office, the Grand County clerk/assessor, faced off with the county treasurer's office.

Betty Paxton, the treasurer since Ronald and Nancy kissed in the Lincoln bedroom, shot from her office into the hall at the same time Ethel, still wearing her rubber rain boots, scurried after her, squeaking and leaving wet footprints on the linoleum.

"Morning," I sang at them. It wouldn't hurt to be friendly.

Betty reluctantly slowed to say good morning, and Ethel edged in front of her on the way to the commissioner's room, where the communal coffee pot spewed. "Look at you here all bright-eyed and bushy-tailed."

I normally showed up about this time. "Always try to get a good start on Mondays."

Betty's gaze dropped to Poupon, who ignored us. "Who's this beautiful boy?"

Ethel appeared in the doorway of the commissioner's room, having scored the first cup of the day. She scowled at Poupon. "No dogs allowed in the courthouse."

As if not understanding *no dogs* and *courthouse*, I gave her a cheery smile. "I'm babysitting him for Diane. I'll keep him in my office."

Betty patted him on the head and murmured happy dog talk.

Wanting to move beyond potential war, I managed the old standby, "Get any rain out at your place?"

Ethel must have decided not to fight the Poupon issue, but then, she'd always liked Diane. "If you'd bothered to check the radar, you'd know the rain hasn't started yet."

Temptation clawed at me to reach my hand out and tip the bottom of her cup. Instead, I made a point of looking at my rain-pocked brown jacket. "You're right." We stood as natural as ketchup on ice cream, neither of us finding another word.

Betty straightened from her conversation with Poupon. "My cousin, over to Dunbar, said they got nearly a quarter inch."

Ethel challenged her. "Your cousin doesn't know anything. I heard they only got one-tenth."

I brought it to a halt when I said, "Any rain is good rain."

Ethel stared at me as if I'd said the stupidest thing she'd

ever heard, so I plunged ahead with an intellectual discussion. "How's the coffee?"

"It's crap. But it's all we've got." Ethel pushed past me to her office.

Betty frowned after her. "It's my day to make the coffee. She swears I make it like weak tea."

I had to agree, but I kept it to myself.

Betty, now the clear loser in the daily race for the first cup, took her time going to the pot. I followed and Poupon stayed in the hallway. She reached for her #1 Grandma mug and filled it. She handed me a NACO (Nebraska Association of County Officials) mug, the one I used because I didn't have a cute one of my own. "You notice on Tuesdays and Thursdays we go through a lot more of the creamer."

Betty made coffee on Mondays and Wednesdays and Ethel had Tuesday and Thursday. Fridays alternated between the two battle axes. I'd thought to do my part and made coffee one Friday when I'd arrived first. Ethel had blown up and Betty nearly cried because I hadn't trusted her to make it. I vowed not to get between them again. If I could help it.

I sipped what tasted like hot tap water, hating Roxy all the more for denying me my Long Branch fix. I leaned against the wall with my cup, acting casual. "Who owns the old Olson place north of town?"

Betty looked over the rim of her cup. "Since the old man died?" She leaned back, cradling her coffee cup. "Assessor should have records. But that's hit and miss in this county."

Never one to miss a dig at her fellow county official. "Thanks, Betty. Try to stay dry."

She laughed as if I'd spewed a great joke. "We'll all be waterlogged before this storm passes. At least it'll make the grass grow." She cleared her throat. "Uh. Kate."

I winced, knowing what was coming and already feeling guilty. "Yes?"

Betty's expression steeped in apology. "I really hate to nag, but you know, your budget was due last week and...?"

"Of course. It's on my list for today. I promise to get it to you." I carried my mug into the hall and back to Poupon, who sat in the same spot, continuing to ignore everyone. "Come."

He didn't.

His neck reached my thigh, so I grasped his collar without bending, and at my gentle tug he stood and walked with me to my office. After unlocking the door and pushing it open, I waited for him to sashay inside before closing the door and sneaking down the hall into Ethel's office. I didn't want Betty to hear me and feel betrayed.

Brittany Ostrander, Ethel's assistant, stood at the coat rack in the corner, shaking out her raincoat. She settled it on a hook and welcomed me.

Brittany was a year older than Carly. The girl on the phone last night, would she be about the same age? Was she huddling in the rain somewhere? Locked in a basement listening to it fall on the ground, maybe dampening the dark basement walls? Probably at home, snuggled under blankets, sleeping late and dreaming about rainbows.

Brittany rubbed her arms for warmth. "It's really settling in out there. How much did you get at your place? Dad said we had three-tenths."

I hoped Ethel heard Brittany report about rain. "None before I left." I slipped around the counter on my way to the vault, where Ethel sat on her throne behind a heavy government-issue desk piled with files and bound ledgers. Brittany was supposed to guard the threshold of Ethel's inner sanctum and deal with the citizens' business. But Brittany didn't have the fortitude to question the sheriff, so I broke through her weak barrier.

Ethel had heard me in the outer office and was ready. She'd taken off her rain boots and left them to dry before the radiator in the corner behind her desk. The vault, twice as large as the outer office, smelled of musty books and dust from the hundred and fifty years of records locked in here. A banana smell hung heavy, along with burnt popcorn. Ethel not only ate lunch at her desk every day, but a constant flow of snack detritus filled her trash can. The vault had no windows or ventilation, and that could account for Ethel's troll-like personality.

Ethel folded her arms across her bosoms. On most women, they'd be called boobs, or breasts, or even tits. But Ethel had bosoms. "This is restricted access. You need to respect the rules of the office. Talk to Brittany, and if she can't help you, she'll ask me."

I tried to look contrite despite comparing her behavior to that of Poupon. "Of course. Normally I would, but this is confidential sheriff business."

However reluctantly, Ethel showed interest. "How so?"

I looked over my shoulder, not because I cared whether Brittany overheard, but to make Ethel think I did. "There's something fishy going on at the Olson place. I need to know who's living out there."

Ethel's face fell. She wrenched open the top drawer of her desk and rummaged inside, finally pulling out a packet of Taster's Choice. "No one is living out there. Unless they're in tents or campers. We haven't had any requests for building permits."

It didn't surprise me Rhonda and Marty hadn't been in for permits. "Can you tell me who owns it now?"

She snatched a pair of scissors that could be used as hedge

trimmers and violently snipped off the top of the instant coffee package. "A Delaware LLC owns it."

"Can I get the records?"

She dumped the coffee into her full cup and shoved some papers around until she found a spoon. She stopped and stared at me. "Do you want some instant? Betty's excuse for coffee needs a boost."

Why she didn't just heat up her own water instead of wasting the brewed coffee seemed irrelevant. I made a point of taking a swig from my cup and smiling. "No, thanks. Where are the records? I can look them up."

She shoved back from her desk with the attitude of the long put-upon. Sighing with annoyance, she pushed her puffy feet into scruffy blue slippers. "It's not going to tell you anything." She rose and stomped to a shelf, hauled a ledger the size of a surfboard to a sturdy table in the middle of the room, and smacked it down. It took two hands to open the book and flip through the lined pages. Seemed like all this stuff should be filed digitally, and it probably was. But Ethel probably distrusted computers and kept her records the way they'd been doing it in Grand County since the 1880s.

She plopped her wrinkled finger onto the middle of the page. In her spidery handwriting, the parcels and tracts of the Olson ranch filled line after line. It had been purchased from Tyrell Olson over two years ago. The owner was, indeed, an LLC from Delaware listed as Hidden Valley Ranch. Really?

"How do I get in touch with the owners or board members or whatever?"

She stomped back to her desk. "I don't know. Call the Delaware Secretary of State, I guess."

"I sure appreciate your help," I said, somehow keeping the sarcastic tone in my head.

Brittany stopped me before I escaped into the hall, her

face full of hope. "Um, Kate? Have you seen Jeremy around lately?"

"He was at Dugans' roping yesterday."

Her face fell. "Oh. I haven't seen him for a while, and I thought maybe he'd been out of town."

Do I give her the sisterly advice to find someone more stable than my youngest brother? Jeremy loved everyone. All at the same time. Or consecutively. Brittany would do better to find a more consistent heart.

With the mysterious caller and Carly already on my care-taking failure list, I didn't need another girl to worry about. Saving Brittany wasn't in my job description. And yet.

I walked over to Brittany's desk and set my cup down. "Jeremy is something of a free spirit."

She nodded, but her eyes started to glisten with tears. "I know."

"I love him to bits. Everyone does. But he's not big on commitment."

A lump the size of a Bartlett pear made its way down her throat, and she nodded some more.

Dang it. I wasn't helping. I put a hand on her desk and leaned in. "You deserve to be someone's one and only."

That did it. Two buckets of tears drained from her eyes. "I-I-I knew that, I guess. I just needed someone to tell me."

Glad it could be me. Hey, maybe I could set my family to finding Brittany a beau and get them off my trail. I backed out while Brittany plucked a Kleenex from the box on her desk and dabbed at her tears.

The front door rattled opened to the sound of pattering rain and clanked closed. It could be any number of citizens on a hundred different missions at the courthouse.

What did it say about me that I expected the worst?

10

Before I took more than three steps from the clerk's office, a magical aroma of fresh, strong coffee hit me. I'd left my cup on Brittany's desk, considered it a casualty of war, and went forward to find the source of the smell.

Kyle Red Owl wiped his boots on the doormat. Kyle had the well-toned physique of the Marine he'd been less than two years ago. He held a soda case cardboard box with two giant Styrofoam takeout cups and accompanying white boxes.

I almost ran to him. "My savior!"

He tilted his dark face in surprise. "Why don't all the women welcome me like this?"

I pulled one of the cups from the box and flipped off the lid. "They would if you brought them coffee and rolls from the Long Branch."

He handed me the box and shook out of his wet jacket. "Uncle Lloyd Walks His Horse always told me a way to a woman's heart is through her stomach."

"Wise man, your uncle."

Kyle grinned. "Naw. He was single. Couldn't cook."

He took the box back and I sipped the magic brew. The hot liquid melted tension between my shoulder blades.

"How's your morning?" he asked.

"I'm just destroying the hopes and dreams of young girls." Wouldn't it be nice if I could save one once in a while?

The front door opened again. Why was I so jumpy? I didn't relax much when Pete and Tammy Grainger stepped in from the gloomy morning.

Tammy wore a belted red rain jacket, her blond hair looking stylish despite the wind. Pete had on jeans and a fleece, no sheriff's duds in sight. He vibrated with his usual energy, his dark crew cut glistened with moisture and his perpetual tan made him look more like a coach than a sheriff in the manner of the full-bellied profiles of Milo or Barnett.

Tammy broke into a wide-mouth smile when she saw us. "Kate! It's great to see you."

Pete stuck his hand out. "Well, look here. Great to run into you."

It's not like I was an elephant in the alfalfa patch. A sheriff's natural habitat was the county courthouse. On the other hand, it was my county, and Pete belonged to Chester County. "What brings you back this way?"

Pete's attention focused on Kyle. His eyebrows dipped before he pulled out his full-on happy again. "Working on weekdays now?"

I fielded the question. "He's making up hours from Saturday when he was at the sweat."

Pete's face tightened slightly but he never lost his grin. "Gotcha. I need to slip in and talk to Ethel. She had me scout out a new pole barn on Dempsy's place. It's on the border between our counties, and she wanted to know if she should assess it or leave it to Chester County."

His eyes lingered on Kyle. He'd probably report to his

buddy Lee, and there would be general discussion about Kyle working on a random Monday. As if it were any of their business.

Kyle lost his ease. He motioned toward my office. "I'll be down..." He walked away, leaving me with Tammy.

She waited a beat, her Vanna White smile easy. "We're on our way to Broken Butte. District music is today. Rusty has a trumpet solo, and Becca is singing with swing choir."

I tried to look interested. "Nice you can go."

She batted her blue eyes. "Don't you love the flexibility of this job? Pete is so lucky he can be such a part of our children's lives. Of course, he's a lot happier when we're following sports. Especially basketball." She looked stricken, as if mentioning family and jobs might have insulted me.

Before I answered, she patted my arm. "I know I haven't been a very good friend."

I didn't know we were friends.

She quit patting and squeezed my arm. "But, you know, I feel so awful about the way Ted treated you."

Where was my cloak of invisibility?

Her voice lowered. "I don't understand cheating, I really don't. I mean, if Pete ever did that...Well, I'd do exactly what you did. I'd leave."

I wanted to jerk my arm from her grasp and run away. No, I really wanted to tell her to shut up. But she meant well, I was sure, and besides, Pete would return soon. I hoped.

She gave me a knowing look, as if we were soul sisters. "I mean, Pete was dating someone when we met, and I found out he hadn't broken it off with her. I forgave him that one time, because, as I understand it, she just wouldn't let him go. But he knows. Never again."

Pete's footsteps sounded in the hall, and if I knew it wouldn't send Tammy into a jealous fit, I'd have thrown my arms around him. To say I was relieved to wish them a fun day would be like calling Lake Michigan a puddle.

I headed toward my office, where Kyle waited outside the locked door. I unlocked it and pushed it open to Poupon sitting in my desk chair with impeccable posture.

One hand holding my coffee, I waved the other. "Get down."

He slowly turned his head away.

Kyle raised his eyebrows at me and the dog. His lips barely moved, and even though he sounded fierce, he spoke so quietly I strained to hear. I couldn't understand the harsh syllables and sounds in the back of his throat, the melodic Lakota language.

Apparently, Poupon understood perfectly. He whipped his head toward Kyle and immediately jumped off my chair, trotted to Kyle's side, and dropped down, head on paws.

"What did you say?"

Kyle bent over and scratched Poupon behind the ears. "A dog doesn't have to grow up on the rez to understand the concept of soup."

Kyle settled in the oak chair, and I sat in the preheated chair behind my desk. "I'm going to ask Pete to switch weekends with me next month. That work for you?"

"Sure. Got a romantic getaway planned?"

We tucked into Aunt Twyla's cinnamon rolls, all warm and gooey with slathers of cream cheese frosting and melting pats of butter.

"Not you, too?" I licked my finger. "I signed up for scuba lessons in Denver."

He gave me a "you're crazy" eyebrow raise. "It's your weekend."

My phone rang, and I wiped my sticky fingers before picking up.

Stormy sounded irritated and sorry at the same time. "Can't get that car until this afternoon. Donna's refusing to leave that little turnip until after her bath."

I thought the car would be on its way in by now. "Get to it as quick as you can, then." I hung up, a little irritated myself.

Kyle tore off a small bite of roll. "What's that?"

I spoke around a sweet nibble. "Someone rolled a car up north on the county line. I think it might be a rez car. Let's drive on up there. Maybe you can ID it."

Kyle took his time swallowing a sip of coffee. "As the token Indian, I know all the rez cars?"

Pete's subtle disapproval hadn't been lost on Kyle. Levity might help dilute the insult. "Exactly."

That earned me a half-smile.

"You could stay here and clean out the jail cell if you'd rather."

He gave me a cute grin that made him look about twelve. "I didn't say I wouldn't take a look." Kyle studied his frosting-covered finger. "Barnett spends more time on the rez than I do. He'd know whose car it is."

"Except he doesn't." I nearly groaned at the goodness of the cinnamon roll. "Do you know anything about folks moving onto the old Olson Ranch?" I wasn't ready to call it Hidden Valley Ranch. "It's owned by a Delaware corporation, but I don't know who's living out there."

"I can ask around." Kyle wiped his fingers on a paper napkin.

I picked off another gooey portion. I should have started with the middle, the tastiest section, and left the doughier outside. I felt stuffed, but no way was I leaving the most delicious part. "Let me finish this and we can head out to the wreck. I got a call from a girl, and she sounded pretty scared.

I'm not sure it was the driver, since no one was at the wreck. But I feel jumpy about the whole thing."

"Was it a sheriff call?"

I shook my head. "Not sure. Sounded more like she thought I was someone else."

A roar, sounding like the sky fell, filled my office, and Kyle and I both turned our heads to the ceiling, then at each other. It probably looked like choreography in a cheesy comedy. "It's really coming down."

Squeaky tennis shoes on linoleum warned us of someone heading down the hall. I hadn't heard the front door, but I had a moment to hope it wasn't more bad news before Susan (Go Big Red) poked her soaking head into the office. "Hope you're building a big boat or we're all gonna drown."

Susan was a younger version of me, compact and sturdy, with tons of wavy, dark hair. She popped into the office, took one look at my roll, and pulled a line off. Between chews, she said hi to Kyle and shook her head, sending drops of water in all directions.

"Poupon!" She offered him a bite of my roll, which he accepted with no thanks. "It's good you're taking him. Diane and the kids never pay attention to him."

"I'm not taking him. Just watching him for a week." I offered her the box with the remainder of the roll. "I thought you were heading back to Lincoln today. When's your job start?"

She waved to indicate I should wait until she swallowed. "My shift is five to midnight, but the other bartender will cover for me if I'm late."

Charming Susan, the youngest of nine. She could work hard when she was motivated, and the rest of the time, she knew how to use her smile. Who was I to judge? The kid had a 4.0 after two years in pre-med at the university.

She had a way of getting people to fill in the blanks for her, so I figured she hadn't stopped in to say goodbye. "Hope you don't have heavy rain the whole way."

She shrugged and swallowed the last of the roll. "I've got a favor to ask."

Didn't take a psychic to predict that, so I didn't score points for my forecast.

She tossed it out in a casual way, though her eyes looked anxious. "I need to borrow two hundred bucks."

I didn't say anything. Kyle looked from her to me, his expression clearly wondering how I'd react. I waited.

She started to show a little more angst. "I have to pay my share of the cleaning deposit on the apartment, and I don't have the money until I get paid."

"How long have you known you owe this?"

She went on the defensive. "I had a lot of expenses at the end of the semester."

I nodded. "Uh-huh. I'm sure that road trip to San Francisco wasn't cheap."

She gave me big eyes. "It's not like it was a vacation. I *had* to go. Emmy didn't have anyone else to help her move."

I could play this game with her all day. In the end, she knew and I knew I'd give her the loan. I wouldn't buy beer for them when they were underage. I wouldn't fix tickets or bail them out of jail. But I'd lend them money, babysit their kids and dogs, let them move in with me, and just about anything else they'd need. I pulled out my checkbook.

"Thank you."

I'd been saving for that vacation. The one I'd been dreaming about since Ted and I went to Cancun two years ago. Not like our trip sitting on the beach and drinking margaritas, hitting all the tourist sites along with honeymooners and families with sullen teenagers and whining kids. I wanted to learn to scuba dive.

Since divorcing Ted, I decided to do this one thing for myself. I'd even picked out the resort on Cozumel where they'd finish my open water training and certify me after I passed the basics in Denver. The only thing holding me back was time and money. With Kyle on board, the time off could be managed. But last month, Jeremy needed help paying for a saddle he'd had made, and the month before that, Esther, Louise's middle child, wanted desperately to go to drama camp. They'd all do the same for me.

Susan hugged me, dripping water and smelling like damp dog. "Thank you so much. I promise to pay you back with my first paycheck."

Except there would probably be some other emergency. I'd get my $200 back eventually. Maybe after she began practicing medicine.

Susan folded the check and stuck it in her hoodie's front pocket, where it had a high likelihood of getting lost. "Just for the record, I voted for you to stay single and strong."

"Voted?"

"When the sibs were debating whether you should go with Trey Ridnoir, Heath Scranton, or Josh Stevens."

Kyle snickered, and I gave him The Look. He wasn't any more intimidated than Rhonda had been. I might need to work on my technique.

I picked up the budget worksheets scattered around my desktop and patted them into a neat stack, as opposed to letting out a string of curses. "Can't see as how that's anyone's business."

"I told them you should date Tori Engseth and that shut them up for about two seconds. With our family, that's saying a lot."

Kyle looked at me with a puzzled expression. "Isn't that the new English teacher? I didn't know she's gay."

Susan wound her hair into a wet ponytail. "I don't know that she is. Neither is Kate." She addressed me. "Got a ponytail holder?"

I slipped mine off my wrist and handed it to her. "Hey, have you met any new guys around here lately?"

She laughed. "I'm not the old maid who needs fixing up."

Grr. "I wondered if you'd seen or heard about a guy around your age. Tall, geeky-looking with a lot of dark bushy hair."

She fawned. "Sounds dreamy. But no."

It was worth a try. "Be careful driving in this weather." My heart squeezed at the thought of another young woman in trouble. Was this the price of being sheriff? Suddenly every situation screamed danger.

She shook her damp hair. "It's just rain."

I nodded. "And you could hydroplane or lose visibility."

Kyle took up the warning, using a haunting voice. "Flash floods and washouts."

Susan gave me a hug and kiss, took the last swig of my coffee, and flew out the door.

Kyle grinned. "They are a pain in the butt, but we love them."

"You've got brothers and sisters?" Kyle and I didn't spend personal time together. He filled in on my weekends off, so aside from work-related conversations, we hadn't shared much.

His face lightened. "I've got a sister that just graduated from high school."

Another woman starting out. I liked hearing good news. Maybe this one wouldn't find trouble. "Congratulations."

His eyes gleamed with pride. "She's going to Chadron State on scholarship in the fall."

I didn't ask if she graduated from a rez school. Maybe she didn't live on the rez, though I knew that's where Kyle grew up. If she did, it would account for Kyle's glowing pride. The dropout rate on the rez hovered around 70 percent, and going on to college wasn't a given, as it was in the Fox household.

I considered my own numerous clan. "Is it just you and your sister?"

That happy expression vanished. "I've got two brothers. Both younger."

If I were Louise, I'd jump all over that mood change. She couldn't help but search out family trauma. I pulled my coat from the back of my chair. "Let's go check out that car, see if we can find something to help us identify the driver."

Kyle wadded up the napkin, placed it in his food container, and snapped the lid. He picked mine up, I assumed to deposit them in the Dumpster at the parking pad in back.

He surprised me by sticking with our conversation. "Shelly was valedictorian of Sand Gap. I didn't want her to go to a rez school, but she took college courses online and went to some academic summer camps, and I think she's ready."

"That's pretty dedicated."

"Shelly always knew what she wanted. When she was three, she carried around these two Dr. Seuss books everywhere she went. My brother, Darrel, tried to take them away once, and she beat him up." Kyle laughed at the memory. "He was two years older than her and about twice as big. You do not want to get in Shelly's way."

"My sister Diane is like that. When she sets herself to something, she's one-track." Like getting me to watch her dog. Which reminded me. "Come."

Poupon didn't move. His gaze shifted to Kyle.

Kyle gave his head the slightest twitch, and Poupon jumped up and followed us out.

We clambered down the back stairs. "Shelly worries me, though. She's kind of like you. She'll do anything for her family, even if it gets her into trouble."

"I don't let my family get me in trouble. But yeah, if I can help them, I do."

He accepted that. "But do they help you?"

"Of course. They campaigned for me. Mom and Dad let me move back in when I needed it."

He poked at my shoulder. "You're crazy for your clan, admit it."

Yeah. Maybe. I couldn't imagine anything I wouldn't do to bring Carly home.

I opened the back door to rain pelting the pavement. We dashed to the cruiser, with Kyle stopping to toss the breakfast remains into the Dumpster and me opening the back door to let Poupon in. With my wipers beating a steady pulse, we drove north, speculating about the preppers and about the caller. Kyle thought Barnett had the right idea, that the caller got a ride back to the rez and left the car for dead.

Kyle leaned back in his seat. "I ever tell you about Uncle Lloyd Walks His Horse and the flood?"

"Why, no. You haven't."

Kyle folded his arms. "Uncle Lloyd was a finder of lost things. One day, a man heard Uncle Lloyd tell someone where to find a ring they had lost. The man didn't believe Uncle Lloyd had this gift, and he called Uncle Lloyd a liar. The man told Uncle Lloyd that he'd believe in the gift if Uncle Lloyd could find the marbles the man said his old man had lost.

"It was well known the man's father was crazy, but Uncle Lloyd, he said okay, he'd find the marbles.

"That night it started to rain, and it rained for a whole

week. There were floods, and the rivers overflowed their banks. Then finally, a flash flood roared down a gully and knocked the old man's house off its foundation. When the man went out to help his father, the old man was sitting in the mud with a buckskin bag in his lap. He was so happy because when the house fell, the old man found his stash of toys from where he'd hidden them as a boy. He was especially glad to have his marbles back."

I glanced at Kyle. "You just made that up, didn't you?"

He gave me an innocent face and crossed his chest. "It's the truth."

We sped past the turnoff to the Olson place, and I stared at the hills hiding their compound. This storm had erased the motorcycle tracks, of course.

The rain didn't let up as we closed in on the county line. The flashing lights of a wrecker shone through the watery morning. Maybe Stormy had broken free of his domestic duties after all. I squinted, suspicious because the wrecker didn't look familiar.

Kyle jumped when I slapped the steering wheel and shouted, "You're kidding me."

Poupon let out a yip in his sleep but, other than that, didn't budge.

Kyle leaned forward and squinted out the wet windshield at the tow truck, its yellow lights flashing, backing into the pasture at the side of the road. "What?"

"I told Barnett I'd handle this. That SOB called Schneiderman." What a snake.

"No," Kyle murmured. Then louder: "Oh, no!"

I pulled up to the wrecker and slammed on the brakes, but before we'd come to a full stop, Kyle's door flew open and he jetted from the car.

Red and blue flashed on the other side of the wrecker. I

tucked my gun into my holster, forced myself into the rain, and walked a few steps closer. The light bar of the Spinner County sheriff's Bronco only made my temper rise more. I swiveled and headed down the barrow ditch.

Before I made it to where Slim Schneiderman knelt to attach the hook, Barnett caught up to me and grabbed my arm. He raised his voice above the rain. "He's about got it loaded."

I squinted as cold rain pelted my face. My brown uniform spotted, bled, and deepened all over as it took on an ocean. "Oh, I'm not going to stop him."

Barnett's lip curled. "That's the first smart thing I've heard you say."

I yanked my arm from his grasp. "Gonna tell him to haul it to Hodgekiss. On Spinner County's dime."

Barnett drew himself up, no doubt to give me the business, but something at the wreck drew his attention. Kyle rushed around the car, throwing himself to his knees in the wet grass and shimmying to peer into the back windows.

Barnett raised both hands in the air and flicked them toward me as if batting a beach ball. He looked like he'd swallowed a cup of acid. "Fine." A greyhound might have had trouble keeping up as he hurried to his Bronco.

I trotted toward the wreck. The wheels of the Bronco threw gravel as Barnett spun out. He crossed the county line as I bent over to shout to Kyle. "What is it? Do you know who owns this car?"

He answered in one anguished word. "Shelly."

11

By the time I dragged Kyle to his feet, we both looked like we'd swum a lap or two around Grand County. A big rain in the Sandhills meant an inch over the course of a day, maybe a ten-minute downpour resulting in a quarter inch. This kind of unrelenting storm system was not normal.

Kyle sounded breathless. "You got a call from a girl? It had to be Shelly. What did she say?"

As if I could forget. "Please help me. We need you. I'm on my way from the rez.'" I didn't tell him how the fear in her voice froze my blood. Or the helplessness that had tugged at me ever since.

His dark eyes looked like they wanted to suck the memory from me. "Is that all she said?"

Even if his bridled violence wasn't directed at me, I stepped back. "'I don't know what he wants.'"

He narrowed his eyes on my face as if answers were written there. "Who?"

All I could do was stand in silence and shake my head.

"Why did she call you? Why not me?" He ran a hand through his hair and shifted from foot to foot.

"Did she think you were working Saturday?"

A thought occurred to him, and he yanked his phone from his pocket and bent to shield it from the rain. "Saturday night. I went to the sweat on the rez. I wanted to put my phone in airplane mode so it wouldn't ring. But Leonard Stands with Heart dropped the grandfathers." He paused to explain. "The hot stones used to make steam are called grandfathers. I hurried to help Leonard. I must have automatically transferred the calls to your sheriff line out of habit since I do it whenever I work for you."

Technology at work. "So Shelly meant to call you."

He swiped his phone and punched a speed dial number. He stood still as a portrait. I wanted to pace the wet pasture. A girl came on the line, and he shoved the phone at my ear. "Is this the voice you heard?"

"...I'll call you back."

I gave Kyle a helpless look. "It wasn't enough to tell."

He dialed again, and this time while we waited for the voicemail message, he said, "At least her phone is ringing."

A thousand scenarios ran through my mind where a ringing, unanswered phone didn't mean good news. This time I was ready when he handed me the phone. "*Hoka Hey*. This is Shelly. I'm probably in class or asleep. Leave a message and I'll call you back."

"Well?"

"Maybe. I don't know. She was shouting and upset."

He grabbed the phone back and hit another number. I figured he was trying to locate Shelly, so I checked on Slim's progress and gave him instructions to tow the car to Hodgekiss, then called to cancel the towing with Stormy. That was fine because Donna had decided they were staying another day.

Kyle jettisoned past me and rammed the phone back into his pocket. "Let's go."

I trotted after him to the cruiser. He started for the driver's door and I shouted, "I'll drive. But you have to tell me where we're going."

He balked at giving up the reins, but after a moment's hesitation, in which we both took on another gallon of water, he stalked around the nose of the car.

I started the engine, cranked the heat, and slid the car into gear. Poupon didn't seem to notice our return.

Kyle spoke quietly, quickly. "Head to the rez."

Tension roiled off him and filled the car. We drove in silence until I couldn't take it anymore. "What's your plan?"

His neck looked like the trunk of an oak. Only his eyes moved as they watched the road beyond the windshield wipers. "My brother Alex didn't answer, either. We're going to my mother's house on the rez. Seems like the best place to start."

Knowing Carly and how many times she'd slipped her halter and ran, I couldn't stop myself from asking. "Has Shelly been in trouble before? Run away?"

His lips flattened, but that was all the movement on the surface. I imagined he was twisting on the inside. "No. She's a good kid."

This felt like poking someone's bruise. "You said she would do anything for her brothers. Would she be helping out one of them?"

A tick in his jaw. "I've only got one brother."

I glanced at him. He'd said he had two.

His nostrils flared, and he said, "I've got one now. Alex is fifteen."

No sense in rushing him, since we had a ways to go before we reached the rez.

After a time, Kyle spoke. "My other brother, Darrel, died two years ago, when I was in Afghanistan."

I hated that he'd gone through the pain of losing a sibling. I really hated that I knew what it felt like. Glenda's wasted face flashed through my mind. Not her radiant, grinning expression, so full of mischief like her daughter, Carly. But the wan, pale skin stretched in agony across her bones. Eyes closed, struggling to stay alive and failing. I felt that gaping crater again.

Glenda had died eight years ago, and sometimes life filled in the hole and I didn't ache with sadness. But then something reminded me of the way she laughed or how she loved peaches, or someone mentioned losing a brother, and I felt the sucker punch of loss all over again. In many ways I'd learned to live with it, not crying every time I thought of her but letting that first wave of grief crash over and going on.

"I'm sorry. It's awful to lose a sibling."

Another jaw tick and this time, he turned his head to his side window. "The waste wasn't his death. The real waste was his life."

I thought I understood but wasn't sure. "What's that mean?"

His words shot out in angry volleys. "He was a drunk. Eighteen years old, high school dropout, unemployed. Another dead injun."

"Wow. That's harsh."

He turned to me. I'd never heard him so bitter. "Yeah. That's how life can be on the rez."

The windshield wipers whapped back and forth and water splashed from the road. "You're a really great role model. I'm sure you did all you could. Sometimes kids are hell-bent on destroying themselves." God, I hoped I wasn't talking about Carly.

He wanted to say something. The words dammed up behind his eyes, and I wondered if the lead sentence would go something like this: "Keep your patronizing comments to yourself and your happy white family."

That's what I might have said if our positions were reversed. And I'd have been right. What did I know about growing up on the rez? But I went ahead and pushed more. It's what Grand County paid me for.

"If she wasn't in trouble, why would she be on her way to see you?"

His attention returned to the road ahead. "That's what we're gonna find out."

By the time we reached Dry Creek, the shabby settlement two miles from the reservation's border, the rain retreated, huddling in the heavy, angry clouds, building strength as if to attack again.

On the outskirts of the settlement, a brick ranch house lurked behind a tall cedar fence, only visible through the open driveway gate. This belonged to Frankie Delrose and his wife, Starla. They owned the largest of the four liquor stores and accounted for one half of the population of Dry Creek. They'd raised four kids; all had flown the nest but still counted in the last census.

Technically, the owners of the other three stores claimed Dry Creek as their home, but they'd anchored single-wide trailers in the lots behind their stores and kept an old junker parked out front to meet the county residency requirement. Their substantial profits bought them beautiful homes in Rapid City or Broken Butte. They only stayed in Dry Creek if they opted not to drive the two-hour commute to a cheerier environment.

Far from washing the town clean, the spring rain clogged the roadside with muddy runoff, making half-submerged boats of the snack wrappers and six-pack cartons. An abandoned Quonset hut with a metal overhang to shelter a concrete slab, and a house that burned down mysteriously a decade ago, welcomed us to Dry Creek. The carport and Quonset served as shelter and hangout for anyone too drunk to walk the two miles back to the rez. Every year, those spots served as the final resting site for a few unfortunates.

There was nothing redeeming in Dry Creek. Since alcohol was prohibited on Antelope Ridge Reservation, Dry Creek fed off addiction. It was nothing but a sinister, sad, wide spot on the road to death.

Kyle's voice barely rose above the growl of the tires. "I'd like to burn this place down."

"I think that's been tried a time or two."

His mouth turned up as if he'd smelled something rotten. "They've tried all kinds of things. When the reservation was started, the law said there couldn't be liquor sales within fifty square miles of the rez, but then, in all his wisdom, Teddy Roosevelt took away the buffer zone."

I thought for a moment. "Didn't someone try to get the buffer zone reinstated?"

"Oh, sure. But our favorite sheriff, Lee Barnett, rallied everyone in Spinner and Choker counties to lobby the state to keep the status quo. He's got a good buddy in Frankie Delrose, probably getting kickbacks."

Dry Creek made my heart hurt. "Anyone who thinks this town isn't here only to serve alcohol to the rez is blind."

"Money can cause blindness, I've heard."

A Lakota man in baggy canvas pants and an unevenly buttoned shirt staggered across the parking lot of A-1 Liquor. He looked up, and it took him a moment to focus on the cruiser. He spun around and tottered in the opposite direction.

Kyle closed his eyes. "They won't shut this place down.

They say the liquor stores will just pop up on the border, wherever they set it."

"It's what, a two-mile walk to Sand Gap from here?"

"It's too close."

I drove down the middle of the road, feeling depressed and dirty. The rez and its problems of poverty, addiction, and early death didn't factor into my daily life. Just over a hundred miles from where I'd complained endlessly about a small refrigerator with no functioning freezer compartment, and where I'd felt deprived because I'd never owned my own home, people were dying on the streets, alone and in pain. They didn't have enough to eat, a decent roof over their heads, or cars that ran. No jobs, sketchy health care, and schools that might be more holding pens than places of education.

Poupon sat up, stretched his front legs, and yawned. He gazed out the window, and as if it were too depressing to witness, he plopped back down and closed his eyes.

Three Indians in saggy jeans and jackets colorless with filth and rain sat on the front porch of a boarded-up building with a wood awning and concrete steps. A forty-ounce Colt 45 can stood like a guard at the hand of one man whose head hung from his neck as if holding on by a stretched Slinky. The other two men rested their heads on the building, their legs splayed in front of them, eyes unfocused.

Tucked away from the road, next to the boarded-up building with the optimistic Arts and Crafts sign, Frankie's Smart Shop announced itself with a Pepsi sign that glowed against the dark sky. Frankie might sell a bag of chips or maybe a Mountain Dew from time to time, but his real business was beer.

"Hell of a way to make a living." My words slid out.

Kyle's eyes stayed on the wasted men on the step. "They

say four million cans of beer are sold from Dry Creek every year."

Helplessness and defeat weighed me down.

"Four million cans. The population of Dry Creek is twelve." I had to strain to hear him.

A stucco house, probably vacant longer than lived in, marked the edge of town. Large splotches of black paint pocked the side, covering graffiti, I imagined. A hand-painted sign stood a few feet from the highway showing a Jack Daniel's bottle with "We Own You" stenciled in black.

What words could I form to express my sorrow at the despair so visible? Trash, weeds, plywood-adorned buildings, bars on the windows, and men and women so hopeless.

Tension drew his voice tight. "The life expectancy on this reservation is something like forty-seven for men, fifty-two for women."

Two miles from Dry Creek we came up to Sand Gap, the biggest town on the reservation. Not quite four thousand people, it had a school, a health center, and a few sad businesses. A gas station convenience store sat on an intersection, doing what appeared to be a big business. The sign out front identified the business as The Stop. The cars and pickups out front looked like abandoned vehicles, but anything with an engine that ran was sporting on the rez. We broke through the other side of town and Kyle directed me to an oil strip, a one-lane blacktop.

Nothing but wet prairie stretched on either side of the cruiser. Here, in the middle of nowhere, I could imagine we drove through any ranch, not a depressing pocket of poverty. Grass greening in the rain, wildflowers waiting patiently for the sun so they could burst out like debutantes at their first ball. But Kyle's words made it feel so very different.

"You know the suicide rate here is one hundred and fifty times higher than the average."

I knew very little about the rez except we'd been warned since childhood to avoid it. We'd take a different route to Rapid City or for a weekend in the Black Hills. I'd been to the Wounded Knee memorial once many years ago. All I remembered was a rickety sign by the side of the road. It made me feel sad.

And then I'd driven away.

Kyle directed me to turn north on a dirt track. Roads in Grand County, even rarely used ones such as the road into the Olson place, were plowed, constructed, layered, and packed with heavy equipment. They might deteriorate to washboards and potholes, but even then, they were better than the muddy trail I followed to where Kyle grew up.

We wound around a low hill and nearly hit a rusted hulk of a Chevy four-door. Two other vehicle carcasses littered the grassy road, keeping watch over the plastic Walmart bags skittering in the wind.

Kyle pointed to a rusted house trailer. Black trash bags covered two of the windows, and a bent screen door dangled by twisted hinges. "That's it. Home sweet home."

I kept my mouth from hanging open and held back my incredulous exclamation. Broad-shouldered, proud, and cheerful Kyle, always clean, shirt tucked in, hair combed. Smiling, confident Kyle, healthy, smart, handsome. He'd come from this place?

I parked in front, eyeing the cinderblocks that served as a front porch. "Your mother lives here?"

"Ma, Shelly, and Alex. I tried to get my brother and sister to live with me in Dunbar, but Alex doesn't like me much, and Shelly wants to keep an eye on Ma."

My old Boxer, Boomer, had had a more welcoming dog house than this trailer. "Doesn't look like anyone's here now."

Kyle stared at the trailer. "She's here."

"Shelly?"

Sadness swallowed his face, and his dark eyes seemed black. "Ma."

With a steel set to his face, he pushed the car door open. By the time I scrambled after him, he was yanking back the useless screen. The morning air smelled fresh with the rain, and I wanted to stay out here, where the world seemed right. The grass wet my boots as I hurried after him.

He pushed open a scratched and mud-smeared metal door. "Ma?"

Right behind him, I caught a whiff of cigarettes, a century or two of greasy meals, and dirty clothes. The front door opened directly into the space between a grungy kitchen and cramped living room. My eyes adjusted to the dim interior, where a tiny woman with more gray than black in her hair, and a face like a dried peach pit, sat at a splinter-topped wooden kitchen table.

The single-wide trailer held the night's chill but none of the morning's freshness. Dark, scratched paneling lined the living room, and a torn, rust-colored plush couch with no legs rested on carpet that peeled from the walls. A woven aluminum lawn chair comprised the rest of the furniture, along with upended plastic milk crates for tables. It made our backyard treehouse look like Club Med.

The mite of a woman pushed herself to stand and hobbled toward Kyle, arms reaching up. "Kyle!" She wore faded and stretched black sweatpants and an old, long-sleeved sweatshirt with a ripped collar.

He tensed and allowed her to hug him, gingerly patting

her back. With her still clinging to him, he spoke. "Is Shelly around?"

She stepped back and her arms dropped. Her smile looked strained. "No. She stayed over with Kim in Sand Gap."

An eight-by-ten graduation portrait hung in a cheap gold frame tacked to the paneling. It showed a young man, similar in looks to Kyle, but darker skin and eyes. I stepped closer and noticed another grainy framed photo of the same young man in a basketball uniform on the corner of the kitchen counter. A braided loop of grass draped over the corner of the frame. This must be Kyle's brother Darrel. No other attempt at decorating was evident.

Kyle inventoried the kitchen table, strewn with junk mail, dirty dishes, more than a few Budweiser cans, and various odds and ends. "Alex?"

The woman turned to me with forced cheer. "Is this the woman you work for? Down to Hodgekiss?"

He didn't seem excited to make introductions. "This is Grand County Sheriff Kate Fox. Kate, Rita Red Owl, my mother."

I'd figured she was his grandmother. The wrinkles and way she seemed tired and used up made me think she had more than one generation on him. I extended my hand. "Glad to meet you."

Her dry hand felt like an empty leather glove, and after a mumbled greeting, her eyes shifted back to Kyle. "You should have told me you were coming out. I'd have cooked something."

Kyle ignored that, making me ache for Rita at his rejection. "Where's Alex?"

Rita looked up from a lowered head in an almost coquettish way. "You didn't happen to bring groceries?"

Kyle's jaw ticked.

Rita smiled. "That's okay. You're busy. Do you have any cash? We could use some gas money."

I wanted to jump in for Kyle and give her a few bucks. He seemed so cold.

Rita took hold of his hand. "Sit. I'll make some coffee. I think I have a cookie or something here."

Kyle jerked his hand away, stood motionless for a beat, then lunged past me, streaking down the narrow hallway. His boots clumped on the threadbare shag carpet, and the trailer shook. He threw himself against a closed bedroom door.

I reached for my gun and started after him, but before I had it out of the holster, Kyle shot from the room and knocked into me on his way out the door.

What the—?

I sprang into the room, saw the open window, and figured someone had recently shimmied out. I whirled around to follow Kyle.

Rita screeched behind me as I hit the door in time to see Kyle sprinting across the wet prairie in pursuit of a black-haired kid. It looked like those Animal Planet videos where the cheetah races the gazelle and throws itself on the poor beast, tackling it to the ground.

I caught up with the two of them rolling in the sand and grass. Kyle grabbed the kid by the back of his hoodie and hauled him to his feet. He gave the boy a shake and let go. "Where are you going?"

The kid, a spittin' image of Kyle, except darker skin, glared at him. "Away from you."

No denying this was Alex, Kyle's younger brother, even though Kyle's skin was lighter. Their matching faces shot rage at each other.

I tucked my gun into my holster, noting that I'd actually drawn it.

Kyle scratched the back of his head as if trying to resist smacking the kid. "Why weren't you at the sweat?"

"Why were you there?"

Kyle practically vibrated with his effort at restraint. "Because Shelly asked me."

The kid's mouth twisted in bitterness. His eyes were nearly black, without the warmth of Kyle's. "Sure. For Shelly. You'll do anything for her."

The same hand that scratched his scalp dropped to slap his thigh. He won the battle and spoke with a calm voice. "The sweat was for you, *misúŋka*." Kyle thumped Alex in the chest. "For you."

Rita hurried toward us, her scruffy Kmart tennis shoes gathering moisture from the grass. Her thin arms lost in the sleeves of her sweatshirt, she shouted at Kyle. "You leave him alone. He done nothing wrong."

Kyle and Alex both ignored her, so I stopped her. "We're not here to arrest Alex. We're looking for Shelly."

Rita looked at the ground, not at me, like someone used to being disregarded. "Shelly's a good girl."

I nodded, keeping my eye on Kyle and Alex as they exchanged barbs and harsh words. "We only want to talk to her. Do you know where she is?"

Rita's head whipped up, and she shot me a hateful glance before rushing forward, putting a hand on Kyle's chest and shoving him away from Alex. "I said to leave him alone."

Kyle's eyes flashed but he didn't move.

Like a dog that attacks a badger as soon as you shoot it, Alex raised his chin and shouted at Kyle. "Don't come out here acting like you give a shit about any of us."

Rita's face, prematurely aged with alcohol and hard living, sagged. She pushed baggy sleeves up skinny arms and stepped forward. "If you cared, you'd have brung us something."

I might've agreed with Rita. She lived in such poverty, would it kill Kyle to give her a few bucks?

His face looked like a bronze statue. "Look, I'm only here to find Shelly. Do you know where she is?"

Alex sneered, his dark eyes so much like Kyle's except filled with unchecked rage. "Right. The golden girl. She gets the grades and the awards. Makes you look good in your white world."

Rita's sleeves slipped down, making her look like a child in her father's clothes. "You keep pushing her to be like you. Making her lose her culture."

Steel edged Kyle's voice. "The Lakota culture isn't alcohol and filth."

The whites of Rita's eyes were shaded a dull yellow from alcohol. "Go away. We don't need you here. If you were a real Lakota, you'd be finding Darrel's killer, not getting all your big white dollars and kissing up to the other sheriffs."

Alex stepped forward, his face full of bitterness. "You think you're some kind of Lakota warrior. Medals and fucking Marines bullshit. But Darrel, man, he knew what being Indian was."

"Go away," Rita repeated, her voice like a terrier's bark.

Alex flopped his hood over his head. "Look at you, Apple. You forgot where you came from. Listen to me, man. Red lives matter."

Kyle bristled with impatience. "What's that mean?"

Alex pointed. "If Shelly's gone, it's on you. She knew Darrel didn't accidentally get killed by some hit-and-run. Someone wanted him dead. And the white man, he let it all go. Just another dead Indian. But Shelly. She wants justice for her brother. You think the white man's gonna let that stand?"

Banded together, Alex and Rita generated their own pool of animosity. Rita thrust her chin out. "Hell, no."

Kyle seemed baffled. "What's Darrel have to do with Shelly disappearing, and what do you know about it?"

Alex lost some of his bravado and glanced nervously at Rita. "I don't know where Shelly is, man. She's all white-washed, like you. She don't tell me nothing."

Frustration and irritation made Kyle growl. "Then what are you talking about?"

Alex acted as if he'd rather be throwing punches than words. "What I'm sayin' is you shoulda found Darrel's murderer. Not get your paycheck from the people who hate us."

12

Kyle stared at them for a moment, then turned and strode toward the cruiser.

I hurried after him and flopped inside. "What was he talking about? Your brother's hit-and—"

"Just drive."

"But—"

"Damn it, Kate. We're not *Leave It To Beaver*, okay? It's the rez. It sucks." If I kept poking him, he might explode.

I kept my mouth shut.

When we drove through Sand Gap, Kyle nodded toward The Stop. "Pull in."

I found a space between a rusted Toyota about Diane's age and a low-riding Frankenstein of a pickup. Kyle jumped out and slammed the door.

Since the rain had let up, I opened the back door to let Poupon have a break. He didn't make an effort to sit up but gave me an expression that clearly told me he'd prefer I left him alone. Before I got to the front door, a group of teens burst out. They scattered like my badge carried the plague.

The door dinged as I entered the clean and well-lit convenience store.

Kyle stood at the counter addressing a round woman about Susan's age, with a glorious fan of black hair hanging to her waist. She stared at Kyle without expression.

He acted casual. "Have you seen Shelly around lately?"

It took her several beats to give him a deadpan answer. "She don't hang out here no more. Too good. You know."

Kyle maintained good cheer. "How about Alex?"

Her weight fell to one hip, making her hair sway. "Someone die? That why you're here?" The girl picked up an apple from a basket on the counter containing browning bananas and dusty fruit. She bit into it and spit the bite on the floor. "We don' like apples in here."

Kyle lifted his arm toward her. "Kate, this is my cousin, Kim."

An obese man lumbered from a room behind the cash register. His wide grin was the first welcome I'd seen on the rez. "Kyle Red Owl. Don' you look pretty in dat uniform."

Kyle's shoulders relaxed, and he met the man as he came around the counter and they clasped hands, slapping each other on the arms. "Gordon."

Gordon spoke with a thick Lakota accent. "What brings you here, man?"

Kim dug behind the counter and brought out a wooden baseball bat. She slapped it in her palm. "Rotten apples."

Kyle held up his hands and gave her an exasperated sigh, as if dealing with a naughty child.

Gordon's laugh boiled from deep in his belly. "Be nice."

Kim sneered at Kyle and me and sauntered to the back room.

Gordon shrugged. "Sorry 'bout my li'l sis. She don' like cops."

Kyle gave a friendly snort. I didn't think much would be gained if I got all indignant.

Kyle and Gordon gossiped about people I didn't know, passing the time as if they had no cares. I wandered down one aisle filled with every imaginable snack food. Up another aisle with a deli and soda fountain, along with espresso and slushy machines. Clean floors, neatly stocked shelves, bright lights, everything you'd expect from a highway quick shop.

I approached as Kyle finally got to his point. "Seen Shelly around lately?"

Gordon shook his head. "Naw. Haven't seen her much for a coupla months. Quit comin' in with the other kids."

"How about Alex?"

Gordon grinned. "That little shit. Tried to beg gas off me las' week."

Kyle looked irritated. "That Marquis burns twice what it should."

Gordon tipped his head back. "Not Shelly's car. That new one he got."

"Alex got a car?"

That deep rumble from the bottom of his core. "An old Chevy, like a '84 long bed. You ain't seen it?"

There hadn't been a pickup parked at Rita's trailer. Kyle frowned. "Wonder where he got the money for that?"

Again, Gordon's mirth boiled over. "I don' think he got the money. Way I heard, he tol' Hersh Good Crow he had money comin' and Hersh, he believed Alex. But the money didn't come. Alex couldn't even get gas. I heard Hersh took the truck back."

Kyle and Gordon chatted back and forth before Kyle dug in his back pocket and brought out his wallet. Flipping it open, he pulled out three twenties and laid them on the counter. "Put this on Ma's bill. Tell Aunt Birdie I said hi."

Kim plodded out, still holding the baseball bat, and looked at the bills. Her lip curled back. "Oh, cuz is suddenly concerned about his mother. Don' spend his Sundays talkin' to her about old times. Jus' want to pay her off. And using *those* bills. You suck, cuz."

Kyle reached for the cash. "Forget it."

Kim smashed the bat on them before Kyle could pick them up. "Leave 'em. Rita's got a big bill."

I gave Kim a tough look before sauntering after Kyle into the gray afternoon.

Poupon ignored us as we climbed back into the cruiser. I pulled out on the highway heading east. "What did Kim mean about 'those bills'?"

Kyle didn't look at me. "Indians don't like twenties. Andrew Jackson's picture."

I squirmed, embarrassed I hadn't thought of that.

"They'll be happy to get it." He sighed. "They won't tell Ma I paid it, but they'll keep giving her credit."

"Why didn't you just give her the money?"

It took him a minute to answer. "It wouldn't have gone for food or gas."

The rain pelted down again. "You don't suppose Shelly's car broke down or ran out of gas and she caught a ride with a friend?"

"She would call me."

"She did."

He slammed his palm on the dash. "And I wasn't there because I was trying to help Alex by going to the sweat. Now she's in trouble."

We came to the Nebraska state line. Up ahead the Pepsi sign for Frankie's showed a pinprick of light in the heavy sky ahead. I glanced at the familiar sign that highlighted every highway entering our state. Most places it said, "Nebraska...

the Good Life. Home of Arbor Day." But someone had spray-painted over it, declaring this place the Dead Life. Home of Death.

I tried to sound reasonable. "Shelly might not be in trouble. She's a teenager. They're so wrapped up in themselves they don't care about anyone else. Maybe she's with a friend and didn't even think you'd be worried."

His voice rumbled. "Not Shelly. She's always thinking of other people. She wouldn't go to school off the rez because she had to look after Ma."

I knew a thing or two about wacky mothers. "Your mother didn't seem like she needs someone to look after her."

"Ma was having a good day."

"What is Shelly's plan for your mother when she goes to college next fall?"

He closed his eyes and let out a breath. "Shelly thought she could get Ma's sister to take her in." He paused to explain the relationship. "Gordon and Kim's mother." He opened his eyes and stared at the upcoming disaster of Dry Creek. "Birdie's not a whole lot better than Ma. I'm worried they'll suck Shelly back to stay with them."

I blurted it out without thinking. "You can't let that happen."

His frustration hit me full face. "Right. I need to get her out of there. But every time I try, something drags her back. And Alex, he's even worse. Fifteen and headed for an early grave just like—" He cut himself off.

"Like Darrel?"

He didn't respond, and I slowed to the speed limit to pass through Dry Creek. But I jerked the wheel and pulled into Frankie's Smart Shop instead.

Kyle stirred. "Craving a Colt 45 for the drive home?"

I yanked the keys and opened my door. "Let's see what Barnett is up to."

Kyle scanned the parking lot that contained a white Toyota that chugged and sputtered with no driver and an old silver-and-red flatbed Ford F-150. He scrambled from the cruiser, still looking confused.

I hurried through the rain to the barred glass front door. Coors Light, Miller Genuine Draft, and the ever-present Budweiser signs flickered and glowed, promising the hopeless patrons forgetfulness for a few bucks. A bell above the door jangled, and I entered a dimly lit, cluttered room. A fluorescent light fixture flickered overhead. The gloom wasn't enough to mask the grimy old linoleum floor. An overpowering cloud of cigarette smoke allowed only the slightest hint of wet dog.

Kyle pushed in behind me, and we both made way for a staggering man, mumbling to himself as he headed outside. His odor of unwashed body and urine cut through the smoke and lingered after the door closed behind him.

Barnett stood at the counter wearing his sheriff browns and cowboy hat, a black slicker glistening with rain. His mouth opened in surprise when he spotted us. "For the love of...What are you doing here?"

Frankie's store was a little bit liquor store and a lot like a fortress. The cash register was barricaded behind a counter with bars and a smooth cutout to slide money and change back and forth. Alongside the bars, solid shelves held pocket-sized liquor bottles, cigarette racks, snacks, and other items, effectively blocking the view behind the counter. A few feet away from the register, a door—no doubt locked—provided access to the area behind the counter. My guess was that Frankie had an office somewhere behind the safety of the door and bars.

A skinny man in a plaid pearl-button shirt poked his head

from behind the cash register. Tufts of white hair spiked from his scalp. His teeth seemed too big for his face and hard not to focus on when he gave us a fake smile. "Officers. What brings you to Dry Creek?"

I slid my hands into my jacket pockets to seem friendly and casual. "Checking out an abandoned vehicle."

Barnett huffed in annoyance. "Still gnawing that splintered bone?"

What a jerk, but I didn't take the bait. "The car belongs to Kyle's sister. She's missing, and we're afraid something happened to her."

Impassive, Barnett leaned against the counter. "That so?"

Kyle sounded like a dangerous rez dog. "You knew that was Shelly's car. She drives it around every day."

Frankie pulled his lips over his front teeth. "Shelly Red Owl? That your sister?"

They say still waters run deep, and Kyle was as still as death.

Frankie passed a knowing look at Barnett and raised his eyebrows to Kyle. "She was in here Saturday night, late. Wasn't in too good of shape."

Kyle snarled. "That's a lie."

Frankie's white hair looked like dandelion seeds threatening to launch in a wind. He turned to Barnett for backup. "You've seen her around lately."

Barnett folded his arms across his barrel chest. "Running with a bad crowd."

Kyle seemed ready to spring. "She just graduated valedictorian. She's a good kid."

Barnett tsked. "I've seen it happen before. The good kid breaks out and celebrates and that's it. You know how you people can be. Sometimes all it takes is one drink to get you hooked."

Quicker than I thought possible, Kyle jumped at Barnett. I grabbed his collar as he flew past me and yanked hard enough that his first punch missed Barnett's nose and barely grazed his chin.

Barnett yelled and put up his fists, ready to swing. Frankie hollered and dove for something under the counter. I threw myself between Barnett and Kyle, pushing on Kyle's chest, backing him toward the door.

We hit the cold rain, and it seemed to douse some of Kyle's anger. He spun away from me and stomped several paces into the muddy parking lot and stopped, his back to me.

The drunk we'd passed on the way into the store leaned against the side of the building, joined by a ragtag woman wearing an unraveling stocking cap and ripped wool jacket. They passed a paper-bag-wrapped forty-ounce can between them.

"You going to be okay?" I called to Kyle.

He ran a hand through his hair. "Okay?" He spun toward me. "Look at this place. These people." He pointed to the couple sharing the malt liquor. "My mother."

Any words I had wouldn't help him.

He lowered his voice, eyes anguished. "The world wants to write the population off as drunks and losers, and I can't do anything about it."

All I had for him was my willingness to listen.

He closed his eyes for a moment. "My motto has always been to save myself first, then my brothers and sister." He gazed beyond the tacky store. "So far, I'm failing."

I could point out his success. Stellar military record, police academy certified, employed, responsible. But he didn't need that. One glance at Dry Creek told me the awful battle he waged on behalf of Shelly and Alex. I reeled away from him, fueled by contempt.

The door jangled as I stepped back into the dank store, under the winking light. Barnett still leaned against the counter. Frankie, all wispy tufts and teeth, stood behind the cash register. A shotgun rested on the counter next to Frankie. Guess that was what he'd reached for when Kyle went after Barnett.

I was a tiny spark away from explosion. "What's the deal?"

Barnett smirked. "With what?"

I addressed Frankie. "The man you just sold to is obviously drunk. That's one offense. He is out on your property drinking, another offense." I shifted my attention to Barnett. "Why aren't you arresting Frankie for selling to an inebriated man, and why aren't you arresting the people in the parking lot for drinking illegally?"

Barnett scoffed. "First time to Dry Creek and you're turning into some kind of activist. Save the red man."

"Laws are on the books. It's your job to enforce them."

Barnett straightened. "I'm not here in an official capacity. Just visiting my buddy."

"Oh, brother."

A bolt of anger shot across his forehead. "What? You think I ought to round up every drunk Indian and haul them into my jail? How do you suppose Spinner County would pay for that? Cleaning up this place is a job too big for one county sheriff."

"So you just give up?"

Frankie watched this exchange go on before jumping in with the ingratiating voice of a snake oil salesman. "I know it looks bad. You want to help these people. Don't you think it breaks my heart to see them come in day after day and know they're ruining their lives?"

No, I doubted it ruffled his conscience at all. "Then why do you stay here?"

"If I didn't, someone else would. And that someone wouldn't know the people here like I do. I keep an eye out. Like that Shelly Red Owl. I sold to her, sure. If I didn't, she'd go to A-1 or one of the other stores, or down the road to Potsville, or maybe up to Rapid City. She'd get her beer, for sure. But then she'd have to drive. When they buy it here, most times they walk back to the rez. No one gets hurt."

That was about the biggest lie ever told. "Everyone gets hurt. Except you. You get rich."

Frankie faked a sad smile through his big teeth. "You see? That's what everyone thinks. I'm exploiting the poor Indian. But here's the truth. We're in America, and we believe in people's right to make their own decisions. I'm not twisting anyone's arm to buy their beer from me."

If I'd ever wanted to puke on demand, this was the time. All over the front of his shirt, on his cash register, on the floor of his gold mine.

He shrugged. "I'm not to blame that they voted over a hundred years ago to make the reservation dry. The people have a right to drink if they want. I'm allowing them personal freedom."

He was probably still justifying his motives when I pushed through the door.

Kyle waited for me in the cruiser. I slammed the door and started the engine.

A sad grin flitted across his face. "He pissed you off, too, huh?"

"He's a jerk."

Kyle laughed. "Is that what you call it?"

No, actually. "Prick. Asshole."

"That's more like it." He sat up. "I've had more practice than you at dealing with this crap. It's wrong, yeah. You can fight it. But you won't win."

Black, hot, boiling over. Grab me a can of spray paint and I'd color my rage over storefronts and cop cars.

I backed out and eased toward the highway. A newish white pickup heading from the east slapped on a signal to turn into Frankie's. I focused on the driver. A ball of dark hair.

"Holy. Is that—"

Kyle leaned forward. "What?"

"It is. It's the kid from the Olson place."

When he got close enough to see us, the blinker stopped, and he slinked down and kept driving. "What's he doing up here?" I said.

Kyle watched in the side mirror. "Guess Indians aren't the only ones Frankie sells illegal beer to. That kid didn't look anywhere near twenty-one."

Maybe. Probably right. But I did wonder if Barnett being here in his pickup instead of his official ride had anything to do with the kid. "I saw him at the preppers' place yesterday and then at the fairgrounds. Do you know him?"

Kyle shrugged. "Nope. Why would I?"

Weird. "My niece said he was looking for you."

Kyle twisted around at the taillights disappearing in the gloom. "Your niece say what it was about?"

"Nope."

Kyle turned toward the front, wound as tight as a rattler. "I'm not that hard to find. He can call if he wants."

I glanced at him. "How do you keep it from getting to you? The rage, I mean."

He looked like cold steel. "I got out. I can't tell you why I fought to get out and so many of my family and friends let it wash over them. It was in me from as far back as I remember. I never wanted to stay on the rez."

We left Dry Creek behind. "So, you're trying to help Shelly and Alex?"

Kyle stared at the hills, but I doubted he saw them. "And Darrel. He was stealing beers from Ma and skipping school before he turned ten."

"What was Darrel like?"

Kyle hesitated and then spoke in a husky voice. "He loved to draw. Had pictures taped all over the trailer."

I stayed silent.

"Ma got drunk one night after he died and burned them all."

After several minutes of silence, he drew in a breath. "Darrel was always in trouble. I never could help him. He wanted to beat me up, didn't want to listen to me."

"But Shelly and Alex are different?"

He swallowed as if pushing down the pain. "I was ten when Shelly was born. Ma wasn't so bad then and had a job, and Dad didn't hang around much. I took care of Shelly most of the time. She looked up to me."

Half of my brothers and sisters were older and half younger. I was both the look-upper and the one being looked up to. "That's a big responsibility."

He grunted. "Probably why I kept straight. I wanted to show Shelly how to be. I wanted her to make a good life, maybe more than I wanted one for me."

"So you got good grades and then enlisted?"

"I didn't plan on going into the Marines. I wanted to go to college. Stick around to help Shelly and Alex."

"What changed?"

"Dad moved back. He was drinking bad, and I was his preferred punching bag. My existence pissed him off. I thought if I left he'd be better."

"Was he?"

He didn't move for a moment. "He died in Dry Creek a couple of months after I enlisted."

"Why did he pick on you?"

Kyle grunted again. "Pick on me." The tires rumbled on the road, and the occasional swish of the delayed wipers kept us company for several moments. "No one ever said, but we all knew. Dad wasn't my real father. I'm eight years older than Darrel, and the other two came along pretty quick."

"Do you have any idea who your real father is?"

His lips twisted. "Probably some worthless piece of crap. He didn't stick around to see how I grew up, and obviously, Ma felt ashamed of me."

"You don't know that."

He snorted. "I've got no doubts about that. Ma didn't like me much. Ever. She paid attention to the other kids, hugged them, laughed with them. Not me. She ignored me as much as she could."

I didn't ask for any more details. Talking seemed to hurt him more than silence.

My phone rang, and I reached into my pocket and pulled it out. My sister-in-law Lauren chirped a greeting. "I have this bumper crop of rhubarb, and I mentioned it to Doc Scranton, you know, the new vet."

Yeah, I knew.

"Anyway, he said rhubarb pie is his favorite, so I invited him out for dinner tonight. Michael and I thought we might as well make it a party, and Robert and Sarah are going to be here, too. So, you'll come, right?"

My guess was that Michael had no idea Lauren was trying to set me up. "I'm probably going to be working."

While Lauren absorbed the rejection, I checked on the sleeping king in my rearview mirror. Poupon seemed content.

"Oh." She obviously hadn't counted on me saying no. "Well. Everyone else said they'd be here, so I guess we'll go ahead. I won't say anything to Doc in case you can get away."

I had no intention of changing my plans. "Thanks for thinking of me." I hung up, but Kyle wasn't about to let it lie.

"Got a date for tonight?"

"No."

"Why not?"

I stared at the rain popping onto the windshield. "Not discussing this."

Kyle took notice of our surroundings. "Hey, where are we going?"

I'd scooted past the turnoff to the highway heading south to Hodgekiss and kept going east. "We're going to the research ranch."

He twisted in his seat to look west. "Why? Shelly's not hiding out there."

13

In the 70s, Angus and Mary Magnuson donated their ranch to the University of Nebraska (Go Big Red). Since then, the Magnuson Ranch housed a world-class ag research facility. Mainly, their projects included cattle, range, wildlife, and insect research.

My brother Douglas, an honored graduate from both the university ag college and its graduate program, had snagged the operations manager job two years ago. Something of a big teddy bear, he surprised everyone but his family with his firm management style. We all knew he didn't suffer laziness or inaccuracy, so he rode herd on his graduate assistants. He'd fired his share of day workers and sent a few researchers packing. He might seem easygoing and complacent to others, but he had a perfectionist streak a body didn't want to mess with.

Kyle and I were lucky to find his university pickup parked at the headquarters. I opened the back door and demanded Poupon get out this time.

He didn't move until Kyle growled, "*Ločhíŋ*." Then he jumped up, tail wagging, and hopped out of the car. We waited while he trotted off into the pasture to relieve himself.

"What did you say?"

Kyle raised an eyebrow at me, and I was glad to see humor glint his eyes. "Reminded him I'm hungry."

After Poupon had done what he needed to do and we let him sniff a few smells, all three of us tromped through the damp air to the ranch headquarters.

Douglas's office took up most of the ground floor of the old ranch house with his bedroom upstairs. I knocked and opened the door to the savory, welcoming scent of beef stew. My stomach sat up and begged.

Kyle's nose twitched, and he licked his lips.

Douglas sat at his kitchen table propping a veterinary journal open with his fleshy elbow while he clasped a spoon in his other fist, halfway raised to his lips. He dropped the spoon when he saw me, his eyes flew open in surprise. "Kate. What are you doing out here?"

He jumped to his feet and stuck out his hand to Kyle. "Have you eaten? I've got a bunch of stew."

"Hell, yes." I hurried to a cabinet and found two bowls and plates while Douglas yanked out a drawer and grabbed spoons. Over my shoulder I addressed Kyle. "Douglas is the best cook of the Foxes." To Douglas I said, "Don't tell Louise I said that."

He gave Poupon a skeptical appraisal. "New deputy?"

"Temporary."

"Not much of a cow dog."

I set the bowls on the counter. "I don't have any cows."

Douglas tipped his chin toward the window. "How about this rain?"

Keeping sarcasm out of my voice, I answered, "It'll make the grass grow."

Douglas nodded with enthusiasm. "Damn right!"

Kyle plucked two paper napkins from a holder on the

table and set them at our places. "I was about to die of starvation, so this is appreciated."

Douglas spooned hot stew into the bowls. "You're in for a treat today. This might be the best batch I've made yet. Dorsey Minden gave me an indoor herb garden and it's making a big difference."

I lifted my brows. "Dorsey? Anything I should know?"

He placed the steaming bowls on the table, and we both sat. "I don't suppose you need to know much."

Poupon flopped under the table at Kyle's feet.

I punched Douglas in the arm. "Come on. Are you and Dorsey a thing?"

Kyle blew on his stew and, without looking at me, said, "You sure you want to open up the topic of who's dating who?"

Douglas's eyes sparkled. "Yes. Let's talk about that. My vote is for Trey Ridnoir."

I shoved the spoon into my mouth. The rich, thick beef broth mingled with potatoes and onions, a hint of garlic. "Is that thyme? Or marjoram?"

Kyle tucked into his stew and kept his head down.

"A little of both," Douglas said. "Along with a touch of cinnamon. So now, about Trey."

"Dorsey enjoy your cooking?" I spooned in another delicious bite. "You'll make her a fine wife someday."

Douglas laughed. "Okay. Just let me say I've known Trey for a while. We served on a youth committee together a few years ago. He volunteers with troubled kids."

Kyle scraped his bowl. "This is the best stew I've ever had."

Douglas indicated the pot on the stove. "Help yourself. There's plenty."

I buried my spoon and pulled up a potato bit, celery, and a chunk of beef. If heaven had a taste, this would be it. "This is amazing."

"It helps that you're a coyote," Douglas said. "If you'd learn to cook for yourself, you wouldn't have to rely on your family to feed you."

"I can cook." I'd managed to put meals on the table for eight years when I lived on Frog Creek. Some of them pretty good, if I do say so myself.

He lifted an eyebrow. "Still, when someone invites you to dinner, you ought to accept."

I jerked up straight. "Lauren called you?"

He shook his head. "Michael." Michael and Douglas were twins. They didn't look alike and rarely agreed, but if one knew something, it was a sure bet the other did, too. They were close as salt and pepper. "We disagree on who's right for you."

That ought to take my appetite away, but I kept eating. "I figured Michael didn't know Lauren was setting me up."

Douglas laughed. "Oh hell, I think it was Michael's idea. He's voting for Heath Scranton."

I kept eating. It tasted too good to waste over personal discomfort.

While Kyle's spoon scraped the bottom of his bowl again, I swallowed and got serious. "Do you ever go into Dry Creek?"

Douglas looked surprised. "As little as possible."

Kyle caught him in his sights. "But you do go sometimes?"

Douglas shrugged. "Yeah. It's not great, but Frankie's carries butter and milk."

I swallowed another spoonful of deliciousness. "Been there lately?"

He tensed. "What is this about?"

Kyle leaned forward. "My sister went missing Saturday night."

"Shelly Red Owl?"

We both stared at him in surprise.

He shrugged. "I helped out with an FFA project at Sand Gap High. Shelly's a good kid." To Douglas, everyone in the world was a good guy or a good kid or a hell of a good hand—unless you worked for him, of course.

Kyle jumped in. "So you know she wouldn't just run away."

Douglas frowned. "Well, young girls can get skittish." He tipped his head my way. "Like Carly. They get a notion, and all of the sudden they're gone."

The stew soured in my stomach.

Kyle was firm. "Not Shelly."

Douglas stared at him as if debating whether to argue. "How often have you been around her in the last couple of months?"

Alarm flashed in Kyle's eyes. "She's been busy with end-of-school stuff. Graduation and college prep. But we talk on the phone."

Douglas picked up a spoon and set it back down. Raindrops splattered on the kitchen window. "I'm not like a school counselor or anything. Only there a couple of times a week and I see the kids for maybe an hour at a time. But something changed with her."

Kyle focused like a hawk on a mouse. "What are you talking about?"

Sweet Douglas. The compassionate Fox. If I had to receive bad news, I'd want it to come from him. "I noticed she seemed distracted and tired. Times she actually dozed at her desk. And we were doing aquaculture, so there wasn't a lot of sitting around."

"Aqua, as in fish?" I asked.

Douglas kept his eyes on Kyle. "Salmon hatchery. Last year we experimented with mushroom farms. We're trying to find entrepreneurial ventures that can create new economies on the rez."

Kyle ignored me. "Everything she had going on, she was probably worn out."

If Shelly had been trying to take care of Rita, and Alex was acting up, that might drag her down.

Douglas's voice grew softer, not quieter. "A couple of the teachers told me her grades had fallen off. She hadn't turned in her last English paper, and her math teacher said she barely passed the last trig test."

Kyle shook his head. "That's not true. She was valedictorian."

"That's why I heard about it. The staff was upset she'd dropped off like that because all the announcements had been made and graduation programs printed. Her grades were high enough even with her messing up like that, so they let it go."

Kyle barely stayed seated. "That's only been a month ago. If she was doing so bad, why didn't I know about it?"

It was only after Carly vanished that I realized she'd been acting strangely. Her sudden interest in her father's death. Asking questions about how he'd afforded the new house and indoor arena for his wife, Roxy. Maybe she'd be here with me now if I'd been paying more attention.

I wanted to pat Kyle's hand but didn't. "Who knows what goes on in someone else's head?"

Kyle stacked his empty bowl on the others. "Do you know anything about Lee Barnett?"

Douglas studied us before he spoke. "Why are you suddenly interested in Barnett?"

Kyle's voice sounded strained. "My sister is missing."

Douglas looked alarmed. "And you think Barnett has something to do with it?"

I held up my palm. "No. But Barnett acted like he didn't recognize her car when he should have."

We waited, the sound of the rain tracking time. Finally,

Douglas folded his hands on his belly. "I don't know anything for a fact."

"Got it," I said.

He shifted. "You asked if I go into Dry Creek." He paused.

I pushed. "Right."

"A couple of times I've seen Barnett there." He toyed with one of the spoons.

I prompted him. "He was there just now. Hanging out with Frankie Delrose."

Douglas looked up at me. "Who else was there?"

Kyle answered, "Sammy Good Crow, Graham White Lance, a couple of guys I didn't know."

Douglas seemed satisfied. "No girls?"

Kyle jumped on that. "Why?"

Again, Douglas seemed reluctant to say. "I don't know anything, really."

"Say it," I said.

He swallowed. "A few months ago I was in Dry Creek after dark. Barnett was there in his pickup."

He stopped, and I nudged his shoulder.

"He was helping a drunk girl get in."

This felt all wrong. "Did you ask him about it?"

Douglas nodded. "Sure I did. And he said she was underage and he was taking her to Potsville and charging her with MIP."

Both of Kyle's hands showed white knuckles.

"But when I watched the newspaper, I never saw the booking record. She was underage, so they wouldn't publish her name, but they usually say someone was picked up. And I didn't know the girl, so I couldn't check up with her."

Kyle pushed his chair back. "Let's go."

"Where?"

"Back to Dry Creek. That bastard knows something."

I didn't get up. "I'm not taking you with me."

"Then I'll go myself."

"Calm down, will you? We can't go barging in and accusing Barnett of kidnapping your sister."

"Why not?"

I folded my arms, planting myself in Douglas's kitchen chair. "We've got no proof of anything. We don't even know Shelly is missing. She's eighteen, so legally, she's an adult and can go where she wants."

"I'm not going to sit on my thumbs while you play diplomat with a damn racist."

Douglas stood, filling the room with authority. "You're jumping to conclusions. Barnett is an ass, all right. But for all we know, he might have been taking that girl home."

Kyle snorted. "This is the man I've seen finish a can of beer, crush it on the bar, and shout, 'Another dead injun.' And you think he might be out helping young drunk Lakota maidens?"

Douglas held up his hand. "Lee Barnett isn't a great guy—"

Kyle ground out his words. "Something about the whole story bothered you or you wouldn't have thought twice about it. Come on, man, you know he wasn't helping her out."

I stayed sitting, hoping to keep emotions lowered. "Before we go knocking down Barnett's door, let's talk to Shelly's friends. See if maybe something was going on with her."

Kyle's breath came hot and fast. "We're wasting time. Barnett took her. I know it."

A sharp bird's chirp rang out, startling me. Douglas perked his head. Kyle's hand dove for his pocket, and he pulled out his phone.

He swiped it and stared at the screen, alarm in his eyes.

I couldn't wait. "What?"

He sounded as if I'd sucker-punched him. "Shelly." He handed me his phone.

I stared at the green dialogue box from Shelly on Kyle's phone. As if she'd been sitting in our conversation at Douglas's kitchen table, she'd written, "I'm okay."

Kyle snatched the phone from me. He tapped back, his face scrunched and his breathing fast.

The bird chirped again. He read.

He might be used to living alone and not having anyone around to talk to, but I wanted to know. "Tell me."

"She said, 'I'm good. Alex is cool.'"

He typed again, and in a second the phone chirped. His shoulders slumped and he handed me the phone.

I read out loud to keep Douglas in the loop. "Kyle asked her where she was. She said, 'Not your business, leave me and Alex alone.'"

Kyle took the phone I offered him and typed again. Douglas picked up the bowls and set them in the sink. No chirp.

My phone rang and I jumped, answering quickly as if I thought maybe Shelly might be calling.

Sarah didn't wait for me to finish announcing myself as sheriff. "You better frickin' get yourself to Michael and Lauren's tonight."

Douglas turned from the sink, obviously hearing Sarah yelling through the phone. He pointed and laughed. "Busted."

I sighed. "You know how much I appreciate you all meddling in my life and telling me how you think I should live, but I'm really busy working a case and can't make it."

Douglas raised his voice so Sarah could hear. "That's a lie."

"It is not," I said to him.

Douglas pointed to Kyle. "Shelly may not be found, but she's not lost, either."

Kyle didn't bother looking up as he typed away. Still no answering chirp.

Sarah latched onto Douglas's announcement. "Don't be a douche about this. Maybe you aren't interested in Heath Scranton. I get that. I'm voting for Josh, myself."

I burst out, "What is this voting BS?"

She ignored that. "But Heath is a nice guy, and Lauren is a great cook. Think about it. Lauren, Michael, me, Robert. And Heath. Sitting there at a table all alone."

Lauren was a great cook, and even though I hated rhubarb and didn't consider it food, she'd probably pair it with her famous homemade ice cream. "I'm not responsible for Heath Scranton's feelings."

Sarah wasn't going quietly. "Oh, right. It's not like you owe him anything. Like maybe for stitching up that stupid hard head of yours. And it barely left a scar. You ingrate."

Douglas pumped the air. "You gotta love a sister-in-law who tells it like it is."

I glared at him. "No, you don't." She was right that I owed Heath hospitality at least. My head got bashed in when I was attacked last winter, and Heath had stitched up my forehead, saving me a call to the ambulance or a drive to Broken Butte County Hospital's emergency room.

"Besides," Sarah wasn't quite done. "Even if you don't care about Heath, you love me, and you wouldn't send me out there, in all my pregnant glory, to make small talk with Lauren all night long. Even you aren't that cruel."

"Even me?" At least now, until the baby was born, Sarah still wanted me around.

Sarah sighed. "You did make me double-date with that nerd from Omaha."

"And you'll never let me forget it."

"And you didn't stop me from marrying into this crazy family."

"You can't pin that on me."

"So you'll come to Michael and Lauren's tonight."

"Fine."

She brightened and in a singsong said, "See you soon!"

Kyle didn't bother looking up as he typed away. Still no answering chirp.

14

We thanked Douglas for the delicious stew and slogged through the drizzle to the cruiser. I considered our options. The shortest route to Hodgekiss took us deep into the hills. "With all this rain, I'd rather go back to the highway and around instead of dirt roads."

Kyle nodded, clearly distracted. "That's fine. I want to stop in Dry Creek again."

I tapped my finger on the steering wheel. "What about the texts from Shelly?"

Kyle's voice sounded as tight as his neck looked. "She's in trouble."

"The texts didn't make it sound like trouble. More like a kid acting out."

"It's not like Shelly."

We were back on the merry-go-round where I repeated that Shelly had been acting different than normal and he told me she was a good kid. "You think the texts aren't legit?"

He rubbed a hand through his hair. "Maybe whoever has her forced her to text me. Or maybe he texted himself."

That was true. "Why mention Alex?"

Evidently, he didn't have a theory on that, because he answered, "Sammy Good Crow's sister used to be a friend of Shelly's. He might know something or at least know where his sister is."

Twenty minutes later we cruised into Dry Creek, and it hadn't changed in the last two hours. Probably much the same as in the last two decades. Or more.

We pulled into Frankie's parking lot. Sammy Good Crow still sat on the pavement to the side of the store along with three other men. A rusty black beater car, filled to overflowing with people, sputtered out of the lot and turned toward Antelope Ridge. A knot of younger people, maybe in their twenties, headed out of the parking lot on foot, along the highway toward the rez.

Kyle got out, and I tagged along behind him. Sammy sat with his legs in front of him as if the bones had been removed, head resting on the side of the building, eyes closed.

Kyle stopped in front of Sammy and tapped him on the bottom of his grungy tennis shoe. "Sammy, wake up, man."

Sammy wagged his head from side to side and slowly opened his eyes. "Kyley Two-Shoes."

"Good to see you." Kyle's cheery voice covered his worry. "Hey, you seen Shelly around lately?"

Sammy stopped moving his head and stared at Kyle as if trying to bring several images into focus. "Shelly, your sister? Whaddya wan' from her?"

Kyle looked way more relaxed than I knew him to be. "Ma's worried, you know. She's been gone a couple of days. I told Ma I'd try to find her."

Sammy snorted and left his mouth open, like a door he'd forgotten to close. He roused himself. "Saw her a while back. It was that cold night. Remember?"

Because there'd only been one cold night in Nebraska, ever.

Kyle didn't press on the timing. "Was she with anyone?"

One of the other men, who seemed more alert than Sammy, offered information. "Dat Shelly, she comes aroun' sometimes. She tries to get the kids to stop partyin'. She's like a Indian narc."

Kyle focused on the talker. "You see my sister around here? Shelly Red Owl?"

He nodded like his neck was rubber. "I seen her haulin' off girls that come to have a good time. At leas' those girls come back."

Kyle alerted like a sniffer dog on a joint. "What do you mean, those girls come back?"

Sammy snorted. "Man, I hate this rain. How long you suppose it's gonna keep this up?"

Kyle nudged the foot of the other man. "Are there girls who go missing?"

The man sat up straighter, though that made him list toward Sammy. "All the time, man. Poof. Like smoke."

Kyle prodded the man. "Who?"

Sammy squinted at Kyle as if trying to sharpen his image. "There was Ginny Two Guns."

"Yeah," the other man said. "An' that cousin of hers. An' what about Missy Iron Cloud?"

Sammy shook his head. "Naw. She wasn't the one. It was that, what was her name?"

The two men lost interest in Kyle and mumbled back and forth, disagreeing with each name they threw out.

Finally, Kyle raised his voice. "Hey. What about Shelly? Was she drinking or hanging out with a bad crowd?"

The man took a few seconds to concentrate. "Naw, she's

like you, bro. Kyley Two-Shoes." He snickered. "Shelly Two-Shoes. Sounds better."

Kyle spoke to Sammy. "Your sister around?"

Sammy leaned his head against the building and mumbled. "They went to Lead for a track meet."

"She and Shelly still good friends?"

Sammy closed his eyes. "I'm kinda thirsty, man."

Kyle tapped Sammy's foot. "Think about that night you saw her. Maybe Saturday night."

Sammy's tongue snaked out and licked his lips. "Shelly drive that car of Darrel's, huh?"

Kyle's effort at easygoing cracked at the edges. "His old Marquis. Yeah. So, she was here in the car. With who?"

The guy sitting next to Sammy swiped his arm under his nose. "Heard she was working for the ranch."

Kyle zeroed in on the guy. "What ranch?"

The guy blinked. "That place, you know. Where Darrel worked. You know."

Sammy nodded. "Yeah. They come get us sometimes. Want us to work for them. Pay us cash. Pro'ly Shelly's planting corn or somethin'."

It made sense now, how Marty and Rhonda found labor. "Guy drives a white pickup?"

Sammy smacked his lips. "If I wasn't so thirsty I could think better."

I considered bringing him a Mountain Dew and figured that wouldn't get us any more information. Still, it wouldn't hurt Sammy. I spun around to enter Frankie's. The flicking overhead light and cloud of cigarette smoke made me hurry.

Barnett and Frankie no longer parlayed near the front counter. Now, Frankie's wife, the ever-bubbly and beautiful Starla, lasered me with her angry stare. She didn't offer a hello but crossed her arms over her breasts and thinned her mouth to invisible, leaving her caterpillar eyebrows her dominant features.

I didn't feel like conversation anyway, so I opened the soda cooler near the front door and grabbed some bottles.

I dropped four twenty-ounce bottles of Mountain Dew in front of the cash register, and Starla banged on the keys, croaking out a total several dollars higher than the gas station in Hodgekiss would charge.

Starla still hadn't so much as grunted a conversational word by the time the bell jangled on the door announcing my departure.

From the frustration lining Kyle's face, I gathered he hadn't come up with any more information.

He stepped back to give me space to distribute the Mountain Dews. As expected, the guys weren't thrilled with the freebies. Grumbling and leaving them on the pavement seemed the generally accepted thanks. Maybe they'd soak down the calories after we left, but not while there was still a chance I'd come to my generous senses and supply them with forty ounces of real charity.

The heater felt good after the damp air, though Kyle didn't seem to notice. Far from defeated by lack of progress, his thumbs drummed on his knees, an outward sign of agitation I hadn't seen from him before.

I glanced to the west before pulling out of the parking lot and heading back to Hodgekiss. Just beyond the speed limit sign outside of town, two old Monte Carlos, one turquoise and one gold, parked end to end at the side of the road. I headed toward them.

Kyle glared at them. "Now what?"

"Gonna check this out."

Eyebrows ducked. "Let's get back to town. You've got a date, and I've got stuff to do."

"It's not a date," I grumbled. Not enough of a date to put Baxter into a saddle, anyway.

Two dust motes of men tumbled on the roadside in front of the gold Monte Carlo, a whirl of camo, gray hair, and flying weeds rolling toward the ditch.

I pulled behind the turquoise car and shut off the engine. "Newt and Earl."

"Newt and Earl," Kyle agreed, with the same resignation in his voice.

Bachelor brothers, not more than a year apart in age, they'd gone to high school with Dad. After a tour in Vietnam, they lived together in the decrepit ranch house they inherited from their mother. Mostly, they got along all right. But when they didn't, Nelly bar the door.

Rain had begun in earnest again, and we stepped out into it.

I squinted to avoid direct raindrop hits to my eyes as I advanced on the wrestling brothers. "Nice day for a civil war."

They froze and, in unison, whipped their heads to me with expressions best described as "duh."

Newt, the younger brother, scrambled to his feet. Despite a smear of mud down his left side and grass ornamenting his hair, he looked about as clean as I'd ever seen him. With the rinse from Mother Nature, he smelled a darned sight better, too. He smoothed his camo jacket over what appeared to be five feet, eight inches of bones. "Katie."

Earl jumped up next to him, and slapping the back of Newt's head, he corrected him. "Sheriff Kate, you pencil dick."

Newt didn't return fire, just ducked his head toward me with a grin that reminded me of the skunk saying to Bambi, "He can call me Flower if he wants to."

I sensed Kyle's impatience next to me.

I folded my arms in a stern way, like I'd do with Zeke and

Mose, my eight-year-old twin nephews. "What are you doing up here?"

They looked at each other as if afraid to reveal the secret location of buried treasure.

Newt opened his mouth and Earl elbowed him. Newt kicked back and Earl cocked his arm for a punch.

"Knock it off." I had to bring out The Look, and this time it worked as intended.

Newt tucked his chin and blinked in righteousness, the same expression I'd seen on Grandma Ardith's face when she trumped Aunt Tutti's ace to win a pitch tournament at the Long Branch. "We come out here on Mondays and Thursdays usually and collect the beer cans from here to Sand Gap."

The Fox kids collected cans along the roadsides for years. We never made more than enough to take us all to Pizza Hut in Broken Butte. "That worth it in this rain?"

Earl's hand snaked out and latched onto my arm. "Look it."

He pulled me to the front of the gold car to a mass of flattened beer cans on the ground. A good majority were the forty ouncers. "We collect 'em, roll over with the cars here, and take 'em to the recycling center over to the 'Bluffs."

He dragged me to the back of his car and inserted a key in the trunk, slammed the side of his fist in two places, and it creaked up. He lifted it to reveal the trunk filled with black trash bags. "All of them are full of crushed cans. This is the easiest pickin's we have."

Newt startled me by speaking right behind my shoulder. "But don't tell no one. It's our gold mine, don't you know."

"You get this haul twice a week?"

Kyle held himself rigid, like a comment might blow him to bits.

Newt and Earl nodded. Their take of four million cans a

year might not make the Johnson brothers rich, but it probably kept them in gas for the Monte Carlos.

Newt brought the lid down to keep the rain from filling the trunk. "Why are you up to the rez?"

I glanced back at Kyle. His jaw twitched, and I figured I'd better take over. "You guys know Shelly Red Owl?"

They looked at each other and shrugged in unison. "Nope."

"She's eighteen. We're trying to find her."

Earl grew serious as mashed potatoes without gravy. "She get abducted by aliens?"

That wasn't what I expected.

Newt nodded. "It happens out here. There's this connection between the Indians and the aliens. It's documented."

"I don't think that's what happened." I shouldn't have added, but I did, "Although we found her car abandoned south of here on the highway."

Newt's eyes widened. Earl took the pragmatic approach. "What's she drive?"

"An old Grand Marquis."

They both brightened. "Red?" Newt asked.

Kyle jerked forward. "Yeah. You know it?"

"That girl that drives it. She's a good one," Newt said.

Earl continued from Newt. "She stopped one day. Thought she was going to get after us about collecting cans on the rez. Some folks think we ought to be saving them for the Indians, but it's a free country."

Kyle leaned forward. "What did—"

I placed a restraining hand on his arm to shut him up. It was best to let Newt and Earl tell it their own way.

Newt took up from there. "She just stopped to help us. She was kind of down about there being so many lying around."

Earl jumped in. "She was real curious about us and how

long we been collecting cans. Asked lots of questions about what and who we see."

Less like ping-pong and more like a relay, the conversation continued. Newt spoke. "Mostly she wanted to know about her brother."

"Kyle?" I interrupted the flow, and it took them a moment to pick it up again.

Earl started. "Not that one. The other one. The one that died out here a couple of years ago."

Newt: "But we weren't out here when they found him. So we couldn't help her."

Earl: "Then she asked about the preppers."

That startled me. "You know about them?"

The rain nearly sizzled on Kyle's intense gaze.

Newt and Earl both gave me a disappointed look. "We know a lot of things."

I was more than a little curious. "Who are they?"

Newt screwed up his face. "They don't have a dump, and they haven't lived here long enough to have thrown out anything good."

Earl nodded at me. "That's the truth."

Now it was my turn to be disappointed. "That's all you know about them? What about when they moved in? Who repaired their house and barn? What do they do for a living? Their names? How many people live out there?"

They seemed to consider all those questions. Then Newt said, "They showed up somewheres around two years ago. In March and it was damned dry. Didn't get any rain and the pastures dried up."

Earl agreed. "Nobody had hay. Govamint did that drought program." He pronounced *drought* with a *th* on the end.

Newt laughed. "City slickers, that's for sure. That whole

place under that hill, and they put their cistern on top, above it all."

Not fluent in Newt and Earl, Kyle looked lost.

Earl explained in a patient voice, as if trying not to embarrass Kyle. "Dry year, they didn't know that meadow tends to fill up on a wet year like this 'un."

Newt got enthusiastic. "And that hill is like to give out on that cistern. Too much weight. Too much sand."

As long as no one drowned, I might get a chuckle out of Rhonda and Marty getting a soaking. "That's all you know about them?"

Earl shrugged. "That and they got a bea-u-ti-ful '72 Road-runner. And they offered to buy the Monte Carlos."

Newt nodded. "Both of 'em."

Earl: "Our girls don't have computers and whatnot that will ruin when the bomb drops."

They both shrugged again. Earl said, "Told you we know a lot of things, not everything."

Kyle had been remarkably restrained throughout, but he finally jumped in. "Did Shelly say why she wanted to know about them?"

Newt looked at his boots again, then up at me. "Sorry. Me and Earl didn't ask."

Earl threw his head back and let out a yelp. "What in hot tamales is in your back seat?"

I whipped around in alarm. Poupon sat up, the eyes in his fluffy head trained on Earl. "That's Diane's dog."

Newt sneaked toward the car like he feared I'd let a monster loose. "A dog, you say?"

Earl, the more worldly of the two, waxed wise. "It's from a city. Not like the good dogs out here."

"He's okay. Just has a silly haircut." I don't know why I defended Poupon. He wasn't my dog.

I thanked Newt and Earl, left them to their can collecting, and took my waterlogged self back to the cruiser.

My phone let loose as I eased behind the wheel, and I pulled it out of my pocket. As usual, Diane started in before I even said hello.

"For Mom and Dad's anniversary, will you find a good resort—and make sure it has a decent restaurant—and get them a reservation?"

I took a second to untangle her request. I spoke slowly to irritate her. "Poupon is spending the day in the back of my car because I'm not set up for dog sitting."

She paused. "Yes. Thank you."

I did my best Diane imitation, complete with impatient sigh. "'Do me this one favor. I owe you,' she said. I believe it was right after telling me you had the anniversary all taken care of."

"I know, I know. Look, I'm swamped and can't do it. I emailed you my credit card number." Now she sounded exactly like my earlier impression. "Just help me this one time."

The wipers slapped a few rounds. "You said, and I quote: 'I promise to plan Mom and Dad's anniversary weekend so Louise won't make us do a family reunion.'"

She spoke faster as if to compensate for my pace. "Jesus, Kate. I know what I said. But I've got a life! Should I tell my billionaire clients I can't make those buys this afternoon because I promised my little sister I'd get hotel reservations?"

I felt Kyle's focus from across the cruiser and refused to look at him. "I have a job, too. Involves life and death and citizens' safety."

Diane laughed. "In Grand County, Nebraska. Never mind. I'll see if my admin assistant can do it. But he gets all bent when I ask him to do personal stuff."

And now guilt coated my throat. Mom and Dad deserved someone who loved them to consider where and what they'd like for their anniversary. But this was Diane's party. She'd insisted she could pick out a great weekend getaway for their surprise. Louise, of course, balked and lectured Diane on her crass, over-consumption ways and how Mom would feel bad about basking in luxury. How Dad would rather be with his kids than anything.

Diane beat Louise this time.

So how did I end up making the arrangements? "Okay, I'll do it."

"You're an angel. I owe you."

I slapped my trump card. "You can pay up by telling me who is on the board of the nonprofit Brian set up."

Dead silence. One, two, three. Her voice rose three octaves. "I can't tell you that. And you shouldn't even ask."

"Carly's been to see at least one board member. I need to know who it was and everyone else on the board so I can track her down."

"No."

"It's Carly, you—"

"No. Bye." Connections didn't get any deader than that.

Kyle's tone was crankier than I'd ever heard. "If you're done having lunch with your family, talking with them on the phone, and chatting up junkyard dogs on the highway, do you think we can get ourselves to the Olson place and see about finding Shelly?"

If I hadn't been shivery wet, nervous for a date I didn't want to admit was a date, and getting a little fed up with people telling me what to do, I might have let his rudeness pass. He was worried about his sister. Of all people, I should understand that. But I popped off anyway. "I'm not the one who lost your sister, so back off the attitude."

He looked up, startled. "You're right. Sorry. But the preppers keep coming up. I think we need to go out there."

I turned on the highway heading south. "I've been out there. I didn't see anything, and I can't go back out without probable cause."

Kyle banged the dash. "Shelly missing is cause." His voice lowered like a cat in a midnight alley. "You wouldn't let it go if it was your family."

He was right. The tires splashed through puddles on the highway as I thought. "Fine. We'll check it out."

We approached the turnoff to the Olson place, and I slowed, slapped the turn signal, and bounced off the highway.

Tracks from a pickup on the gravel road led up to the gate. Whoever we followed hadn't closed and locked the gate, so we passed through and up the hill overlooking the Olson compound. The tracks led to the covered parking, where a white pickup dripped rain.

Kyle's keen eyes took in the details of the barricaded house, the barn, chicken house, and corrals, all empty. I scanned all directions for Marty or anyone else sneaking up on us.

We hadn't gone more than a few steps from the cruiser when the front door flew open and Rhonda stepped out, arms folded and a grim expression on her face. She wore a faded blue tracksuit that probably looked nice on her a few years and dozens of cannoli ago. "You better not have cut the lock off the gate again."

I tried for the kind of dopey grin an arrogant city person might expect from a country bumpkin. "Gate was open as a welcome home sign. How are you, Rhonda?"

She glared at me, then turned it on Kyle. "What do you want?"

Kyle offered a hand she didn't take. "Deputy Kyle Red Owl. I hear there's a young man out here looking for me."

"You heard wrong." She clamped her lips closed and gave us dead-fish eyes.

I nodded cheerfully. "Kids in town told us that. You know how kids can tease. Mind if we check it out anyway? Can I talk to the kid?"

"No kids here."

"Well, now, Rhonda. That's not true. I saw him the other morning."

Kyle matched her deadpan. "We won't keep him. Just want to make sure he's okay."

With no inflection, she said, "He's not here."

"Huh." I pointed to the carport. "'Cause that pickup was just in Dry Creek with the kid driving it."

She held up her hands and widened her eyes. "I don't know what to tell you. Sorry you came out here for nothing."

Still faking country charm, I said, "Mind if we look around?"

She barked at me. "I told you yesterday not to come back without a warrant. I'm trying to be nice about this, but we like our privacy. We aren't hurting anyone. So if this is all you've got, you've got nothing."

The three of us stood in silence for a full minute before I finally broke it. "Okay, then."

"If you're feeling friendly, go ahead and close the gate and lock it on your way out. We don't want the cattle getting out on the highway." Her lips pulled back in a scary imitation of a smile.

15

I dropped Kyle off at the courthouse and watched him hurry to his 1996 teal Chevy Silverado. Like Shelly's car, despite some wear, it was clean and taken care of. I hadn't put the cruiser into gear when, with a roar and rush, the sky opened up and great waves of rain crashed onto the hood. Everything beyond my windshield disappeared.

It only lasted a few minutes, but long enough so I thought about the children's Bible in Doc Kennedy's waiting room. If you weren't quick, the other Fox kids grabbed the *Highlights* magazines and you got stuck with the illustrated book of horrors. One of the nightmare-inducing pictures was of Noah on his enormous boat beneath roiling black clouds, the animals apparently tucked away dry and safe, but people bobbing in the wild seas, their arms raised, screaming in terror, their last moments before succumbing to a hideous watery death.

"Good thing you made it onto the ark," I said to Poupon. He didn't open his eyes.

My phone rang, showing Louise's ID. Since I was waiting out the storm, I answered.

"Thanks for picking up. I hardly ever get you without leaving a message."

"Did you need something?"

"I love to visit with you, but yes, this time I'm calling to see if you've talked to Diane about Mom and Dad's anniversary."

Dang. "I don't think she's made any plans yet."

Louise humphed. "I knew it. Let's have a party at Mom and Dad's. Leave it to me. All you have to do is tell Diane not to plan anything."

Looked to me like the problem of making reservations just resolved itself. "She'll be disappointed, but I'll let her down gently."

"Okey-dokey, then." And away Louise went, leaving the strains of *The Wizard of Oz* Wicked Witch music wafting through my head.

When the deluge let up, Kyle was long gone. I headed home without stopping in to say good night to Betty and Ethel. They wouldn't miss me, though Ethel would be sure to tell anyone how unreliable I could be.

Clouds hung low, blocking out the sunset. I craved a warm shower, comfy sweats, snuggling into bed with a novel, and drifting off to a long sleep. After the cold rain and running all over the territory, I felt like the lonely wilted lettuce I'd find in my fridge.

I yawned as I swerved around puddles on the gravel road leading to my bungalow. One of the advantages of the Sandhills was its amazing drainage; the area was basically a twenty-thousand-square-mile sponge. An inch of rain would trickle into the ground quickly, leaving little mud. But we'd had so much rain, the ground had soaked to capacity. As far as ranchers cared, rain, even an abundance of it, boosted spirits. We'd had too many drought years not to rejoice in a downpour.

I parked in front of my house, admiring the sparkling green lawn and making note to mow it as soon as it dried in the morning. At least Poupon cooperated and climbed out without balking. In the dwindling light, I dragged my bag of bones to the back to check on the garden's progress. My mood brightened at the tiny green leaves of radishes, lettuce, and peas.

Healthy eating, that, Douglas. Tomorrow I'd plant another row of peas and maybe even risk green beans. With the rest of the day, I'd finish up the budget and make Betty smile.

Poupon wandered over to me and sat close enough for me to put a hand on his head and tease my fingers through his poof. "What was I thinking to say yes to this dinner? I don't want to start dating again."

He didn't say anything.

"Do I?"

Clouds hung heavy, and a slight breeze sent a fish smell from the lake.

"Let's be honest. I haven't had sex for a year, one month, and a smattering of days. And I'm not counting, because if I was, I'd be more precise. But it's been a long time."

Poupon looked at me.

"I know. I shouldn't start a relationship because I've got spring fever. Sex and a relationship are two different things."

Poupon stood and shook.

"I can't have a one-night fling in Hodgekiss. Everyone knows everything. If I have a roll in the hay with someone, I'll be assigned to them and labeled 'taken.'"

Bored with my problems, Poupon wandered up the porch steps and waited for me to let him inside.

My hair hung in drenched ropes, and it would take me a good half hour to dry it. That's the thing about being married to Ted for eight years. I didn't spend a lot of time worrying about drying my hair, putting on makeup, dressing in anything except practical, comfortable clothes. According to Roxy, that casual attitude caused my marriage to hit the skids.

While I'd hate to think a marriage could be based on something so superficial, I wondered if maybe it would have helped to have made a little more effort at my appearance. And then the whole idea torqued me off and I decided if some guy couldn't take me in my natural state, then he wasn't the right guy for me.

And yet, here I was, stumped about what to wear to a dinner with my family and my non-date. I filled Poupon's dish and set it on the kitchen floor. "I don't care how important you think you are, no table and chairs for you."

My phone rang. Sarah spoke through clenched teeth. "Lauren called me in a panic and said you weren't there yet."

I paused. "You aren't there, either, so I can't be that late."

She sounded annoyed. "I've been throwing up all day. I'm not going anywhere. Damn, I wish I could take pregnancy like Roxy. She had morning sickness at the beginning but she looks great now."

I hated that her words smacked me like a truck. Of course, she and Roxy were comparing notes, being friendly. They had due dates three days apart. Knowing Sarah and Robert were staying home took what little stuffing I had from me. "Honestly, I don't think I can make it. I'm beat, and I haven't even taken a shower."

"You don't need a shower. Wear that flowy black blouse with the cami underneath. Put your hair in a bun. Mascara and hurry out here. Don't be a chicken shit."

"I've got a big day tomorrow and—"

She exploded in the way only Sarah could. "Damn it! Maybe you want to be an old maid, but I won't accept it. Heath Scranton might not be the one, but you've got to practice or you won't be ready when the good one shows up. I feel like crap and can't hold your hand tonight. If you won't do it for yourself, do it for me."

I wasn't sure I'd ever said no to Sarah, and in her fragile emotional state, now didn't seem like a good time to start. "Fine."

I didn't think any further than following Sarah's instructions. I considered Poupon sprawled on the living room rug judging me and decided he could stay home for the night.

Elvis slipped and slid along the dirt road to Michael and Lauren's house. I popped a Willie Nelson cassette into the tape deck. I hadn't actually stolen the tape from Glenda, but I was the only Fox with a car old enough to still have a cassette player, and when she died, I took her cassettes without asking anyone else. They soothed me but were a poor substitute for my sister.

I needed a little soothing right now. I was all shaken up and feeling bad for Kyle. I had brothers and sisters pulling me this way and that, but that wasn't particularly unusual. This whole thing about voting on my next romance chapped me.

I should be plumb happy. The last year and a half included two murders, one divorce, a missing niece, and nine months living with Mom and Dad. Compared to that, a set-up date and Kyle's runaway sister ought to be a summer breeze.

Her sunny smile, blond hair flying, laughter flowing like a spring creek. Carly was ever on my mind. Like one of those hidden programs in the background on my phone, constantly draining the battery, operating even when you weren't aware. Mostly, I was aware. Worrying.

With one hand battling Elvis's steering wheel, I hit Baxter's speed dial.

He sounded pleased to hear from me, even though he said, "We talked yesterday. I've got nothing new."

If Diane wouldn't give me board member names, maybe I could get them from Baxter. "You told me Carly is talking to Brian's and your Kilner classmates. Who hasn't she contacted?"

He hesitated. "You've got to let my investigator handle it."

Night had fallen and the thick clouds parted, suddenly revealing a sky littered with stars. Carly was like one of those millions of stars. You'd have to be an expert, studying for years to learn all the constellations and every nuance of the night sky to be able to identify one lone star. Or be impossibly lucky.

The gnawing worry in my gut grew ravenous. "Why are you holding out on me? Don't you want Carly found?"

"Hold on." The anger in his voice stopped me. "Brian and I met when we were twelve years old. We lived together for nine months every year. No parents, no other relatives. Just us and a handful of other brothers. You, more than most, understand the bond of family, of life-long friends. How can you question my commitment to Brian's daughter?"

The lights of Michael's house appeared ahead, and I pulled over on the muddy road. Guilt elbowed its way next to worry. "I'm sorry. But she thinks someone killed her father—"

Baxter interrupted. "He crashed his plane into a hill. No one killed him."

He couldn't see me nod. "I know. But even so, she's running around ruffling feathers. That could get her into trouble."

He lowered his voice. "I care, Kate. Don't ever doubt that."

Elvis idled under me, with his heater on low, playing oldies and surrounding me in familiarity. "I don't feel any better. But I'll trust your investigator."

"I'm sorry. I wish I could make it right for you." With all his money and influence, it probably frustrated him that he couldn't fix everything.

"You help, believe me. I don't like to let the rest of the family know how worried I am. As far as they know, Carly ran off to find adventure because she's young."

We paused, then he started a new track. "What are your plans for this evening? Reading anything good?"

I wish. "I'm having dinner with my family."

"You don't sound excited."

Ugh. "They invited the new vet and are playing matchmaker."

I heard the grin. "What's the vet like?"

I thought a minute. "He's tall and blond and looks a lot like a Disney prince. Smart, because he went to vet school. He's nice."

He sounded startled. "Is this a date?"

"You know I like to win, but I'm not going to declare victory with a set-up by my family. When I said date, I meant something that could lead to something."

He hesitated. "I hadn't really meant something serious. Just a little fun."

It tickled me he sounded so flustered. I didn't figure he wanted a relationship, but he hated to lose. "As Dad says, 'In for a penny, in for a pound.'"

Baxter didn't sound pleased. "He says that, huh?"

We talked about the rain, Baxter trying to tell me what that meant as far as the end of civilization according to the documentary he'd watched. I enjoyed our conversation, more than I anticipated the dinner conversation. But I'd still have to go in.

We said our goodbyes and hung up. I never talked to anyone about my conversations with Baxter. Partly because of his celebrity—I didn't want to expose him or me to that famous-person weirdness—but more because I didn't want to share this friendship.

Staring at the lights of Michael's house, I shifted my emotional gears from stress and worry to friendly and upbeat. It wouldn't be fair to carry gloom into a party, so I practiced smiling on the muddy drive to the house.

I let myself in the side door and up the steps to the kitchen. The smell of warm bread opened a hole in my stomach. I filled my lungs with the heavenly aroma of beef roasted with onions and garlic. A true Sandhiller, I could eat a variation of beef for every meal. The house seemed unusually quiet for a dinner party and especially a home filled with Lucy and Kaylen, my two young nieces. A worry bell clanged, and I nearly dove for cover.

Lauren, with her blond spiky hair, leaned against the kitchen counter holding a glass of red wine. Across the overheated room, Heath sat at the kitchen table set for two, complete with a thick blue candle. He stood up when I walked in.

Lauren set her glass by the sink, her look of relief obvious. "Just in time. The roast is on warm in the oven. Any longer and it would be dry."

My glance moved from one to the other, and I mumbled, "Sorry I'm late. I was working." I waited a moment. "Where are Michael and the kids?"

Lauren pulled a jacket from the back of a chair and, with only minimal discomfort, spewed the lies. "We forgot Kaylen and Lucy had a birthday party in town for Chisolm Cleveland, and we promised to help. They invited twenty kids, so, you know..."

Holy mother of lost kittens. What could I say?

Heath watched me, all blond, broad-shouldered, masculine tallness. He looked game for the obvious setup.

Lauren zipped her jacket. "Roast is sliced. Mashed potatoes and gravy are in the oven, too. Green beans get thirty
seconds in the microwave. Pie on the counter. Ice cream in the
freezer." She pointed to the bottle of wine on the counter next
to a hand-painted wine glass I recognized from a party Louise
had made me attend. "Have some wine."

She clattered down the stairs. "Just leave the dishes. I'll get
them later." The door slammed closed.

Heath lifted a can of Coors Light in a toast. "It wasn't
smooth or pretty, but your family sure can set a trap."

The temperature in the kitchen soared another twenty
degrees as my skin flamed. Stiff and awkward, I poured a glass
of wine, hesitated, and sloshed more in until it rose to the rim.

I gulped it like a beer, then set the glass down. "I didn't
arrange this. I apologize for their scheming. I totally let you off
the hook."

He crossed the kitchen, picked up my glass, handed it to
me, and clinked his can against it. "I admit it's a weird situation, a not-so-blind date or whatever you call it. But the roast
smells awesome and you're pretty, so why don't we enjoy all
their hard work?"

If he agreed to be a good sport, I didn't feel I had much
choice. He hunted another beer from the fridge and I shuttled
Lauren's feast to the table. With another heaping glass of
wine, I settled in.

Lauren proved her usual prowess in the kitchen and the
food held up its promise. Heath downed half his plate while I
nibbled and drank wine.

He paused and sipped his beer. "Lauren is a great cook. My
mother is a terrific cook, too. So, I've been spoiled. I sure miss
home cooking."

"Me, too. Although my brothers and sisters take pity on me
quite a bit."

He sat back. "You don't cook?"

When I was married to Ted and working Frog Creek, I cooked almost every day. I hosted my share of family dinners, and there was always a potluck contribution or funeral dinner. "Not much anymore."

He answered with a "huh" and went back to eating. He went through seconds. I finished the bottle of wine and opened another.

After the fascinating story of his growing up in Topeka and three tries before finally scoring a spot in the vet program at Iowa State, I feared we'd run out of topics. I'd cleaned my plate and indulged in another helping of potatoes and gravy. He hadn't asked me anything about my past or current life, and I chalked him up as one of those guys who are only interested in themselves.

I got up to slice the pie, wondering how to get him to eat fast so I could go home.

He pushed his chair back. "Now it's my turn to apologize."

My knife stilled. "How so?"

He picked up a fork and set it down. "When you came to the clinic last winter with all that blood dripping down your face and asked me to stitch you up, I thought you were some kind of psycho. But then, I've seen you around, and I got to know some of your brothers and sisters. You seem really interesting."

I remembered to shut my mouth.

He glanced at me and back to the fork. "But you always seem busy or already talking to people. I wanted to get to know you but didn't know how to go about it."

I leaned against the counter, drawn in. "I'm not hard to talk to. All you had to do is say hi."

His skin flushed. "People don't know this, but I'm really shy around women."

I laughed, then felt bad. "Sorry. You've got to know how handsome you are. Women must fall all over you."

"I wish. Most of the time they smile at me and wait for me to make the first move. But I don't know what to say to women, never have. So, like tonight, I get nervous and end up talking about myself. I'm afraid if I shut up, the conversation will die and she'll...you'll...leave." He quit playing with the fork and looked up at me. Worry filled his blue eyes as if he waited for me to let him off the hook.

Huh. "Don't think of this as a date." I knew I wasn't. "Let's just be two new friends having a nice dinner."

His shoulders dropped and his expression softened. Funny, a guy with so much going for him had so little confidence. "That's a good idea." He sat back. "What's your favorite movie?"

"I hate that favorite question. My nieces and nephews are always asking my favorite this or that. There's so much pressure in the answer. I'll tell you a movie I like. How about, *The Big Lebowski.*"

Enthusiasm replaced nerves. "Yes. And *Dumb and Dumber.*"

I slid the pie on his plate. "Ew. No. I hate those stupid movies. But my niece Carly loves them."

I scooped ice cream, giving myself a generous portion to make up for the insult of rhubarb, and we went from movies to TV and wandered off on fourteen paths. I set the wine aside and laughed as he downed two more pieces of pie and compared foods we hated.

Two hours later he watched me finish up the dishes. "Thanks for making tonight fun."

I dried my hands. "It didn't turn out too bad, especially after the awkward beginning."

We left a light on for Lauren and Michael. I stopped short

of writing a thank-you note since I still thought they'd all crossed a few too many boundaries.

Heath walked me out to Elvis. Clouds obscured the moon. "Looks like we've got some more rain heading in."

So that's it. In the tense moments leading up to good night, he'd resorted to weather talk. I felt weary of trying to be pleasant and helpful. "It will make the grass grow."

If he'd thought about a kiss, my response didn't invite romance. "Okay, then. Stay dry."

"Good night." I dropped into Elvis and turned up Willie Nelson, singing along all the way home.

Poupon's tail flopped against the back of my couch when I got home. "No dogs on the furniture." I tried to add a growl to my voice, imitating Kyle. I think Poupon knew I'd had enough of my day and stepped down without hassle. He trotted outside, and I padded down to the basement.

On a high shelf, I found the boxes of Carly's things I'd packed from Frog Creek. She'd kept a few items from her parents, and I rummaged in several crates until I located that shoe box amid clothes. By the time I'd found the pictures of Brian's graduation from Kilner and brought it back upstairs, Poupon was in the kitchen chowing down on his kibble and sloshing water from his bowl all over the floor.

I carried the picture into the dining room, which was really just a corner of the living room. The picture of Brian and five other boys conveniently listed their names on the back. I trusted Baxter's investigator, but it wouldn't hurt to find out something about these guys myself.

Poupon strolled from the kitchen and pushed his head under my hand for an ear scratch.

No washing his dishes or folding his laundry. No bolstering of his ego. His supper required my pouring from a bag. There's a lot to be said for the company of a dog.

16

Tuesday dawned with low clouds. It would take a few hours for the yard to dry enough to mow, and working in the garden would be more comfortable after the chill lifted. Instead of a hot breakfast at the Long Branch, I grabbed a granola bar when I fueled up at the Conoco.

Even though both of the courthouse dragons were long past their first cup race, I crept into the commissioner's room as quietly as possible for Ethel's muddy roast. I wasn't quick enough.

Betty swirled from the hallway and startled me into sloshing coffee onto the carpet. "Did you try to slip the budget under the office door last night? You weren't here when I left, and I didn't want to leave my door unlocked."

An adult person, especially an elected county official, should not feel like a kid without her homework. I carried a gun, for the love of brown gravy. "I wanted to check it over today before I turn it in. Make sure it's perfect for you."

Betty handed me the powdered creamer. "That's nice, but if you could get it to me—"

My cell rang and I shot Betty an apologetic look, set the

creamer down, and thumbed the phone on while carrying my coffee out of the room.

Kyle's voice sounded tight. "I can be in Hodgekiss by noon. That'll get us up to Sand Gap to talk to the Chapter police chief and over to the school when it gets out. We can talk to Shelly's friends."

I motioned Poupon to vacate my chair, and he ignored me. "The rez is so far out of my jurisdiction I can't justify snooping around."

He sighed. "Humor me, okay? As a friend. We could go up there this morning, but I'm vaccinating heifers for Rocking L." The part-time deputy gig didn't pay his bills.

I set my coffee on my desk and surveyed the budget papers. "Why do you need me to go with you?"

He hesitated. "In case we find something. Do you think the legal system in western Nebraska will favor a case investigated by an Indian?"

Even if he knew it was coming, Poupon waited for me to tug his collar before he climbed out of my chair. "If you find something illegal, sure they will. We wouldn't hire you for deputy if we didn't think so."

He scoffed. "I fill in for you guys. Patrol, keep the peace. Not lead investigations."

He had a point. If he didn't get here until noon, I'd have a few hours to work on the budget. How long could it take?

"I have to get out to the corral. See you at noon?"

Guess my yard and garden could wait. "Sure."

But Mom's neighbor, Beverly, called me because her lights went out. Not my job, but I went over to replace a fuse and share the musty chamomile tea she'd already steeped. Jim Bingham locked his keys in his car, again, and I spent another hour breaking into his car and chatting with him about the meat-packing companies taking over the world.

Brittany Ostrander cornered me in the bathroom at the courthouse to commiserate with me about the awful state of being single in Grand County and how all she wanted was to share a home with a man. That led me to thinking about setting the table, serving pie, and doing dishes for the pleasure of sharing a few laughs. And I hadn't even cooked all afternoon for the privilege.

When Kyle showed up at twelve thirty, I hadn't so much as shuffled the budget papers. Good thing Betty always ate lunch at the Long Branch, so she didn't waylay me on my way out.

Poupon settled into the back seat without comment. Kyle and I didn't have much more to say than the pooch. The clouds hung heavy, making me worry they'd spring a leak and the whole sky would crash down on us again. Kyle and I studied the hills surrounding the Olson place.

Eventually, we pulled into Dry Creek. We both focused on a group of half a dozen young people gathered under the awning of an abandoned craft store. Mixed boys and girls, I pegged them as late teens, early twenties. With an unemployment rate of 80 percent on the rez, a roaming group like this didn't seem unusual.

When we reached Sand Gap, Kyle gave me directions to the tribal police station. A brick building on the outskirts of town, with the entryway tucked back between jutting walls and very few windows breaking up the surface. The grass in front looked challenged, despite the rain. Two Oglala Sioux Antelope Ridge cop cars were parked in front.

We entered a cramped lobby and approached a uniformed woman behind a glass panel. Kyle stepped to the glass. "Can we see John Yellow Bird?"

The woman didn't greet him or smile. She shook her head. "Naw. He is busy."

Kyle looked behind her as if trying to see into the narrow hallway leading toward the back of the building. "Is he here?"

She took her time answering. "Naw. He jus' left."

Frustration wrinkled his forehead when he spun from the window and shot outside into the gray day, with me on his heels. Without warning, Kyle took off, running down the wide sidewalk toward the parking lot.

A compact man, with nearly gray hair, hurried from the side of the station toward one of the cars.

Kyle shouted, "Captain! Wait. I need to talk to you."

The man spun around, clearly surprised.

I trotted to them as Kyle finished introducing us. I shook Captain Yellow Bird's hand.

Dark circles draped under his eyes as if sleep were foreign to him. His belly drooped over his belt, and he had the irritated expression of a busy man. He put a hand on his cruiser door. "I really don't have time—"

Kyle launched into it. "What do you know about young girls going missing?"

Captain Yellow Bird sagged. "Yeah. Girls go. Boys, too. Kids are kids."

Kyle lowered his eyebrows. "Ginny Two Guns? Missy Iron Cloud?"

The older man jerked on the car latch and opened his door a few inches. "I don't know those names. Far as I know, no one reported them missing."

I jumped in. "Is this common? Minors disappear and no one investigates or cares?"

Fire ignited in his eyes. "This ain't Disneyland, okay? By the time they hit fifteen or sixteen, there's not much holding them down. Some find things they like to do better than go to school. Drink, drugs, sex." He let go of his door and advanced on me. "Do you know six months ago a thirteen-year-old girl was shot on the street in Sand Gap?"

Kyle closed his eyes and inhaled, then started again. "I'm looking for my sister, Shelly Red Owl."

Captain Yellow Bird sagged again. "Hey, man, that's tough. I'm sorry. But these girls, you don't know what they're thinking. They're selling hummers behind Frankie's for a forty. They take a few days and go with their boyfriends to Rapid City." He shrugged.

"What about sex trafficking? Or kidnapping?" I asked.

He spoke to Kyle as if I didn't exist. "I got a force of thirty-two officers to take care of three million acres. Eighty percent of our calls are alcohol and domestic abuse. I can't go looking for rebellious girls. Are they taking off on their own? Getting stolen and sold? I don't know, man. I'm running as fast as I can, trying to keep the people as safe as I can."

Kyle didn't stop him when he reached for the car door, hefted himself inside, and started the engine. We watched him drive away, the cool, heavy wind boxing our ears.

Kyle stomped to the car, and I hurried to join him.

The muscles in his jaw flexed. "I don't believe Shelly would run away this close to graduation. Not when she is supposed to give the valedictory speech. Not with Alex acting up like this."

The logic evaded me, too. "If other girls are missing, no one is looking for them."

He flinched. "That makes the rez a perfect place to get girls." He tapped the dash. "Let's go to the school. Talk to Shelly's friends."

With more grunts and pointing than words, Kyle guided me to Sand Gap School. We parked in angle parking on the street in front of a sprawling one-story brick building with the tall block of a gym on the western end. A wide band of yellow, red, black, and white geometric designs wound around the whole structure. It looked to have been built about sixty years ago, with little upkeep in the interim.

Kids of all ages, from six or seven years to high school seniors, headed down the sidewalk-less streets, milled in small knots, or roughhoused on the sparse front lawn. Typical after-school gathering.

Most of the chatter faded when we got out, and their eyes tracked us. I kept up as Kyle marched the length of the school toward the west end, dodging mud puddles and trash. The squeak of tennis shoes on a wood floor and bouncing of basketballs filtered from the open gym doors.

Gym smell of sweaty kids, hints of cafeteria meals and concession popcorn drifted on the air. A half-dozen boys and girls played half-court ball, yelling and throwing elbows, their laughter and exertion a happy contrast to all the sadness on the rez.

A tall, thin girl with tangled long hair held the ball to her chest and searched the court for someone to toss it to. She caught sight of us, her arms dropped, and her face registered surprise. The other kids spun around to see us.

Kyle raised his hand. "Hi, Amanda. Got a minute?"

The girl shifted her attention to the group of kids around her, and acting as put-out as only a teenager can, she tossed the ball to the nearest kid. The guy caught it. "I'll be right back."

Everyone watched us as we slipped out the door and around the back of the school.

Amanda stood with her hip thrust out. "What?"

Kyle fired back. "Where's Shelly?"

More teen attitude. "Do I look like her secretary? Call her yourself."

Kyle's two-second stare started to unravel her, and his words finished it. "I haven't forgotten that night. Have you?"

Called to the carpet with his words, she colored and dropped her eyes. After all the episodes where I'd helped out a brother or sister and their friends, I figured Kyle had enough blackmail fodder to last a good long time. "I don't know where she went after she left here. She was looking for Alex."

I jumped in. "Today?"

She glared at me, and I wished I'd stayed quiet.

Kyle's voice faltered. "Is she okay?"

A defiant fire lit Amanda's eyes. "Like always. Mad 'cause Alex isn't doin' exactly like she thinks. Even though she, like, skipped school all week, she was askin' us why we wasn't at the sweat on Saturday." She folded her arms and notched down. "Kind of weird she wasn't there."

"Was she planning to be?" Kyle asked.

Amanda nodded and sniffed indignantly. "Kind of a hypocrite. Like, you know, she's always complaining about us being crabs."

Kyle looked confused. "Crabs?"

Amanda rolled her eyes. "She says Lakota are like crabs in a bucket. Everyone tryin' to get out, but when one climbs to the rim, the others pull him back down. She says we gotta learn to help each other. So, like, she does all this stuff to try to help kids out."

I waited, and Kyle asked for me. "What kind of stuff?"

Amanda twisted her neck, checking on the kids in the gym. They'd gone back to their game. "She goes to Dry Creek sometimes when she knows there's gonna be a party. She takes rubbers and hands them out to the girls behind Frankie's. You know, the ones that get into trouble."

My stomach flipped. These girls Captain Yellow Bird and

Amanda talked about would be Ruthie's age. Selling sex for beer.

Kyle didn't breathe for several seconds. "But she's around town today? Looking for Alex?"

Amanda's eyes cast a belligerent gleam when she looked at me, and I wondered if she'd made that last comment to shock me. "You know her. She's always tryin' to do the right thing. Gettin' good grades and playin' sports. She said we need to set an example."

Kyle's tone pinned Amanda like a gigged frog. "What's going on with her?"

Amanda glared at the ponderous clouds, then at Kyle. All blistery and tough, she swung her gaze to the kids in the gym, then seemed to give in. "Somethin'. I don't know. In the las' coupla months she changed. Like inside her head all the time."

Now that he'd broken in, Kyle tried again. "How was she today?"

Amanda focused on his face. "She acted scared. Kept lookin' around and really wanted to find Alex."

I bulled in. "She wrecked her car. How was she getting around?"

Amanda didn't rebuff me this time. "We was in the gym. I didn't see."

Kyle sounded frustrated. "She didn't say where she was staying or what she's doing?"

Amanda studied him with intelligent eyes. "Does this have to do with Sheriff Buttface?"

"Who?"

She exhaled. "Barnett Buttface."

Intensity radiated off Kyle like heat from a revved engine. "Why?"

"'Cause Shelly was askin' if he'd been here and stuff."

Kyle shot back, "What stuff?"

She shrugged. "I don't know. Buttface is creepy. Always watchin' us girls. A real perv."

"Does he ever hurt you?" Kyle asked.

Amanda looked up at the clouds again with impatience. "No. Just kinda there all the time. What's goin' on? Is Shelly in trouble?"

Kyle sighed. "I'm trying to find out. She hasn't been home, wrecked her car, and won't talk to me."

The kids in the gym shouted, and their shoes squeaked. Amanda kept eye contact with Kyle. "That's not good. Shelly loves you. Always talks about how great you are."

Kyle switched to small talk about classes, friends, and sports. Amanda had nothing more to help.

I peeled off and wandered into the gym. In the corner next to the opened door, a collage of photos hung behind a protective plexiglass sheet. I studied the action shots of dark-haired kids, alive in their determination. Jump shots, drives, passes, posed championship portraits, candids. Looked like a collection of decades, with the shorts lengths going up and down, baggy and tight.

"Can I help you?"

The man's voice startled me, and I flinched. The white guy, maybe in his mid-forties, wore pocketed sweatpants, a whistle around his neck, and a collared white T-shirt. He took in my uniform with questioning hazel eyes. "Coach Henderson. Is there a problem?"

"Kate Fox, Grand County sheriff." I shook his hand. "Wondering if you know anything about a couple of missing girls?"

The smile fell from his face. "Who?"

Shelly wasn't really missing, since she'd been here within a few hours. I had to think a minute. "Ginny Two Guns and Missy Iron Cloud. Heard anything?"

His bushy eyebrows dove over his eyes. "They're back. If they ever went farther than Dry Creek. I had to chase them off school grounds this morning. Both drunk. Before eight o'clock."

My attention focused a moment on the kids playing ball at the far court. I needed to see happy, healthy students, laughing, running, doing normal things. Amanda loped from the open door and joined them.

Coach Henderson's face lit up as he saw Kyle approaching us. "Here he is!"

Kyle grinned. "Coach. Good to see you."

Coach seemed to put it together when he saw Kyle's uniform. "Right. I heard you'd taken a deputy job." He addressed me. "Kyle was one of my stars."

Kyle frowned and rolled his eyes.

Coach tapped my arm. "Look." He pointed at the collage. "Here he is, '05 state champs."

I leaned close to see Kyle, the lightest-skinned player in a group of grinning boys, his compact energy coming through. "Aren't you cute?"

He squinted at the pictures and tapped the plexiglass. "This is Shelly."

She stood at the free throw line. If determination could make that shot, it was a swish. She looked lankier than Kyle, long legs, straight black hair in a ponytail down her back. "She's a beauty."

Coach sounded nearly as proud as Kyle usually did when talking about Shelly. "She is a force on the court. I got a bunch of marginal athletes on the girls' team this year, and Shelly had a way of making them all better. She led the team onto the court every game with the Lakota shawl dance. Made the other teams take notice. We weren't ever going to win a championship this year, but we ended with a pretty good season."

Kyle's eyes shone. "Like I told you, she's not a quitter."

Coach indicated another player. There was a clear similarity to Shelly and Alex, with the tall, skinny build.

"Darrel?" I asked.

Coach nodded. "Not as good as Kyle, who had more talent, despite him being short. Didn't have the heart of Shelly, but all the Red Owls can play basketball. Just wish I could get Alex on the court."

Kyle and Coach slapped backs and promised to get together, and we slipped out the open door. With heavy footsteps, we retreated to the cruiser, still under the watchful eyes of the few kids left on the school grounds.

We drove down a series of potholes with a few feet of blacktop scattered about that passed for a road. Before we turned on Main Street on our way to The Stop, we passed a faded car that had probably started out as a champagne-colored Taurus about the time Susan spit peas in my face the first time.

Kyle threw himself toward the dash, then hollered, "There! Follow him."

I checked the houses lining the road on either side, made sure the road in front of and behind me was empty, and squealed a U-turn in the middle of the street. I accelerated after the dumpy car.

I gave up dodging potholes, and we gained on the car. "Who is it?"

The driver must have realized I followed because he suddenly got a jump on us. Kyle ground his jaw. "Alex."

I flipped on my lights. Now that I knew we were in full pursuit, I didn't spare the speed. We quickly closed the gap.

Alex took us back toward the school. With students milling around, my heart climbed to my throat and I backed off. Only a couple of teens sat on a low brick fence in front of the school, and the yard was empty.

Alex turned at the east end of the school, zooming behind the building. I jerked the wheel to the left to follow him. A thud and yelp sounded from the back seat, and I guessed I'd disrupted Poupon's nap.

A parking lot stretched behind the school, with as much attention to maintenance as the street in front. Alex must have realized he'd boxed himself in. He squealed to a stop before a low cable barrier to the open prairie. Maybe he thought he could run, but Kyle blasted from the cruiser and I tried to do the same.

Alex didn't make it more than a few steps before Kyle grabbed the back of his hoodie and spun him around like a game of crack the whip. Kyle slammed him against the side of the car.

"Hey!" I pulled Kyle back.

He stood in ready position, panting. Kyle and Alex resembled each other, but after seeing the pictures of Shelly and Darrel, Kyle looked like the odd man out.

Alex struggled to regain his bravado. "What the hell?"

"Where's Shelly?" Kyle's words came out ragged.

Alex managed a little swagger. "Haven't seen her since Saturday."

"What's going on with her?"

Kyle's growly voice reminded me of Poupon. I backed up a few steps and opened the rear cruiser door. Poupon hopped out and trotted a few feet, then stopped and lifted his leg against a post from the cable fence. He gave me an accusatory stare.

Kyle demanded, "What?"

Alex's first comment had been spoken with the sharp

consonants and swishy sounds of Lakota. He glared at Kyle and enunciated slowly. "She don't need to answer to you."

"Why is that?"

Alex's lip pulled back. "You turned your back on your people. That means Shelly. You left, so you don't get to mess in our lives no more."

The stuffing went out of Kyle and he stepped back. His eyes traveled over the Taurus. "Where'd you get the car?"

Alex lifted his chin. "I bought it."

"With what?"

Alex spoke with the teen belligerence that made adults want to punch them in the face. "Money I earned."

Kyle nodded. "Like what you promised Hersh Good Crow?"

With temper he hadn't learned to control as well as Kyle, Alex shot back. "Hersh knew I was good for it. He backed out of the deal 'cause his old lady didn't want to sell." Alex patted the car.

"Where do you plan to get the money?" Kyle asked.

Alex tugged on his sweatshirt and stood tall. "Not your business, bro."

Kyle might have had more to say, but he didn't stop Alex from climbing into the Taurus.

I whistled to Poupon. "Get in."

He didn't move until Kyle grumbled to him in Lakota. While I waited for him to saunter over and lift first one paw on the back seat, then the other, and slowly pull up his back two legs, I watched Alex peel out of the parking lot.

A slow-moving splash of white drew my attention to the corner of the school building. I squinted into the stiff breeze to see a shield and *Spinner County Sheriff* printed prominently on the side of the Ford Bronco as it rolled slowly out of view.

17

We drove through Sand Gap and Dry Creek without conversation. Then I broke the silence. "We don't have much to go on.
According to her friends, and from what Douglas saw and
heard, Shelly's been acting different."

That jaw worked. "Girls are disappearing on the rez. I
think she's been taken."

"That's a pretty big leap. Especially when we just saw a
couple of those missing girls were off partying."

He gripped the armrest. "We need to talk to Barnett."

"Because the high school girls think he's creepy? We
thought our chem teacher was a zombie when we were in
high school, but I'll bet now he never ate anyone's brains."

Kyle looked at me with a familiar anguish. "I've always
tried to protect her, and I feel helpless."

He wrung my heart in his hands. I saw Carly, ten years old,
baggy flannel pajama pants and her dad's sweatshirt, curled
into the corner of the old couch Ted and I inherited from his
grandmother. Glenda was in day two of another round of
chemo, so I'd brought Carly to Frog Creek for a few days.
She'd wanted to stay home, but the adults vetoed her.

It had been snowing since before dawn, and we'd baked cookies and watched movies, and still the day stretched ahead of us.

Ted had burst through the back door, tracking slush and mud across the living room. "Let's go!"

Carly jerked off the couch. "Where?"

He grabbed her hand and propelled her toward the attic stairs. Carly always stayed in a room we'd made for her up there. "Long johns, wool socks. We're going sledding."

Her eyes lit up, and she bounded for the stairs.

Ted patted my butt to push me toward our bedroom. "You, too. I'll get the snowmobile and pull you guys up the hill."

I hesitated, eyeing the accumulation on the yard outside the kitchen window. "Doesn't look like enough snow. We'll hit yucca and rocks."

Ted lowered his voice. "Carly needs this. Isn't a broken leg better than a broken heart?"

I hadn't thought of that day in a long time. It had been a grand day, despite me getting a fat lip and Carly smashing a finger between the sled and a fencepost. The laughter and activity had helped her far more than the pain hurt.

What meaning should I take from this? That I ought to let Carly go? I couldn't be her protector? What about Shelly?

I sighed. "Okay. Tomorrow we'll talk to Barnett."

Kyle's hand tightened on his thigh. "Now. We need to go now."

I glanced at him. "I need some time to think how to go about this. I'm out of my jurisdiction, and Barnett doesn't like me. If I go barreling in without a plan, I won't get anywhere."

"Let me do the talking. I'll get somewhere."

I shook my head. "Nope. You aren't going."

"Screw that."

His reaction didn't surprise me. "You're too hot. I'll figure something out, maybe ask his advice about something. Go in through a window instead of breaking down the front door."

There was serious danger of him pulverizing his jaw. "We should go now."

With my calmest voice, I said, "We know Shelly is okay. She was at the school today. Tomorrow is soon enough."

Kyle didn't speak for the rest of the drive back to town, and I didn't have anything to add. As usual, Poupon kept his own counsel, only emitting a deep sigh occasionally. I didn't bother sneaking into the courthouse, since Betty and Ethel would have foxtrotted out the front door ten minutes ago.

Voices at their end of the corridor surprised me. Ethel shot from her office, closing her door with more violence than necessary. She jabbed her key into the lock and, with a great show of annoyance, huffed and muttered and sped by me and Poupon and out the front door.

A gurgling cough preceded May Keller's exit from Betty's office. May ranched north of town and had survived husbands, drought, bad cattle prices, and blizzards. Wrinkled and shrunk, like an apple forgotten in the fridge, May gave me a once-over as I stood in the corridor.

She ambled to me and assessed Poupon. "What the hell kind of pony is that?"

I patted his head so he wouldn't feel insulted. "Diane's dog. I'm keeping him for a few days."

Her voice sounded like shaking a bucket of gravel. "Not much of a dog."

Betty scurried from her office and locked her door. She glanced at Ethel's door, probably feeling the agony of defeat that Ethel had checked out before her.

I winced when she bustled up to me, hoping to deflect what I knew was coming. "Did it rain here all afternoon? Kyle and I went back up to the rez on official business."

Betty's smile looked as if strained through a lemon. "I know you like to help with the other jurisdictions. But, truly, I need your budget."

Another anvil of guilt dropped in my stomach. "I'm sorry, Betty. I'll get it done tomorrow."

She patted my arm. "I'm sorry to be so grumpy. It's been a long day." She gave May a pointed look, smiled at us both, and practically ran out the glass doors.

In her faded plaid cowboy shirt and pearl buttons, May fingered the ever-present cigarette package in her breast pocket. "I love coming in here at closing time. It gets the hens all rattled."

"That's not very nice."

May gave a wet cough. "It does the old biddies some good. Everybody ought to get shook once in a while." She pointed a bony finger in my chest. "Like you."

A few fat raindrops splashed into the puddles on the walk outside the doors. "Looks like another shower."

She pulled out the cigs. Addicted as she was, I couldn't believe she'd lived so long. A true testament to ornery, though she was barely more than twigs and bark. "I'm talking about you, missy. I know the whole damned town wants to mate you up like you're a prize heifer."

I didn't want to have this conversation with May Keller, whose no-good husband had mysteriously disappeared during the Eisenhower administration. "Did you—?"

"They tried to do the same with me and I fell for it. Didn't last long and that's all I'm going to say about that."

Gone without a trace. And May Keller a happier woman, with some secrets.

"It's not—"

She wasn't here to listen to me. "You don't need to have some man mucking up your life. Oh sure, you need to bang boots once in a while. And for that, get up to Rapid City or Denver every now and then. Get the itch scratched."

A roar that sounded like an ocean hit the roof. May's head jerked to watch a curtain of rain out the front door. "This'll damn sure make the grass grow."

"That's—"

Without hesitating, she strode out the front door into the driving rain.

I waited another ten minutes to let the worst of the storm pass, then loaded Poupon and yippee-ki-yi-yayed home. The ditches along the road ran in mini rivers, and small lakes formed in the dirt road. A duck's paradise, the cold, damp, and gray seeped under my skin. My encounter with May didn't fire me up with Women Power. Was I destined to end up like May, alone, shriveled, getting my kicks by teasing old ladies and passing out wisdom to whippersnappers?

"I've got to find a—" My phone rang, and I interrupted myself to answer. "Sheriff."

"Thank God." Relief washed from Sarah's voice and flooded anxiety into me. "I need you."

My heart clogged my throat. "What's wrong?"

"It's the baby. I'm losing it. Hurry!"

"Where's Robert?"

She grunted in pain. "He had a meeting with bull buyers at the golf course. Must have…" She paused for another cramp and started up again, panting. "Must have left his phone in the pickup."

"I'm on my way." I squealed into a U-turn.

Another scramble because of a phone call. More heart-pounding uncertainty. More pleading with the universe for everything to be okay. Six months pregnant and none of it easy, they'd started trying for a baby at the same time as Ted and me. They couldn't lose it now.

I pushed the cruiser and cut the drive from the usual twenty minutes to ten when I rocketed to the front of Sarah and Robert's house and slid on the gravel. I might as well have teleported to the living room for all the awareness I had of running up the porch and through the front door.

Sarah lay on her side on the navy leather couch, her knees drawn to her chest. Tears streaked her face and she gasped. "Damn, it hurts!"

My insides turned to curdled milk to see her moaning and writhing. I'd known her to take a tumble from the saddle, climb back on without a word or even a wince, ride five miles home, then drive herself an hour and a half to the emergency room in Broken Butte to have her broken wrist set.

I knelt beside her and placed my hand on her forehead, not even sure why. She didn't feel hot. "It's okay." Those words came out without any meaning, just something to calm her.

She arched and grabbed my hand, crushing it in hers. "It is anything but okay."

Panic threatened, and I mentally slapped myself. Sarah and her baby needed me. "Do you think you can stand and make it to the car? I'll take you to the hospital."

She blinked tears and pulled her hand from mine to swipe at her wet nose. "Pretty much have to. You're too weak to carry me."

Sarah never caved to panic. I squatted for her to sling her arm over my shoulder and hefted her up. Her belly barely bulged under her sweatshirt. She had a couple of inches on me, and though more statuesque (and the one who always drew the guys over to our table), she carried more weight, and it landed firmly on me as another contraction wracked her.

Her moan sounded low, like a heifer laboring with its first calf. But she never needed to know that. "The baby, Kate." She started to sob halfway to the door. "What if something is wrong with Tigger?"

I made up something so stupid even I cringed. "Tigger is fine. It takes a lot to harm a baby that's all safe and secure in a woman's stomach."

Sarah let out a guffaw and doubled over, almost sending me to my knees. "Damn it, Kate. Don't make me laugh. That was the lamest thing I've ever heard."

We waited for the contraction to pass. How long had it been between them? Why did I even concern myself with counting? Six months was too early for any of this. I had to get Sarah to the hospital, and they had to save Tigger.

No tears, shaking voice, or sympathy from me. That would only make it worse for Sarah. "Of course I was making something up. I admit it wasn't good, but it's hard to think when a giant is crushing you."

Still bent, Sarah shuffled with me toward the door. "Screw you, pipsqueak. Get me and Tigger to the hospital and let the professionals handle this."

We made it to the cruiser. I flipped on the light bar and drove like a jackrabbit with a 'yote on its tail. "Did you try Robert again?"

She winced in pain and waited a beat. "Yeah. No answer."

I raced down the highway and pulled out my phone.

Sarah put a hand on my arm. "What are you doing?"

"Calling Jeremy. Sending him out to the golf course to fetch Robert."

She shook her head and wrapped her arms around her belly. "Wait. Robert will freak out if Jeremy flies out there."

"He needs to know what's going on." I hated arguing with her when she felt so terrible.

She squeezed her eyes closed and panted a moment. With

her head tipped back on the seat, her voice came out scared and small. "Let me do it my way. Please. Just stay with me."

I didn't know what to say and kept my speedometer over 100 mph on the straight, empty road.

She squeezed out more words. "I need all of me to do this. I can't spare anything for Robert. If he's here, I'll worry if I cry, he'll panic."

I understood how he'd feel. I was close to falling apart at the thought of losing Tigger, or watching Sarah in such pain. "Okay. But he'll be mad when this is over and you're fine."

Tears streaked down her cheeks. "Don't pull that bullshit with me. You know this isn't good. And you're going to have to help me deal with it."

Sarah and I never skirted around reality, and this wasn't the time to start. "We'll get through it together. We always do."

She whimpered and squirmed, panting and squeezing the door handle as contractions came and went, and I got us to the Broken Butte County Hospital as fast as possible and screamed into the ER bay. I had radioed ahead, and the crew met us with a wheelchair and whisked Sarah away.

I parked and by the time I found her, she lay on a bed in an exam room. They'd hiked her sweatshirt up and strapped a fetal monitor across her belly. A heart rate monitor clamped her finger, and I thanked my stars I'd missed the PICC line insertion. A nurse hung a drip bag on a pole next to Sarah's bed.

I grasped Sarah's ankle. "How're you doing?"

Her eyes, still watery, were wide with fear. She swallowed slowly and held my gaze.

"Should I call Robert?"

She nodded. "Text. Use my phone."

She lifted a hip and jerked the hand with the IV attached. I jumped forward and reached under her to clasp the phone from her back pocket. "Got it."

She gritted her teeth. "Say, 'I'm okay. Tigger's okay. At hospital. Come pick us up when you can.'"

I stared at her. She could be losing her baby. "That's what you want to text?"

She growled at me. "Don't want him driving too fast."

Oh, brother. She needed to quit worrying about Robert. But she could handle this however she needed. If it made sense to her. I sent the text.

It took a stressful ten minutes for the on-call doc to drag herself from her workout and reach the hospital. Docs didn't man the ER 24/7 in Broken Butte. On the occasion one was needed, the on-call doc was usually minutes away. I met her at the doorway since I was on my way to escort her myself. With extreme self-control, I didn't rip into her about how I'd called ahead and why had it taken her so long to arrive. She was here now, and all my righteous frustration wouldn't contribute to her helping Sarah.

She hurried into the room ahead of me. "I'm Dr. Brainard."

I glared at her, even though she had her back to me. I'd never heard of a Dr. Brainard and wished Doc Kennedy, the man I trusted above all others, had been the on-call doctor. I tamped down my urge to ask her where she'd come from, where she earned her degree, what experience and qualifications made her worthy to treat Sarah and Tigger.

Dr. Brainard stared at the heart monitor and read from a chart. She studied the fetal monitor.

I had to admit, Sarah seemed much more comfortable now than when we arrived. The fluid must have helped and she seemed less tense, which probably minimized the cramps.

Sarah's phone dinged, and I glanced at the screen. "Robert says he's on his way."

"If he calls, let it ring. Text him back that I'm ready to go."

It felt like lying not to tell Robert the whole truth, but I did what Sarah wanted.

Dr. Brainard put her hand on Sarah's belly. "Your heartbeat was elevated when you came in. But it's normal now. How do you feel?"

Her eyes still topped the worry chart. "Better. Still having cramps, though."

Dr. Brainard considered that. "What did you eat today?"

Sarah thought a minute. "Not much. I've had morning sickness pretty much all day, every day."

Dr. Brainard appeared to be about the same age as me and Sarah. Pale and thin, she didn't look all that healthy herself. She wore black capri workout pants and a ratty fleece, slightly damp from sweat, despite all the massive amounts of time she'd been alerted before she got here.

"One problem is that you're dehydrated. Even if you can't eat, you need to drink."

Sarah wasn't taking the abrupt manner very well. "I drink a lot."

Dr. Brainard didn't seem to notice Sarah's bark. "Sure. But what? If it's coffee or tea or caffeinated soda, you're doing more harm than good."

Sarah narrowed her eyes at the doctor. "I drink plenty of water."

"How about chocolate? That's a diuretic, too."

Sarah started to say something, then stopped. Her mouth formed a surprised *O*.

Dr. Brainard raised a thin eyebrow.

Sarah gripped the bar of the bed. "Oh my God. Grandma sent me a box of dark chocolate from Germany. It's the only thing that's tasted good for ages. I ate some this afternoon." She choked. "Did I hurt the baby?"

"How much is 'some'?"

Sarah glanced at me and away, as if embarrassed. "She sent two pounds, and there's not much left."

Dr. Brainard broke into a grin, and her eyes sparkled. I suddenly liked her a lot more. "Bingo."

"What are you saying?" I butted in.

Dr. Brainard laughed. "What you have is stomach cramps from too much chocolate, coupled with caffeine rush and dehydration. You're fine. The baby's fine."

Sarah's tears gushed like the recent Sandhills' weather.

"Talk about death by chocolate." I laughed.

It was too soon for Sarah. "Shut up. And I mean shut up. You can't tell anyone about this ever."

Dr. Brainard and I laughed harder. "I mean it."

A clatter of footsteps brought Robert on the run into the room. He didn't seem to see me or doc but ran to Sarah. He had hold of her hand and leaned toward her before I could swallow my mirth.

"Are you okay? What's wrong?" So much for Sarah's downplaying. I guess if you tell your husband you're in the hospital, no amount of lying can calm the panic.

Sarah sobbed, unable to tell him anything. He gathered her into his arms, somehow keeping the IV inserted into her wrist. "I love you. It's okay."

Sarah buried her head in Robert's chest and let out all the fear she'd been toting around for the last few hours.

Dr. Brainard and I backed out of the room. We stopped in the hallway. "Thank you," I said. "I had no idea eating chocolate could cause this much trouble."

Dr. Brainard shrugged. "I've seen it before. We'll keep her here until morning to get some fluids into her. But she'll be fine."

I introduced myself and learned Laura Brainard came

from Denver to join Doc Kennedy's clinic. I welcomed her to Nebraska, and we chatted briefly before she excused herself to go back to her workout.

I turned for one last look. Sarah and Robert held tight to each other and spoke quietly. Even though Sarah had been my best friend since kindergarten, she and Robert hadn't started dating until our last year at the University of Nebraska (Go Big Red). Now I couldn't imagine one without the other. They had the kind of marriage I'd hoped for with Ted.

Feeling happy for them and sad for me, I tromped out to my car and woke up Poupon so he could take a break. We wandered through the dark parking lot to the wheat field behind, and I forced him to romp, probably doing me more good than him. With the fresh air and smidgeon more optimism, we settled in for the long drive home.

Halfway home, dark clouds blotted the moon, probably hanging above my house. Rain hung heavy, waiting to break loose again and create havoc, washing out roads, flooding basements. Don't give me any of that malarkey about making the grass grow, this was a Genghis Khan rain. It wanted to destroy everything in its path.

The closer I came to Hodgekiss, there was more evidence a good toad strangler had passed. Ditches ran with highway runoff. My dirt road was crossed with thin ravines and deep ponds. I swerved and braked.

I finally pulled up in front of my old dumpy house and stared in the darkness.

What the what?

18

Already wet, feeling lonely and depressed about Shelly and Carly, and worn to nubbins, what little fortitude I had left withered. I tried to make sense of the disaster in front of me.

My yard was a sandbox. It didn't matter that I hadn't mowed the grass, because now it was buried under a foot of sand that had washed from the hills behind my house.

How?

My cottage sat on a slight rise above the lake. It wasn't supposed to flood from behind.

In the dark, details weren't clear, but sand had washed through and over the wire fence separating the wild pasture from my garden and yard. Like a lava flow, it kept coming, spreading across the grass and creeping up to the house.

I parked on a sandy moraine, the old gravel of the parking area buried. I might as well have been walking along a Mexican beach, except I didn't even want a margarita. A breeze still carried Nebraska's spring chill, several degrees colder now since the sun went down.

I checked the rain gauge nailed to the fence post of my yard. It could register up to five inches, but that puppy overflowed. The old place had been built a football field away from the northern-most hill. In anyone's imagination, that ought to be far enough away to avoid any wash from a summer storm. But who plans for a five-inch downpour? Far as I knew, Nebraska didn't qualify as a rainforest.

Poupon trotted off, not showing much solidarity as I plodded on soggy sand to where my sweet garden had been planted. Not even a tip of a lettuce leaf poked through.

As bad as the outside looked, my stomach did that flip and sink, like a boat in heavy seas, when I focused on the house. What kind of mess waited for me inside?

The cement of the bottom step of the porch was buried, not a good sign. Aside from the damp that caused the wood frame to swell, the screen seemed to hang straight and the front door opened without a problem. So at least the house hadn't been knocked off its foundation.

I hit the light switch, not surprised it didn't respond. REA, Rural Electric Association, put in place by Roosevelt so many years ago, was truly a wonder. But out in the great American West, it often cut out. Again, not a crisis, since someone would fix it. In the meantime, I could sleep here. Since I hadn't stopped at Dutch's grocery store, I had to get morning coffee at the Long Branch anyway. If it took longer than a day for the juice to come on, I could always stay with Mom and Dad.

Poupon's claws clicked on the wood floor as he beelined for the couch.

I took a little of my irritation out on him. "No dogs on the furniture."

He immediately plopped his butt on the floor and gave me a look of surprise. I countered with, "I mean it."

I didn't think dogs could shrug, but it kind of looked like Poupon did.

I slipped into the heavy evening air to retrieve Big Dick

from the cruiser and once back inside, braced myself for the trip to the basement. Along the way, I inspected the eight windows, and they seemed leak-free. No drips from the ceiling in the two tiny bedrooms, the living room, and the kitchen.

Wincing, I opened the door to the five-foot-wide back porch that protected the basement steps. The pond smell hit me first, confirming my fear. With growing trepidation, I pointed Big Dick down to see rippling dark waves.

Drat. No, not drat. Damn. Not even. Damn it to hell.

I perched on the step above the water line and inspected my basement from wall to wall in the beam. Washer and dryer would be toast. I wasn't an amateur when it came to basements and had taken the precaution to not leave any belongings on the floor. So things like boxes of old tax returns and pictures and all that stupid crap you couldn't bring yourself to throw away but didn't know what to do with were stored on steel shelves. I wasn't so lucky with other things· I'd tossed downstairs intending to put away later. Such as laundry, muddy boots, ice skates, and who knows what else.

I plucked my phone from my pocket, dialed, and waited for Michael to answer. Lauren picked up instead. "Glad you called. How did the date with Heath go?"

"Uh. It wasn't a date, but fine."

She giggled. "I knew you'd hit it off. He's such a cutie, right?"

It was cranky of me, but I cut her off. "Is Michael around?"

She sounded hurt, and I immediately felt like a jerk. "He's in the barn. I'll take the phone out."

I brushed my damp curls away from my face. "Don't do that. Do you still have that sump pump?"

"Huh?" I waited while she shifted gears. "What do you need that for?"

"I take it you guys didn't get that gully washer. My basement looks like Stryker Lake threw up in it and smells like a pool of Michael's dirty socks."

She thought a moment. "I'm sure we loaned that to Twyla and Bud when they had that leak at the Long Branch."

"Okay. Hey, thanks for dinner the other night. It was delicious."

She giggled again. Apparently we were still friends. "You guys make the cutest couple."

I started up the steps, already tired out and with a long way to go before the day ended.

Ten minutes later I pushed into the Long Branch. Most of the tables were full. Must have been a program at the school, maybe awards night or Baccalaureate. Since Bud had hired the wife of the new guy at the feed store, Twyla stood behind the bar in a fine mood. Waiting tables tended to ruffle her fur, so until another waitress turnover, she was in tall cotton.

I headed straight for her and plopped on my favorite bar stool. From the mirror over the bar, I spotted a few regulars and diners scattered around the tables. A good Sandhiller would stop and say a few words to friends and neighbors. Especially if they happened to be an elected county official who might want to run again. I'd reached my social limit for the day, though.

Twyla saw me coming and tossed a bar rag toward the cash register. It landed on a coffee can, which I assumed held donations for the Dugans. I'd be sure to take it off before I left.

Twyla reached for the cooler under the bar. She brought out a bottle of beer with a logo I didn't recognize. "Got this new microbrew from a place in Ogallala. Try it out."

With a flick of an opener, she popped the top and set the bottle in front of me. Twyla rested her hip on the bar. "So, you've got a flock of ganders pitching woo. Who're ya gonna settle on? I got my vote, but I'm not going to tell."

I took a draw on the beer to keep from baring my teeth. The cold bubbles hit my mouth with a burst of hops that could choke a bull. I coughed with my lips clamped and swallowed.

Twyla waited a second, and when I didn't answer, she shrugged. "Keep the mystery alive while you can. So, how's Sarah?"

Sarah would be irritated word got out. "Going to be fine. Nothing wrong."

Twyla accepted that. "I didn't figure I'd get details from you. You're like your dad that way, keeping information to yourself. Sarah's lucky to have you in her corner."

That seemed overly mushy coming from Twyla. I wanted to save us both from embarrassing tenderness. "Lauren said you've got their sump pump. Can I borrow it?"

Twyla lifted an unlit cigarette to her lips and stuck it in the corner of her mouth. She glanced at the ceiling, though I doubted the pump hung there. "Let's see." She swung her head toward the back of the bar, where it opened into the kitchen. "Bud! Where's that ol' sump pump?"

Nothing.

"Bud!" That siren could wake a sleeping teenager, but it didn't have any effect on Bud.

Twyla spun around and stomped to the kitchen. "Damn it, Bud." There was more, but I turned my attention to the hoppy goodness in front of me.

Someone slid onto the bar stool next to mine. "Are you here for supper?"

I looked up at Josh Stevens next to me. If I had to talk to anyone, Josh would be better than most. In fact, I actually brightened to see him.

I returned his grin. "Just stopped in to talk to Twyla. What are you up to?"

He set a half-filled bottle of the same microbrew in front of him. "On my way from branding cleanup for Shorty Cally. Thought I'd get sandwiches for me and Dad so I don't have to cook."

My muscles unwound a click or two. "How's Enoch?"

He took a pull on the beer, and his face fell. "He's going to that lost place more and more. I'm not sure how long I can keep him home."

Josh's MO seemed to be a caretaker. Loyalty and protection almost got him thrown in jail for murder a few months back. "Sorry to hear that."

He shrugged. "I'll figure something out. Why don't we get a bite to eat?"

I wouldn't have minded relaxing here and having another beer with Josh, talking about nothing over a greasy burger and fries. That'd be fine. If I didn't have a drowned house to resuscitate.

Twyla stomped back out stuffing a French fry in her mouth. How someone could live on the grease and dubious nutrition of the Long Branch food and stay so skinny is a question for the sphinx. She eyed me, stopped for a rocks glass, and filled it with one, two, three fingers of Jack Daniel's, taking her time.

She finally sauntered over, a wicked gleam in her eye. "Bud took the damned pump to the house. He thinks it's in the shed."

"I can go find it," I said.

She shook her head, her dark hair flapping back and forth. "A hound couldn't find a dead rabbit in that shed. Bud'll bring it tomorrow. You sit tight and eat. Bud's got some good hot beef sandwiches tonight."

Josh brightened, maybe thinking there was hope for dinner after all.

My phone rang, and I pulled it from my pocket, only half-irritated to see it was Jeremy.

He sounded chipper, as always. "It's a lovely day in the Sandhills, don't you think?"

"If you like the rain."

"It makes the grass grow."

Here we go again. "What do you need?"

All charm and sweetness. "What makes you think I need anything?"

I waited.

"Okay. Yeah. The alternator went out on my pickup."

My diving vacation spun further away. "How much?"

He hurried to assure me. "No. I got this covered."

"Then why are you calling me?"

He sounded hurt. "Jeez. You're so hard."

"And?"

He huffed. "Okay. Can I borrow your car for a few days while mine gets worked on?"

I burst out in disbelief, "Elvis?"

He sounded like a little boy. "Well, I can't really drive the cop car, can I?"

I shook my head. "Elvis is like my child. I've had him almost as long as I've had you as a brother, and I think I like him better."

"Ouch."

I didn't feel bad.

He tried again. "I promised Bill Hardy I'd break that colt and help him get his hay machinery ready. I can't let him down."

My fight woke up. "Hardys live twenty miles from town."

"That's what I'm saying. I need wheels to get there. It's not like I'm taking the car to Broken Butte to cruise Main. It's a job."

No. Not Elvis.

He sounded desperate. "I really need the job. Especially if I have to pay for a new alternator."

Damn it. I sighed. "Okay."

All happiness and sunshine. "You're the best. I promise I'll make it up to you."

"I'm sure you will."

He'd known I'd say yes. "I just picked it up. Man, your place is a mess."

"Maybe you could help me clean it up?"

"I'd love to, but the job. Starts really early."

He hung up, and I turned back to Josh, who gave me a silly smile.

Oh, what the heck. I needed a new plan, and a girl's got to eat. "Sure. Hot beef sounds great."

Twyla gave Josh an expectant look. "Two?"

His mouth ticked up. "You bet."

When Twyla left, he leaned on the bar and gave me his whole focus. "What do you need the pump for?"

The beer and company relaxed me some. "Basement sprung a leak with that last toad strangler."

"Are you heading back out to your place? I could help."

Wow. "That would—" Something wrapped around my middle and weighted on my shoulders. High-pitched squealing startled me, and before I could pull my gun, which wasn't my first reaction, I glanced in the mirror above the bar.

Louise's youngest boys, twins Zeke and Mose, continued their ambush, making gun noises and yelling in their eight-year-old outdoor voices.

Louise stomped through the glass door and positioned herself behind me. She clapped her hands, like Thor's thunder. "Mose. Zeke. Stop that."

Amid their "aws" and "mans," they let go.

I ruffled their messy heads. Louise had strict rules, which included homework and an early bedtime on school nights. "Are you little dudes here to eat?"

Louise folded her arms and watched the boys, avoiding eye contact with Josh. He'd helped her out of an embarrassing situation a few years earlier, and she'd never been comfortable with him since. "We're on our way home now."

"Mom said we could stop to give our money tonight." Zeke dug a fist into his jeans pocket.

Mose copied him. "Yeah. We saved a whole bunch."

Zeke pulled out a handful of quarters and dimes. Mose produced a neatly folded five-dollar bill. They held them out to show me. Zeke gave a solemn nod to his brother's treasure. "Dad changed our money into dollars at the gas station. I got the leftover money, and Mose gots the big dollars."

Josh gave them an appreciative grin. "Wow. That must have taken you a long time to save up."

The boys looked adorable in their seriousness. Mose spoke for them. "It's from chores and birthday money."

"What are you going to do with it?" I asked.

Zeke's little face dropped even more. "It's for Dugans' baby. She's got a disease and she needs help."

A lump stuck in my throat. I jumped from my stool. "I think the donation can is here."

Twyla stepped from the kitchen carrying two plates heaping with burgers and fries. When she lifted her head and saw me reaching for the bar rag covering the donation can, her eyes flew open. "Hey, wait."

I stopped mid-grab and stared at her. "Mose and Zeke are donating to Dugans."

Twyla's eyes took on a frantic glint. She set a plate on the bar and held out her hand to the twins. "I'll take it."

It wouldn't mean as much to them to hand it over to Twyla

as it would to drop it in the can. "Here." I grabbed the rag with one hand and closed my fingers on the plastic lid of the coffee can. I swung around and held it down for the boys.

Mose's little fist clutched the five dollars, and he reached out to slip it through the slot on top and stopped. He looked at the can, then up at me.

Zeke's eyes opened wide and his mouth followed. As if someone flipped a switch, both boys howled with laughter.

I turned to Twyla. She stood stone-still, holding the plate, a look of horror on her face. Even Josh looked rattled.

My attention drew back to the can I held. I smiled back at myself. Or, rather, a candid shot of me taken a few years ago at Robert's branding beamed from the side of the can where it had been pasted.

I gulped and twisted the can around to see the lettering. "Vote Now!"

The jukebox kept cranking some country caterwauling, making it feel as though the whole bar held their breath to see my reaction. I probably held my breath, too.

How? What? I didn't even...

Twyla stuttered like a car trying to turn over. "You. It's. We thought. You have to..."

My jaw opened and shut, then opened again. "I have to what?"

"We thought. Well, you're gonna start dating, and we kind of just thought it would be funny."

I might burst into flames. Mad? Hell, yes. Embarrassed? More than I'd ever thought possible. Betrayed. That's where I stuck.

Twyla's face looked pale. "It was a joke. You weren't supposed to see it."

My mouth felt full of sand, hot wind blowing through my head. "But the whole rest of the county?"

"Oh, honey, I'm sorry."

I didn't know what the twins thought. I couldn't look at Josh or anyone else in the Long Branch. My goal was to exit with dignity. I brushed past Louise, who might have been as mortified as me. Probably not.

19

I drove outside of town about six miles to Bud and Twyla's house. They lived in an old stucco house, one of the first prefab kits Sears sold in the 1930s. A few disused corrals surrounded the place, along with an old shed that probably housed a Studebaker in its day. It was packed full of junk and as messy as Twyla said it would be.

It didn't make me proud, but I admit to throwing a few things around while I searched for the pump. A series of broken railroad ties flew from a pile to land in a heap a few feet away. One cracked terra cotta flower pot might have shattered against a corner.

How was I supposed to instill confidence and capability to the people of Grand County after a stunt like this from my own family? Who would take me seriously?

I carried a gun, for the love of cheese. I was the law. The Law. You couldn't put a can with my name on it in the bar to vote for my next husband.

Except if you were a Fox in Grand County. Then, your brothers and sisters, cousins, friends, and relations could whoop it up at your expense. Damn it. I fumed and fussed. Cursed and howled. It didn't solve a thing.

One after another, my brothers and sisters and sisters-in-law called. I didn't answer. But when I saw Kyle's number, I punched it on.

Kyle sounded winded. "Can you meet me in Dry Creek?"

More problems. "What? Now?"

The sound of wind brushed the phone. "Yeah. There's stuff I need to tell you."

"Is this about Shelly?"

Impatience beat in his words. "Not just her. I don't want to talk about it on the phone."

His demand hit me like needle grass on bare legs. "Why not?"

"Because I need to show you or you won't believe me."

One more person wanting something from me. "This has to do with the sister who doesn't want to be found?"

He didn't increase his volume, but the urgency amplified. "She's in trouble and trying to protect me and Alex."

I was bone-tired, my legs ached, my eyes felt like all the sand on Wild Horse Hill had settled into them. "You're going to have to tell me more than that if I'm going all the way up to Dry Creek tonight."

"Just do me this favor."

Wrong thing to say to me tonight. "No. Just no. No to you. To my family. To all the girls out there telling us not to find them. I'm tired, I'm sick of racking up IOUs that will never be paid and getting slapped for it. I'll talk to you in the morning."

I hung up. Yeah, Kyle didn't deserve the consequences of my family's joke. It wasn't his fault I hadn't drawn better boundaries with my kin. But Dry Creek was not my jurisdiction. Shelly was not my sister. And damn it. I'd had my fill.

Sarah called and I let it go to voicemail, then listened. "I just heard what happened. The can is a pretty shitty thing to do. I don't know who set it up, but it wasn't there for more than a day. This isn't nearly as embarrassing as the time your skirt got stuck in your thong at the student council assembly junior year. Okay, maybe it is. But you survived that, and this will go away, too."

I stared up at the night sky, finding Orion's Belt and the Big Dipper. You'd think with complete lack of light pollution and all the time I'd spent gazing at the sky while checking pregnant cows at night and sitting on the old porch swing at Frog Creek, I'd be able to name more constellations. The constant stars, the rolling hills on either side of the road, the fragrance of rain on sand. Same. Familiar. Home.

I spoke some of Dad's wisdom. "It'll stop hurting when the pain goes away." My words echoed in the cluttered shed.

Only because Poupon would need to go out, I gave up the search and drove my sorry butt home. The puddles on my road still forced caution, and I meandered down the road to my shanty.

With no pump, I'd start bailing, if that's all I could do. While I bailed, I'd recover from the Kate Fox Dating straw poll and maybe find some humor in it. Though laughing seemed a stretch.

Then I'd go ahead and feel like a stinky butt, as Lucy would say, for blowing off Kyle. In fact, before the home repair, I'd check on Poupon, then meet Kyle in Dry Creek. If he thought I could help, it was my job to be there.

I pulled my phone out and called Kyle, but he didn't answer. I left a message that I'd be on my way soon and hung up.

Lights winked at me when I topped the hill that led to my house. I'd probably left the switches turned on when I'd tested them earlier. Once REA restored electricity, everything burst to life, whether I was there to rejoice about it or not.

Josh's old black Ford parked outside my fence not only explained the lights but piqued my curiosity.

As soon as I stepped from my car, the low rumble of an engine broke through the usual night's solitude. I followed the sound to the east side of my house and a blue hose about two inches in diameter snaking from a basement window. It spewed water to create a mini creek cutting through the new sand, away from my house.

Josh met me on my screened front porch. "I didn't know you had a dog."

The naturalness of him walking out of my front door struck me. "Only keeping him for Diane."

He accepted that. "Not really a cow dog."

"I don't have any cows."

He held a scoop shovel. "I'd hoped to have your front walk cleared before you got here."

"What are you doing?"

He passed me and descended the porch steps, sliding the shovel under the sand and scooping it away from the cracked cement walk. "I had a sump pump at home. Thought you could use some help with your basement."

I almost wept. Well, no, I didn't. But it was damned good of him to help me out like that. "Thanks for bringing the pump. But you don't need to dig me out, too."

He kept shoveling. "That's why I'm here."

I went around back to the decrepit wood garage and found my own scoop shovel. Actually, it came from Frog Creek, along with other tools I figured wouldn't be missed.

I changed into a T-shirt and met Josh out front. He'd made good progress, and I pitched in to finish scooping my front walk.

He grunted and tossed a shovelful of sand. "Sorry about that. Well, the voting thing."

My shoulders heated up from the work. "It's the curse of being a Fox."

Scrape, toss. "You're taking it pretty well."

Scoop, lift. "I can either get over it or die."

We worked in companionable silence, with a few comments about the roping, the benefits of working cattle with horses or ATVs, the prospects of next year's Husker football.

By the time we'd finished the walk, the sump pump had done its best on the basement, and we tromped down into the dampness and shoveled, hauled the sand out in buckets, and swept.

The moon snuck up on us so that when we finally climbed the cement basement stairs a few hours later, the sliver cast ripples of light across the lake. We plopped down on the metal lawn chairs. My body felt like it weighed twenty tons and it would take an act of Congress to make it move again.

"It's beautiful out here," he whispered.

I loved that he seemed as much in awe of this scene as I did. As if we sat in church. "It's really peaceful."

At that word, the whole day fell down on my head. I reached for my phone and remembered I'd set it on the dining table to keep it from falling out of my pocket into the water. I pushed myself up, letting a groan escape, and lumbered to find it. Kyle had probably called back, wondering where I was.

I'd kept my mind busy while I was working, and now suddenly, worry blossomed. I snatched my phone from the table and swiped it on, expecting an irritated voicemail from Kyle, not to mention apologies or explanations from my family.

One message from Kyle, nothing else. When the voicemail

engaged, there was only the sound of wind against the phone, then Kyle's quiet words. "You're wrong. Shelly isn't okay."

I took my worn-out bones into the kitchen and jerked open the fridge door. Just as I suspected.

I pulled out the bottle, grabbed two juice glasses, and headed back out to the porch. I spoke in a quiet voice so as not to disrupt the night too much. "Sad to say, I've only got one beer."

Josh took the glass I handed him and let me divide the beer between us. "That's probably a good thing. It's late."

We sipped in silence and Kyle's last phone call began to eat at me. The longer I sat, the guiltier I felt until I couldn't stand it. "Do you mind if I make a call?"

Josh looked startled. "It's really late."

I held my phone. "I know. And I'll probably wake him up, but Kyle Red Owl needed me earlier and I want to make sure everything is all right."

Josh sat back. "Sure. Sheriff business isn't a nine-to-five, or even ranchers' hours, I guess."

I hit speed dial and waited three rings for Kyle's voicemail. I left a message. "Okay. He's probably fine."

I downed the last gulp of beer, wishing we had at least one more. I fell back in my chair, head resting on the wall of the house. My eyes dropped closed, and my muscles ached with release. My brain only allowed two exhausted breaths before my eyes popped open and I sat up. "You know, I'm not going to sleep tonight until I hear from Kyle."

"Did he sound like he was in trouble earlier?"

"No." If he had, I would have hurried to Dry Creek. Wouldn't I? Of course I would. Unless I was in a snit from my family's prank. "I'm sure it's because I'm tired I feel anxious, but I know I won't relax until I prove to myself what a ninny I am."

Josh laughed. "I can't imagine using Kate Fox and ninny in the same sentence. But if you want to go up to the rez, I'll go with you."

I stood and took his glass. "You've already done too much. Thanks, but you should go home."

He tagged after me to the kitchen. "I'm not even tired. I wouldn't mind a ride on a nice spring night."

I set the glasses in the sink. "This isn't a drive for fun. It's me being sheriff."

He gave me an easy grin. "Sure, but it likely won't amount to more than a drive up to Dry Creek and back. I can help keep you awake."

Why did everyone question my every move? My voice came out harder than I intended, and not as rough as I felt. "I appreciate you coming out here to help me. I really do. But now I need you to go home so I can do my job."

His smile froze, and I felt like a skunk for hurting his feelings. "Okay. I've got to go back to Shorty's tomorrow pretty early, so I'll take off."

"Let me get your pump."

He was already halfway to the door. "We can get it later. If you're going all the way to the rez, you should get started."

I had to skip to make up for his long strides and catch him before the screen door banged shut. "Come out tomorrow night. I'll make some dinner to thank you for shoveling and pumping."

He turned and studied my face. "That's okay. You're busy. You don't need to cook for me."

Now I was on the begging side. "I mean it. I'd like for you to come out, and we can relax. It'll be fun." The more I talked, the more I convinced myself.

I must have done a good job because Josh hesitated.

"Sounds great. I don't know when I'll get done at Shorty's, so maybe a little bit later?"

"Perfect." That might give me time to dust and vacuum and maybe even fix my hair. What a girl I was turning into.

He gave it another shot. "Sure wish you'd let me go with you tonight."

The tight lips and narrowed eyes I shot him let him know what I thought of that comment.

He laughed. "Okay. See you tomorrow."

It's not that I would've minded his company on the drive. That little twinge in my belly told me this cruise might not be a joy ride.

20

I changed back into my sheriff browns and cowboy boots. I tried Kyle's number several times on the way up to Dry Creek and got nothing for the trouble. The more he didn't answer, the tighter my gut curled. To unravel it, I analyzed the last encounters I'd had with Kyle.

He was upset about Shelly, of course. He'd been frustrated earlier today when we left the rez. Kyle wasn't likely to do something dangerous. So why was I jittery and nervous?

I expected to sail through a quiet and dark Dry Creek now, a little after two a.m. But my hands tightened on the wheel when I saw Frankie's store lights on and a few cars in the lot. I slowed and pulled in, identifying Barnett's and Pete Grainger's sheriff Broncos. This couldn't be good.

The moon hurried to the western horizon, but the stars still blazed, probably happy the rain clouds decided to hike out of the area. It felt more like March instead of May, my breath puffing ahead of me.

I made sure my gun was firmly in my holster and I had both pairs of cuffs on my utility belt before I hurried into the liquor store.

The bell jingled, and I walked into fluttering fluorescent lighting and the smell of a dank, moldy dishrag with hints of spoiled cabbage. At first, the place looked deserted, then a movement near the front counter caught my eye.

A black cowboy hat poked from behind the cash register, giving me a dose of dread when I saw Barnett's scowl beneath the rim. "Damn. You're like a bad penny."

Scuffling and a muffled cry. Pete Grainger swung the door behind the counter with a squeak. He stepped out, body giving off energy like a coiled spring. "How did you know to come out here?"

This was all too strange. "I didn't know. What's going on?"

Frankie's voice carried from the room behind the counter. "Now what?"

Barnett's face and hat disappeared, and he spoke above the clack of his boots on the old linoleum as he stomped to the back room. "Kate Fox poking her head where it doesn't belong."

Another muffled grunt. Men's voices murmuring.

Grainger's face looked pale, his brown eyes like tiny alarm buttons.

I walked to the cash register and leaned over the counter, trying to peer into the back room. "What's going on, Pete?"

It was easy to see the athlete Pete must be, with tension coming off him like a runner in the blocks. "A kid. Tried to break in while Frankie was working on his books."

Thank goodness Pete was here, instead of only Frankie and Barnett. "Wow, Frankie works late. How did you find out about the break-in? I didn't hear anything on the radio."

Pete shook his head. "Maybe dispatch only called me and Barnett since we're up here."

Something seemed wonky. "It took the both of you?"

Pete glanced behind him. "Frankie called. Heard a noise and didn't know. I guess he called us both."

I started toward the door to check out this crazy story. "Frankie called? Not dispatch?"

Cockamamie, that's what Dad called stories like this that we made up to avoid getting in trouble. But this wasn't kid mischief, and a time-out probably wouldn't correct whatever Pete was hiding. I rested my palm on my gun and steadied my nerves.

Pete nodded. "That's right. I forgot. Anyway, no need for you to be here, too."

Without waiting for any more explanation, I squeezed between Pete and the doorjamb. The door to Frankie's office stood open only a few steps away.

Barnett and Frankie spun around with surprised faces. Someone sat in a chair behind them.

Barnett held up his hand and growled like a dog protecting his dinner. "We've got it taken care of."

"Okay," I said as agreeably as I could. "Kyle called me about something going on up here, and I came to check it out."

Frankie looked like an old pot starting to boil, the lid rattling. "It's damned near daytime. I'm sick of the lot of you. Get out."

I put a hand on Barnett's shoulder to nudge him out of the way. He resisted, so I slid around him.

Alex Red Owl sat in a ladder-back chair in the middle of the small office. Not as a guest, since his arms were arched behind him, wrists caught in handcuffs with a red bandana shoved into his mouth.

What the hell? A teen break-in didn't call for two sheriffs and a well-armed Frankie. Certainly not tying a kid in a chair. It couldn't be a coincidence this was Kyle's brother.

My hand tightened on my gun, but I couldn't OK Corral this, even if I wanted to.

Without letting my nerves get to me, I yanked the soggy bandana from his mouth and dropped it on the floor.

His eyes round and black like hockey pucks, Alex started to yell in Lakota, the vowels thrown back in his throat, harsh consonants rushing forward. I didn't need a translation to understand his hatred and outrage.

Barnett stooped and picked up the bandana. "You see why we gagged him? The kid won't shut up, and it makes no sense." He shoved the red cotton toward Alex.

I grabbed it from him and tossed it over my shoulder. I might be outnumbered, but I was right. "What's he done?"

Alex shouted, "I ain't done nothing. These assholes grabbed me for nothin'."

Frankie slammed a key ring onto the desk that was piled high with invoices, receipts, folders, and flyers. "Drop these off when you're done with this polka. I'm going home."

He brushed past Pete, who stood in the narrow corridor between the office and the door into the store.

Pete spoke to his back. "We're darned sure sorry about this, Frankie. I'll stop in tomorrow to take your statement about the attempted robbery."

With Frankie gone, and Pete being a reasonable person— even if Barnett was his best friend—we might be all right.

Alex's voice cracked. "What? It wasn't me! I was at the rec center in Sand Gap. You ask Benji Pourier. We was there together. And Kyle called me to meet him."

Barnett raised his arm, poised to backhand Alex. "Shut your trap."

Pete stepped into the room. "Hey, hey. Come on, Lee. Take a breath."

Barnett lowered his arm but huffed in and out with his nostrils flaring like a mad bull.

I gave Alex a twice-over, then a third time for good measure. "Have you seen your brother?"

Alex's eyes, black and dilated, took on that teenager flat glare, the one that said they were so much smarter, cooler, better than you in every way. His lip curled like some tough guy, but his voice sounded like the kid he was. "I had a brother, but he's dead."

Barnett stiffened, and his eyes grew even meaner. "What did you say?"

Alex didn't move his head, but his gaze shifted to Barnett. "Darrel was my brother. True Lakota."

Barnett responded with a scary smile. "True Lakota, right. Drunk and dead on the side of the road."

Alex tried to jump to his feet, but Barnett's paw on his shoulder slammed him back down in the chair. Pure black hate shot from him toward Barnett. "It was probably you who dumped him there. No one hit him on the road. Dude, he had a car. He wasn't a walker."

Exhaustion pulsed behind my eyes. I couldn't piece together what was really going on here, but I'd had enough. "Where's Kyle?"

He gave me a smirk. "Where's Kyle? Where's Shelly? You're sure full of questions." He finished this with a string of Lakota that took little imagination to know what he thought of me.

Barnett leaned down in Alex's face. "So where are they? Huh? Kyle? Shelly?"

Alex drew in a giant snort, getting ready to spit a glob into Barnett's face.

Barnett's ham of a fist shot out and closed on Alex's neck.

I jumped in. "Stop it!"

Pete stepped between Alex and me and Barnett. He gave

me a tight smile to say he'd take over. "Let's all calm down, okay?"

Barnett held his ground for three beats, then exhaled and stepped back. With him tied up and three sheriffs surrounding him, Alex did something surprisingly smart and kept his mouth shut.

Pete's eyes stayed on Barnett, as if holding him back, but he talked to me. "Here's what happened. Frankie called me and Lee about midnight. Said he heard someone trying to break in."

Alex kicked his foot in frustration. "It wasn't me! I was at the rec center, I told you."

Being at the rec center at midnight didn't sound like a great alibi to me.

Barnett's boot shot out and caught Alex's ankle, and Alex yelped. Barnett couldn't have sounded more like Clint Eastwood if he wore a serape and chewed on a soggy cigar. "Shut up."

I surprised myself by snapping at Barnett. "Knock it off." I needed to get Alex to a safer situation.

Pete tipped his head in acknowledgment of Alex's protest. "Don't know if it was you or one of your posse."

Alex snorted. "Posse. Right."

Alex wasn't helping me.

Pete didn't let Alex rile him. "What I know is that when we got here, this kid was lurking around outside, and he tried to run when I gave chase."

Alex's laugh had an edge that could slice leather. "Like I'm stupid enough to stand there and let you motherfuckers grab me without a fight."

Barnett lunged at Alex, feinting a punch. The boy threw himself back in the chair. Barnett sneered.

I glared at Barnett and stepped closer to Alex. "Did Kyle tell you why he wanted you to meet him?"

Alex stared hard at me. "Told me we were hunting some sweet white ass. And here you are."

This time Barnett's palm connected with Alex's temple before I even knew he'd swung. I shoved Barnett backward and he stumbled. He acted ready to go for my throat, and I figured if one of us was going to get beat by Barnett, it'd better be me instead of Alex.

We stared at each other, every muscle inside me jumping and electric. I'd once punched a bull in the nose, but that was only to buy myself some time to run for the fence. It was plain stupid to pick a fight with one.

Alex broke the tension. "Beat the Indian. Go ahead, throw me on the side of the road like my brother. Call it a hit-and-run."

I warned Alex. "Stop talking."

His black eyes shot death but he stayed quiet.

"Okay," Pete said. "I'll take the suspect to Chester County. He can cool his jets in the cell there."

Alex howled like a coyote on the prairie. "No way! I didn't do nothing."

I considered the situation. I sure as hell didn't want to leave Alex in Barnett's hands. "I'll see if I can find Kyle."

Contempt weighted Barnett's words. "What good's a deputy if you can't get hold of him?"

Pete helped Alex stand and propelled him out of the office.

I followed, talking to Barnett over my shoulder. "Kyle is off duty. He's not obligated to answer his phone."

Barnett's footsteps thudded behind me. "'Cept he called you. A responsible human being would be available."

He acted like he didn't know cell service out here was spotty. "It's the rez."

"Exactly."

We caravanned from the corridor, through the door, across the store, and out into the cold parking lot. Barnett grasped Alex's shoulders while Pete locked the front door.

Barnett took the opportunity to shake Alex and give him a shove, knocking him to the pavement.

I jumped forward, planted my palms on Barnett's broad chest, and pushed him back. It was like shoving a half a ton of mad grizzly. I forced my eyes open and my face calm as I watched emotion battle across his face.

Resistance, fight, acceptance. At any moment, a swipe from his paw could send me flying across the broken pavement. I expected to get creamed. And yet, he finally walked backward. Not wanting to get into this again, I kept walking with him until I figured Alex couldn't hear, leaving Pete behind to help him to his feet. "What is your problem?"

He towered above me, all hard temper pulsing. "My problem is this whole tribe." He spit the word as if it were poison. "Lazy, dirty. Drunk whenever they can find a buck to spend on beer. Using girls so desperate for a drink they sell themselves for a buzz. And we're supposed to be nice to them because they are downtrodden. And when a little prick comes in and causes trouble, you want to get him into rehab or some stupid thing. I'm sick of it."

I really hadn't been prepared for such hatred, and aside from pulling out my gun and shooting his knee, I couldn't think of a way to respond. I opened my mouth, not sure what would come out.

Pete let out a yelp. I spun around. Under the light from Frankie's store sign, he pushed himself to his knees. "Stop!"

Alex leaped away from Pete, his hands free.

Pete yelled again. Barnett roared.

Without thought, I dug my boots into the ground and

pushed off, pumping my arms to gain speed. Pete stood and reached behind his back.

Barnett kept bellowing, but everything narrowed to the boy fleeing in front of me. He was only a few feet from the side of the store, where he could slip into the near-total darkness. I strained harder to catch up.

More shouting behind me. I struggled to run faster. Alex was getting away. Even if that might not be such a bad thing, considering the dicey way Barnett was treating him, I didn't question the need to catch him. "Alex!"

His tennis shoes grabbed more traction than my cowboy boots. Barnett's shouts battered me. Or maybe it was Pete. Alex put a few more feet between us. I'd never catch him before he peeled off into the dark.

I gave an extra burst, putting everything I had into my legs, my fingers grabbing, feeling like a cartoon character whose legs spin but they go nowhere. He was one lunge away from disappearing—

Bang.

21

I dove for the pavement, catching sight of the sole of Alex's shoe as he burst from the parking lot around the side of the building.

Barnett shouted, but whatever he said jumbled in noise and shock. I rolled over as Pete rose from his crouch, arm still extended, his service gun straight out. *Bang. Bang. Bang.*

He was shooting in my direction. Real bullets. Dear God.

Three shots in rapid succession, though Alex would be around the corner and long gone. Frustration shots I never expected from Pete.

Barnett ran behind him and swatted his arm down. "Stop!"

Pete raised his face to Barnett, looking shocked and disoriented. "He..." Pete's voice trailed off.

When I was sure the shooting was over, I jumped up and rocketed toward them, feeling like a hornet on a hot day. "What the hell! He's a kid. And you could have hit me! What were you thinking?"

Pete's arm hung down, the gun dangling.

I grabbed the gun from his hand, fighting the urge to bash him with it.

His eyes held shock and despair. "I'm sorry. I don't know what happened. He must have wormed out of the cuffs and he knocked me down. I just...I reacted."

Pete wasn't a big man, but he was solid muscle. Alex had the skinny build of an adolescent with some assembly still required. It seemed odd he'd be able to topple Pete. Surprise and adrenaline must have worked in his favor.

Barnett clamped heavy hands on Pete's shoulders and forced eye contact. "Christ. Those kids are slippery. They can get under your skin."

Pete blinked and sucked in a breath, seemed to pull himself together. "I haven't had a good night's sleep in a while. You know how busy it gets at the end of the school year with all the awards and programs. Then being up all night. I guess I lost my judgment."

Still hot, adrenaline pumping, I shouted, "So you shoot without thinking?"

Barnett took the gun from me and handed it back to Pete. "Yeah. It's late, or early. Whichever you call it. I'm going home."

Sure, forget a wild-assed shooting. Chalk it up to fatigue and take a nap. This was messed up.

Pete zeroed in on the corner where Alex had disappeared. "Maybe we ought to go after the kid."

I followed Pete's focus to where Alex had disappeared into the black. "He knows this place better than we do. You're not going to find him tonight." No way I wanted these bozos going after Alex tonight.

Barnett was already climbing into his Bronco.

Pete's shoulders dropped. "You're right. I let him get away."

Well, thank God. How safe would Alex have been if Pete had taken him to Chester County? I thrust my hands into my pockets to stop their shaking. Not from fear, but from rage. I paced toward my car.

Pete's voice stopped me. "I'm kind of worried about you and Lee."

It caught me so off guard I responded, despite myself. "How so?"

We watched as Barnett flipped his left turn signal on and entered the empty highway toward Spinner County. "Lee is, as my kids say, old school. He grew up here, within a stone's throw of the rez. He's seen the poverty and what it does. But he doesn't focus on the cause, he's more about the effect. Makes him mad."

"He is that."

Pete added sad to his exhausted expression. "But he's got a good heart. Under all that bluster, he does what he can to help them out. Especially the youngsters."

I wasn't buying that. "Like slapping them around when he gets the chance?"

"It's a tough love thing. He uses fear to scare them into being good."

I snorted. "It's not working."

Pete rubbed a hand over his face. "I hate to say this, but it's you who fires him up. He sees you as a bleeding heart who wants to coddle them. Makes him mad and he takes it out on, well, Alex or Kyle."

"That's twisted."

Pete shrugged and started for his car. "Give him a little time and space, especially about Kyle. He'll come around eventually."

"Barnett doesn't get a grace period to stop being a dick."

Pete's head drooped, and he shook it slowly. "I'm so sorry about the shooting, Kate. I know it doesn't seem like it, but the shots never came close to you. I'd die before hurting you." He slid behind the wheel of the Chester County sheriff's Bronco.

He looked so broken I didn't have the heart to do anything but wave it away.

I didn't wait for him to drive to the west before hurrying to my cruiser, jumping inside, and firing up the heater. The run and the scare over being shot at, or around, had worn off and I was downright cold.

I ought to head back to my house, snuggle under my covers, and fall into a deep sleep. But that wouldn't take care of the reason I gallivanted around the countryside. Even if I climbed into my warm bed, I'd wonder what Kyle was up to. I pulled out my phone and tried him again. And got the same nothing I'd been getting all night.

Alex said Kyle had asked to meet him in Dry Creek, and the last time I'd spoken to Kyle, he'd asked me the same. I stared at the oil-stained pavement under the glow of Frankie's Pepsi sign. Another job for Big Dick. Heavy in my hand, I cranked the heat, opened my window, propped my arm up to aim the beam, and began a slow cruise out to the road, then weaving into the other liquor store parking lots, shining the light behind the abandoned buildings and around the burned-out house.

This late, maybe Kyle had decided to stay at his mother's house. If I grabbed an hour or two of sleep in the car, I could drive out there early. If Kyle wasn't there, I'd go home. I wanted to check on Alex, anyway. Chances were slim he'd be hiding somewhere easy, like his house, but I'd feel better if I at least looked.

I pulled under Frankie's Pepsi sign and, with the cruiser running for the heat, closed my eyes. Josh's face floated to mind. That shy smile. Warmth spread from my chest at the image of his strong back and arms shoveling, doing what he could to help me out.

My eyes popped open. If Kyle had told me and Alex to meet him in Dry Creek, and I couldn't raise him on his cell after all this time, something was wrong. I shut off the cruiser, and Big Dick and I stepped into the predawn chill. Alex had disappeared around the east of the store, so I went west. My boots crunched on broken glass and kicked through trash in the weeds. Frankie had his own collection of dead cars, even a pickup, waiting eternally for the sand to bury them. The first trill of a robin rang out. I loved the sunrise, but I was getting tired of spending it looking for a Red Owl.

Wait. That pickup parked next to the rusted sedan. That was no abandoned vehicle. Kyle's Chevy. I spun around and ran to it. Something caught my eye under the bed.

A man's body. An arm flung out, a hand curled and still.

"Kyle!"

Splayed under the pickup on his back, his eyes closed, no movement. I crawled next to him, placing my hand gently on his neck, first relieved to feel warm skin and then a weak pulse.

I put my face close to his, smelling the metallic scent of blood, praying I wasn't too late. "I'm here, Kyle. Hang on. Gonna get you some help."

I ran back to the car and threw myself inside, closing the door, turning the key, grabbing the mic, and driving around the store at the same time. I called for an ambulance, knowing it would take nearly a half hour to get here from Potsville, but not willing to move Kyle. My cruiser bumped over the trash and weeds, and I positioned it to shine the headlights in Kyle's direction. I grabbed a blanket from my trunk and hurried back to him.

I inspected him as carefully and thoroughly as I dared. His

face looked bad. Eyes swollen, a bruise on his right cheek, cuts on his neck. Obviously, something harder than fists had created an ugly lump covering Kyle's forehead. I gently probed for more injuries and found nothing. Most of the bleeding had stopped and clotted, and I didn't know what else to do.

"You'll be okay. The ambulance is on its way," I murmured close to his ear, repeating the same words, letting him know he wasn't alone. I held Kyle's hand and thumbed Barnett's number on my phone.

He growled into the receiver. "Sheriff."

"How far away are you?"

He sounded groggy. "Who is this? Kate Fox? What do you want?"

I assumed he'd be alerted by dispatch to the ambulance in Spinner County. "Frankie's. Kyle's here. He's in bad shape."

He grunted. Even sleep was an effort for him. "Ambulance on the way?"

I squeezed Kyle's hand. "Should be here in another ten." I meant minutes, but it felt more like years.

More strange struggle noises. Tricky bed, I guessed. "Okay. Thanks."

I watched Kyle's chest barely moving. "How long will it take you to get here?"

He paused. "Don't see any reason for me to drag myself out there again."

Shocked by his nonchalance, I blurted out, "It's Kyle."

He cursed. "He might be your deputy, but he's an Indian. I'm not inclined to ruin what's left of my night over some Indian who got beat up over a beer and passed out."

"He's not drunk."

Barnett's sigh was deep and irritated. "What does he say happened?"

"He's not conscious. Looks like he was attacked and beaten. Are you coming out here?"

He didn't hesitate. "I think you've got it under control." The phone went dead.

Asshole! The lowest, meanest excuse for a human being. I wanted to yell and curse at him and tell him any decent person would care. But Barnett wasn't my immediate problem. Kyle deserved all of my attention. I bent over him and kept talking.

I shoved the phone into my pocket, held Kyle's hand, and encouraged him until finally, the ambulance arrived. I wished I could give Kyle into the capable hands of Eunice Fleenor and Harold Graham, but the Spinner County squad seemed competent. They loaded him onto a hard board and into the ambulance in short order.

We took off at full speed, me following them in my cruiser, my light bar flaring in the weak dawn light.

I punched in Milo Ferguson's number to let him know what happened. And then alerted Pete Grainger.

Grainger reacted with concern. "You go ahead to Broken Butte and keep us updated on Kyle's condition. I'll go to the accident site and see if I can gather any evidence about what happened."

Bitterness rang in my voice. "Barnett isn't going to help out."

Grainger clicked his tongue. "You can't really blame him. This kind of thing happens all the time up there."

"What kind of thing?" If he brought up the phrase *drunk Indian* again, I might call the ACLU on the whole lot.

Grainger sighed. "Cut him some slack. It's on account of..." He trailed off.

"On account of what?"

Grainger hesitated, then started out, sounding sad. "Happened a long time ago. But Lee's parents were killed in a head-on up there. They were real nice folks. The driver, a Lakota man, was drunk."

Oh. Man. No denying that senseless tragedy would leave a deep scar. With more understanding, I said a little more gently, "If he can't be impartial, then he shouldn't have the job."

In a level voice, Grainger said, "You know how hard it is to find a sheriff in our counties. In most ways, Lee's a good sheriff. He's not usually quick to temper, he's brave and smart. None of us are perfect, are we?"

The way he said it sent a shiver up my spine. What secrets was he hiding for Barnett?

22

Dull morning sun filtered through the glass doors of the emergency entrance at Broken Butte County Hospital. I paced the empty corridor, hating the weird hospital smell of cleaning fluid, cafeteria food, sick people, and worry. They'd whisked Kyle into the inner sanctum a few hours ago and I'd been restless, my stomach a mass of acid and stress. My muscles twitched from lack of sleep, eyelids like sandpaper, my head buzzing.

He'd looked pale and lifeless when the EMTs pulled him from the back of the ambulance into the garish overhead lights of the hospital. A surgeon waited in a prepped operating room when we arrived.

Since then I'd been dozing and staring at the door, waiting for news.

The double door where they'd spirited Kyle away pushed open. Aunt Tutti tottered out, her violet-colored scrubs looking like she'd worn them for a week of Sundays. Her permed gray hair twisted close to her scalp, and dark circles ringed her eyes. Tutti didn't usually work ER but she knew everything that went on at the hospital during her shift, and she'd understand my need to hear about Kyle.

I jumped up and hurried to her.

"He's still alive."

A steel rod inside me melted with the release of a pent-up breath. "Thank God. How is he?"

She licked her lips, looked around the open corridor, and waddled to the row of hard plastic chairs bolted together against a wall where I'd perched earlier. She plopped down. "I'm too old for this double-shift nonsense."

I lowered myself next to her. "You look exhausted."

"Honey, I'd make the Grim Reaper look good. Looks like you been rode hard and put up wet, yourself." She glanced at her watch.

I leaned in, my nerves jangling with dread. "Well?"

She massaged the bridge of her nose. "He's got a couple of busted ribs. His shoulder was dislocated, but it's set now. Lots of bruises. Somebody worked him over pretty good. All in all, that stuff will mend."

I hated the inevitable "but."

She rubbed her eyes. "The real problem is the knock to his head."

He'd been through a war in Afghanistan with nothing more than athlete's foot. It was so wrong that he'd been nearly killed behind a liquor store just off the rez. "How much damage?"

"We don't know. There is some swelling, but not enough we need to drain it. Doc is going to keep him in a coma for twenty-four hours just to be sure."

"So even if he could regain consciousness, you'll keep him under?"

She nodded. "In the meantime, he's in ICU."

"Can I see him?"

"Yep. I'll take you down."

The hospital was a beehive. Once morning hit and the sun came out, everyone buzzed and flew on their missions. Food trays appeared in the hallways, staff doubled as one crew came on before the night shift left. The administrative people turned on lights, cranked up coffee pots, greeted and conversed and started their day.

ICU took up a small section of the hospital, around the corner from the ER. Kyle wasn't aware of the morning bustle. He lay swaddled in the soft hums and beeps of monitors and equipment, which I prayed helped him heal quickly. His beautiful copper skin had taken on a gray pallor. I ached to see him open his eyes and tell me how his uncle Lloyd Walks His Horse had roped a tornado or talked a cow into letting milk flow like a faucet.

I settled for watching his chest rise and fall with regular breaths. Situating myself close to him, I kept up inane chatter for the five minutes allotted me and promised to return that evening.

Before I left the hospital, I wandered into the cafeteria for coffee, hoping for eggs and toast. I'd assumed I'd find an institutional breakfast I'd merely choke down, but I wanted something fast, and finding a decent breakfast would take time.

The happy surprise of fresh cooked scrambled eggs, hot toast with lots of butter, and coffee that tasted like a little bit of Columbian heaven could only have been ruined by who sat down at my table before I'd even finished half of my breakfast.

Gulping a mouthful of eggs, I said, "Ted. What are you doing here?"

He placed a tall to-go cup of coffee on the table and sat across from me. "Milo called me, said you were down here with Kyle."

"Why would Milo call you?"

"It's a sheriff thing."

"But you're an ex-sheriff."

Another cup landed on the table along with a loaf-sized cinnamon roll. Milo pulled out another chair a couple of feet from the table to make room for his belly. He settled himself in. "Morning, Katie."

I didn't have a chance to respond before Pete Grainger sat down with his coffee and Lee Barnett dragged a chair from the table next door, spun it around, and straddled it. So much for the one pleasure I might have enjoyed that day. I shoved my plate aside and gripped my coffee, not sure what to expect.

The buttons of Milo's shirt strained at his belly, showing his white undershirt. He spoke around a bite of cinnamon roll. "They say Kyle's not looking too good."

Barnett didn't have food or coffee. He hunched over the back of the chair like a trained bear.

Milo's prognosis irritated me, so I defended Kyle. "He's doing pretty well. His bones are going to heal."

Grainger thrummed with restless energy. I wondered if he'd had enough sleep to do him any good. "But that head injury. We just don't know."

I looked around at each one in turn. "What is this convention about, boys?"

Ted's hands cradled his cup, and he engaged me with one of his serious, understanding looks. I remembered that particular expression from when he asked me to marry him, and a few years ago when we'd discussed having a baby. Most recently, it was the face he used when we'd oh-so-civilly negotiated our divorce. It was the face of fake compassion I hated worse than cooked cabbage. And that was a lot.

He added a sincere eye blink before he began. "Couple of reasons we're all here. First, of course, is to see how the deputy is doing, give our support."

Bull malarkey.

"The other reason is to talk to you." He paused.

Again, I let my gaze rove around the table. "And it takes all of you for that?"

Ted laughed even though I hadn't joked. "It's that stubborn streak you're famous for."

Air pushed through my lips like a bored horse. "I'm not stubborn."

Milo's eyebrows shot up in amusement and his belly jogged with a silent chuckle. Grainger's leg jiggled and he pondered something fascinating on his coffee lid. Barnett had the look of a teen whose mother dragged him to church.

Ted reached out a hand and lightly gripped my wrist. "Just listen, okay?"

I whisked my arm into my lap and gave Ted my stone face.

He sat back, sipped his coffee to show his command, and then started. "Pete got out to the site a few minutes after you'd taken off. He looked around, got an idea of what happened, and, well, why don't you tell her, Pete."

Pete pushed his coffee cup from one hand to the other and fidgeted enough to make his chair squeak. "You're not going to like this, and I hate to have to say it. But what I found out there...well. I found a whole lot of beer cans."

"It's right behind a liquor store. Of course you found a bunch."

He glanced at me, then back to his cup. Each word struggled out as if it pained him. "These were still wet, and three of them weren't even open."

I turned to Milo, who chewed his roll and nodded as if some vote had been taken.

"What are you saying? That Kyle was drunk?"

Barnett's paw slapped the table, and a big green toad jumped up my throat. "For chrissake. That's exactly it. Kyle went on a bender, some Indian clocked him and took his money for beer."

My jaw dropped at the preposterousness of this claim. I finally found my voice. "Kyle wasn't drinking. He'd called me earlier to meet him in Dry Creek."

Barnett guffawed.

Ted reached for me again, but I shifted away. He paused. "You're going to have to face it. Kyle wasn't the guy you thought he was."

I shoved my chair back. "Is. Kyle *is* a good deputy. He's not a drunk." I paused to remember. Had I smelled beer on him? I would have noticed. "They had to check him when they treated him. If he'd had alcohol in his system, they wouldn't have induced a coma."

Pete tilted his head. "He might have been out there long enough it went through his system."

I glared at them all in turn. "You're wrong."

Milo put his fork on his plate. "Now listen. I got a call last week from Frankie. He thought I ought to know that Kyle had been in for three days in a row buying beer."

My turn to laugh. "No, he wasn't."

Barnett glared at me. "That's good sheriffing, Fox. Ignore what all of us—with how many years of experience—know. Pay no attention to the citizens giving you fair warning. You just keep believing your fairytale because you don't want to admit you're wrong."

Ted still had that sincere look I knew to be anything but. Grainger had given up on his coffee cup and offered me sympathy. Milo seemed to be waiting for my agreement.

Barnett flexed his arms and leaned away from the chair back before he passed final judgment. "Just like a Fox."

Milo cleared his throat and patted his belly. He spoke to

me. "I think we can wait to see what Kyle has to say about his drinking when he comes to."

"If he comes to," Barnett threw in, and I thought I might actually hate him.

Milo ignored the interjection. "But the fact is he's laid up and not going to be able to deputy for a spell."

Oh, now I knew where this was heading. I'd been clever... until now. How had I got suckered into this? They blew the whistle and the engine chugged toward me. I was tied to the tracks with no escape. Mad didn't seem like a big enough word.

Barnett gave me a smile I hankered to slap off his face. "We've taken a vote."

I'd had about enough of elections in my life. "I haven't voted." I couldn't have sounded more pathetic.

"Don't matter how you vote. It's four to whatever your bleeding heart says," Barnett said, slapping the back of the chair.

I gave a last-ditch plea to Pete with my eyes. He was back to reading his coffee cup.

Barnett crowed, "Ted is going to be the new sheriff."

There was silence before Milo corrected him. "Deputy. Ted is our interim deputy."

23

I'd given them the satisfaction of all the rise they were going to get out of me. With my most businesslike nod to Ted, I said, "Great. I can use the help if you're available."

Not sure he looked surprised or disappointed by my acceptance. "Sure. What do you need?"

The other three sheriffs passed off nonverbals to each other. Relieved, pleased, and in Barnett's case, only slightly less irritated than usual.

Tutti hustled into the cafeteria carrying a coin purse. She seemed surprised to see a whole herd of sheriffs and wound through a few tables toward us. "This looks like trouble."

Pete jumped to his feet, fired with his usual friendly fuel. "You must live here."

She beamed at him. "Pert near. Kyle's gonna be under for a while. No need for you all to hang out here."

Milo pushed back from the table and tossed out a goodbye.

Barnett stood and yanked up his pants. "I got court here this afternoon. Sure messed up my day having to come up here this morning. Now I've got a couple of hours to kill 'cause it makes no sense to drive home just to turn around and come back."

Cry me a river, you big baby. I watched him trudge out.

Pete paused with Tutti. "Please keep us informed if there's any change."

Tutti nodded. "Sure will." She watched the three men walk out and nodded at me. "That Pete Grainger is a good guy."

If you don't mind being shot at. I kept that to myself.

She didn't wait for consensus and scurried off to the concession.

Ted sipped his coffee, a satisfied expression settling on his face. "Are you wanting to take some time off? I can fill in for as long as you'd like."

Mr. Helpful and Sincere. I figured he was sincere in helping himself back into my job.

Calving was over, but he'd still have lots to do on Frog Creek, not to mention planning his branding, fixing fence, and getting hay equipment ready. Maybe he'd hired someone and I hadn't heard. That would eat into the small profit Frog Creek managed every year.

Sheesh. It was none of my business if the spring ranch work didn't get done or if Frog Creek went tits up. "I need you to go to David's Lifestyles class and talk about law enforcement jobs."

His face fell. "You're not serious."

The fake smile I sent his way matched him for sincerity. "You'll need a PowerPoint presentation."

His eyebrows dipped in skepticism. "What are you going to do?"

I gave him wide-eyed innocence. "Nothing."

He pinned me with his disbelief.

"Okay. But I don't want you ratting me out to the others."

He drew an imaginary cross on his heart.

I used to talk to Ted about most things. Old habits and all that. I couldn't trust Ted with my heart or job, but he wasn't stupid or mean and I needed someone on my side. "I don't care what they say, Kyle isn't a drinker. Something is going on, and I'll bet it has to do with Shelly's disappearance."

"Shelly?"

"Kyle's sister. She went missing Saturday night. She sent him a message Monday, telling him she was fine. But I know he didn't believe her. We found out she's still around, but she's hiding."

Ted took that in. "How do you explain Kyle being in Dry Creek, getting beat up and all the beer cans?"

The evidence was circumstantial and stupid. "I don't believe he was drinking. I think he was lured out there and someone was waiting for him."

"Why would someone want to hurt him?"

"Because he'd found out where Shelly is and what happened to her." I threw it out to see how he'd take it. "And whoever it is didn't want the information getting out."

Ted shook his head. "You're reaching pretty far just to deny Kyle is a drinker."

Why wouldn't he listen to me? "Kyle isn't a drunk. Period. If this accident doesn't have to do with Shelly, then it has to do with his brother Alex."

Ted gave me a pitying look. "Now you're making up things."

"You've met Kyle. You know he's a good guy." I didn't know why I appealed to Ted's good sense. One look at Roxy proved Ted was no character judge.

"You've always been like this."

A geyser of anger started in my gut. I narrowed my eyes, ready for the fight. "Like what?"

Ted leaned back, coffee cup in hand, as if he wasn't

insulting me but simply having a pleasant chat. "Believing in everyone. You'll march in a pride parade in Lincoln, hand out money to beggars on street corners, hell, I've known you to vote Democrat at least once."

He said it all like it was a bad thing.

"Hiring Red Owl without the consensus of the other sheriffs, especially when you're the most junior member and only in office a few months, well, that shows you're more interested in doing the PC thing than the smartest thing."

I spoke slowly, struggling to hold back my temper. "I shouldn't need to keep saying this: Kyle is an excellent deputy. Trained, reliable, smart, hardworking. And if that wasn't enough—which it is—he's the only one out here qualified for the job."

Ted tilted his head to the side and stared at me, waiting for me to acknowledge my mistake.

I bit my cheek, and when he didn't yield, I said, "At the time we hired him, you were using a cane and had months of physical therapy ahead of you."

"Because I'd been shot in the line of duty."

I shouldn't, but I did. "Duty? That's what you call conveniently being at the crime scene because you were screwing your girlfriend?"

That ignited a spark in his blue eyes. "Careful, your bitterness is showing."

I slapped my palm on the table. "Frankly, your affair with Roxy was the best thing you ever did for me. Because of that, I have a job I love, and I don't have to deal with your lying and narcissism every day."

"You stole the best things in my life from me. You didn't even want to be sheriff before you ran against me."

I stole...what? "I had to make a living once you kicked me off Frog Creek."

"That was your choice. I never wanted you to divorce me."

Did he hear himself? "But you didn't want to give up Roxy. You can't have us both."

He didn't seem to draw the lines. "Still, you didn't have to steal the job I loved."

Oh, for the...just...ugh. "Poor you."

A hand on my shoulder made me jump. Aunt Tutti, in her violet scrubs, frowned at me. "I think you two ought to take this outside."

I let my gaze shift from her around the cafeteria. People in scrubs and street clothes sat at most of the tables, and they found sudden interest in their food or each other. They were curious enough to watch our spat and probably whisper it to their friends and relations, but polite enough to pretend they hadn't noticed.

I stood. "Will you be at David's class this afternoon or not?"

Ted sighed and nodded at me.

With a peck to Tutti's cheek, I walked out with as much dignity as any humiliated ex-wife/sheriff could and went to check on Kyle once more before throwing myself into another bad situation.

24

Fresh, clean ozone rose into the air as I crossed the hospital parking lot to my car. Lilacs pushed their sweetness into the cool air, and I wanted to bury my nose in them, wishing Kyle's pale and motionless body wasn't in his hospital bed. The forecast called for several more days of rain, so the sight of sun flashing across the hills, highlighting the neon green of the new grass, was a gift, although wasted on me.

I should have rushed to help Kyle when he'd called me last night. Why did I let my foul mood answer for me? My basement could have waited. What kind of sheriff was I to let my personal life interfere with the job?

Something Kyle found out got him in trouble. Kyle was tracking Shelly. The kid from the Olson place, Max, wanted to talk to Kyle. Barnett was lurking around the school in Sand Gap. Alex said Kyle had asked to meet him in Dry Creek. Barnett and Frankie had Alex cornered. Max had been on his way to Frankie's yesterday morning. How did this all tie together?

If there was a connection with any of this, I couldn't find it. Thinking felt like the click when you turn the key on a dead battery. Every muscle twitched with fatigue, and I had to roll down the windows and sing to keep myself awake.

After what seemed like a lifetime, I made it home to my cabin on the lake. Poupon jumped from the couch, anxious to go outside and do what dogs do. The house smelled damp, but no water rippled on the basement floor, and the fans Josh and I had set by the windows kept up their roar. A bag of groceries sat on my kitchen counter containing coffee, bread, a jar of peanut butter, and orange juice. Someone in my family felt bad about the voting can. Maybe I didn't feel like forgiving anyone, but the coffee made me happy.

I fed Poupon, and he accepted my apologies for leaving him alone. Kyle deserved a friend to find his attacker, but I couldn't help him unless I slept at least a little. I bargained for three hours, hoping that would revive me enough to go on.

When my alarm sounded, I'd been running from house to house on a busy street, leaving bits of myself behind. My arms, ears, nose, and one eye were goners, so I wasn't too upset to wake up and get going.

I phoned the hospital before I swung my feet to the floor. Aunt Tutti must have slipped home for her own nap because I talked to a different nurse. She told me Kyle's condition hadn't changed, not the best news, but I suppose it could be worse.

I stared at the ceiling while late morning air seeped through the curtainless window. Redheaded blackbirds squawked in the orchestra, and it seemed the day had set the table and invited the sun over for coffee.

My mind was like a stormy lake, questions floundering in white caps of worry. Someone had brutally attacked Kyle. On purpose. I intended to find out who.

The extra scoop of coffee I'd dropped into the coffeemaker helped clear my head. I picked up my phone and dialed Josh, feeling like a turd in a bucket. "I've got to cancel our dinner tonight. I'm in the middle of something for work."

Josh sounded happy to hear from me. "Glad you called. I wondered how everything worked out last night, and then I worried when I heard Kyle's in the hospital. Sure wish we could get together, but I understand."

I'd spent scads of time this past year wound up about people worrying about me. I was the damned sheriff, after all, and I should not be worried over. But it felt kind of good when Josh said he'd been concerned. Different, somehow. "I really appreciate your help last night."

"No problem. Sounds like a few folks had flooding. It was a big rain."

"I'll be running around today. I could drop your pump at your ranch if I get out that way."

He hmmed. "Dad might get spooky if you showed up out there. He likes his routine. I'm putting in a dog door for Olin Riek. Why don't I meet you in the Long Branch in an hour and buy you lunch?"

Showing my face in the Long Branch made me cringe. Still, I had to get over the voting can, and putting it behind me right away was better than letting it fester. Having lunch with Josh sounded nice, if I didn't have a deputy and friend with his brains bashed in and a need to find out who did it. "I really can't take the time for lunch, but I'll meet you there with the pump." That would give me time to run to the courthouse and see about building permits for the Olson place. I hoped that information would provide probable cause.

I scarfed down a peanut butter sandwich, sipped my extra-strong coffee, showered, and loaded Josh's sump pump into my trunk.

Before I left the house, I grabbed the picture of Brian and his classmates. I wanted to start checking into those friends.

"Baxter's guy might be the best, but..." I couldn't simply sit and do nothing. That's the truth.

I propped the screen door open and left the front door ajar. Poupon sat in the middle of the living room, and I was sure he understood exactly what I said. "I can't take you with me today. You have a full food dish, plenty of water, and can go outside. Don't run off." As if there was a chance he'd expend energy if he didn't have to. Diane's cockamamie story about a new fence because Poupon ran away frayed at the edges.

At the back of the courthouse, I used care to quietly click the door closed, then held my breath and snuck up the stairs, hoping to avoid Betty and the Case of the Missing Budget.

The commissioner's room still emitted the stench of scorched coffee, and a few papers littered the long conference table. A new commissioner had been appointed to fill out Clete Rasmussen's term. Clete had been commissioner for decades until the scandal that broke moments after he swore me in last January.

Illogical though it may be, a few people held me responsible for Clete's downfall. People in Grand County didn't cotton to change, and with an institution like Clete, the crash could hit hard.

While I debated the wisdom of another cup of coffee and contemplated the state of affairs in Grand County, Betty zipped into the room, face set.

"Budget?"

Guess I hadn't been as stealthy as I'd hoped, either that or Betty's Sheriff Detector Ring worked great. "You heard about Kyle, right?"

Her face fell in sympathy. "I am sorry for that boy. But that was last night, and you promised me the papers yesterday."

The front door opened, and I almost prayed for an emergency to get me out of this. Betty and I turned in anticipation.

Trey Ridnoir glanced inside the room, probably on his way to my office. He altered his path and poked his head in. "Hi, Kate."

That didn't sound official, but I jumped at it. I gave Betty a serious nod. "Excuse me."

She planted her hands on her hips. "Of course." Her motherly frown followed. "Today. I need those papers today."

I refrained from making her a promise I wouldn't deliver and hurried out to Trey. I led him out the front doors into the fresh-smelling spring air. It held moisture but was a darned sight warmer than yesterday. "What are you doing up here again?"

Crimson started at the base of his neck, where his gray uniform collar buttoned tight, and colored his face. "Heard your deputy got worked over. Wanted to check up on you."

I gave him an exasperated look. Last time we'd worked together, Trey's concern over my welfare cost him a bullet to his leg. "We aren't going to get into that again, are we?"

Duly chastised, he shrugged. "It was an excuse to see you."

It felt like the floor dropped. My mind stuttered and looked for the ladder out of this pit. "Oh. Have you had a lot of rain in Ogallala?"

He glowed like a branding iron in the fire. "Um. Yeah. Four inches in the last few days."

We stood in silence, and I tried to think of something to say.

He got there first. "I was wondering. If you?" He hesitated and swallowed. "Ted called."

Oh for the love of moldy mildew.

Trey swallowed and started again. "He, well, I imagine Roxy put him up to it."

No doubt.

"He said you might be interested..."

His throat closed, and I wanted to help him out. "Half the darned town is trying to set me up. I don't know why they think it's any of their business. I'm officially letting you off the hook. I'm not a prized pig on auction."

I didn't think it was possible for him to turn redder, but he looked like a Husker flag. "Of course not. No." He let out a breath that must have burned his lungs. "I think you're great. I do."

Ted might not have been a prince, but if being married saved me from conversations as painful as this, I had another reason to regret my divorce. "Thanks."

"But I don't think I could stand being with you."

Ka-wham. It wasn't that I carried a torch for Trey, but admittedly, that stung.

He babbled on. "That didn't sound right. I mean, I like you a lot, and if we were together, knowing that you could be in danger, well, that would make me crazy."

I laughed. "Thank goodness. I thought maybe it was because I was a slimy monster who slithered on shore looking for my first meal."

Tension eased from his face and shoulders and rolled onto the pavement. "Far from it."

Now was a good time to swerve from the personal and get to business. "Have you dealt with preppers before?"

It took him a moment to catch up to the change in subject. "You mean end-of-world, religious types?"

I tipped my head to catch the sun. "Not really. Maybe people who want to live off-grid."

He thought about it, his skin turning a more natural color. "I'd say most of them are harmless. They distrust the government or society or what have you, want to rely on themselves, so they find someplace like the Sandhills."

I walked him toward his trooper car parked at the curb. "The preppers I found seem pretty secretive and mean."

He mulled. "There are places I've heard of where a group of militia get together and plot the overthrow of a government, maybe send bombs or anthrax."

Marty and Rhonda didn't seem like overthrowing types. "How can I get a warrant to check it out?"

Trey shook his head. "You really can't, unless you've got some compelling evidence of a crime or intent to commit a crime."

Hiding an eighteen-year-old runaway wasn't a crime. "What else?"

He leaned back on his car, arms crossed. "There are weird cult things, like Waco."

I pictured Rhonda kowtowing to Marty or worshipping anything. "I didn't get a sense of religion going on."

Trey grinned now as if we were playing a game. "How about organized crime?"

He'd hit closer to their personalities. "Mafia? What could they be doing out here?"

He leaned forward, getting into it. "I don't know. Maybe they're laundering money or running from the law."

That seemed more like Rhonda and Marty.

"Or they could be hiding stolen goods."

I needed to have a look around that big barn and the chicken house with no chickens. "Thanks."

He stood close, looking down at me. "Whatever you're planning, I would be happy to go with you."

I started to protest, saw he was teasing, and grinned. He surprised me by landing his palm on my shoulder and pulling me in for a one-armed hug. "Glad to have you as a friend and colleague."

That put a fine period to the end of any romantic notions.

Another one bites the dust, but I couldn't generate remorse. I slapped his back.

A black pickup pulled up Main Street and turned toward us. Josh.

Dang. "What time is it?" I pulled out my phone and realized I was twenty minutes late to the Long Branch.

Josh pulled a U-turn at the intersection and glanced our way. He registered me and Trey looking all chatty. Like a stupid teenager, I snapped my hand up and plastered an eager look on my face, trying too hard to show that I was glad to see him, not guilty or embarrassed, as I was, but didn't want to be.

Without stopping for his pump, Josh continued back down Main Street.

Trey spun toward the street to see why I'd gone spastic. He looked back at me. "Where you meeting him? Here?"

"I, well, not really." That sounded lame, and I felt my face heat up.

A "bye," "see ya," a few asides about the next training and the flood damage he'd seen on his drive up—your basic ten-minute Sandhills' goodbye—and I watched Trey drive off.

I should chase after Josh on the pretense of giving him the pump. But really, I wanted to make sure we were still...what? Friends?

Didn't matter. I had sheriff work to do.

It started with some quick Internet searches of the names on the back of Brian's class picture. Easy enough, since at least three of these guys were lit in pretty bright spotlights. A lawyer, a real estate broker, and a rich guy who sat on about two dozen boards. Within an hour of sitting at the computer, I'd contacted the offices of those three and given messages to their gatekeepers.

It was a start.

25

Not that I doubted the cliché about the rain making the grass grow, but, holy fat cows, the blades practically shot up a foot and deepened three shades of green since last we'd had full sunshine. The hills popped with yellow and blue wildflowers, the roadsides dripped weeds onto the gravel shoulder.

What a waste of a perfect day—poking my head where it decidedly would not be welcomed. I turned off the highway at the unmarked dirt road to the Olson Ranch and rolled down my window to soak up as much budding spring happiness as I could, fighting guilt that Kyle would miss this—and probably more perfect days.

Because I hadn't taken him seriously. I owed Kyle more than duty. I owed him justice.

A brown long-nosed curlew let out her shriek and dove in front of the cruiser. Maybe because they were so ugly, or because they showed up as if bringing spring with them, curlews were one of my favorites. A meadowlark let out her trill, so beautiful. Mom said it always sounded to her like, "There's jelly in the courthouse." This was the sort of day I loved to be out working cattle or mending fence. Not tracking violent criminals.

Thinking of people who steal girls and attack my friends hardened my resolve. When I reached the locked steel gate, I grabbed the bolt cutters and made short work of it. Marty and Rhonda would spend a small fortune on padlocks if they didn't start cooperating. On the way back to my car, I glanced at the flattened grass of a trail road heading over the hill to the east. The tire tracks veering from the main road must have been made since the last rain, possibly that morning.

I topped the hill, gazing down on the headquarters. Far from the abandoned feel when I tromped into the ranch at dawn two days ago, now the place buzzed with activity, all centered around the house. Obviously, I surprised them when I slipped over the last hill because no one fired a cannon at me.

The hillside had collapsed in a scene similar to those you see on the news from Malibu. But instead of some movie star's mansion, the cistern lodged halfway down on its side. Beneath the three-thousand-gallon barrel, it looked like a thousand-year flood ran its course. Marty and Rhonda darted from the front of the house, around the back, then to the front again.

By the time I pulled up, Marty and Rhonda stood in front of the house, arms crossed, legs spread wide in challenge, their deranged version of *American Gothic*. I had barely climbed out of the car, pocketing my keys, since I'd learned a valuable lesson about leaving keys in cop cars—may my old cruiser rest in peace—when Rhonda advanced on me.

She wore a shabby turquoise velour sweat suit, and her dirty blond hair with inch-long dark roots looked like she hadn't washed it in a week. "What the hell are you doing out here? I know the gate was locked this time. You goddamn owe me a lock if you cut it off."

I watched her hands and kept an eye on Marty to make sure he didn't reach for a gun, either. They gave off a dangerous stink. "Police business. Since I have no way to contact you, I had no choice." I pulled the lock from my jacket pocket and held it out to her.

She folded her arms across her chest and curled her lip. "What do you want?"

I pocketed the lock and took in the sand dunes butting up against the house and the open basement windows, the giant cistern overturned with the wrecked top laying downhill, the cylinder empty like a spilled beer glass on the hillside above the house. Looked like the same cloudburst that wreaked such havoc at my cottage had settled over their place.

Marty joined Rhonda in front of me. "If you don't have a warrant, you need to get your ass out of here."

That Jersey accent in the middle of the Sandhills sounded mighty strange. "I'm here to see your building permits."

Rhonda shot Marty a can-you-believe-this look.

He took an intimidating step toward me. "This ain't no city or suburb with an HOA. This is our land, and we can do anything we damned well please out here."

"More or less." I gave my words an airy tone. "But you're required to register building with the county assessor and have the place inspected for code."

He raised his hand and unholstered his finger to poke it toward my face. "That's bullshit, and you need to leave."

I considered biting his finger, but not seriously. "You have some flooding?"

It worked. He dropped his hand and looked confused.

Rhonda joined us, a little too close for my taste. Her breath hadn't improved much since the other morning. Stale coffee and permanent garlic. "Not your business, honey."

"Building inspection, remember?"

Rhonda let her lids half close in menace. "Send the county assessor or building inspector. Make an appointment."

I studied the hillside and toppled cistern. "My basement flooded in that storm. Made a big mess."

Marty held up his thumb and forefinger and gave me the world's smallest record player and a completely unsympathetic grimace. "Your doctor called and said you're late for your lobotomy."

"Are you having a hard time bailing out your basement?"

"We don't have a flooded basement, and everything out here is peachy," Rhonda said.

I nodded. "Okay. You can see how I might jump to that conclusion, what with the buckets scattered on the ground, the basement window open, and the upturned cistern."

"You're seeing things," Marty said.

Their words weren't frightening and I didn't see any guns or knives, but they scared me. Threat wafted off them with the garlic and body odor. One thing I'd learned from growing up a Fox, though: Never let them see you flinch. "Probably. But, coincidently, I have a sump pump in my trunk."

"A what-what?" Rhonda asked.

I gave them my back as I retreated to my trunk. I hefted the pump out. "See? You set it in the basement and hook up a hose. Crank it on and let it pump for you."

Marty jerked his head toward the pump and spoke to Rhonda. "That's what I was trying to tell you. That's gonna work a whole lot better than buckets and mops."

She swatted his arm. "But we got buckets and mops. We ain't got a *sump pump*." She said the last two words with an exaggerated Western accent. I wanted to tell her I didn't sound like that.

Instead, I lit up with a Sandhills' smile and set the pump down. "It's right here. You can use it."

Marty narrowed his eyes. "How much?"

I shook my head. "Not for sale. But you can borrow it." I leaned on the grill of my car. "I'll wait."

Rhonda eyed the pump and then her house, obviously weighing whether to trust someone to help or go it alone. Resigned to accept a favor, she gave her regular sneer. "If you just can't help yourself being a do-gooder, then fine. We could use the damned pump."

Marty offered a humph and picked up the pump. He scuttled with it up the walk and into the house. Rhonda muttered a grudging thanks and sauntered after him.

I didn't think she'd let me, but I had to try. I followed her to the concrete slab and had a foot poised to cross the threshold. She blocked the door before she opened it and turned to me. She glared until I backed all the way off the concrete pad of a front porch.

"You wait in your car." She walked me toward my car.

"It's a really beautiful day. Do you mind if I wait outside?"

She aimed her finger at me. "Suit yourself. You got no permission to go anywhere but right here by your car. We got signs posted. Trespassers will be shot."

I propped myself on the fender. "Posting a sign doesn't make killing someone legal."

"You think I give a shit about legal, Rizzoli and Isles?"

"That's two women, right?"

She slashed her finger in front of me, then showed a wolf grin and spoke in a singsong way. "Stay put. I'll get your pump back to you in a jiffy."

They went to work. Rhonda's unhappy cat screech pelted from the basement window and Marty's answers sounded like a boxer's punches as they fired the pump and eventually opened up the front door and began hauling things from the basement.

Crates of dried food, plastic fifty-gallon barrels, and sealed boxes accumulated on the concrete porch.

"You guys want some help with that?" Ever so cheerful, I hollered from my perch on the car.

My offer didn't merit a shut up from either of them. I didn't know how big their basement was or how much water had seeped in, but I figured it would take at least two hours, maybe longer, to pump it.

They bickered, hefted boxes and containers outside, and retreated inside. The gaps of time between appearances on the porch lengthened, and I figured they were wearing down. They weren't paying any attention to me. Like a baseball player stealing bases, I ventured farther and farther from my car.

My goal was the chicken house. The kid had taken a plate of food out there a couple of nights ago. I hadn't heard so much as a cluck, and yet, it was locked up tight. The windows blacked out. Obviously, they were hiding something in there. The barn, too. No animals in sight.

I'd snuck halfway to the chicken house, and still they hadn't noticed. Together they hauled a wooden crate the size of a coffin and placed it on the porch. I couldn't hear their words, but they shot them at each other like bullets from ten paces.

The chicken house had a hundred-square-foot yard fenced with chicken wire and two low water troughs along with a metal pan—all the normal setup for chickens. And yet, no birds. The prefab shed was made of pressed wood with an asphalt shingled roof that sloped forward, creating a nice shelter for the entryway. It snugged up next to the barn, which was also shut tight.

I let myself through the wire gate in the fence. The contraption felt rickety, as if constructed quickly or without expertise. A padlock hung from the door of the shed, not like any Sandhills chicken house I knew. Who needed to lock in their hens?

No one. But if you stored stolen goods—or people—you might want to protect them. I inched toward the door, not sure what I planned to do, but maybe I'd see some clue.

"What are you doing?" The angry voice stabbed between my shoulder blades. I whirled around.

Marty hadn't misplaced his gun after all. There it was, attached to his hand and pointing at my head.

Nothing like that feeling of your heart slamming into your chest and the air knocked from your lungs. Guns pointed at me tended to do that.

The string of curses flying from Rhonda wilted the new grass. "I told you to stay put. You've got no right to go snooping around."

Hand up. I regained my breath, though my heart still pounded. Would he shoot me and bury me behind the barn?

Rhonda must have thought Marty's gun had it covered, because her hands were empty. "You have a chicken fetish or something."

Might as well call it. "You don't have chickens in here." I casually lowered my hands, inching my right hand toward the gun tucked behind my hip.

Rhonda's shrewd eyes watched my hand rest on my gun. "We don't?"

Marty seemed curious. "What makes you think we don't have chickens?"

They weren't going to shoot me, since Rhonda let me touch my gun. Feeling brave, I wasn't above a little belligerence. "Aside from the fact you don't seem like chicken kind of people?"

Arrogance spit from Marty. "Yeah, aside from that."

"It's afternoon, and there's not a peep from the hen house. If you had birds, the roosters would be going crazy and the hens would be carrying on."

Rhonda swatted Marty's arm. "That damned kid forgot to let out the lousy birds."

Marty lurched toward me, and I managed to not flinch. He grabbed the padlock and twisted, making me feel like a dope that it hadn't even been locked. He popped the lock off and flung open the door. "We trained them to sleep in."

Amid a blizzard of feathers and a chorus of clucking, hens fluttered from the shed, squawking and pecking, admonishing one and all.

I stared at them.

Rhonda plastered on her custom sneer. "Blackout paint, lights on a timer until midnight. We're not morning people."

Marty got behind me and herded me out the gate and toward my car. "Just because it's always been done that way doesn't mean we have to. We're smarter than any dumb birds. They can adjust to our schedule."

I swung my head back to see the hens happily pecking in their yard. Though I liked to hear a rooster crow first thing, I couldn't argue with the logic of putting chickens on a human schedule. Different didn't always mean wrong, even in the case of Rhonda and Marty.

I made a point of looking around. "Where's Max?"

Marty and Rhonda went still and cold as a gravel pit lake. They passed a tense look between them, and Marty said, "He's not here."

"How old is he, anyway?"

Marty moved toward me, heading me toward my car. "Not your business."

I slowed my steps. "Because he looks like he ought to be in school, but I've never seen him at HHS."

Rhonda whirled around and bumped into me. "He's homeschooled, so not your problem."

I backed up a pace to give myself personal space. "Why so secretive? Is there something you're hiding?"

Marty poked me in the back. "We're not hurting anybody. We came out here to be left alone. Get it? So leave us alone."

Rhonda scuttled to the house. "I'll get your damned pump and you can be on your way."

While she was gone, Marty prodded me toward my car. I could have put up more of a fight than I did, but one of the white pickups was missing from the carport. I had an idea where it might be and who was driving.

Rhonda returned in a toot and opened the back door of my cruiser. She tossed Josh's pump onto the seat, ignoring the water soaking into the upholstery.

Marty leaned over, his breath hot and stale on my face. "Fair warning, Sheriff. You come back here again and we're going to shoot first."

26

I didn't bother closing the steel gate on my way out and swung my cruiser off the road onto the trail. Pete and Barnett had their matching Broncos, but my ol' Charger held its own cross-country, even without four-wheel drive. I followed the tracks of crushed grass up one hill and around another. Marty and Rhonda weren't real ranchers, but they might have a few head of cattle and therefore a windmill or two that might need checking.

Around one more hill, I hit the jackpot. The white pickup sat next to a half-filled stock tank, the windmill clanking overhead. Max's fuzzy head bent over the overflow pipe, and he yanked a soaking tumbleweed free, tossing it to the side.

A handful of motley cattle milled around the windmill. If anything proved to me Marty and Rhonda weren't here to raise beef, it was this collection of rangy critters passing for a cattle herd. Thin, a couple had one horn, even a mixed-breed bull mingled in the bunch.

Max's head jerked in my direction when he heard the car.

He hesitated a moment, and even from a hundred feet

away, I saw his panic. He looked from me to the pickup and finally got to his feet and ran toward it. I gunned my engine.

His door shut and the pickup's engine turned over, but I pulled up in front of him. This guy wasn't nearly as slick or quick-thinking as I imagined his parents were. For instance, he didn't seem to consider backing up to escape.

On the other hand, where was he going to run? Maybe he wasn't quite as dense as I thought. I jumped out of my car, made sure my gun nestled on my back hip, and walked to the pickup.

Max sat with his hands on the wheel, watching me with scared eyes.

I stopped a few feet away from his door and let the windmill clank a few times. The cows wandered away, not too disturbed but not wanting to be close to the commotion.

"Step out of the pickup."

Max's shoulders dropped, and he lowered his head. The door opened, and his tennis shoes plopped into the sand. He backed up and closed the door. "Don't shoot me."

That's not what I expected him to say. "Why would I shoot you?"

He didn't look at me. "Aren't you working with Barnett?"

This surprised me even more. "Why would I be working with him?"

Max ventured a glance at me. "I don't know. I thought maybe he sent you here."

What was going on? "I'm looking for Shelly Red Owl. Do you know where she is?"

He seemed to catch a breath before he answered, his voice strained. "No."

"But she was here."

He didn't answer, so I bluffed. "I know she was. You brought her food to the chicken house."

He looked confused by that. "I feed the chickens every night."

Okay, that hadn't worked. "I saw you bring her here on your dirt bike after the car wreck."

His eyes looked like that of a colt after he sees his first snake. "Okay. Okay, yeah. But she's not here now."

"Where is she?"

He shook his head.

"Did your parents hurt her?"

That threw him. "My parents?"

"Marty and Rhonda."

His jaw dropped. "They're not my parents. We aren't even related."

A cow mooed as if Max had surprised her, too. "You'd better explain."

Max looked at me a moment, then shifted his focus to the tank. "Yeah, so we moved out here about two years ago. Rhonda and Marty came first, then us."

I waved him to continue. "Who is we, and what are you doing out here?"

"Dad and the guy who owns this place had an accounting business in New Jersey. Marty had a bunch of money he needed to..." Max paused and searched for a word. "Invest. So, about that time, Mom started reading all these books about EMPs and, you know, just kind of what happens if the electricity goes out."

"EMPs?" I asked.

Max looked disappointed in my ignorance. "Electromagnetic pulse. Could happen because of a sunspot or terrorism or just about anything. It can knock out the power grid and then, you know, the zombie apocalypse."

This might or might not bring me to what happened to Shelly. "Right."

The windmill clanked in the light breeze. Max rocked a little as if burning off nerves. "So Marty comes in with all this money, and he's kind of interested in getting out of town. You know, far away."

I was starting to get the gist. "So, the Olson nephew sells Marty and Rhonda this land, they get your folks to come out here and help them set up to be totally off-grid. Your family is protected from EMPs, being the prepper types. Marty and Rhonda get to be in their own private witness protection program."

He nodded. "Something like that. But my folks went home last winter. They couldn't take the isolation and, well, they hated Marty and Rhonda."

I could understand that.

Max went on. "Mom and Dad did all the work. They had a big garden and canned vegetables, took care of the chickens and butchered them. All the maintenance. It was too much work to keep it all going. And then, I think Mom got lonesome out here."

This sounded so farfetched. There had to be more going on. "Your family came out here and you weren't allowed off the ranch? Ever?"

"Marty and Rhonda were afraid if anyone knew we were here, the guys they were hiding from would find them. They let us hire people from the rez if we needed extra help."

"And your parents agreed?"

"Marty owns this place." Max raised his fingers in air quotes. "He *let* us live here for free because no way my folks could afford a ranch like this."

"But now your folks are gone. Why are you here?"

His rocking accelerated, and his eyes flicked from the tank to the cows to my car and back, everywhere but on me. "I...I like it here, so I stayed."

That was a bald-faced lie. "Why were you looking for Kyle Red Owl the other day?"

"I wasn't. Well, yeah, I was. But, you know. I just kind of wanted to talk to him. About, well, about some Indian stuff."

"Not about Shelly?"

He clenched his fists and looked directly into my eyes. "Shelly isn't here. Stop looking for her."

"Where is she?"

He turned cherry red under his mop of hair, and I thought maybe he'd start throwing fists. "You want to know where the trouble started? Find Alex. It's him."

27

I didn't hold out much hope I'd find Alex at home, but it seemed like the place to start, so I took to the road. A meteor slammed into my windshield, and I flinched. Expecting spider-webbed glass and flaming upholstery, I was surprised as a heavy film of water spread across the windshield. Another burst exploded, more water. These weren't raindrops but some kind of celestial weaponry. I rolled my window down a crack to smell the rain on the warm road. Making the grass grow? We'd be lucky if it didn't leave craters in the hills to become blowouts when the rain quit. Unless, of course, this was the start of another Noah's flood incident, and then it wouldn't matter if I found out who attacked Kyle or not.

The rain settled into a steady rhythm as I drove through Dry Creek, noting the same people hanging out on the street, a few rusty vehicles scattered at the liquor stores, the same general feel of despair. The wipers carried the conversation on my way from Sand Gap, past the vehicle carcasses and sailing Walmart bags to Rita Red Owl's trailer.

Sun burst from behind a cauldron of black clouds. Typical bipolar Sandhills weather.

Rita's place looked every bit as forlorn and empty as it had before. If any vehicle had been there in the past two days, all traces were wiped out by the last squall. I parked close to the trailer and made my way across the mud and weeds and up the cinderblock steps to pull the decimated screen back and knock on the door.

No one answered. Maybe Kyle's Aunt Birdie had taken Rita to her house after all. I waited a moment more, then tried the doorknob. It turned, and I creaked the dented door open.

"Hello?" I hollered through the crack.

A slight moan greeted me, and I shoved the door open. Whoever beat up Kyle might have taken Shelly and was after the whole family. The smell of spoiled potatoes and puke hit me full force and stopped me. It took a second for my eyes to adjust to the dim light, and when they did, I saw Rita on her side on the living room floor.

I rushed to her and put my head close, nearly retching at her smell. "Rita. Wake up. Are you okay?" All the while I tapped on her cheeks, soft with wrinkles.

No blood on her clothes and she didn't have a fever. A line of dried saliva and vomit ran from her mouth down her cheek, where it puddled. She moaned again and opened her eyes.

"Rita. It's Kate Fox, Grand County sheriff."

Her mouth opened and closed a couple of times, and her eyes fought for focus. "Sheriff?"

I put a hand under her shoulders and helped her sit up. "Are you okay?"

Her feet collided with a pile of beer cans, making them rattle. She squeezed her eyes closed and rubbed her temples. "He's not here."

"Alex?" I squatted in front of her, trying to ignore the stench of stale beer breath, unwashed body, and the puke.

She squinted at me and rolled to her hands and knees. "All of them. No one left here but me."

I helped her to stand, and we wobbled toward the front door. "What do you mean?"

She leaned on the doorframe and swayed. "It was that man. He ruined me. I had a life and something to look forward to. You think Shelly had a future? What about me? I was gonna leave the rez."

Rita's blood alcohol level had to be well on the way to pickled. I wouldn't get anything useful from her, but that seemed less important than getting her some help. "I'm going to take you into Sand Gap. Maybe go stay with your sister for a while?"

She let me lead her outside before her legs gave way and she plopped on a cinderblock. "He promised me. Said he'd love me and take care of me. And then what?" She swayed, and I clutched at her arm to keep her from careening off the side of the step.

"Leave me with a baby. I can't do nothing with a baby. So I gotta stay on the rez and get married to some drunk."

Tears sprouted. "I was gonna go to college, jus' like Shelly. Had a scholarship. Gonna be a nurse."

I managed to hoist her to her feet and drag her arm over my shoulder. I had to stoop to keep her feet on the ground.

"That man. He don' care. Not abou' his son. I tried to get him to pay, but he won' give me nothing. Says he'll send me to jail if I tell anyone about him." She stopped and tugged on my arm so I looked at her. Her eyes widened to drive home the point. "An' he can do it. He can."

I dragged her a step before she staggered along with me.

She pounded the air with her free hand. "He don' love Kyle. And tha's what's wrong with him."

My heart stuttered. Kyle? I tried to keep my voice even. "Kyle's father doesn't love him?"

She flopped over, making me bend along with her. She jerked her arm from my shoulder, planted both hands on her knees, and retched before dropping to the ground. "Then they took Darrel." She started to cry. "He was gonna take care of me. He promised."

I wanted to get back to Kyle. "You mean Kyle's father? He was going to take care of you?"

She twisted her head to look at me. "Darrel. My good boy. He wouldn't leave me. But they killed him."

For a tiny woman, Rita took a lot of wrangling. I succeeded in pulling her to her feet and began our trek to my car. A ding alerted me to a text, but I didn't have an extra hand to check it. It would have to wait.

Rita wasn't making any sense, and every time I asked about Kyle's father, she wandered behind another hill.

I opened the back door, wedged the pump on the floor, and settled Rita into the back seat. She kept a running monologue about Darrel being the best of the lot, until we reached the highway and I tried to redirect her. I doubted I'd get any real information, but I'd had enough of her glowing tribute.

"Do you know where Shelly is?" I watched her in the rearview mirror.

She slouched against the back seat, her head barely above the windows. Her face contorted. "I tried to tell her. I said to leave the white boys alone. But Kyle got hold of her. Got her thinkin' the white world is good. And they took her."

An electric current shot through me. "Who took her?"

Rita started to cry again. "They got her. Gonna treat her like a whore. Gonna ruin her life. Like mine."

Rita didn't give me much, but her rambling made a kind of sense. It solidified a nagging thought I'd been inching toward.

"And Alex? Do you know where he is?"

She sniffed and wiped at her eyes. "He's the one that did it. He made this happen."

I took Rita to The Stop, and Gordon helped me get her into the store. We made a bed for her on a broken-down loveseat in Gordon's office. He assured me he'd call his mother and get Rita to her house. With any luck, they'd keep her from going back to her trailer when she sobered up.

I practically ran to my car and pulled out my phone. I meant to call Pete but was stopped by the text I'd forgotten.

What a sucker-punch to the gut.

"Leave me alone." Even though I knew, I texted back, "Who is this?"

I stared at my phone, and against all laws of physics, willed her to appear by my side. A toucan icon appeared on the screen to the ding of the new text alert.

Carly. I'd given her a stuffed toucan when she was tiny. Birdy Bird was her best friend, and she knew I'd understand the icon.

I typed fast. "Come home. I love you."

I waited. Nothing. For a full five minutes, I clutched my phone. It took me a while before I realized I'd been repeating, "Please, please, please."

Still nothing.

The calls I'd made to the men in Brian's picture. Is this why she contacted me? Had news gotten back to Carly? If so, how? Who?

My first impulse was to call Baxter. But he'd climb all over me about interfering in the investigation. We'd have a go-around about the professional knowing how to work a missing person case and about how I was too emotional and hot-headed.

What I needed to do now was find Kyle's attacker. This was my job.

I continued with my original plan. I tapped my feet while I waited several light-years for the two rings it took for Pete Grainger to pick up.

After I identified myself, I started right in. "Did you get some rest?" The last thing I needed was a muddle-brained sheriff.

He hesitated. "Well, yes. I'm sorry about the shooting. But I'm better."

"Can you meet me in Dry Creek?"

He didn't question me. "Of course. When?"

"Now. I need you to go with me to Barnett's place before he gets back from court."

Grainger sounded grave. "Why?"

Wished he was driving and not jawing. "I'll explain it all when you get here, but I need you to help me."

"You know I'll do my best, Kate. But can you tell me what this is about?"

I took a deep breath, every bit of me thudding with what I feared. "I think he's involved in human trafficking."

28

When Pete pulled into Frankie's parking lot, I quit pacing and jumped in the passenger seat of his Bronco. He left it in park and turned to face me. "You're wrong about Lee."

I'd expected this. "I know you and Barnett are good friends. But everything points to this. I think it started a couple of years ago when these people moved onto the Olson place."

Grainger gave me a quizzical look. "I thought no one lived there."

I nodded. "They've been hiding out. Kept all the buildings looking abandoned on the outside but fixed up on the inside. They have it all barricaded like they expect World War III."

"And you think Lee's got something to do with them?"

"Barnett picks up the girls on the rez and hands them off to Marty and Rhonda, probably through the young guy who lives out there."

Pete was full of explosive energy trapped behind the wheel. "Sounds farfetched."

I was losing him. "I think they took Kyle's sister and Kyle figured it out. That's why they tried to kill him."

Pete put the Bronco in reverse and backed out. He straightened the wheel and started us down the highway toward Potsville.

After a long time, he pulled in a deep breath and said, "Lee isn't selling girls. I'll show you what's going on."

Lee and Sally Barnett lived about two miles outside of Potsville, a twenty-minute drive from Dry Creek. On the way, Pete spoke in bursts. "Lee has a lot more bark than bite."

"His teeth look pretty sharp to me," I grumbled, watching the play of sunlight on the prairie as bear-like clouds tumbled across the sky. Would it kill Mother Nature to give us one whole sunny day, without driving rain and wicked wind?

Pete was like a dog without his daily run and yet he drove exactly sixty-five, the speed limit. "He's not had an easy life."

After seeing the folks in Dry Creek and on the rez, I didn't feel a lot of sympathy for Lee's harsh experiences. "Whatever he's been through is no cause to treat people, especially the Lakota, worse than livestock."

Pete rubbed his chin. "Lee's got a lot more compassion than you give him credit for."

"Ha." I didn't try to hide my disbelief. "I see him more like the Bad Samaritan."

In his starched shirt, Pete hinted at a smile. "You don't know him."

I folded my arms and considered when the clouds would dump again. "He doesn't seem like a terribly deep man, more like a mean dog with a broken leash."

Pete flashed dark eyes at me and lectured as if talking to his kids. "Lee doesn't hate the Lakota. Just the opposite. It kills him to see the poverty and wasted lives."

"Uh-huh." This attitude showed the same lack of clear thinking as shooting wildly in the parking lot last night.

"Lee would probably kick my butt for telling you this, but I think you need to know so you'll understand him better."

Understanding why a wasp stings didn't make me want to invite one into my bedroom.

"When Lee was a kid, he fell in love. Hard. This wasn't any young love thing, like the kids that have a different girlfriend every two months. They fell true and deep."

This was like telling me tarantulas are sweet, just misunderstood. "Did you know Barnett then?"

Pete reddened and nodded. "Yeah. We got to be friends because I didn't bust his balls over dating a rez girl. At that time, you gotta understand, it wasn't accepted. A white guy dating an Indian. But Lee didn't care."

If Pete had stood by him then, no wonder they were such good friends.

"Lee and his girl decided to run off and get married. It was senior year, in the spring. About this time of year, actually. But Lee's folks caught wind of it. They flew into a rage and took off to the rez, going to stop Lee. Guess Lee's dad was so upset he wasn't paying attention."

My foot pressed against the floor of the Bronco, putting on phantom brakes.

"They had a head-on somewhere north of Sand Gap. His folks both died. The Indian that crossed the line and hit them was okay." Pete paused. "Luck of the drunk." That last bit came out more bitter than I'd ever heard from him.

To lose your parents in a sudden, violent way was a terrible thing. Still. "So Lee hates the Lakota because one man killed his folks?"

Pete's eyes flicked to me and back to the road. "He doesn't hate the Indians. Trust me."

"What happened with his girlfriend?"

Pete's tight ball of energy made me jumpy. "The accident

hit Lee hard. He blamed himself for it, because that's the way he is. Tortured. For a long time, maybe even still, he didn't feel like he deserved happiness. And the girl faded from his life."

A few moments of silence followed, and I left Pete to reminisce about his teenage years. Clouds scuttled across the sun, making a slow strobe of light. Pete broke the quiet. "Have you heard how Kyle's doing?"

The image of his passive face against the white sheets tightened my chest. "No change when I called a couple of hours ago."

He clicked his teeth in sympathy. "His sister is still missing as far as you know?"

I considered Pete. If he didn't believe me that Barnett was kidnapping and selling girls, he'd still think Kyle's injuries resulted from a drunken brawl. "I don't know where she is."

Pete sighed. "That's too bad. Maybe if Lee had been able to find her, he could have helped her."

I didn't know Shelly, but I doubted having Barnett in her life would be helpful.

Pete slowed as we closed in on Barnett's turn. "What about Alex? Do you think he knows something about the sister?"

"I haven't been able to find him, either."

Pete shook his head. "My kids aren't much younger than Kyle's sister. In fact, my boy is the same age as Alex. I can't imagine them running around like that. They stay busy with school and church and 4-H. It's a shame the way these rez kids are so neglected."

Pete turned left onto a gravel road. Barnett's house squatted on an acreage hidden from the highway by a low hill. The midcentury red brick ranch huddled close to the south base of the hill. A garage, small pole barn, and empty corrals made up the operation.

Pete stopped in front of the house. All that rain-fed grass

grew so deep Barnett would need a machete to cut it back. Winter's tumbleweeds and dead leaves choked the flowerbeds lining the house. A porch swing dangled by one chain, and an unraveling wicker rocker junked the entryway.

Neither of us moved. "You think Sally's home?" I asked.

Pete seemed ready to shoot from the Bronco. "I didn't know it was this bad."

"What do you mean?"

Pete popped out and I followed, keeping an eye on the road. He walked away from the house, toward the barn. "Sally left a while back. Not long after both girls moved out."

Barnett had two daughters. I didn't know them well. I'd played against them in volleyball and basketball, but after high school, I didn't keep track. "Barnett is divorced?"

Pete studied the house and grounds on our progress toward the barn. He rubbed his fingers together with nerves or impatience, or maybe they itched. "Could be. She's gone is all I know. Wrecked Barnett. I know if Tammy ever left me, I'd die."

Most people say that figuratively, but for Pete, it might be literal. "Barnett talks about Sally as if she still lives here," I said.

"Well, Lee's a loyal man. He doesn't give up on those he loves."

We reached the barn. "What are you showing me?"

Pete watched my face as he opened the door and swung it wide. He stepped back to let me see.

I'd figured the room would be an office off the side of the barn. Maybe a workroom or studio of some kind. Lots of ranchers have a place set up for a bunkhouse, maybe for night calving help. But Barnett wouldn't need that since he only owned a couple of acres.

I didn't expect the cheery room. Yellow ruffled curtains

hung at the window, and a double bed with a flowered quilt made the place look like a girly bedroom. A small desk and lamp and well-worn velvet recliner completed the furnishing.

I turned to Pete. "What's this?"

Pete's eyes jumped to the window, and his smile strained. "This is where Lee brings the girls he kidnaps and sells."

What? Did Pete say I was right?

Pete chuckled. "The girls in trouble. Not just girls, by the way. Lee collects the strays. He brings them out here and tries to help them. Sometimes he finds them schools and programs and sends them away. Sometimes they head right back to the rez and waste their lives."

I walked into the room and ran a hand along the desk. "Lee is into rehabbing teenagers?"

Pete's usual black-Lab exuberance faded. He frowned. "Mostly from the rez. Kids like Kyle's brother and sister who don't have anyone who cares about them."

Kyle cared. So did Gordon. Shelly cared and even planned a sweat, which had been well attended. "If he's such a do-gooder, why is it a secret?"

"If anyone knew about this, they'd shut him down. He's not going through social services or the tribal agencies. I'm sorry to say that some people on the rez don't want to see young people succeed and get out. They make it hard for kids to get away." He moved to usher me out, looking at the road and rubbing his fingers together.

My skepticism must have shown, because even though I hadn't said anything, Pete rushed on. "I know Lee comes off gruff and uncaring. But I've known him almost my whole life. You won't find anyone kinder or more generous. And loyal. By God, Lee would do anything for a friend. Lee is the salt of the earth."

No matter what Pete said, I'd caught Barnett lying to me.

That killed my trust. "I'm not sure about this Underground Railroad or whatever he's got happening here."

Pete spoke about loyalty and family and the closeness between him and Barnett. What lengths would Pete go to protect Barnett?

I let my attention wander over the room. From the window looking out on the thick clouds to the reds and oranges of the poppies decorating the bedspread. Did Barnett really choose the red, yellow, and orange striped area rug covering the fake wood floor? I couldn't imagine he had that kind of whimsy in him.

A wood floor? In a pole barn? Even one converted would probably still have a poured concrete floor. I studied the rug, noting a small bulge toward one edge.

I looked away, afraid Pete had noticed my scrutiny. But he was staring out the window at the house. He jumped when I spoke. "Thanks for bringing me out here. It explains a lot. I guess Barnett isn't such a bad guy after all."

Pete put his arm around me and steered us out of the room, clicking the door closed behind us. I was eager to get out of there as quickly as possible, and I stepped away from him and led the way to the Bronco.

Small talk on the way back to Dry Creek turned easy when I asked about his kids. Pete galloped off about Rusty's new roping mare and Becca's barrel horse and how the high school rodeo team needed a new coach. Silently, I urged him to exceed his strict sixty-five miles an hour, but my powers of suggestion didn't penetrate his enthusiasm for his kids' activities.

He dropped me at my car, and before I climbed out, he put a hand on my arm. "Please keep me posted on Kyle's condition. Tammy and I will go to the hospital when he comes to.

Take him flowers and see if he needs anything. I don't suppose he's got any family to help him out."

I nodded, too distracted to say much. "Thanks, Pete."

I climbed into my car and started the engine and waited for Pete to head back to Chester County. He sat in his Bronco with the engine running, maybe waiting for me to take off. I gave it another few seconds, and when he didn't go, I put my car into gear and turned right, toward Hodgekiss.

When I was out of sight of Frankie's, I took a quick detour around the back of the boarded-up craft store. Two men dozing on the concrete step didn't look up as I executed a U-turn and stayed half-hidden behind the building. Ten long, painful minutes later, Pete cruised past on his way out of town.

I gave it another five minutes, then I pulled out, heading east. Back to Barnett's, hoping his court appearance would be a long one.

29

I sprayed gravel as I slammed on the brakes and jetted from the cruiser to the door of the bunkhouse. With swift movements, I jerked the striped rug from the center of the room, revealing what I'd suspected.

A trapdoor. Just as I'd seen on a thousand TV shows. This one was marked by crudely cut boards and latched, but not locked. Barnett would have no reason to lock anything around here. It's unlikely anyone, not even the Schwann's man, who delivered frozen food to remote ranches, would come snooping at his place. No one lived close enough to hear a scream.

I flipped the latch and jerked on the door. It didn't weigh much, and when I opened it, light streamed into the hole. A set of steep stone steps descended into a shallow room with wooden shelves. A storage cellar. Most of the older ranches had something like this to keep canned goods and root vegetables. I leaned over, sure this one held more than summer's harvest.

Although the daylight illuminated most of the cellar, my eyes didn't adjust quickly enough to identify the shadows.

Before I could make out details, a lump rose from the corner of the cellar and burst toward me.

It knocked into me, and I fell back with an "umph."

The kid scrambled over the top of me, making a run for the door. I reached up and caught his ankle, and he crashed to the floor, crying out.

He fought like a tiger cub, kicking and writhing, making it nearly impossible to keep my hold and to get purchase on my knees. I threw myself on top of him, pinning him under me while I struggled to grab his wrists.

I finally looked at his face. "Alex!"

He didn't stop fighting. "Lemme go."

We wrestled for a second. "Knock it off or I'll put the cuffs on you."

His fear was so real I could touch it. His voice cracked. "What do you want from me?"

I panted from the struggle. "Why are you here?"

His heavy breathing sounded like a steam engine. His words were meant to be tough, but they came out squeaky. "You and Barnett gonna kill me like you did Darrel?"

I sat back, staying alert in case he bolted. "I've got nothing to do with Barnett. Did he kidnap you? How long have you been here?"

He panted, eyes still wild and searching the room. "Last night. He found me after Frankie's. Brought me here."

Whether Pete believed his lies about Barnett's goodness, the truth was here before me. "Did he say why?"

Alex calmed a little, maybe starting to understand I wasn't going to hurt him. "He wants Shelly. Said if I took him to her, he'd let me go."

I knew it. With her beauty and exotic Native American mystique, I'd bet she'd bring a lot on the market. "Where is she?"

Alex's mouth clamped shut, and he focused on the corner of the room.

I stood up, positioning myself between Alex and the door so he couldn't make a run for it. "I'm trying to help Shelly. Shut Barnett down."

Alex sat up but didn't say anything.

I leaned closer to him. "Barnett nearly killed Kyle last night."

Alex jerked as if struck by a snake. "No. Is he? Is Kyle...?"

"He's in a coma at the hospital, but he'll be okay." Kyle might or might not be okay, but Alex didn't need to know that. I barked my words so Alex would focus. "Barnett might have killed Darrel. Now he's after Shelly. You need to trust me."

Alex switched from scared to belligerent in a blink. "Trust. That's the white man's line."

With effort, I kept my voice low and calm. "We don't have time for this BS. Help me find Shelly. That'll give us the proof we need to lock Barnett up."

He lifted his chin. "Shelly don't need your help."

"Where is she?" How long would court last? Was Barnett on his way home now?

"She's safe."

I ground my molars. "How safe can she be if she's hiding from Barnett and from the preppers?"

He looked confused. "Preppers?"

I wasn't getting anywhere with this kid. "The Olson Ranch."

He shrugged as if he had no idea.

We needed to get out of here before Barnett returned. With clenched teeth, I said, "Hidden Valley Ranch."

He opened his eyes wider. "You know about them?"

"I think they're in this with Barnett."

He might as well have called me a moron. "They don't

know nothing about this shit. It's Barnett, all the way from the beginning."

"What are you talking about?"

He shut up again.

I grabbed the front of his T-shirt and jerked him toward the bed, pushing him to sit. I stood above him. "You know something, and if you want to save your sister's life and find out who tried to kill Kyle, you'd better tell me."

"I know who went after Kyle. Same as who killed Darrel. I just don't know why."

He stopped and I waited. When he didn't pick up again, I pulled out my cuffs. Whether he talked or not, we couldn't hang out here any longer. "Guess you can sit in jail until you feel more chatty."

He glared at me.

I lunged at Alex, had his arms behind his back and cuffed before he had time to swing. I'd learned the skill at the police academy and practiced it on brothers, sisters, nephew, and nieces. It was my best real sheriff move.

I pulled him up and jerked him toward the door. "Might have to keep you locked up awhile. Won't matter because no one knows where you are."

He pulled back. "You can't do that. I'm a minor."

I opened the door and leaned on him to push him into the drizzle. "Gosh. I hadn't thought of that."

I opened the back door of my cruiser and placed a hand on the back of his head. "In you go."

He resisted. "Okay. Okay."

I applied a little more pressure to his head. "Okay, what?"

He raised his voice. "I heard Ma and Shelly fighting about a month ago."

I quit pushing, even though I wanted to throw him in the

car and peel out before Barnett showed up. I held him close to the door. "What were they fighting about?"

He didn't look at me. "I didn't hear the start. They were yelling and crying, all that drama shit. Then Ma said something about Kyle's dad and how bad sheriffs were, and staying away from the law. It's the kind of crap she's said forever. But I never heard her say anything about Kyle's dad before. She hates cops, and that's why she hates Kyle."

I backed up a step and nodded for him to continue, one ear on his speech and the other listening for Barnett's Bronco.

He scowled and went on. "Then she says Darrel was gonna make the sheriff pay for what he done. Ma and Shelly raised hell fighting and stuff, but what I got was that Darrel knew something and he was gonna use it to get Ma what she deserved."

"Do you know what or who Darrel found?"

Alex shook his head. "No. But I figured Shelly would because she's smart. After that, she got all weird. Hardly home. Secret as hell. Ma wouldn't talk to her."

"What happened a couple of nights ago? The night of the sweat?"

Guilt splashed suddenly across his face, like the squalls that had washed over the Sandhills. "Shelly was done with school and gonna go to college or leave home no matter what. She knew something about a sheriff, and I figured that was worth some money. So I sent a text to Barnett and told him I knew what happened and to give me five thousand dollars and I wouldn't say nothing."

I nearly choked. "You tried to blackmail Barnett?"

"Yeah. And next thing I know, Shelly's gone. Then Kyle wants to meet. And Barnett grabs me, throws me into a spider hole with a bag of peanut butter sandwiches and a case of juice boxes."

I needed to find Shelly. She held the key to Barnett's secret.

Max. Scared and lying. He knew something. Maybe he was hiding Shelly. Or something.

I unlocked Alex's cuffs. "Get in the car."

He backed away. "No way."

"I can lock you in the back seat, or you can grow up and sit in front with me."

We had a couple-second stare down. "Do you really want to hang around here and wait for Barnett to get back?"

Alex dragged his feet getting into the front seat, and when I slid behind the wheel, he said, "Where are you taking me?"

I hurried out of the ranch yard and to the highway. "Your cousin Gordon."

He crossed his arms. "Another apple."

Good thing I'd developed teenager tolerance from being part of such a big family. "When Kyle recovers, he'll be able to tell us what happened."

Alex sneered. "Kyle's like Superman. Dude won't die."

I fought a battle to keep my mouth shut and lost. "Kyle loves you."

Alex scoffed. "He doesn't know anything about me or my life."

"He's done everything he can to help you. Try to get you off the reservation."

"Yeah, take me away from my culture. My people."

I squeezed the wheel and frustration tightened my chest. "You could do worse."

"Says the rich white bitch. You ain't had some cop pick you up and give you shit because you're Lakota. You ain't had grocery store clerks do everything but spit on you because you got food stamps. You got no idea what it's like to be Indian."

"Right. I don't. But that's no reason for you to push away Kyle's help. Why not try to make your life better?"

"Better according to Kyle? To you?"

I opened my mouth, but his words popped it closed again. He was right. Better to me meant getting an education. So he could get a good job off the reservation. So he could live in a nice house, eat big meals, take dive vacations. I glanced at him. "What kind of future do you want?"

Hope lit his eyes for the first time since I'd met him. "Like my ancestors. Right? They knew the land. They hunted and lived free. Didn't need money. Or government housing. No diplomas and jobs. Just living. Real life."

I thought about that. "You know that's impossible."

He folded his arms. "It's not impossible, man."

Time to be real, even if it was ugly. "Your ancestors weren't relegated to some seriously questionable lands. They could follow buffalo and elk herds. The world is different for you. There are fences. The prairie is settled. The buffalo are gone."

Alex's passion frothed. "You don't understand. You got your paycheck and your big house and car. I got nothing and not going to. What I got is screwed."

I nodded. "Yeah. You're right. It's easier for me. It's always going to be easier for me. I can be sorry about it, but I can't change it. Living in poverty to spite me is just stupid."

He rolled his eyes.

"Kyle has a good life."

Alex's eyes, so much like Kyle's, drilled me. "And he still has to put up with bullshit from the white world."

Whatever else, Alex was teenager through and through. So, because it was something Mom repeated to me often when I was a teen, I recited from her code of living, *The Desiderata*, "Everywhere the world is full of treachery and broken dreams. But don't let it blind you..."

We debated, with less animosity, all the way to The Stop in Sand Gap.

Alex didn't put up any ruckus when I escorted him to the back room. Kyle's cousin Kim made it clear I wasn't welcome. She smacked her bat into her hand and curled her lip at me when I passed in front of the cash register. I gave her a friendly hello, because, as Dad says, there's never any reason to be rude.

Gordon walked me out. "Tha's two of the four Red Owls safe and soun'. You got someone keepin' an eye on Kyle up there in that hospital?"

Worry throttled my innards. "My Aunt Tutti has Rottweiler in her blood. If someone comes sniffing around who doesn't belong, she's got sharp teeth."

He raised an eyebrow as if that didn't account for much in his view. "Bes' you can do is fin' Shelly. Rita isn't in good shape, and Alex is gonna need someone to look after him."

If I did find Shelly and get this mess straightened out, I didn't think I'd urge her to take on parenting her younger brother. But that was an issue for another day, another caretaker. For now, finding Shelly topped my list, and there was only one place she could be.

I checked my gun to make sure it was loaded and turned south.

30

Kyle's swathed head filled my mind, and my pulse raced. With determination, I raced down the highway. I pulled out my phone and punched in Ted's number.

I explained my encounter with Alex and Max and laid it all out for him. "I'm nearly there now. You need to get here so we can protect Kyle and arrest Barnett."

Ted sounded too relaxed. "You're wrong. There's no way Barnett would kill anyone."

Arguing with Ted was taking up too much time today. "Fine. I'll call Milo or Pete. Maybe I *am* wrong. But I'm not going to give Barnett the benefit of the doubt and maybe lose Kyle."

He did not yawn, did he? "You're overreacting."

I shot back my response before thinking, the way you can with someone you'd been married to for eight years. "And you're a pig-headed blowhard, jerk in the mud."

"Jerk in the mud?"

"I'm mad." I sucked in a few breaths. "Are you going to back me up, or should I call someone else?"

He sounded entertained. Damn him. "I'm halfway there now. But we're going to talk first, arrest later."

I'd grown up with compromise. However, you'd think once I was the lone law enforcement officer in my county, I could make the rules. "Get here fast."

I cut another lock off the gates into the Olson Ranch. Now it was just getting irritating. This time, when I topped the hill heading down to the headquarters, there was no activity. One pickup was parked outside the main house. The hen house door stood ajar, and the birds pecked happily in their yard.

I pulled up in front of Marty and Rhonda's house, a chill crawling up my spine and tugging the hairs on my neck. The basement windows were propped open, but sand hadn't been dug back far from them. Another goose-drowner would create a beach in the basement again. The cistern still rested on the hill. Most Sandhillers I knew wouldn't have done such a half-assed job. Out here, you couldn't rely on someone else to finish a chore or clean up after you.

More than the sorry state of repairs, the headquarters felt ominous, like a weight hung overhead, waiting to fall. Fear billowed in the air as menacing as if rain clouds still hovered.

I pushed my car door open and sat a moment. My good sense screamed at me to stay put. But a meadowlark trilled and blackbirds chirped in response. The hens clucked. A slight breeze whispered across my cheeks, and the sun twinkled with spring seduction. Maybe I'd let my imagination run rampant.

Right after I'd been sworn in last winter, Milo advised me to trust my instincts. Right now, those puppies told me Shelly was here, or had been here. She needed me. Kyle needed me to find her.

I pulled my gun, and with my stomach flipping, sweat

dripping down my sides, and a dry mouth, I stepped out of my cruiser. No gunshots or laser missiles. I walked around their pickup.

The peephole in Marty's front door dropped, and a gun barrel poked out. I nearly dove for the ground but stopped myself. No one was going to shoot the Grand County sheriff. They'd never get away with it. Marty and Rhonda wouldn't risk it.

Rhonda's harsh voice vibrated through a hole in the shutters of the front window. "We told you if you ever set foot out here without a warrant, we'd shoot your ass. We weren't joking."

My palm sweated where I clutched my gun. "Tell me where Shelly is."

Rhonda shouted back, "Drop your gun."

The slipshod repairs, cistern cast off like a broken Christmas toy, the locks continually being replaced. Chickens with blackout curtains. Why did I think I could count on Marty and Rhonda's rationality when it came to shooting me? "I can't leave until I find Shelly."

"We warned you." Rhonda's tone was like a fist in my gut.

I heard the clack of metal on metal, maybe a lock opening, a gun engaging, something or anything from my imagination. I twisted and dove behind their pickup. Dirt puffed and a whizz of a bullet split the air where I'd been standing. I lunged from the ground where I'd landed under the pickup, opened the door, and threw myself inside, a coon's hair before a bullet thunked on the ground close to where my foot had been.

Shots zinged and whipped through the air. The barricaded doors of the house muffled the sound of firing, so the bullets made about as much noise as a bumblebee. But that didn't mean they weren't deadly.

I knew the pickup's frame wouldn't protect me from the bullets. If they wanted to kill me, they'd have to damage their vehicle, though. Maybe that kept them from shooting me. Marty and Rhonda probably didn't mean to kill me, just scare me off. Small comfort.

Their house was fortified. No sense in me firing off a round. Ted was bound to show up soon, so at least I'd have backup. He had a phone, and in an hour or two we could have us a regular Ruby Ridge situation.

A commotion started from the barn behind me. Shouting, a girl. Max's cracking voice. Banging and knocking. I snaked my head out of the pickup, with the scant protection of the door.

A girl with black hair struggled to break free from Max's grip. It had to be Shelly. They both yelled. With one giant yank, she tore from Max and ran toward my car.

"Get down!" I jumped from the pickup, my gun up, poised to shoot if Max attacked.

She ran straight at me, arms raised. Still shouting, but I couldn't make out what she said. I raced to meet her, not sure whether to throw myself between her and Max or her and the house.

I reached for her, but she swerved away from me, hands waving overhead. "Stop it! Stop!"

I tackled her, and she struggled beneath me. "Get off of me!"

The door to the house flew open and Rhonda ran out, Marty close on her heels. "What the hell are you doing?" she screamed. I didn't know if she addressed me, Shelly, or Max.

I scrambled to my knees, and the girl squiggled away from me. Confused, I held my gun on Rhonda, since she seemed the biggest threat.

Tears streaked down the girl's red face, and her mouth contorted. "Quit shooting. Stop."

Rhonda glared at her, the Glock in her hand pointed to the ground. "I'm trying to protect you."

Marty's mole-like face pinched tight in rage. "I told you we shoulda turned her over that first morning."

Rhonda flashed irate eyes his way and swiped her hand out to swat his rifle's barrel to the ground. "Be careful with that thing."

I decided against holstering my gun. "Shelly?"

She nodded, sucking back sobs. Max rocketed behind us and put an arm around Shelly, helping her up. I pushed myself to stand, and we all took stock, eyeing each other warily.

"What's going on here?" I finally asked. "Did they kidnap you? Are you okay?"

Rhonda's lips curled back like a growling terrier. "Kidnap? What kind of crazy are you? She's been nothing but trouble since she set foot out here."

Shelly sniffed and struggled to get control. "Why didn't you and Kyle let it go?" She stood with her jet-black hair tossing in the breeze, her skin a deeper bronze than Kyle's, but the same fire flashed in her eyes as in Alex's and Kyle's eyes.

"He can't." Any more than I could let Carly go. "He loves you."

She swiped at tears.

Rhonda looked from me to Shelly. She pointed a finger at Max. "You did this. You brought all this to our doorstep. We wanted to be left alone."

Max hugged Shelly to him in a protective way. "They were after her. We had to take care of her."

With a roar of a powerful engine, Ted popped over the hill

and careened down the gravel road toward us in his ranch pickup.

As if someone had hit pause, we stopped and waited for him to race into the yard and slide to a halt. He jumped out, gun pointed toward us.

I gave a curt nod in his direction. "Glad you're here. Put these two yahoos in my car and take them back to the courthouse."

Marty raised his barrel a couple of inches.

Ted shouted, "Drop the gun!"

I was surprised to see my arm up, gun pointed in Marty's direction. Since two guns were trained on him, he took the path of least resistance and dropped his rifle.

Ted kept his eyes on Marty and Rhonda, but he spoke to me, softening his voice like he spoke to a puppy. "Good decision to call for backup. Glad I could be here for you."

With effort, I kept from turning my gun on him.

Rhonda had the good sense to let her gun fall to the ground. "You can't take us in. You've got nothing."

I shuffled behind Rhonda and, while Ted held his gun, pulled her arms back and cuffed her. "Shooting at a police officer is enough for me. Then we'll see about money laundering, extortion, and stolen goods."

She didn't fight me with her body, but words flew fast, most of them the kind Dad would find offensive. Marty didn't have much to add, but his expression made it plain he wished he'd shot me when he had the chance.

Ted did that tough lawman scowl he'd honed from old spaghetti Westerns. "You speak to your mother with that mouth?"

Rhonda spewed a particularly foul expletive at him, and I pretended it was from me, too.

We loaded them into the back of my cruiser, and I handed

Ted the keys. "I'll talk to Shelly and Max, get what I can, then we can make a plan about Barnett."

Rhonda shouted something about intimate relations between Barney Fife and Sheriff Andy.

Marty raised his voice above hers. "Sheriff. Hey, I got to talk to you."

I leaned down, making sure to stay clear of the door or their reach in case one of them had escaped the cuffs.

Marty spoke quietly. "We weren't going to hurt you. Just wanted our privacy, right? So, look. How about we call it a truce, huh? Rhonda and me, we've got some means."

I must have looked surprised.

He rushed on. "You got kids? On the sheriff salary, college can be tough to pay for, right? So, we help you out, start a nice account, take care of you, huh?"

Rhonda jumped on board. For the first time, I saw real fear in her eyes. "We don't want trouble. You help us, we help you, everybody wins."

I stepped back and swung the door closed. "All yours," I said to Ted.

Ted went to the driver's door and stopped. "I still think you're wrong about Lee. Don't go getting all hot-headed until I can get these two processed in Ogallala."

I didn't say it, but I bet he figured it out. I'd darned well do what I felt needed doing, and I didn't need his permission.

He bent to get in my cruiser, straightened, and backed out. He leaned into the car, adjusted the seat back all the way, and slid inside, giving me the stink-eye. Some nitpicks hang on, even after a divorce.

I turned back to Max and Shelly, who stood side by side watching Ted take Rhonda and Marty away.

I started with Max. "You said they were after her. Who?"

Shelly lowered her head. "No."

Max bent to her. "She's a friend of Kyle's. I think we can trust her."

Shelly pleaded with me. "If you're Kyle's friend, get him out of here. Fire him. Make him leave."

I softened my voice. "Kyle was attacked last night. He's in a coma in Broken Butte."

Shelly gasped, and her hands flew to her mouth. She shook her head in denial.

With a gentleness at war with urgency, I said, "Your mother and Alex are safe now, but I found Alex locked in a cellar at Barnett's house."

One sob escaped from her.

Now I pushed. "What's going on?"

Max waited a moment. "If you don't tell her, I will."

I kept my eyes on Shelly. She looked healthy, no bruises, clean clothes. "Are you okay?"

Tears pooled in her eyes but didn't fall. "I'm good. It's safe here."

Shelly wiped her eyes and straightened her shoulders. A bit of Kyle's determination sparked in her. "You can't help Kyle. Or me. We come from a different world."

I'd had about enough of that. "Bullshit."

Max nudged Shelly. "You need to tell her."

Her hand lifted to her belly, and she massaged it as if her stomach ached. She raised dark eyes to mine. "Okay. But I need to sit down."

Max leaned into her. "Are you going to be sick?"

She paled and her throat worked. "It's the—" She bent over and puked.

I jumped back, barely avoiding the splash, then stepped forward, helping Max half carry Shelly into the shade at the side of the barn.

"Not here." She waved at the chickens. "The smell—" Off she went again, bending over and letting a stream hit the dirt.

Max and I took Shelly into the barn, leaving the door open for the sunlight and fresh air. Unlike my shop at Frog Creek and the barn where I'd kept the stalls lined with sweet-smelling hay, Marty and Rhonda's barn smelled of grease and the tools lay in heaps. We settled Shelly onto a tall shop stool. Max held her hand and stood close enough for her to lean against.

"Okay, tell me what's going on."

With one long silent exchange with Max, Shelly began. "My brother, Darrel, was killed two years ago."

I nodded. "A hit-and-run."

She swallowed as if fighting another bout of nausea. "That's what they said."

"You don't believe that?"

"I did. But then..." She gripped Max's hand and paused.

While I waited for her to upchuck again, I kept the thread going. "What changed your mind?"

The wave must have passed. "Ma. She told me something."

Shelly leaned against Max and closed her eyes, her skin the green tint of spoiled ham. "When I t-t-told her I was pregnant and what we were going to do, she went off. She said my life would end up like hers because the white people use us and leave us."

Her revelation of pregnancy only confirmed my suspicion.

Max hugged her tight, bending to kiss her. True love wasn't thwarted by vomit breath. "I won't leave you."

She gave him a watery smile. "Then she said all this stuff about the white man killing Darrel and it should have been Kyle. And, God, I don't know. Ma's brain doesn't always work right. But what I came up with is that Darrel found out who

Kyle's dad was and decided to get some money from him. And the sheriff killed him."

A bomb exploded behind my eyes. "The sheriff? Barnett?"

She swallowed and waited a beat. "I think so."

As much as I disliked Barnett, enough that it could fill Husker's Memorial Stadium, my brain stalled out on this one. "You think Barnett killed Darrel to keep him from telling everyone Barnett is Kyle's father?"

Shelly gave Max a look that said she'd been right not to tell me. "Everyone knows how much Barnett hates Indians. How would it look to his white world if he admitted to being Kyle's dad?"

I needed to think that one over. Murder was a big thing, and if Shelly was right, Barnett had not only killed Darrel, he'd tried to kill his own son.

I changed the subject, hoping I might get a feel for the reliability of Shelly's assessment. "How did you two meet?"

Shelly leaned on Max. "A few months before Darrel was killed, he started spending money. He bought that car. When I asked him where he got the money, he wouldn't tell me."

She paused for a deep breath. I inhaled with her.

"I kept bugging him, and he told me he got a job with some new white ranchers and they paid him cash. He was laughing about how they wanted his Indian knowledge. Like that he was supposed to be so connected to the land and all that."

"He was working for Rhonda and Marty?"

"No. Max's parents." She smiled for the first time, showing her youthful beauty. "Newt and Earl Johnson. They told me about this place out here. I thought if they hired Darrel, they might hire me, too."

Max took over again. "I was the only one here because everyone else was fixing a windmill."

They squeezed each other's hands and smiled. Teenagers.

"Max told me that Darrel helped drywall their house. They paid him cash and swore him to keep quiet. They've had a bunch of Indians help out."

She stood up and twisted, stretching her back. "Max and I, well, it was like, that's it. We took one look at each other and we were kind of together after that."

Max pulled her to him. Love was love, whether you were eighteen, thirty-five, or eighty. "So you kept your relationship secret?"

Shelly gave a rueful laugh. "Until recently."

She stepped a half foot away and let Max's arm drop. "So yeah. I got pregnant. And that's when it all got bad."

"My brother Douglas told me your grades dropped and you'd been feeling lousy."

She offered a wry smile. "I wish that was all."

I bit my lips while she plopped down again. She clearly felt miserable.

"I went to Ma when I found out. I told her about the baby and that I was going to finish school. Then Max and I planned to move in with his parents in New Jersey, and we'd figure out how to go to college and work and raise the baby."

Max's face hardened with determination, older than I'd seen him.

"Ma came apart. She started screaming about how I couldn't have a white man's baby. She wasn't drunk, so the way she blew up scared me. I couldn't get her to calm down, and what I got out of it was that Kyle's father was some white guy."

She shrugged. "We always thought Kyle had a different dad. But Ma said Kyle's father promised he'd marry her and take care of the kid and then, poof. I guess he disappeared and never gave her anything.

"Ma was screaming about me getting an abortion. And I left. You know? I just got in my car."

"So was this the night you ran away?"

Shelly shook her head. "No. This was, like, two weeks before. I was trying to figure out what to do about Darrel being killed. I tried to talk to Kyle about it, but he wouldn't listen."

She paused as if waiting for a wave of nausea to pass. "Then Alex started being big trouble, and I got worried about him. He started acting strange."

What constituted strange for that kid? "How so?"

She shifted and arched her back. "Like a total douche asshole."

"That tells me nothing."

She reconsidered. "He bought a car from a guy and promised to pay him but had to give it back. I asked him where he got the money, and he wouldn't say."

My heart sank. "He planned on blackmailing Barnett about being Kyle's father."

She shook her head. "He didn't know that."

I told her Alex's story.

She closed her eyes and opened them. "That explains why Barnett showed up that night."

"The night of the sweat?"

She leaned into Max. "Yeah. I heard someone pull up, and when I looked, I saw the cop Bronco. The lights weren't on or anything. It was really dark, but the sheriff got out and you could tell he was pissed. He didn't knock, just ripped open the front door."

"Your mother wasn't home?"

Shelly glanced at Max. "She was drunk."

I hated making her tell me that.

Shelly continued her story. "He came in and started yelling

at Ma. Asking her, where was Alex. But Ma, she was at that stage where she couldn't answer.

"I had to get us some help, so I crawled out the back window. I ran to my car and took off."

Max leaned into her. He whispered to her, "It's okay."

She inhaled and ignored Max. "That's when I called Kyle. I knew Alex was in trouble but didn't know what for."

"Kyle's phone was on transfer because of the sweat. I got your call."

She took that in but didn't comment. "Then Barnett was following me. I kept looking at the Bronco in my mirror, and my front tire dropped off the road. The car flipped. I don't even remember climbing out, but then I was running. I called Max and hid over the hill. He came and got me."

"Why didn't you talk to me when I came out here?"

She gave me a look telling me what she thought of the question. "You're a white sheriff. I didn't trust you. I'm still not sure I do."

Max apologized to me with a geeky smile. "Sorry." To Shelly, he said, "She's okay."

Shelly focused on me and her eyes filled again. This time, the tears escaped. "He killed Darrel. And he hurt Kyle." She trembled. "And he had Alex. It's my fault."

Max rocked her. "It's not."

She sniffed. "It's because of me that Alex found out and tried to blackmail Barnett. And it's my fault that Kyle..." She choked back a sob.

My heart broke for her. Too young to carry such a burden. "I'll stop him, I promise."

My phone rang, and I pulled it out. The hospital. "Sheriff."

A sweet voice I didn't recognize answered. "Hi, Kate. Your Aunt Tutti asked me to call and tell you that Kyle Red Owl is waking up."

Relief, like a soft breeze. Immediately followed by a jolt of fear. "Thanks for calling. But do me a favor and don't tell anyone else about this. I'm on my way."

The caller hesitated. "Really? 'Cause Tutti told me to call all the sheriffs."

My mouth went dry. "I'm the first call, right?"

Her voice shook. "Um. You're the last one."

I spun from Shelly and Max and sprinted for Ted's pickup.

31

I'd been so quick to advise Kyle to let Shelly go. But seeing her today, frightened and young, trying hard to be grown up, hammered home the inexperience and vulnerability of an eighteen-year-old. Shelly had taken on the responsibility of Alex and her mother, carrying them on her thin shoulders. She thought of herself as Superwoman, but she needed help.

I raced down the highway and reached for my phone. When the hospital operator picked up, I asked for Aunt Tutti.

Bright spring sunshine coaxed the hills into a dazzling green, highlighted with wildflowers. Black cows dotted the prairie, and the sky burst in deep blue. The whole day looked as if it'd been drawn by a kindergartner with a new eight-pack of crayons. Too cheerful and hopeful for what was going on.

After a few minutes on hold, Aunt Tutti picked up. "What?"

"How's Kyle?" I sounded breathless.

Aunt Tutti ground her words like pepper. "Didn't Brianna call you? Damn it."

"She called. I just want to know from you."

Tutti sounded irritated. "His heart rate and temp are

normal. Respiration good. The swelling is down, and he woke up for a few minutes. Honestly, I'm busy with patient care. Don't have time for phone calls."

Ted's pickup had power and felt like driving a tank, but it didn't have a light bar or siren. "Sorry. This is important. Is anyone visiting Kyle?"

"For the love of Pete. I don't know."

I hated leaving Kyle alone. "You've got to check on him. Make sure only hospital staff goes into his room."

"Why?"

Should I tell her I suspected Lee Barnett was a murderer? I had no proof, and if I accused him falsely, it would be bad. On the other hand, if I was right, I couldn't take a chance of giving him access to Kyle.

"Just don't let anyone in, okay?"

Aunt Tutti sounded weary. "I've got patients that need care. I can't stand guard over one because you're paranoid."

My voice rose a few decibels. "The person who hurt him might come back."

Now she sounded interested. "Who?"

Well, damn the torpedoes... "I think it was Lee Barnett."

She laughed. "No, really. Who?"

I wanted to scream. "Please."

Lucky for me she didn't have the time to argue or gossip. "Whatever. You can explain when you get here."

I passed the Flying T ranch sign. "I'll be there in twenty minutes."

But it seemed more like two hours before I flew by the sale barn on the outskirts of Broken Butte. Within ten minutes I whipped into the lot for Broken Butte County Hospital. There were only two public entrances into the hospital—the main one opening into a lobby and the reception area, and the emergency entrance in back with sliding doors. I parked in the lot behind the hospital, close to the emergency doors.

Right next to the Spinner County sheriff's Bronco.

Damned good thing I'd made Aunt Tutti promise to keep Kyle safe.

There seemed to be an abundance of vehicles in the back lot. By that I meant two pickups, a blue Suburban, and a black Malibu station wagon, besides Lee's Bronco and Ted's pickup. I raced to the emergency room entrance. Aunt Tutti would be keeping a good eye on Kyle, but I needed to find Barnett. What I'd do then, I wasn't sure.

I pulled out my phone. Since Ted had Marty and Rhonda, I hit speed dial for Milo. "Can you hurry to Broken Butte?"

Milo grunted. "Can't. My danged back went out again and I'm down. But I just talked to Pete, and he said he's on his way down to say hi to Kyle."

I didn't want to tell Milo my suspicions until I talked to him in person. I'd stand guard over Kyle in the meantime. "Right. I'll be here."

He sounded concerned. "Well, okay, then."

I'd made it across the parking lot and checked to make sure my gun was nestled on my hip.

The glass doors of the emergency entrance slid open, and I walked into chaos.

Two middle-aged women in jeans and T-shirts sat in the molded plastic chairs where I'd talked to Aunt Tutti earlier that morning. They were covered in dirt, their hair in disarray. People, also grungy and disheveled, sat on tables in both the exam rooms. Medical staff bustled around them. It was a small ER, so it took only a few people to fill it and make it seem like an all-out disaster.

No one wailed. I saw no tears, and not even any blood. Aunt Tutti scooted out one exam room on her way to another. I jumped toward her and caught her arm. "What's going on?"

"The ladies auxiliary were cleaning the Legion, and Guy Compton ran his Cadillac through the kitchen wall."

I must have looked flummoxed.

She pulled her arm away. "Says it's a new car and he couldn't find the brake. They ought to take away his license, is what I think."

I spun around and raced down the hall. Barnett was in the hospital, and no one was protecting Kyle.

My boots clacked on the shiny linoleum until I hit the

hallway leading toward the front door and administrative offices. I dashed down the corridor, skirting a woman locking an office and slinging a purse over her shoulder. She gasped and muttered something as I raced past. A young man in scrubs carrying a yellow plastic tray full of vials flattened against the wall to let me pass.

I rounded the corner and poured on the speed. Nurses and other staff crossed in front of me or hurried on their own business. It could've been a shift change or maybe it was the emergency, but the place seemed to whir with activity. No one would notice Barnett slipping into Kyle's room.

They barely paid me any attention, except to get out of my way. After what felt like an elephant's lifetime, I reached Kyle's corridor and his room.

I grabbed the doorway and propelled myself inside. Like plunging into flames, I reacted without thought. Barnett stood over Kyle, a grimace on his face. Within reach of the IV running into Kyle's veins. "Stop!"

Barnett flung his head up. Our eyes met. "Stay out of this."

Kyle lay motionless on his back, eyes closed, his skin a chalky version of his usual bronze. A bandage turban glowed white against wisps of his black hair. Defenseless, vulnerable, so alone.

Desperate to protect Kyle, I lunged across the room, catching Barnett off guard. Ambushed, Barnett's defenses never really kicked in. I didn't know how, but I'd already clutched my cuffs, and before I knew what I planned, I snapped cuffs closed around one wrist and yanked it, along with his other arm, behind his back. Adrenaline and flat-out rage at him for threatening Kyle gave me strength I didn't know I had.

The spindly IV rack crashed to the side, tossing the half-full bag of fluid across the room, jerking the end from the back of Kyle's hand. I was probably yelling, Barnett roared, but who knew if either of us used real words.

Whether the racket from the toppled IV hook or our struggles caught her attention, an older nurse in dark green scrubs scurried into the room. "Dear Lord, what is going on?"

I clamped the cuffs on Barnett and he fought to escape, kicking the bedside table so it rolled toward Kyle's head.

"Stop it!" the nurse hollered. "Get out!"

I clasped Barnett's cuffed hands and took hold of his collar and started propelling him from the room. "Kyle's IV got pulled out. I think Barnett might have put something in it."

Barnett twisted from side to side attempting to break away. "I didn't touch it."

Barnett was a big guy. Even cuffed he took my full strength to control.

The nurse seemed more annoyed than worried. "You can go to jail for tampering with his meds."

"He's going to jail for more than that," I said.

Barnett wasn't making this easy. "You don't understand. I'm protecting Kyle."

"From what, staying alive?" Kyle looked so fragile in his crisp sheets, white bandages, pale skin. "Is Kyle going to be okay?" I asked the nurse.

She righted the rack. "Not if you don't get out of here."

I shoved Barnett ahead of me. "Let's go."

Barnett planted his feet. "Damn it, Fox. You're going to get Kyle killed this time."

I routinely wrangled two-hundred-pound calves, so one overweight, soft-bellied sheriff wasn't going to get the better of me. Since I didn't have an electric cattle prod, I used the standard Fox control method. I pinched hair at the nape of his neck and snapped it up.

"Ow!" He flinched and took a few steps forward.

"Did you think you could get away with it?"

"I haven't done anything I need to get away with."

"Kidnapping Alex is definitely something."

He whipped his head toward me. "You were at my house?"

"Don't worry. Alex is fine and ready to testify that you locked him up. And as soon as Kyle comes to, he'll confirm you're responsible for beating him. After that, it's a matter of compiling evidence that you killed Darrel."

Barnett swiveled to look at me. "You're insane. Remand me to Ted's custody."

I reached behind his head and gave his hair another yank. "All because you don't want the world to find out that Kyle is your son."

The nurse stopped her checking and patting and repairing for a split second. Barnett's lips curled back. "You don't know what you're talking about."

"Let's go." I shoved him, and he stumbled a few feet.

I manhandled Barnett out of the room, and now a small crowd formed a circle around us. "I found Shelly and she's safe from you."

He looked alarmed. "Where is she?"

I kept shoving him down the corridor.

He balked. "You need to tell me where Shelly is. If you don't, I can't protect her."

I grunted, cold rage taking root. "You kidnapped Alex, tried to kill Kyle, and now you want me to tell you where Shelly is?"

Barnett sounded equally wrathy. "I didn't do any of that. I'm only trying to stop it from happening again."

"If you didn't do it, who did?"

He closed his mouth. After a moment, he said, "If you're going to haul me away, at least call Milo to come sit with Kyle."

"When you're locked up, Kyle will be safe."

"Damn, you're stubborn. Now I know why Ted left you for Roxy."

He was not making me feel any better about him as a human being.

We struggled down the corridor, him cuffed and belligerent, me pretending I had the situation under control but really just happy to have Barnett away from Kyle and wishing Pete would hurry. Taking Barnett to the Broken Butte cop shop temporarily would be best.

He eyed the gathering looky-loos and quit fighting me. "Okay. Let's get out of here."

We tromped back through the ER, where the ladies auxiliary had vacated, assumedly none the worse for Guy Compton's driving.

What was taking Pete so long? "You say you didn't do this, but you won't say who to blame."

Barnett spoke as if his jaw were stone. "I won't blame anyone."

"You'd rather go to jail?"

He fired up, his eyes going all Godzilla. "Your generation is out for yourselves. You've been coddled and given the big red participation ribbon all your lives, so you have no idea about friendship and honor and loyalty."

Yep. That's me to a T. So pampered I had that nice diving vacation coming up, as soon as I quit bailing out my family. My walls could be lined with the Divorce ribbon, Unemployed one, Single and Childless, Niece Missing, and oh, and don't forget the Pathetic Pity Party one with all the streamers and stars.

He'd hit a nerve, for sure. "Loyalty, huh? I'm pretty sure murder cancels your nobility."

We made our way out of the ER without running into any

more shocked citizens. By now, the gossip would be spreading through the Sandhills. I kept a hand on Barnett's back because he remained reluctant to leave the hospital.

He bucked me. "You can't leave Kyle unprotected."

"It's touching how much you care." We crossed the parking lot. "I'll need your car keys." I couldn't haul a prisoner in Ted's pickup.

Barnett halted midstep.

Around the corner of the hospital, Pete drove his Chester County sheriff's Bronco into the front parking lot.

Barnett sucked in a quick breath. He shook his head and turned to me, alarm shooting from his face. "Let me go." He jerked out of my grasp.

"Knock it off."

The humiliation of having Pete see him cuffed, or maybe revealing Kyle as his son, seemed too much for Barnett. He twisted and spun, like a calf at a rodeo. Before I knew it, he flew past me, heading back to the hospital. With his arms pulled behind his back and his wrists tied together, he ran like a rooster. Still, he had the jump on me, and I took off after him.

While the hallways had been bustling before, now no one ran interference for me. Barnett made it through the ER before I grabbed his arms and threw him backward.

He bounced against the wall and fell to his knees.

He roared at me. "Stop him!"

I stared at him, not comprehending. He struggled to his feet. "Don't let him get to Kyle."

My thoughts started to shift into a new perspective. "But Alex?"

Barnett's slick-soled boots slid on the linoleum. "I had to hide him. I was trying to find Shelly for the same reason."

Shelly said she'd been chased by a Bronco. Barnett had been at her wreck in his pickup.

Oh my God. I'd been so wrong.

33

I left Barnett struggling to his feet and raced down the hall. Kyle's room felt like it was ten miles away and I was floundering through neck-high cut-grass. I slid around a corner and opened up on the last few feet to propel myself into his room for the second time.

Again, a sheriff stood by Kyle's bedside.

This time, it was Pete Grainger, his skin mottled, eyes glassy, and lips pulled wide in a mask of horror. His arms were braced, and he leaned his weight into a pillow covering Kyle's face. Meanwhile, Kyle's arms slapped weakly and his body contorted beneath the thin hospital sheets.

Grainger lifted his head and focused on me. "Get out!"

I threw myself across the room as Pete backed from the bed and reached his arm behind him. With a fluid movement, he pulled out his gun and held it straight, barrel pointing at my heart.

The pillow over Kyle's head slipped to the floor.

I slid to a halt, arms raised. "Hey, Pete. Easy."

A cornered animal, he sweated, and his focus flicked

around the room. "I'm sorry. I'm sorry. But it's your fault. You should have let it go."

Breathe, Kate. "Come on, Pete. You don't want to do this."

His dark eyes pleaded with me, and for the first time, I noticed they were same umber color as Kyle's. "I don't. You're right. But what choice do I have? Tammy, she won't understand."

What would he need to hear? "She loves you. She'll forgive you."

He seemed to consider that with some hope. Then his eyebrows fell and tears pooled. "No. She won't. If I'd told her a long time ago, sure. She might even have adopted Kyle and raised him like her own. But not now. She'll never forgive me for not claiming Kyle. Not giving him a father."

I stepped toward Kyle's bed. Pete startled and shoved his gun at me. I didn't flinch, even though instinct told me to dive for cover. I kept eye contact. "He's your *son*." Then whispered to him, "You can't kill your own son."

Frantic eyes shifted from Kyle to me. "It's the only way to fix this. He should never have been born. He ruined my life."

I spoke low. "Too many people know."

He choked a sob. "My kids. This will destroy them."

"Kyle is your kid!" Damn it, why didn't that sink in?

His face sloppy with tears, his mouth opened in a silent scream. I'd never seen someone so broken.

He stared down at Kyle and drew in a shocked, shaky breath.

Kyle's eyes held Pete.

Pete looked at me, pleading for something I couldn't give. He slowly raised his gun to his temple.

Crashing behind me, a heavy body thudded into the wall and slammed into the door. "No!" Barnett shouted.

It was enough to make Pete hesitate.

Barnett righted himself and stood inside the doorway. He advanced on Pete. "You can't do that. Your kids, Tammy. Hell, me. We've had each other's backs since high school."

Pete's eyes seemed unfocused, as if he couldn't quite make out Barnett. "You knew, didn't you? All along you could have turned me in for killing that Indian. But you didn't."

Barnett inhaled with a pain, as if Pete thrust a knife into him. "No. I hoped it was what they said, a hit-and-run."

Pete pleaded with Barnett. "He said if I didn't pay, he'd tell Tammy, tell everyone. I couldn't let them know about—" Pete's face contorted with hatred as he glared at Kyle. "*Him*."

Barnett held out his hand. "Don't you leave me now. Not like this."

Pete's shoulders heaved with his sobs. "I can't."

Barnett walked past me, his hand out. "I'll be with you. No matter what happens. I'm your friend. Always."

Pete dropped to his knees, his gun clattering to the floor. He collapsed weeping, his sobs so wrenching they swallowed the room.

Barnett kicked Pete's gun my way, and it slid behind me. I turned to pick it up, but Aunt Tutti got there first. She held up the gun in one hand and the key to the handcuffs in the other. Of course Barnett would have the key on him.

I hurried to Kyle's bedside. His mouth worked, but he made no sound.

"They're fine. Alex and Shelly are safe."

He let out a long breath and closed his eyes.

34

Gentle rain pattered on the porch roof. I sat with my feet up, sipping a cold beer, listening to the frogs croak in the dusk.

My phone rang, and I tensed. My plans for the evening didn't involve sheriffing. One look at the ID and I relaxed again. "Baxter." I hadn't told him about Carly's text, deciding it wouldn't advance the investigation.

He answered the same. "Kate." A pause. "Why is it you never call me by my first name?"

I sipped my beer and patted Poupon's fluffy head. "Never thought about it. Baxter sounds like a first name. Kind of."

"But Glenn sounds friendlier. I know we didn't start out as friends, but we are now, right?"

I'd lived in Grand County my whole life. Accounting for births and deaths, I'd known the same people forever. Sarah and I had been inseparable since kindergarten. Yet Baxter, who entered the scene as a suspected murderer, seemed as much a part of my life as any of them. "Sure, we're friends. That doesn't mean I'm going to call you Glenn."

I heard his smile. "Anyone ever tell you you're stubborn?"

The rain tapped a happy tune, and soft spring growth floated on the evening air. "Might have heard it a time or two."

He chuckled. "I guess it won't do me any good to plead again for an exclusive interview about Marty and Rhonda."

I snarled. "It hasn't worked for the *Omaha World-Herald* or the *Wall Street Journal*."

"Damn. The *Journal*?"

The warm temperatures of the last week had gone a long way to encouraging the grass in my sandy yard, and I concentrated on that instead of the irritation of almost constant harassment from the press. "They all have an angle. Everything from Marty and Rhonda to what I know about the trend of preppers in the Sandhills to the criminal charges for Barnett and Grainger."

Something sounded different in his voice, slower, maybe lower than normal. "Looks like you'll be spending time in court."

My stomach tightened. "I'm writing reports and gathering evidence for the cases against the sheriffs. But they tell me I won't have to testify against Marty and Rhonda, so I won't have to hit the big city. Whew."

"Hey, the city's not all bad." He switched the subject. "Is Kyle out of the hospital?"

"Got out a couple of days ago. He's going to be okay. He bought a little house on the rez, and Alex agreed to move in with him. Shelly is going to New Jersey with Max, at least until she's done with college."

Baxter sounded surprised. "On the rez? Wow. Are you surprised Kyle is going back?"

"It's not going to be easy. But Alex wouldn't leave, and Kyle is determined to keep him straight." I thought about it. "Kyle and Alex want to reconnect. Rebuild the family."

Baxter chuckled. "If anyone knows about family, it's you."

He had that right. Brothers and sisters pulling me here, pushing me there. Nieces to love and lose. A new generation swelling the Fox herd. And me, building fences and walls around myself. I changed the subject. "How's Chicago?"

Baxter hesitated. "Spring blizzard. Icy wind so cruel it could draw blood. Thank goodness I'm not there."

I sat up. "Did you hear anything about Carly? Are you on your way to get her?"

"No." He answered quickly. "I didn't mean to get your hopes up."

"Oh." I settled back into my porch chair. "Hope runs high, I guess."

"I'm in LA. Sitting by a pool and a bucket of chilled champagne."

That didn't sound half bad, though I preferred the moon glow on Stryker Lake and a hoppy beer.

"And packing a box of DVDs on climate change. Just in case you don't own a player, I'm sending one of those, too."

Well, shut my mouth. "Holy cow. You've got a date!" If he flew to LA for the gig, that meant his dinner partner was probably someone famous, elegant, and beyond imagination.

He laughed. "You issued a challenge. I like to win."

Headlights cut the gloom and pointed my way. "When is the lucky lady supposed to arrive?"

His voice sounded like satin. Dating might be good for his blood pressure. "I sent a car for her an hour ago, but with this West Coast traffic, she might not make it here for another hour."

The black pickup rumbled to a stop in front of my gate. "Then I'd say you can quit packing the DVDs and your personal assistant should book an appointment at the nearest stable. Unless, of course, you'd like to make a stop in the Sandhills on your way home."

The laidback tone vanished. "What do you mean?"

Josh unfolded from the pickup, reached inside, and brought out a bouquet of Sandhills' wildflowers. My favorite. He flashed me a shy smile.

"It's time for me to rip down walls and maybe start remodeling my life."

EASY MARK
Kate Fox #4

With her ex-husband, Ted, working nearby in an adjoining county, Kate Fox is eager to prove she's the better sheriff. And when the less-than-popular ex-foreman of a local ranch is found dead, Kate gets the opportunity she's been looking for.

But as it turns out, the case hits a little too close to home. The dead man's body is discovered in Kate's brother Jeremy's truck —and her brother is missing. Evidence left at the crime scene leads Ted to suspect the ranch's new foreman, but Kate isn't convinced he's responsible for the crime.

Kate dives into her own investigation. But the mystery only deepens when a herd of horses disappears and threatening strangers are seen in the Sandhills. It seems like everyone close to the ex-foreman has secrets to hide and reasons to kill —including Jeremy.

As Kate races to eliminate suspects, a shocking realization leads her to the truth. But is she too late to prevent the next murder?

Get your copy today at Shannon-Baker.com

YOU MIGHT ALSO ENJOY...

The Kate Fox Mystery Series

Stripped Bare

Dark Signal

Bitter Rain

Easy Mark

Michaela Sanchez Southwest Crime Thrillers

Echoes in the Sand

The Desert's Share

The Nora Abbott Mystery Series

Height of Deception

Skies of Fire

Canyon of Lies

Standalone Thrillers

The Desert Behind Me

Never miss a new release! Sign up to receive exclusive updates from author Shannon Baker.

Shannon-Baker.com/Newsletter

As a thank you for signing up, you'll receive a free copy of

Close Enough: A Kate Fox Novella

ACKNOWLEDGMENTS

My biggest thanks is to everyone who picked up Stripped Bare and Dark Signal and this book. I hope you like hanging out with me and Kate for a while. All writers start out as readers (and we continue as readers) and it's the best feeling in the world to create a story others want to read. So thank you, for giving me that thrill.

There were a lot of eyes on this book helping it along the way. Thanks to Dave, who inspired the original plot with his doomsday predictions, and for reading and brainstorming and every other thing. To Janet Fogg, as always and forever, thank you. Thanks to Alan Larson for critique as well as beers and commiseration on hot Scottsdale afternoons. To eagle-eye Roni Olson who knows the difference between Norwegian and Swedish.

Heartfelt gratitude to the editorial professionalism of two women. Terri Bischoff is an amazing editor and an even better friend. Jessica Morrell is so freakin' smart about writing, and the best investment a writer could make.

Thank you to Christie Haney, Grant County Clerk, for her expertise about permits and parcels and all that technical stuff. I owe thanks to Betty Gentry, the county treasurer and my boss for two years while I worked at a courthouse "very similar" to where Kate's office is located.

This story borrows heavily from the realities of the Pine Ridge Reservation on the border of Nebraska and South Dakota. I played fast and loose with the geography to make it fit Kate's world. White Clay (Dry Creek in Kate's world) is a horror, but since the time of this writing, liquor sales have been banned. I don't mean to minimize the problems on the reservation, but this book is meant to entertain, not depress the heck out of readers.

Thank you for the Desert Sleuths Chapter of Sisters in Crime, who lives by the national motto, "You write alone, but you're never alone with sisters."

Huge appreciation for the information, handholding, and support of Rocky Mountain Fiction over the course of twenty-five years: you were my K-6, secondary, undergrad and Masters in writing. (I've got degrees to earn, so we're not done with each other.)

To Maegan Beaumont: Wow. Friend, taskmaster, cheerleader, *sensei*. You make my life so hard. Thank you.

Thank you to Andrew Watts, Amber Hudock, and all the crew at Severn River Publishers. You are masters of the publishing universe.

To my daughters, Erin and Joslyn, pandemic life would surely be dismal with you!

ABOUT THE AUTHOR

Shannon Baker is the award-winning author of *The Desert Behind Me* and the Kate Fox series, along with the Nora Abbott mysteries and the Michaela Sanchez Southwest Crime Thrillers. She is the proud recipient of the Rocky Mountain Fiction Writers 2014 and 2017-18 Writer of the Year Award.

Baker spent 20 years in the Nebraska Sandhills, where cattle outnumber people by more than 50:1. She now lives on the edge of the desert in Tucson with her crazy Weimaraner and her favorite human. A lover of the great outdoors, she can be found backpacking, traipsing to the bottom of the Grand Canyon, skiing mountains and plains, kayaking lakes, river running, hiking, cycling, and scuba diving whenever she gets a chance.

Arizona sunsets notwithstanding, Baker is, and always will be a Nebraska Husker. Go Big Red.

www.Shannon-Baker.com

Made in the USA
Monee, IL
06 February 2021

59877095R00196